# Riot Street

ALSO BY TYLER KING

*The Debt*

# Riot Street

## TYLER KING

**FOREVER YOURS**

New York  Boston

Copyright © 2017 by Tyler King
Excerpt from *The Debt* copyright © 2016 by Tyler King
Cover copyright © 2017 by Hachette Book Group, Inc.

Forever Yours
Hachette Book Group
1290 Avenue of the Americas, New York, NY 10104
forever-romance.com
twitter.com/foreverromance

First published as an ebook and as a print on demand: May 2017

Forever Yours is an imprint of Grand Central Publishing. The Forever Yours name and logo are trademarks of Hachette Book Group, Inc.

The publisher is not responsible for websites (or their content) that are not owned by the publisher.

The Hachette Speakers Bureau provides a wide range of authors for speaking events. To find out more, go to www.hachettespeakersbureau.com or call (866) 376-6591.

ISBNs: 978-1-4555-7130-7 (ebook), 978-1-5387-4426-0 (print on demand)

*For Jeff*

# Acknowledgments

I'd like to thank my husband and creative partner, without whom I might still be writing this book. Thank you to Hadley, my constant cheerleader and occasional therapist, and my agent, Kimberly Brower, for her guidance and support. Finally, thank you to Megha Parekh, Alex Logan, and everyone at Forever Yours for being so gracious and easy to work with; you've all made these past two years a true pleasure.

# 1

# THE VIRAL PROSTITUTE

You know who I am, but my name escapes you. It's filed away in the back of your mind with Tot Mom and Those Brothers Who Killed Their Parents. I'm one of those people you read about online under a headline like I WAS RAISED IN A CULT. Or when the essay was reprinted on another site, I ESCAPED THE MASSASAUGA MASSACRE. Four days ago I sold my soul for a chance at my dream job at an important magazine. This isn't what I had in mind.

The editor's name is Ed, which is unfortunate. He should be a Ted, maybe, or Teddy. With a thin, bony frame, he looks like Iggy Pop with a gray David Beckham faux hawk. His Patti Smith T-shirt says he was down with the scene at Max's Kansas City in '69, and his loafers suggest his edges have softened with age. In his office, he sits on a stool beside a sculpture of Ikea components cobbled together to create a standing desk. It is a minimalist contraption smartly appointed with sleek and shiny Apple hardware and one of those little potted plant impulse buys you pick up with the subconscious knowledge that taking home this living organism is an exercise in homicidal mania. Because you're going to kill it—eventually. That's a foregone conclusion. The entertainment is in seeing how long the withering thing will cling to life. Like a goldfish.

But Ed hasn't done much talking. Amid a backdrop of *Rolling Stone* and *Village Voice* covers hanging on his office wall, he stares at the iPad in his lap—perhaps reviewing my scant résumé or reading emails or searching for micro-living retirement options in Nepal. Whichever it is, he looks bored—while Cara, the web editor, gives her spiel. She talks about page impressions and verticals, demographics and target markets. She's said *Millennials* eight times in six minutes. I've stopped listening and now spend most of my cognitive function on creating different versions of the same pleasant facial expression that says, *Yes, this is fascinating. Please, tell me more, wise one, so that I might assimilate into your collective. Hail Hydra.* Oh, and I nod. When her inflection changes and her shaped eyebrows rise, I nod and tilt my head with a little smile. It's my "charming" smile. I do want a job here, but this android woman spewing analytics is sucking all the joy from my being.

I don't know why I'm in a shit mood, but from the moment I walked into this job interview, I had a sinking feeling I'd made a mistake. That I had committed the fatal error of peeking into the factory to see how the sausage is made, and now I can't stomach the truth. Terms like *cost-per-click* and *conversion rate* being tossed like darts at the balloons of my naïve journalistic dreams. It started in the lobby with Cara, a thirty-year-old Gwyneth Paltrow in tailored Calvin Klein and deadly heels.

She made me feel inadequate and underdressed, though I had spent a combined eight hours schlepping through three different malls to put together what I thought was a convincing version of myself as a young, smart, hip journalist. It only cost me a small fortune and three exchanges to come up with the T-shirt, jeans, casual blazer, and flats ensemble. And I fucking hate every thread of it. But whatever.

She sits on a stool on the other side of Ed's desk. His perfect opposite. I get the distinct impression that, given Ed's obvious lack of interest as he remains slouched over his iPad, she was installed as a strategic upgrade by the publisher. A harbinger of the Instagram age of journalism come to pry his print edition from his cold, dead fingers.

Among the print magazines still functioning in America, *Riot Street* could be voted most improbable to exist. It has operated as an independent news and culture publication since 1964, all from a cramped brick building on Liberty Street in the shadow of Lower Manhattan's Financial District. It's the scrappy kid sister still making noise long after its bedtime. The little monthly that refuses to quit. And it has been a crucial part of my career plan since I graduated journalism school last year. Because *Riot Street* has a reputation for breaking out top talent that lands at name-droppable places. But first, I must survive Cara's droning seminar on digital media synergistics or some shit.

Mostly I'm just bummed out, I think. I had imagined the inner sanctum of the magazine as something a little dangerous and destructive, wild and frenetic. So far, what I've seen is more San Francisco disrupt than Chelsea subversive.

"So, Avery…" Cara folds her hands in her lap and clears her throat, which gets Ed to wake up from his iPad trance. "Tell us about yourself."

My mouth goes on autopilot: "Well, I graduated from J-school at Syracuse University last year, where I was a beat writer on student government for the *Daily Orange*." Ed still looks bored, his wrinkled face drawn with deep lines around his mouth, but at least he's making eye contact. "I did my senior internship with the *Post-Standard*, and since then I've mostly been freelancing for an ad agency, writing blog copy, social media posts, that sort of thing."

Saying it out loud sounds even more depressing than the reality. I have former classmates who are already getting clips in the *New York Times* and *Vanity Fair*. Meanwhile, I sling SEO copy for real estate agents and car dealerships while also working part-time at the mall. In the past year, I have pitched *Riot Street* ten times looking for a freelance assignment. Always to no response.

"But I maintain a blog on Medium—I sent over a few links with my résumé—where I write about politics, entertainment…" I've run out of words and now see myself sliding down the cliff into desperation as Ed glances out the window and Cara stares at me with her semi-permanent semi-smile.

"As a matter of fact, while I was at the *Daily Orange*—"

"We saw your first-person essay on Vice.com," Cara says with a perky inflection. "Everyone here is a big fan of that piece."

"Oh, yeah, right," I say, nodding like a dashboard bobble head. I want to smack myself. "I was kind of surprised, actually.

I got so many Twitter notifications I had to shut off my phone for a few hours."

"It got over a hundred thousand hits in the first three days. We checked." Cara likes this. Her plastic smile turns ambitious. "Very impressive."

I can't help that her approval gives me a warm fuzzy all over. I mean, I hate that it comes from a woman whose cornflower-blue eyes twinkle with ad revenue, but all writers are essentially self-hating praise whores. I won't claim to be above it.

"Have you written anything else on the topic?"

"No. First-person essays aren't really my niche." My stomach sinks as her eyes dim. "But I've prepared a list of pitches in other areas," I offer like a defense.

"Would you consider diving back into that well?" Cara asks.

My eyes flick to Ed, who doesn't seem to have much to add to this conversation, though he leans forward as if interested in my answer. Or his sciatica is acting up. Either way, any hope of employment hinges on my response.

The essay in question, my first and only byline since college, was a Hail Mary pass into national publication. After twelve solid months of soul-crushing rejection, I decided to take a stab at what they call the Confession Economy—writers earning a few bucks in exchange for doling out the most sensational or controversial anecdotes from their life story to hang on a line for public view. Now, I'm not sure it was worth it.

"I could be open to the idea," I say, offering what I hope sounds like reluctant agreement. Something to the tune of *If you held a gun to my head while placing my feet in a vat of acid, yes, I would consider it.*

Cara's eyes light up again and she looks at Ed across the desk, a greedy smile spreading over her nude-gloss lips. His response is something like a facial shrug. Ed doesn't want to be here.

"Why Echo?" Cara asks.

"My given name," I say. "My mom is…" Cara gets the gist without making me say it out loud. "So when I was born, she made me Echo Avery Avalon. I go by Avery, but I didn't want this essay linked to my professional persona."

Because I plan to have one of those. At some point.

Cara holds up her hands. "Completely understand. In fact, we're comfortable if you'd prefer to keep the—I don't know if we can call it an alias—but you could keep writing as Echo within the first-person vertical. It would be a shame to abandon the traction you've gained with that identity."

She makes Echo sound like a character I created, but a few years ago she was a real person. Part of her still lives in the corner of my memory. And she isn't for sale. Not again. Publishing the essay felt like giving a blowjob in a back alley for an eight ball of coke. I have regretted it every minute since then. But I cashed the check. When you have rent to pay and student loan debts, dignity and pride are something only the wealthy can afford.

Cara waits for a response. Her straight back and crossed legs stone-still. She stares at me, into me, with the sort of intense concentration of a woman attempting to will me into assent. If she could lunge across the room and shake me, she would.

And Ed. Poor Ed. In this instance, he is a man not in control of his own destiny. His office has been hijacked. As his eyes glaze over, I am convinced this wasn't his idea. That perhaps he doesn't want me here at all, or couldn't care less either way, except even Ed has bosses who make demands and expect him to carry them out.

My heart breaks as I consider what I'm about to do, but this isn't the sort of place I want to work in every day. Not if it means selling off a piece of myself bit-by-bit for no other purpose than generating a good cost-per-mention for the ad department. I've still got a seven-hour train ride back to Syracuse ahead of me. Best not to draw this out any longer than necessary.

"Thank you for inviting me today, but—"

The office door to my left flies open, making me flinch. Noise from the bull pen of reporters roars in on the wake of Ethan Ash.

"Fuck you, Ed," Ethan says with a vicious bite. A tall, commanding presence, he takes the room with complete authority. "You'll print it as is."

Ethan is a big deal, with a list of awards longer than my entire résumé. Only four years out of J-school at NYU, he's written for numerous major outlets and published two books. Strange it's taken us this long to meet.

"I'm tired of dicking around on this one," Ethan says.

Ed isn't impressed. He crosses his arms and leans one elbow on the side of his desk. "Not without a quote for rebuttal in the third graf."

His bland expression and tilted head seem to tolerate Ethan's argument only as the path of least resistance. As if this were a daily occurrence Ed had long since stopped getting worked up about. Let Ethan get it all out of his system until he tuckers himself out.

"So you cut the entire section? Bullshit. That's the crux of the story."

In a heather-gray T-shirt and jeans, Ethan is almost unassuming. But he's got the kind of wavy brown hair and deepwater eyes that sell wedding rings and cologne on TV. Makes it hard not to notice him in a crowd. And I'm sure it doesn't hurt book sales, either. Though it's his shoulders, I think, that define him. The way he carries himself. Ethan Ash is the lone standing larch after the brushfire has scorched the forest black. At the moment, he doesn't notice me hidden behind the open door and staring at his back as he squares off against Ed.

"We can't go to print on that version without a quote."

"That's the *point*." Ethan tosses up his hands like the whole world's gone mad and he's the last sane one among us. "They know that. They're holding up the article until after the shareholders' meeting. Then we'll get a canned denial and three months of research goes to shit."

"Ethan," Cara says like a sigh, "can this wait? We're in the middle—"

He snaps his head toward her. "Piss off, Cara." Then back to Ed. "I'm not changing it. You butcher my story and I'll post my version online today."

"We'll talk about it later." Ed's eyes slide to me with a sympathetic slope to his mouth. "Avery was about to turn down our job offer. You're stealing her spotlight."

Thanks, Ed. Thanks for that.

Ethan turns around and slams the door shut, shaking the

walls, to reveal me sitting awkward and mortified. I'm the little girl clutching her dolly in the shadows while Mommy and Daddy fight.

"Avery Avalon," Ethan says, brow furrowed.

Clearing my throat and sounding half my age: "Yes."

"I wrote you."

"Yes."

"Why?"

Uh…is that a trick question? "You read my essay—"

"Yes, I know." He shakes his head, dismissing my truncated response. "Why are you turning it down?"

"Oh, well, to be honest, I'm not entirely comfortable with the idea of only writing first-person essays. I'm a reporter." Though I don't think my voice is too convincing on that bit. "I want to be a reporter here. But I'm not sure this is a role I'm well suited for."

"Why not?" Crossing his arms, he levels a severe glower at me, which pokes at my more petulant instincts.

"Look, I appreciate the offer. I'm grateful for the opportunity," I say to Ed, because I don't want to burn a bridge, "but I—"

"Give us the room." Ethan keeps his eyes on mine as he gives the order to Ed and Cara. They say nothing and make no move to leave. "Five minutes. Hear me out."

Ed looks to me for an answer, to which I shrug one shoulder. I'm not going to be the one to kick the editor-in-chief out of his office, but I won't tell his golden boy to shove it up his ass, either. Not with an audience.

"We'll wait outside." Ed stands and jerks his head at Cara.

She rolls her eyes as she stands and smooths the creases from her dress.

When they close the door behind them, Ethan picks up a chair from across the room and plants it right in front of me. His knees almost bump mine as he sits.

"Is it me?" he asks.

"What?"

"The reason you're about to make a huge mistake."

I'm not sure what bothers me more, that he places such significance on his tangential connection to my past, or that he might be half-right.

"No."

Ethan wasn't the only person to publish a book about Massasauga and the ensuing trial, but he was the first to land a prison interview with my father. A fact that propelled *The Cult of Silence* to bestseller status when it was published last year and resulted in a new wave of public fascination with the decade-old crime. I saw Ethan once, when he came to SU on his college book tour. Had fantasies of confronting him for hijacking my life story. Threw up in the bathroom instead.

"Then what did they offer you?" he asks.

"Frankly, I sort of tuned out when Cara started talking."

He smirks. "Everyone does."

"I think the gist of it is she wants me to write for one of the online sections. More essays. And I'm flattered," I say so as not to sound like a horrible ingrate, "but I'd rather cut off my hands than make that my career. No one is going to take me seriously as a journalist if my entire portfolio is nothing but diary entries."

"I'm taking you seriously."

"No offense, but you don't count."

"Oh," he says, leaning back in his chair with arms crossed. There's something goading in his expression. A dare. "Why's that?"

"Let's not kid ourselves. You have a financial stake in keeping Echo's story in the headlines."

Ethan was the one to contact me after my essay went viral. He arranged this interview. And while the lure of a job at a major magazine was too tempting to ignore, I'd be an idiot to think Ethan doesn't see some personal advantage in this. Like when a musician dies or an actor goes on a Twitter tirade, publicity sells. How many spots has his book climbed in the Amazon rankings since my essay went live?

"Then why write the essay if you don't want the attention?"

If I'm honest, Ethan's book was at least partially to blame. Response or retaliation, I'm not sure anymore. But in the time since *The Cult of Silence* was released, I had this gnawing urgency to put the ordeal in my own words. To reclaim the narrative and with it what little agency Echo had left. I thought the essay would feel like a victory, a bit of redemption for Echo and all the ways she'd been distorted over the years, pimped by strangers who profited from her tragedy. Instead, I feel like just another john.

Now Ethan wants me to work with him. How am I even considering this?

"I have ambitions," I say. "Why should I abandon them because people like Cara are preoccupied with one brief episode in my past? I'm more than that."

"No one starts out at the top," he says. "You have to be willing to pay your dues."

"I know. I'd be happy grinding it out at some little alt weekly to get a few miles under my tires. At least it wouldn't feel like prostitution."

"So it's about pride? You're too good for us?"

"What? No."

I take a deep breath and slide my hands into my jacket pockets. I'm making a mess of this, and I don't want to leave Ethan with a bad impression of me. He is on a short list of journalists who have reached that rarefied air of influence and respect. The articles he writes shape debates and affect policy. Whatever my personal feelings, it doesn't help my career to make an enemy of him. These sorts of encounters can follow you for a lifetime. Forever known as the brat who spit in the face of Ethan Ash.

"If I take this job now, I don't want to get stuck, you know? I don't want to be typecast in this narrow field. If I don't start getting some professional reporting under my belt soon, I'm never going to get my career off the ground."

He mulls this over, appraising me with intelligent eyes. I can't help the feeling that everything I say digs me into a deeper hole. Ethan's too important a name in this industry to brush off. It's in my best interest to create a professional alliance that I can revisit in the future when a better opportunity comes along. He owes me that much. But as Ethan cracks his knuckles on one hand with his thumb, I realize I'm wasting my time.

"I should go," I say, and reach for my messenger bag on the

floor. "Again, thank you for getting in touch, but—"

"Oh, for fuck's sake, Avery, take the offer." Ethan rubs his hands through his hair and entwines his fingers behind his head. "It isn't a death sentence, it's a job. You put in some time, make friends, and maybe you have an opportunity to branch out, move up. But you won't get that if you walk out. Here you can learn. You can tap into a vein of experience you wouldn't have access to otherwise." Ethan leans forward, elbows on his knees, and speaks with a voice that wrests all the air from the room. "This magazine has a history and a name that will enrobe you in a certain layer of credibility and open doors for the rest of your career. Writing a few essays seems like a small price to pay for that kind of privilege. And they're going to fucking pay you for it." He punctuates this with a hand in the air. "So swallow your pride and be grateful."

He has a point, sure. I'm not oblivious to that, nor the idea that just appearing on the *Riot Street* masthead will be the most significant step in my career to date. And who's to say I can't parlay that into a better gig? When someone is in bed with pneumonia and Ed needs a hungry reporter to drop everything and run down a story. When an associate editor is looking for someone willing to pull an all-nighter tracking down a source or a quote.

But what if I accept and that chance never comes? And one day I realize five years have passed and I've missed my moment? We live in a world where youth is not only a prized commodity, but a prerequisite. If I'm not landing cover stories by the time I'm twenty-five, I can kiss my dream of a Pulitzer goodbye.

In my right pocket, I feel for the shell casing of a Winchester .308 and roll the smooth brass between my fingers. I don't know if it helps, but I've been doing it so long I'd miss it if I stopped.

"I'll think about it."

## 2

# STRANGER ON THE TRAIN

It starts in a subway car on my way uptown to catch the train home. A robust woman with a voice like an outboard motor berates a shameless public masturbator until we stop at Fulton Street and he's chased out the door. Onlookers snap, tweet, and post their videos of the incident while an oblivious stream of new passengers file inside. Among them is a Grandpa Joe type in a light trench coat and herringbone trilby. Water beads off his shoulders and collects in a pool around my feet. A few stops later, he's with me when we exit at Thirty-Fourth Street and take the underground pass to Penn Station. At Hudson News, where I grab a snack before making my way to the Amtrak terminal, he's in line ahead of me counting out exact change for the clerk in nickels and pennies.

That's when I spot it: Ethan's book sitting on a rack below the gum and mints and other impulse buys that rim the checkout counter. Next to James Patterson's latest and Stephen King's fourth this week, *The Cult of Silence* is too loud to ignore. It's been out for more than a year, long since dropped from the featured-release displays and constant marketing push, but someone's resurrected it from the discount grave-yard and left it slotted in front of the most recent page-to-screen adaptation with the new movie-poster cover art.

I consider hiding it. Tucking it behind Patterson or the copies of *Cosmo* and *People*. But as I reach for it, the trilby man grabs it with thick, wrinkled fingers and drops it on the counter. It takes him another two minutes to forage $9.99 plus tax out of his many coat pockets.

I should take the opportunity to ditch him and thus inter-rupt the emerging synchronicity, but I'm weak and can't part with the KitKat and grape soda in my hands. So I wait, pay, and take as long as time will allow to arrive at the platform for my train. When I do, boarding has already begun.

In the economy-class car, I squeeze down the aisle in search of an open row. The car's crowded, but not full, so when I eye some free territory toward the back, I dodge and parry be-tween passengers to claim it. A broken voice crackles through the scratchy intercom as I fall into my seat next to the window. The train rolls forward then back, and with a final announce-ment through the intercom, musters up a great force of deter-mination to surge forward on its seven-hour haul to Syracuse.

That's when my shadow, Trilby, old-man-shuffling right for me, wedges himself past Mother Goose corralling a gaggle of children to drop himself in the window seat opposite me. He pulls down the seatback tray and, from another coat pocket, unwraps a pastrami on rye.

He's like an ex I can't shake. I don't even know his name, but we're trapped in an unhealthy relationship. I could move, but now it's a matter of autonomy. I was here first, and a girl's got to stand her ground. So I put on my headphones and pull out a magazine while I eat my snack, determined to let Trilby have no greater effect on my life than I've had on his.

But my eyes wander, and once he's dusted the sandwich crumbs from his chest, crumpled the wax paper wrapping into a ball, and stuffed it into one of the cavernous coat pockets, Trilby sits three seats away licking his arthritic index finger to flip the pages of Ethan's book.

What did I ever do to deserve this man?

* * *

We've all experienced it. The pattern of coincidence known as the Baader-Meinhof phenomenon, otherwise referred to as frequency illusion. It's when you learn a new piece of information—a phrase like *frequency illusion*, for example—then repeatedly encounter it within a short span of time. Or a song you haven't heard in years makes a conspicuous comeback, following you from the coffee shop to the mall to a busker playing guitar in the park. You've been going about your life, oblivious to this *thing*, then suddenly it's stalking your every step. In my case, it's an elderly man with a book.

Everywhere I turn, Ethan is there.

Hours later, the windows are dark when the train jostles and slugs, slowing on its approach to the Walsh train station in Syracuse. I must have drifted off sometime before sundown. Now while impatient passengers unfold from their seats and relieve their travel cramps, stretching in the aisles and gathering suitcases and small luggage from the overhead racks, I steal a glance at the stark white cover and blurry title font on the seat beside Trilby. The train grunts to a halt, and he catches me. We share a long moment of awkward eye contact.

Does he see her? The version of me created in Ethan's words. The image extrapolated from the hours Ethan spent absorbing a sociopath's reminiscence. Is it obvious?

Passengers move toward the exits and the aisle clears. I'm not sure why, but I don't want to be the first of us to stand. I wrench my eyes from Trilby and his liver-spotted jowls to yank my messenger bag from the floor and pretend to fish through it for my phone. He heaves himself to his feet, grabbing the seat back in front of him for support as he squeezes out from the row. Before his frame disappears from my peripheral vision, something lands on the seat cushion next to me.

He's left me the book.

## 3

# THE RUNAWAY

Eight a.m. Thursday morning and I've got a pillow over my face. On the other side of my bedroom wall, my roommate is into day two of her post-breakup hibernation: the anger phase in which a constant soundtrack of man-hating anthems bellows through our apartment on a loop. Kumi was up at seven to treat herself to her ritual Breakfast Milkshake of Mourning—the piercing *whir* of the blender snapping me awake—to the tune of Taylor Swift.

It's been three days since my interview. I said I would give Ed and Cara my answer by Monday. For whatever reason, Ethan has taken a personal interest. I would be an idiot to pass this up. If I refuse and nothing better comes along, I might spend the rest of my life reading his bylines and thinking about the biggest mistake of my career. Or I take the job and manage to embarrass myself and sabotage any glimmer of journalistic aspirations by falling into the essay abyss. Thus far I've yet to find an off-ramp from this cycle of possibility and doubt. Despite my reservations, I admit there are more items in the Yes column than not.

Either way, Kumi and I are moving to Manhattan tomorrow. Her wealthy but absentee father has recently decided he wants to be back in her life, so his bribery mission begins with paying for an apartment in the city while Kumi attends law school at NYU and I start applying for jobs. She was hesitant to accept until we started looking at rent prices and realized all we could afford was a storage unit in the Bronx or maybe an abandoned car by the river. So she agreed, on the stipulation that I get to come, too. Her dad wasn't in a position to put limitations on his apology for being a catastrophic jackass for the last six years. Having deficient father figures is sort of the basis for everything Kumi and I have in common.

Just as Carrie Underwood launches into the chorus of her revenge fantasy, my phone buzzes on the nightstand.

I haven't spoken to my mom since the essay went up last week—I gave her an advance copy and received her blessing before publishing it—but her name flashing on the screen sends a jolt of apprehension through my chest.

"Hi, Mom," I say, answering the call. I pull the duvet over my head to replace the pillow while Kumi belts over the vocals of Katy Perry.

"Did I wake you up?"

Her voice is bright, airy. Birds chirp in the background and her rocking chair creaks on the front porch. I picture her in jeans stained from her garden, drinking tea while she watches the squirrels run across the yard. The image comes from a photograph, I think. One of her I must have seen years ago. She was younger, barely in her twenties. Hair like a brushfire and eyes green as spring grass, smiling into the camera. People used to tell me we look alike. But she barely resembles that person anymore. I prefer to think of her happy.

"Sorta. No. I'm awake."

"Are you still in bed? Echo, it's such a blissful day. You should be outside getting some sunshine. Come out for a few days. We'll go canoeing at the springs."

"We're moving tomorrow." She knows this, but my mom doesn't adapt well to change. Selective memory is her defense mechanism. "And I have to work." A decision on *Riot Street* aside, I still have looming deadlines for freelance clients. "Besides, the springs are closed. Another bacterial flare-up."

"What, really? Where'd you hear that?"

"Saw an article online."

"Hmm. I must have missed it," she says in a dour tone.

My mother doesn't watch the news. Or read it. Or otherwise acknowledge the crimes and tragedies of humanity. She says it distracts from the "pursuit of wholeness." So I have listened to no small amount of browbeating concerning my chosen vocation.

"You're depriving yourself of felicity with all that calamity and woe," she is fond of saying. And that chronicling society's failures—her concise view of the work of the news media at large—is a distraction from the "human imperative of spiritual awareness."

She didn't always talk like that.

Simply put, I am a disappointment who is wasting the best

years of my life. And I need to find Jesus. Or Allah. Or Buddha. Anyone will do, as long as I find an idol to guide me toward enlightenment. That kind of thing is important to my mother. It gives her purpose and provides meaning and order in a chaotic world. A plan for everyone. A purpose for it all. I don't begrudge her these things. I only wish she'd recognize that our shared history had the opposite effect on me. When you grow up secluded from society, under the autocratic regime of a self-appointed guru—and it all ends in mass casualties—you develop a healthy skepticism about deities and dogma.

"Anyway, honey, the reason I called…" Her rocking chair creaks through the phone and the screen door claps shut. "I went online and looked at your essay."

I close my eyes and hold my breath, bracing for impact. "Yeah?"

"Have you seen these comments?"

A gust of air leaves my lungs and my muscles relax. "Don't read the comments. Ever. People are awful."

"Some of these…" Her voice trails off, in a tone that makes me throw off my duvet and sit up in bed. "The things people are saying…"

"Mom, I knew this would be part of it, okay? I don't look at them and you shouldn't either." Can't put a spent bullet back in the chamber. There's no use flogging myself with the witless snark of internet trolls.

"About me," she says.

"What?" Her muttered statement sideswipes me. "What about you?"

"'This woman should be in prison.' 'How is this not child abuse?' 'Her mother should have done this girl a favor and blown her own brains out.'" Her voice cracks. "'She should—'"

"Mom, stop. Close the page. Just walk away from it, okay? I'm serious."

She breathes heavily through the phone. Stuttering gasps. My mother and I aren't close—she pretends we are and I let her—but I never intended to cast her as the villain. For as fucked up as my childhood was, her experience was far more difficult. And while there's plenty of blame to lay at her feet, it wasn't like her actions were malicious. She was a naïve woman deceived and manipulated by a sociopath. A young mother with no money and nowhere else to go.

"Echo…" A long, pained sigh trickles from her lips, and it cracks my chest open. "Why would you want to do this?"

"Mom, I swear, I—"

"Why would you want to make a life at this? This, letting people peck over your private sorrows, it's noxious. I don't want that for you. I want you to find your joy and be at peace and fulfilled. How can this make you happy?"

"I'm sorry," I say, because I don't have a better answer and it pains me that she takes the brunt of the attacks and feels sympathy for me. "I didn't mean for—"

"They haven't said anything I haven't thought myself. Don't worry about me, honey. I'm happy you were able to express these thoughts and relieve yourself of the burden. It's healthy to confront our emotions and take control of the shadows. But I worry what effect this negative energy will have on you. So much hatred and bile—you can ignore it, but it's there, festering, eating away whether you notice it or not."

I apologize again, and again, and keep apologizing until she's said her piece. I owe her that much. And I understand that when she tears at the shreds of my dreams like she's ripping off wallpaper, it is only because she sees my career path as detrimental to my well-being. At the moment, I can't argue otherwise. So check one more item in the No column.

The difference, however, between my mother and me is that I don't need to be *happy* to be happy. I can settle for being free.

"Come up to the house sometime," she says, knowing that on this point we are at an impasse. "I'll make you dinner."

"Talk to you soon, Mom. Bye."

\* \* \*

For the last five years, since about the time I started college, my mother has lived inside a rural Pennsylvania commune. The town of Aster is infamous as a curiosity that attracts tourists and devotees alike. It is known as a psychic haven for its dense population of mediums, fortune tellers, palm readers, and the like. They are the New Agers, if you will, who set up shop in the "haunted" hotel and entertain visitors with mystic insights. But across the street is the more orthodox clan. The Aster Spiritualist Camp, where true believers have gone since 1884 to engage in a "personal experience with God." In whatever form He/She/They/It might take. So now my mom "talks" to dead people. In one form or another, she's been born again and again and again, and she'll keep trying until she gets it right.

I won't set foot within the camp boundaries.

Not because I take issue with their faith or the form in which they practice it. Not because I suspect some sort of nefarious activities are being carried out within the decaying buildings that sit beneath sagging bows clothed in moss. I won't go in there because, for all its friendly trappings and honest convictions, I can't help but see it as just another incarnation of the place where I was born and raised. A place from which my mother and I escaped the night my father murdered eleven people before attempting to take his own life. Too bad he missed, the bullet went through his cheek.

Anyway, the place gives me the creeps. And I have work to do. So I pull out my laptop, put on my headphones to drown out Kumi's screeching Alanis Morissette at the top of her lungs, and dive into a blog post on the value of saltwater pools over chlorinated. Add one more to the Yes column.

* * *

By afternoon, I've moved on to writing a white paper explaining the benefits and drawbacks to homeowners' associations. Right about the time I decide owning a home is way too much hassle, I get a text message from a number I don't recognize.

Unknown
12:17 PM
It occurred to me that I might have been a bit abrupt with you the other day. Don't let my bad manners scare you off.
E.A.

I suppose that is something like an apology, though no apology is necessary. *Abrupt* is just another word for honest, and honesty goes a long way with me. I could tell him that; assure him my decision on this job is solely about me and not a reaction to anyone else…But his book is lying on the floor next to my desk. I haven't decided yet what to do about it. Leaving it on the train seemed wrong somehow. Like throwing it away. A book in a garbage can is a damn tragedy. Besides, Trilby had spent his hard-foraged dollars on it and gifted it to me in what he must have felt was an act of compassion. Perhaps he believed he'd sniped that copy from me at the counter. That I'd pined over it during our train ride home. Throw the girl a bone, you know?

Unknown
12:20 PM
For what it's worth, today's Thai Thursday.
If you worked here, you'd be eating spring rolls right now.

Yes column.

* * *

A few hours later, I am wrapping up a chat session with a client, sending them revised drafts for approval, when it occurs to me that I haven't heard much sound coming from Kumi's room for the last hour. While the silence is appreciated, I'm somewhat concerned that stillness is a warning sign. It's after five, I haven't eaten yet, and after two days I think it's about time for Kumi to get out of her pajamas and take a shower. So I knock on her bedroom door to invite her out to dinner. We could both use a distraction.

"Kumi?" I say through the door when she doesn't answer. "Want to get something to eat?" Nothing. No movement on the other side. "My treat. You can get loaded on cocktails and—"

The door whips open. Kumi is holding a pair of eight-inch scissors in one hand, the fingers of her other hand combing through what's left of her hair.

"What do you think?" she asks. Her eyes are bright and expectant, a smile on her face that is a little excited and a lot terrified. It's a look that means if I'm not careful, she might stab me or herself. Either way, someone goes to the hospital if I screw this up.

But for fuck's sake, she's left six inches of black hair on the carpet. Kumi has the face for a severe bob, just not the skill to cut in a straight line.

"How about I order delivery and help you even out the back?"

"Oh, please, yes," she says, and yanks me to the bathroom.

By the time I've got her head sorted and she's moved on to the bargaining phase of her post-breakup grief—I threatened to throw her phone in the toilet if I saw her texting her ex—I notice I have a missed text from Ethan.

Ethan Ash
5:27 PM
Do you like karaoke?
This is important.

I sweep up the clippings from the bathroom floor while Kumi searches Netflix for a proper Girls' Night selection. And I smile, because I can't take that message seriously.

Avery Avalon
5:44 PM
I'm judging you right now.
Ethan Ash
5:44 PM
Answer the question.
This is IMPORTANT.
Avery Avalon
5:45 PM
No one likes karaoke.
Ethan Ash
5:45 PM
Blasphemy.
This was a test. You failed.
Avery Avalon
5:45 PM
Oh well. If you change your mind . . .

I'll be at the cool kids' table.
Ethan Ash
5:46 PM
Do they have spring rolls?
My table has spring rolls.

"Avery, food's here," Kumi calls from the kitchen.

I dump the clippings in the trash can and put Ethan in a drawer.

Avery Avalon
5:48 PM
I'll take that into consideration.

In the kitchen, Kumi is unpacking our orange chicken and fried rice. I still don't quite recognize her, but the new look does make her appear taller, thinner. It didn't turn out half-bad for a sudden, scorched-earth approach to hair styling. Sometimes a girl just needs a change and the immediate gratification that hacking off a few inches can provide.

"What are you smiling at?" she asks, turning to hand me a paper plate.

"Nothing. What?"

Her eyes narrow and I have that run-or-be-stabbed feeling again. "You were talking to a boy."

"No," I say, and take my plate to the living room.

"Boys are shits, Avery. Horrible little shits."

* * *

After dinner we finally tackle the last of the packing we've been avoiding. The movers her dad hired are showing up at eight in the morning, and I've warned Kumi that anything not packed by then is getting left behind. Rushing around and last-minute chaos always give me anxiety.

In the living room, we box up her DVD collection, vinyl records from my short-lived vintage phase, and the shelving unit overflowing with books two rows deep. Kumi must have forgotten it was there, *The Cult of Silence* slotted spine-in next to the old textbooks we couldn't sell back to the campus bookstore. When I pull it off the shelf to stack in a box, she turns that nervous shade of red like a kid whose parents found her box of secrets under the bed.

"Busted," I say, tossing it in her lap.

She sits on the carpet, elbow-deep in her collection of true-crime novels. Almost afraid to touch it, as if doing so would claim it and thus admit guilt, she pushes it away.

"Must have picked it up by accident," she says. "One of those bargain-bin buys. I probably didn't recognize it at the time."

So I snatch it back and flip open the cover. Scrawled across the title page in black marker is Ethan's signature.

"You went to his book signing?"

But I can't keep a straight face, and my repressed laughter assures Kumi she doesn't need to find a new roommate.

"I couldn't help myself," she says, all desperate puppy eyes full of regret. "It really isn't as bad as you think."

"I'll take your word for it."

Kumi tops off the box she's working on and tapes it shut. I feel her staring at me.

"You should give it a chance," she says. "It might help you make up your mind about him."

"Pass. Thanks." I get up to pull another armful of books from the shelf. She's still staring. "What?"

"What's he like?"

"You met him." When I glance over, Kumi's giving me her exasperated face. Fine. "He's pushy."

She rolls her eyes. "That all?"

"He's taller in person."

"Oh, well..." Her hands dance between us in a sort of magician's reveal. A very sarcastic magician. "Say no more."

"I don't know. He's..."

She picks up her phone off the coffee table and starts playing with it. "What?"

"Noticeable."

"How so?"

"It's hard to explain." My attention drifts to a scuff on the wall from the day we first moved into this apartment. "Like when he walks into a room, it shrinks. Everything feels smaller around him."

There are those people, the ones born separate from the rest of us. Gifted with an ineffable quality as easily recognized as it is difficult to explain. Some become rock stars or go into politics. Maybe start a cult in the mountains. Most, though, they're the unicorn next door. The charismatic mechanic. The charming shop clerk. Singular personalities who bend the world around them and pervade through the clutter of time and memory.

Kumi stares at me with one raised eyebrow. "You've given this some thought."

"No."

"You know…" There is a perceptible shift in her demeanor. Something almost predatory emerges from behind her eyes. She holds out her phone to show me the photo of him from his *Riot Street* profile. "He's not hard to look at, huh?"

Like I haven't noticed.

"I see what you're doing."

"What?" Kumi applies her contrite face with an octave jump in her voice.

"I know how your mind works."

Feigning wounded by my accusation, she looks away. "I didn't say anything."

"Uh-huh." I get up to hunt for ice cream in the freezer. Because there's always room for ice cream. And because Kumi is a ruthless interrogator when she brings her considerable coercive talents to bear. "You're trying to make this a thing. It isn't a thing."

"Sure, okay."

We still have some chocolate and coffee ice cream left. It shows restraint she didn't clean us out during her hibernation.

"I mean it."

"Yeah." An annoyed clip to her voice. "I heard you."

I pull out two paper bowls and peel open the carton lids. "Okay. Just so we're clear."

Since we met junior year of college, Kumi has had these wild sexual aspirations for me. In her eyes, I'm some stricken, oppressed woman liberated from a convent and in desperate need of fornication. But I think she longs for the days when sex was still exciting and everything was a first time for something. I'm merely an avatar for her vicarious fantasies.

"I'm just saying..." She pauses, and I decide three scoops of each flavor is not unreasonable. Because I'm an adult. "You should totally hit that."

"And now you're not getting any ice cream."

/

# 4

# THE OTHER WOMAN

In the pages of Ethan's book, my alter ego is Enderly Atwood, a spunky eighteen-year-old with curly rose hair and peridot eyes. My fictional doppelgänger. Like other young women her age, she's energetic and inquisitive, traits her father warns must be managed lest they get her into trouble. But unlike most, Enderly's entire world is confined inside the boundaries of Camp Indigo, the secretive commune on the rural outskirts of Doser, Pennsylvania. It isn't until an intrepid journalist infiltrates Indigo that Enderly learns the unsettling truth beneath the empire of ashes she's called home, and must help the journalist reveal the cult's founder, her father, for the dangerous tyrant he is—before it's too late. A work of fiction loosely based on Massasauga and Ethan's interviews with my father, the *Times* called *The Cult of Silence*, "A suspenseful departure from the rational world into a disquieting realm of ego and manipulation, revealing the limits of the human psyche."

But it was upstate New York where we called two hundred

acres of the Adirondack region home. I was only twelve when it all came to an end. And it wasn't an undercover journalist who drove my father to murder eleven of his followers, just his own metastasizing paranoia. Though Ethan does nail my father's tendency toward self-aggrandizing speeches that appeared mid-conversation as if ejected from a passing aircraft. Ethan captures the essence of his natural charisma and the dark shadow of intimidation he cast over us.

Until today, I had never been tempted to pick up Ethan's book. I had convinced myself nothing good could come of it. Now it's after midnight, I'm three chapters in, and more conflicted than when I began.

Sitting in bed, my phone buzzes.

Ethan Ash
12:09 AM
I want to preface this. I'm not drunk.

I put a scrap of paper between the pages to save my place.

Avery Avalon
12:10 AM
Okay…
Ethan Ash
12:10 AM
What are you doing right now?
Avery Avalon
12:11 AM
Is this a test, too?

Ethan Ash

12:11 AM

Yes.

Avery Avalon

12:12 AM

As it happens, I've got a bone to pick with you.

Ethan Ash

12:13 AM

Is that so?

Avery Avalon

12:13 AM

It is.

Ethan Ash

12:14 AM

Go on then.

So far, there's nothing about his book I find offensive, exactly. His writing is clever and thoughtful. But I already knew that. I'm sure Ethan has no shortage of sycophants lining up to kiss his ass. I won't be one of them. And there's just one question that I've been dying to ask for more than a year.

Avery Avalon

12:15 AM

So, how long have you been obsessed with me?

Ethan Ash

12:16 AM

Whoa, ok, shots fired.

Where did this come from?

Avery Avalon

12:16 AM

I'm reading your book.

Ethan Ash

12:16 AM

I see.

Avery Avalon

12:17 AM

And I'm wondering how a 12-yr-old girl you'd never met became the heroine of your novel.

Ethan Ash

12:18 AM

She's 18 in the book.

Avery Avalon

12:18 AM

Didn't answer my question.

Ethan Ash

12:18 AM

You're putting me on the spot here.

Avery Avalon

12:18 AM

That's the idea.

You're the one texting me in the middle of the night.

Ethan Ash

12:19 AM

I keep late hours.

Avery Avalon

12:19 AM

You're avoiding the question.

Ethan Ash

12:23 AM

Well, Enderly didn't sign up for Indigo.

She was born into it, never given a choice.

She's innocent, less complicit than the others.

That makes her more sympathetic to the reader.

Avery Avalon

12:24 AM

I suppose that's true.

Ethan Ash

12:25 AM

But I tried not to write her as hapless or naïve.

She doesn't have a great breadth of experience,

but she survives on strong intuition.

She's a good judge of character.

I'll give him that. Some male writers seem to suffer from a kind of creative paralysis when writing about women. Depicting hollow renditions of the same female tropes regurgitated ad nauseam. But Enderly has dimension. She's complex and at times contradictory—a woman at odds with herself. That much, at least, I can relate to.

Avery Avalon

12:26 AM

I don't hate her.

If we met in real life, I might be her friend.

Ethan Ash

12:26 AM

I consider that a glowing review.

Avery Avalon

12:27 AM

Don't get too excited.

I'm only on the 3rd chapter.

Ethan Ash

12:29 AM

Fair enough.

Any other notes you'd like to share?

Avery Avalon

12:30 AM

Why, working on a sequel?

Ethan Ash

12:31 AM

I'm in a unique position as a writer.

Have to take advantage of the opportunity presented.

Avery Avalon

12:32 AM

You're just burning with questions, aren't you?

Ethan Ash

12:33 AM

Yes, but I do have some tact.

This isn't an interview.

Avery Avalon

12:35 AM

I do have one question...

Ethan Ash

12:36 PM

Shoot.

Avery Avalon

12:36 AM

Was there a reason you texted me tonight?

Ethan Ash

12:37 AM

I was reading the comments on your essay…

I see your point now.

Are you ok?

Avery Avalon

12:38 AM

I don't read the comments.

G'night

Ethan Ash

12:38 AM

Good night, Avery

\* \* \*

I don't hold animosity toward Ethan, per se. Most of the time, the idea of him doesn't even cross my mind. And it isn't his reputation that intimidates me. The breathless vacuum of standing in the presence of fame. That eerie uncanny valley of witnessing in the flesh something that formerly only existed at a comfortable distance through a television screen or in the glossy pages of a magazine. This nervous sensation that tingles my spine and turns my fingertips numb—it's dread. The specific and daunting fear of what's not said.

Three years ago Ethan rose to prominence after publishing a six-page feature about the Massasauga Massacre. The result of his interviews with my father. Ethan was the first to get him on record, for weeks traveling upstate to Sing Sing, where Patrick Turner Murphy sits serving out eleven life sentences for his eleven victims. I don't know how Ethan got him to talk. Neither my father nor any of the survivors had ever spoken a word to the media in the decade since the event. That's where the title of the book comes from. The Cult of Silence was a nickname coined by the press at the time.

But it wasn't reading my father's words that disturbed me. Most of the article painted him as a paranoid narcissist rather than the compelling villain of myth previously portrayed in made-for-TV movies. Instead, it was my father's pervasive preoccupation with me that caused the cold sweat. Though I wasn't mentioned by name, fifteen times I surfaced in the article. Anecdotes of his fond familial memories that bore no resemblance to the reality I remembered. A revisionist history of fatherhood as if he could humanize the monster behind the mask. And yet, that's still not the part that claws at me. Not what Ethan wrote about me for all the world to read. It's what he didn't write.

Eight weeks is a lot of conversation to fit into one article. How much more did my father tell him that didn't make it to print? How many more stories of my childhood has Ethan withheld? The years too young and too long ago to remember. Empty spaces between the lines. To this day, my mother doesn't talk about a time before we escaped Massasauga. And when the memories fade, it's like it never happened.

The fear is that Ethan knows more about me than I do.

# 5

# MODERN RITUALS

I hate moving. No matter how well planned and organized one tries to be, inevitably the whole thing goes haywire. The movers were late, one guy had a cast on his hand and couldn't carry anything heavier than a desk chair, and they put a six-inch gash in the side of Kumi's couch trying to wedge it down the stairwell. But we made it. By the skin of our teeth, we got the last box off the truck by five. If I'd known getting the cable and internet hooked up would be the least painful part of this ordeal, I might have stayed in Syracuse.

The fifth-floor apartment on Bleeker Street is nicer than I expected, though. Nothing fancy, but wood floors and appliances built after I was born are certainly an upgrade from our old place. Plus, the apartment gets great light, has a fire escape over the tree-lined street, and is just two blocks from NYU. There's a café next door and a Mexican restaurant below us. Not a bad commute to *Riot Street*, either. If that becomes relevant.

But that decision can wait.

Despite being exhausted, I've still got work to finish. Once I have my desk and laptop set up, I dive into a tangle of email exchanges with three different clients who all believe their immediate needs require my urgent attention. This always happens on deadline day, and damn me for not spreading these out better. I want to tell them to have a bottle and take a nap. Instead, I reply with some version of *Sure, no problem. I'll get that to you right away.*

I'm neck-deep in revisions when Ethan texts me another nudge.

Ethan Ash
5:25 PM
Today is Food Truck Friday.
This could be you.

He's attached a photo of himself and people I assume are other members of the *Riot Street* staff holding up slushies.

Avery Avalon
5:26 PM
I'm on deadline.
Some of us work for a living.
Ethan Ash
5:26 PM
You could work here.
And have slushies.
Avery Avalon

5:27 PM

You should put that on a T-shirt.

Ethan Ash

5:27 PM

Are you in the city yet?

His question gives me pause. When he first contacted me about the interview, I mentioned I'd have to come in from Syracuse unless we could push it to after the move. Didn't expect him to remember the date.

Avery Avalon

5:28 PM

Got in this morning.

Ethan Ash

5:29 PM

Come out with us tonight.

The staff is going to Peacock Room at 8.

They're good people to know either way.

Even if I don't take the job, making these connections, expanding my networking circle, would be a smart move. All I have to do is pretend hitting a bar with Ethan is a totally normal thing. Simple.

Avery Avalon

5:31 PM

I'm not singing karaoke...

See you then.

That only gives me two hours to push through my assignments while obsessing over how to approach this meeting. Now that I'm faced with confronting the staff, I realize a new dimension of concerns I haven't addressed yet: What if the rest of them think I'm a hack? Sure, Ethan is on board, and Cara has a lady-boner for me, but what's to say the staff didn't read my essay and roll their eyes? All of them sizing me up, appraising, wondering, *What's so fucking special about her?*

Have I earned this job? I wrote something that a lot of people read, but was it good? Was it engaging, articulate, and evocative? I don't want to be that girl in the office everyone whispers about behind her back. The one who *must* be sleeping with someone important to have been hired.

What if they're already thinking it? A newsroom might as well be a high school cafeteria.

Fuck.

My laptop chimes with another "urgent" all-caps email from a client having a complete existential meltdown. One emergency at a time.

\* \* \*

Making friends has never been easy for me. Even Kumi and I were sort of an accident. As far back as I can remember about the commune where I was born, every minute of my life I was surrounded by the same faces. I didn't have to create relationships, they simply imposed themselves. Starting public school after Massasauga at age twelve, I might as well have landed in a foreign country. When every other word out of other kids' mouths is local vernacular and pop culture references, you just smile and nod and try not to say anything stupid, which means you don't talk much at all. I survived the best I could, but by high school I was barely treading water. In tenth grade a group of girls made it their mission to terrorize my every waking moment, so my guidance counselor and principal suggested to my mother that she consider enrolling me in an online charter school. Easier to get rid of the outlier than reshape the social order around her.

Life got dark for a while. I found my breaking point and snapped in half.

Then freshman year of college the world burst open for me. I lived in the dorms, met other weird people with weird histories, and found a little corner of society where I could unfold from my shy, huddled posture. Because in college everyone is figuring their shit out. We all have versions of ourselves we're trying to outrun, deconstruct, or reimagine—all works in progress. But then the research-and-development phase of life ends and we're supposed to emerge as finished products ready for the marketplace. Only I'm still stalled on the assembly line. I know what I'm meant to be, I understand how my parts should fit, yet I feel like I've spent the last year searching for that one missing screw that's supposed to hold it all together.

This job could change all that.

If I can manage not to make a fool of myself.

Later that night, though, I'm having trouble keeping up. Sitting around a table with a selection of the *Riot Street* staff is like walking into the middle of an Aaron Sorkin scene without a script. And the more they drink, the harder it is to follow the conversation. To the point where I'm not certain how, but we've landed on the topic of chimps.

"A chimpanzee throws a stone at a tree—"

"Let it go, Navid—"

"No, listen, there's a paper—"

"They never said—"

"But it was insinuated."

"A chimp throws a stone at a tree, and eighty scientists 'ooh' and 'ahh' and scratch their heads asking why."

Navid is quite likely the smartest person in the room. That's how Ethan introduced him: "Avery, this is Navid Kirmani, our sci-tech writer. He's a member of Mensa, and Monday he has to give his third deposition to the Justice Department. So anything you say to him may become a matter of public record. Fair warning. Also, never open his emails."

"Eighty scientists," Navid continues, "spend hours watching this troop of chimps throw stones at a tree in a 'high state of arousal' and suddenly now chimps have a sense of spirituality. I mean, what? They're calling this ritualistic behavior, but what? When does repetition become elevated to the point of spirituality?"

It's approaching 10 p.m. in a cramped hole called the Peacock Room. One of those bars so dark and crowded you can't see the walls. Overhead are sporadic exposed orange bulbs that throw just enough light to see your drink in front of your face but not enough to make an informed decision about the stranger sliding up next to you.

Sitting on my left, Ethan glances at me and smiles, because

apparently after a couple beers Navid is prone to these irrational rants about...I still don't know what. Ethan's ocean eyes are soft, if a bit glassy from alcohol and laughing, his shoulders relaxed. A lock of hair falls over his forehead as he sips his drink. In this atmosphere, he's almost a regular person. But it's just a trick of the light.

"Ignore him." At my right, C.J. pushes her glasses up to her hairline and rubs her eyes. "Navid just got dumped."

Ethan introduced her only as C.J. because Cynthia Jane Silva needs no introduction. This morning her editorial on the Supreme Court's erosion of equal voting rights was picked up across every major news network. Just one year younger, she's Ethan's natural successor when he inevitably moves on to bigger publications and fatter paychecks. Or she'll eat him alive if he stands still too long. Harvard educated and fierce as fire, C.J. chose *Riot Street* for its independence. They reward her loyalty by letting her write whatever the hell she wants. My goal tonight is not to say anything stupid in front of her. Ever.

"Seems to be a lot of that going around," I answer, because I feel the need to reply.

Ethan pauses mid-sip and stares at me. His eyebrows pull together. "Really, when?"

"Not me, my roommate. Kumi."

Navid perks up. "Does your roommate like Persian men?"

"I don't see why not."

He gives me a satisfied nod and a playful smile. "We'll talk later."

"Did you ask her?" Addison walks up behind C.J. and me to put two handfuls of shot glasses on the table. The black licorice stench of Jägermeister burns my nostrils and tickles my gag reflex. "Navid," Addison says, sitting next to Ethan. "Ask her."

"You ask her." Navid sniffs his shot, winces, then swallows it like a mouthful of battery acid.

"Me?" I don't drink. Never have. It's generally frowned upon that those who've given up heroin take up alcohol. "Ask me what?"

"Don't," Ethan says, leaning back in his chair to run his hands through his hair.

Addison Lee is the senior arts and culture writer for the magazine but also pens a sexuality column for the online edition. Much of the column deals with gender identity and Addison's own experience as a trans man. But there is the occasional letter from a reader asking for advice about a torrid love affair gone wrong or an embarrassing bedroom mishap. Ethan's introduction included a warning that I never be fooled into recounting my private exploits in the presence of Addison, for anything said might next week show up in a pseudonymous paragraph.

Addison plunks his empty shot glass upside down on the table and shakes his head, blowing invisible fire from his lips. "I'm sorry, but this is kind of cool. You're The Girl Who Lived."

"Yep," I say with a patient smile. Never heard that one before.

"So…" Addison elbows Navid beside him, doing a goading head nod. "Navid wants to know—"

"Hey." Ethan sits up and snaps his eyes to Addison. "Don't."

"Best behavior," C.J. says. "Remember? We're not supposed to scare her off."

"It's fine." I push my shot to Addison, who accepts it with a shrug. "What do you want to know?"

"Well…" Addison tosses his head back and swallows the second shot then clears his throat. "We were talking. And Navid was curious…"

"Yeah?"

"In your essay…"

"You don't have to answer," Ethan says, a vexed edge in his voice.

I can appreciate him not wanting me to feel like a circus animal, but the perimeter fence isn't necessary.

"Well, there've always been rumors, so…"

"Ask me."

I've heard this question a lot. Or something similar, at least. In one version or another I've heard every morbid, salacious, bizarre question a person can come up with.

"Were you guys into sacrifices?" Addison leans in to speak in a hushed, secretive voice. "Like serious Old Testament shit? Slitting a goat's throat or…"

See, people can't quite wrap their heads around the *point* of it all. They're looking for complicated reasons for simple acts. Once upon a time, my father quietly ducked out of a career on Wall Street right before the crash of '87. With a hefty stash of other people's money, he moved out to Northern California and spent some time wrapped up with one of those desert spiritual healing centers. But when the IRS and SEC came calling, he took on an alias, skipped out to the Adirondacks, and lured some disenfranchised urchins to set up camp with him on a two-hundred-acre compound in the middle of nowhere. His "philosophy" evolved into whatever was necessary to attract and keep followers. Those who felt somehow abandoned by society or dicked over by The Man. People with access to enough money to keep the polite despot's kingdom operating. He was everyone and anything a person wanted to believe in. Became guru and messiah. The great epiphany, sweet nirvana, always just a breath away. Kept that scam up for fifteen years.

"No, we didn't slaughter a lamb to bless the harvest or execute virgins on an altar. Although…" I lean back in my chair, cross my arms, and stare at the condensation ring around my glass of water. "When I was seven, I had a little brother who was born missing two toes on his left foot."

Navid inches toward me from across the table. "What happened to him?"

"They fed him to us in a stew with lentils."

No one makes a sound. They don't blink. Four pairs of eyes plastered to my face, frozen in shock. Until Ethan's smirk pulls across his lips.

"But cannibalism doesn't count, right?"

"Dammit!" Navid lets out a black licorice gust of air and slumps with both elbows on the table. "You fucking *had* me. I'm staring at you, like, shit, this chick ate her fucking brother like a boss."

I smile when Addison and C.J. erupt in hysterical laughter. Ethan winks at me, shaking his head. It's the closest thing to a stamp of approval I think I could have expected from tonight.

"Girl's got jokes," Addison says.

Humor helps. Letting people laugh relieves the tension and uncertainty. More important, it tells them you're normal. You're adjusted. They have nothing to fear. Otherwise, they regard you as they would a homeless person standing on a street corner with a crinkled cardboard sign. Most of them sympathize, but they don't want to make direct eye contact.

"Remind me sometime to tell you the dragon joke."

A man with a ball cap and cargo shorts stands up at the front of the room to announce karaoke will start in five minutes. I suspect this is the ritual hazing portion of the evening.

\* \* \*

After listening to three hours of off-key melodies with a side of political discourse, Ethan and I end up across the street at an artsy hipster coffeehouse. The kind of place that serves liquor and gourmet, vegan, gluten-free pastries. Cracking gray paint on the plaster walls exposes the red brick underneath. It's like a kitschy consignment shop, all mismatched furniture and lanterns hanging from the ceiling. We take our drinks to a gold velvet sofa in a quiet corner, away from the amplifiers and modest audience of a slam poet free-versing in the front room.

Though my earlier apprehension has evaporated, there's a new kind of nervous energy skittering up my spine.

"I feel like we didn't get a chance to talk." Ethan's face is cast in a soft purple glow from a string of lights tacked along the ceiling. "Did you have fun?"

"I did," I say, blowing on my coffee. "Thank you for inviting me."

"Have you made up your mind?" He sits forward and places both elbows on his knees, coffee between his hands. He closes the space between us, sucking the air from the room in that way he does that insists all things coalesce around him. "Or do I still need to convince you?"

Without a caterwauling drunk doing a rendition of Elle King at the mic and a table of others to pull focus, sitting under the full force of Ethan's undivided attention is somewhat...daunting. The effect of him up close, it doesn't dissipate.

"There's something I'm still having trouble with," I admit.

"Which is?"

"Why? Why is this important to you?"

"Isn't it important to you?"

That's not the point.

"Is this just about your personal fascination with my father? Because I'm not going to cave on an interview. If you're playing the long game here, hoping I'll warm up to you and bring the rest of the scattered survivors out of the woodwork for a big exclusive..."

He smirks. "I'm not sure I'm capable of such elaborate scheming."

Ethan then takes a sip of his coffee when it becomes apparent I want a real answer.

"You got my attention," he says. "If I'd never heard of you, if I'd never met your father, I'd still want to know the person who wrote that essay."

"That much I believe." I watch a man across the room play chess with himself under a painting of Slim Pickens riding the missile in *Dr. Strangelove*. "But what gives me pause, which I don't think is unreasonable, is I want to know if you're more interested in the topic of the essay than the words themselves."

He breathes out through his nose and regards me with something on the self-deprecating side of hostile. "You really have a low opinion of me, don't you?"

"No, I'm being careful. I don't know you well enough to form a complete opinion."

Ethan slumps back and his eyes wander for a moment. When he refocuses on me, his demeanor's changed. The same "abrupt" look that launched him into his lecture during my interview. His no-more-bullshit face. The *I've-run-out-of-patience* scowl.

"You know…" Fingers scratch across his scalp like ants are crawling on him. "It's killing me not to ask, so here it is: Why? I know you said you have ambitions, and that's great, but why *this* essay? Because, I'm sorry, Avery, but it's like you're allergic to it. You put this ball in motion, and now you're backing away from it. I know it wasn't for attention. Right now…" He reaches into his pants pockets and pulls out his phone. "I could call my agent and by morning there'd be a bidding war for your memoir. A year from now you'd have a *New York Times* bestseller with a movie deal. Make your first million by the time you're twenty-five. Go find yourself a house on an island somewhere and live the rest of your life off the royalties. But you sold an essay for, what, a few hundred dollars? Why?"

"I don't know," I say, and fill my mouth with dark bitter

black. My attention wanders toward the chess player again. He's locked in a stalemate. "I had to get my foot in the door."

Ethan's phone clatters on the coffee table at our feet. "Bullshit."

"Excuse me?"

"You're lying to me or to yourself. I'm not sure which. If you don't want to tell me, fine. But let's not pretend I don't know you at all."

My ears go hot. It spreads across my face and stings my teeth. "What is it you think you know?"

"It's starting to eat at you. I think if you could keep this thing bottled up any longer, you would. But it's consuming you from the inside and it won't stop until it's eaten its way out."

I forgot the first rule of talking to another journalist: never engage their curiosity. And never trust someone you can't lie to.

"All I'm saying is…" He lowers his voice and closes in, compressing the swollen bubble between us. "You're a commodity now whether you want to be or not. I know this job comes at a steep price for you," he says, "but you do have an opportunity to control the narrative. Now maybe I'm wrong, but I think there's a part of you that wants to tell these stories. If that's true, you don't have to do it alone."

It's a nice idea, using my pen to become the avenging angel of those whose tragedy has become farce. But there's a reason we've resisted the prospect of a life-changing payday. Everyone who came to Massasauga was running from something, and all were complicit in propping up the façade of their private utopia. They've suffered enough. I have no interest in inflicting any more pain. I think Ethan forgets that I'm still the daughter of a murderer. There are probably a few people out there who'd sleep easier if my parents and I hadn't made it out alive.

"Look, Avery." He takes my coffee from my hands and sets it on the table. As if my undivided attention isn't enough. "You have talent. I didn't just read your essay, I read everything I could find with your name on it. And I think you can only get better at a magazine like ours. But the thing that struck me about your essay was how impersonal it was. It read like you were writing about a different person. Like an outsider looking in rather than a participant. Why is that?"

There isn't a short answer to his question. I don't like thinking of us as the same person. Echo lives back there. I'm here. Better it stays that way. Ethan can't understand what a difficult division that is to maintain.

He takes my silence as a response.

"Fair enough." Ethan scrubs his hands through his hair like reshuffling the deck of his thoughts. "Here's my advice…" He turns to face me, one leg bent on the sofa, his arm draped over the back. "Don't write about Echo. Let Echo write about the world."

"Meaning?"

"You give Cara her essays, but you turn the focus around. You have a unique perspective that no one else can duplicate. What does someone who's survived what you have, who was raised the way you were, dissect and distill from society? You can sell Cara on that. It's a compromise, yes, but we're offering you a platform to say anything you want. What possible good excuse do you have for turning down that kind of freedom?"

Good question.

I spent a decade without the right to fully express myself. Every word manipulated. Every thought stifled. My life was a decaying fantasy created to sustain a megalomaniac's straw kingdom. We were his toys, and nothing good or charitable he ever did was without self-serving purpose. Like free-range chickens, we were kept just happy enough not to skitter away. Just healthy enough to be tasty.

"And Cara will go for this?"

"You have a brief window to exploit her affinity for you. Don't waste it."

"But what about real stories? I want to prove I can be a great reporter."

"I'm not going to let you rot in a basement. If you take this job, I promise I'll find other work for you to do. Other ways you can contribute and show off. I know you're afraid of sinking to the bottom of the pool and being forgotten. I won't let that happen, Avery. Trust me."

I want to. It's quite an attractive carrot he's dangling. But I know better. Never trust a man promising to make all your dreams come true.

"Are you sure you've thought about this?" I ask. "Us working together?"

"I'm game if you are."

Maybe the magazine's first offer wasn't a dream gig, but who am I kidding? I don't have editors lining up and begging for me. Ethan has gone to considerable trouble to convince me to say yes. Nowhere else am I going to find an advocate with as much clout as Ethan has at *Riot Street*.

And perhaps now I can picture more nights like this one. Sitting around a table arguing and laughing at a bar with the staff. Late nights over coffee, Ethan and me combing through public records and interview transcripts. Eating takeout at our desks with Ed breathing down our necks to finalize our copy before deadline. Sitting in front of the TV with pizza to watch C.J. eviscerate some arrogant schmuck on a Bill Maher panel. How can I pass this up?

Yet he didn't answer my first question.

"Why?" I ask again. "Why go out of your way?"

Ethan stares at me for a moment, impassive. "Because you're completely unpretentious," he says. "You don't know how rare a quality that is out there. You're going to do great things."

"Thank you, but I'm not sure that's really an answer."

"Then let me ask you something. Why become a journalist? After everything you've been through, why not live a quiet, obscure life somewhere?"

I suppose it's for the same reason anyone else goes into this line of work. "I want to change the world." It sounds simplistic and immature, I know, but it's the truth. "I want the stories I tell to matter—to do something important and consequential. Because I hate hypocrisy. I hate manipulation, corruption; the things we do to each other. One day I want to write a story that makes a difference. Something people will point to decades later and say, 'That was the day everything changed.'"

"That's why I want to work with you," Ethan says. "That's the right answer."

# 6

# THE ADDICT

I write *MARLA* in bold black marker on one of the blue sticky name tags and slap it on my chest. No one who's anyone in here uses their real name. We're all Jim or Mark or Karen.

Sunday night, after the church ladies have triple-counted the tithings envelope and stuffed it in a safe, wheeled the TV and DVD player into a padlocked closet, a couple dozen people are scattered on folding chairs in the basement rec room of Episcopal Church in the West Village. We sip coffee from little paper cups and nibble on grocery store chocolate chip cookies as a middle-aged man in a green polo shirt and sports coat steps up to the lectern.

"Hello, my name is Gary, and I'm an addict."

"Hello, Gary," the room replies.

"Welcome to the Help and Healing group of Narcotics Anonymous. I'd like to open this meeting with a moment of silence for the addict who still suffers."

Gary bows his head, scabby scalp of new hair plugs staring

us in the face like a teenager's erupted zits. On the wall behind him are bulletin boards with colorful paper flyers begging for church volunteers and announcing the church's food drive, Children's Shakespeare in the Garden, and Parents' Night Out.

Then he says, yellow mustache hanging over graying teeth, "I want to extend a special welcome to newcomers. If anyone here is attending their first NA meeting, would you like to introduce yourself?"

The first six rows all glance at each other, to the sides and behind them, searching for a new face. Several pairs of eyes land on me, but I'm not getting up there.

"Anyone who is new to *this* meeting?"

A tight-and-toned woman in a headband and neon purple tank top with coordinating yoga pants lifts out of her chair, hesitates, sits, then dashes to the lectern. Fingers gripping the edges for support, tendons straining in her tanned arms, she clears her throat and lifts her chin.

"Hi," she says, sharp and neat like a department store clerk who's about to blind you with perfume. Her sandy-blond ponytail sways with the nervous vibration running up her spine. Clears her throat again: "I'm Sarah, and I'm an addict."

"Hello, Sarah."

I sit in the back, out of range of the hyper-fundie twelve-steppers and their evangelic devotion. In the corner, away from the knee-bouncers and arm-scratchers who might mow me down in the event of a sudden escape. The ones still clinging to their doses from the methadone clinic.

"So..." Sarah's lips turn a deep shade of tense, bloody pink as she presses them together with all the force of a gator bite. "I nearly murdered my husband this morning."

An elderly woman in vintage Chanel cackles from the fourth row.

Gary steps in. "Go ahead, Sarah. There's no judgment here."

I do these a couple times a year—in rec rooms like this one with the soccer moms and bankers. The university professors and retail clerks in community centers. Combat vets and retirees in VFW halls. When I have a decision to make, these meetings help me think.

I listen to their stories of cashing out their kid's college fund to go on a week-long bender in a $500-a-night hotel room. How Ron stiffed his convalescent mother-in-law on the nursing home check to score a hit then wound up on a hospital gurney with tubes in his stomach. When the boss just went too fucking far this time, so Megan got a fix on her lunch break and left a Chipotle dump on his leather chair.

"...I thought it was irritable bowel syndrome, always having to get up in the middle of dinner at a restaurant, at the movies," Sarah says. "I thought my husband just had a sensitive stomach..."

But most of the time it's about the craving. The taste on their tongues that won't rinse out. It stalks them, haunts them. They imagine wild fantasies of what they'd do if pain and punishment were no concern. Or they talk about regret: people they've used and abused chasing the dragon. When they need a fix, nothing is sacred, and everyone's expendable.

"...while we were at church this morning, he got up in the middle of the pastor's sermon..."

I never got that far. Not so deep that I couldn't see the surface. I played at the water's edge, watching my only friend drift out with the suction of the ocean, getting smaller, until she disappeared beneath the waves.

"…but the worship band started playing and I got worried, so I went to check on him…"

One would be surprised how easy it is for a lost and lonely kid to become a statistic. When my mother and I escaped Massasauga, we had no money and only the clothes we wore that night. Surviving on charity and government assistance, we lived in shelters at first, then dirty motels once my mom found jobs waiting tables or bagging at the grocery store. I cleaned houses and ran errands for hobbled seniors. Took us a year to earn enough money to rent our first home. Bought an old used car, and a computer from Goodwill.

"…and I found him jerking off in the choir room beside the Easter decorations and clothing-drive boxes…"

Then I got kicked out of public school sophomore year. A social worker got involved, and I was referred to a shrink with a glass eye whose office smelled like kitty litter. That's how I discovered the wonders of Zoloft and Lexapro, Valium and Klonopin. Dabbled a little in Effexor and Cymbalta while my psychiatrist turned me into a chemical experiment, trying to home in on the right combination and dosage for my particular mixture of depression, generalized social anxiety disorder, and post-traumatic stress. But the pills couldn't cure my loneliness. The pit in my stomach grew more desperate and aching every day I spent longing to have just one friend in the world. Funny thing, though. An addict can never be your friend.

They're married to their fix. They're ruled by it, worship it.

"…chronic public masturbator…"

Her name was Jenny. She was the big sister of the block. I became her favorite because I would share my pills with her. In return, she took me to the movies, to the diners and sports bars where the community college kids hung out. We stayed out all night riding around that shit town in her rusted Corolla. She would do my makeup and let me wear her clothes when we cruised the mall.

"…attacked him with a plastic Easter Bunny lawn ornament…"

Jenny was an addict. But not like the sloppy, skeletal, driftwood bodies you see on TV. She had a reliable supply from her dealer boyfriend and a steady job as a custodian at the nursing home. She taught me how to find the happy medium in my self-medication. How to make the nightmares go away. It wasn't getting *high*, I told myself. It was getting *better*. Did you know heroin has anxiolytic properties? Any introvert in recovery will tell you they were never more socially engaged than when they were hooked. Until the fix wore off.

Jenny overdosed in a dressing room at Victoria's Secret wearing six pairs of stolen underwear. She always said she would never shoot it. That was for junkies. But sooner or later they all pick up a needle.

I went to rehab three days later.

That's where I met Maureen, a seventy-two-year-old former stringer for the Associated Press. She'd covered presidents and riots, celebrities and coups. She'd also picked up a coke habit along the way. But she managed to kick it in the nineties and started helping kids like me gain a little perspective. I was fascinated by her stories. Though they were a bit distorted by time and dementia, I listened to her talk for hours, imagining what I could see with a life like hers.

When I got out of rehab five weeks later, my mom brought me home to our new apartment far from Jenny's memory. Clean and straight, I was making another new start.

"…but I didn't use today," Sarah says, her eyes red with stress-tears and pride. "I'm still eight years clean and looking forward to my divorce."

We clap, because today this chick is iron. She's a goddamn steel trap. Sarah's the Hoover Dam.

"Thank you for sharing, Sarah. We're proud of you." Gary is back on his feet at the lectern, coffee stains in his mustache. "Now I'd like to recognize…"

I come here to remember that we're all one stupid decision away from ruining our lives. For some, it's addiction. But whatever our vices or secret inclinations, we're all walking a thin line between order and anarchy. Some have better balance than others. Several years ago I came to a dangerous precipice in the pursuit of affection. These meetings remind me how easy it is to fall over the edge.

At the front of the room, a woman stands to read from the White Booklet: "'Who is an addict? Most of us do not have to think twice about this question…'"

People think addiction is obvious, that it lives on someone like a python coiled around their neck. But that isn't always the case. It can be quiet and patient. It wants to hide. Jenny was a normal, decent person until she got her first taste.

"'…we lived to use and used to live…'"

Becoming an addict wasn't her fault. No one takes their first hit believing it's the first step to the end of their life. That cold, dark place of desperation is born of a certainty that there is no reality in which living and sobriety can coexist. A gun in one hand, and a hit in the other. Because right up to the second we're hooked, we know we never will be.

"'…there is one thing more than anything else that will defeat us in our recovery; this is an attitude of indifference or intolerance toward spiritual principles…'"

I reach into my pocket and roll the shell casing between my fingers, tracing the edge with my nail. This is right about the time I'm ready to leave. The program works for them—so be it. I just don't see how wresting control from an addiction and giving it to a "higher power" accomplishes anything more than trading one crutch for another. How's that taking responsibility?

\* \* \*

Walking home from the meeting, thoughts of Jenny and Maureen follow me. Their memory reminds me how easy it is to get stuck. To become comfortably complacent until one day you wake up and you've pissed your life away. If Maureen were here, she'd tell me to suck it up and quit my bitching. That's what a serious journalist would do. She'd say working with a man whose job it was to expose my family's ugly secrets is a trifling concern compared to professional advancement.

There's a rope tied around my waist, tugging me back and cinching tighter the harder I struggle; the only thing to do is cut it away. Be a razor.

When I get home, I email Cara then send a text to Ethan.

Avery Avalon
9:22 PM
I'm in.

# 7

# THE INTRUDER

Tucked away from Wall Street, in the valley of shadow cast by the big banks and executive corner offices encased in glass, the brick exterior of the *Riot Street* building is unmarked but for simple white lettering on the front door. It's Tuesday morning, my first day as a member of the magazine's staff, and I'm caffeinated to the point of intoxication when I walk in thirty minutes early.

Last night I stayed up until after midnight preparing essay pitches for Cara. It was my mission to start my first day looking like I have my shit together. Then this morning I spent the subway ride over crossing out and revising every idea I'd come up with. Whether from nerves or insecurity, this tends to be a recurring symptom. I get all doped up on a shiny new project, spend days or weeks obsessing, scrutinizing, planning, and prepping, only to dissolve into chaos when the moment arrives. A case of performance anxiety, I suppose. But I try to remind myself, as I sign in at the reception desk and almost misspell my own name, that I don't have to conquer the world on my first day.

Everyone's just making it up as they go along, right?

"This is for you." Andrew, the Banana Republic model in a plaid dress shirt and contrasting bow tie behind the reception desk, hands me a coffee mug with the magazine's logo on it and several fun-size candies nestled inside. "Consider it purely decorative. The coffee here sucks."

"Thanks for the warning." I tuck the mug into my messenger bag.

"You need to go see HR." He gestures toward the hallway behind him. "First door on the left."

Three hours later I emerge from the holding cell of human resources. What I thought would be a quick series of forms and signatures to begin my employment turns into an unending trudge through a dozen major life decisions, like HMO versus PPO and how to allocate my 401(k) contributions.

I walk out of the room—my bag a couple pounds heavier with forms and folders and an employee handbook—to find Ethan leaning against the opposite wall of the corridor. He's glaring at his phone, jabbing his thumbs at the screen while typing what I can only assume from his demeanor is a sincere death threat. I shut the door behind me just loud enough to announce my presence. He looks up, the creases in his brow disappearing, and shoves his phone in his back pocket.

"Ready?"

"Officially official." I hold up the badge hanging from the lanyard around my neck.

"Don't wear that in here." Ethan turns toward the elevator and I follow beside him. "The other kids will blow spitballs in your hair."

"I'm just absorbing the moment," I say, taking a last adoring look at the big bold letters of PRESS PASS above my picture before sticking the badge in my bag. "Let me have my fun."

"You're right." Ethan hits the button for the elevator. He slides me a sideways glance. "I'll resist the urge to smother your excitement with jaded pessimism."

The elevator *dings* and the doors open.

"That's all I ask."

"At least until after lunch."

We exit the elevator on the fifth floor, where the bull pen of blue-gray cubicles hides activity under rows of white recessed lighting. Keyboards clicking in two-dozen swift staccato rhythms. Conversations rising over the fabric-padded cube walls. The air smells of burnt coffee and fresh runs of paper and ink through the copy machine.

"I've got a meeting," Ethan says, pulling out his phone to give it another dirty look.

"Oh, okay." Not that I expected cake and flowers, but...

"Addison will give you the tour and show you to your desk."

Before I can respond, he's walking away. I stand caught in an awkward moment of indecision, follow or wait here, until I see Addison Lee's tall, lanky image materialize in the center mass of cubicles to wave me over. Like an orphaned puppy, I scurry to the familiar face.

"Welcome, welcome," Addison says, setting his headphones on the desk. "I guess you're mine today."

"Sorry you drew the short straw." Babysitting the new girl can't be anyone's idea of a choice gig.

"Nah, no worries. Today's pitch—"

"Addison, got that sidebar?" a voice shouts from somewhere across the room.

"I got you." Addison bends down to his laptop and drops a file into a chat box. "Sorry. It's pitch day, so Cara and Ed are in the Slaughterhouse."

On the back wall, four five-by-eight whiteboards stretch the full length of the bull pen. They're lined in a grid pattern and represent every writer, their stories, and the current stage of production. On the next wall, running parallel to the windows that look out on the street, cork boards are decorated with reams of paper displaying the proposed layout for each page of the upcoming issue. Visualized this way, the operation appears a massive undertaking.

"Follow me." Addison leads me back toward the elevator then down the hallway to where Ethan disappeared. "Online edition meets with Cara for Weekly Wednesday Whippings, so you have that to look forward to."

"Can't wait."

During Addison's rendition of the orientation process, I am introduced to the *Riot Street* offices as a sort of vast landscape of factions and fiefdoms. The cubicle community, where most of the staff writers, associate editors, and the like live, is known as the Farm.

"Pretty self-explanatory," Addison says.

Writers are animals. We subsist on junk food, caffeine, and pats on the head.

The first floor belongs to all things administrative: HR, payroll, that sort of thing. It's a different culture down there, where they all have kids and spouses and are obsessed with their Fitbits. Except Banana Republic Andrew. He is the rare downworlder who transcends the divide between floors.

The fifth floor is shared by Editorial and Advertising, between which is a shaky truce mediated on the neutral and sacred territory of the snack room.

"After *three* meetings between designated negotiators for both sides," Addison says, pulling two bottles of water from the top shelf of the refrigerator and handing one to me, "it was decided that Editorial may occupy the second shelf, Advertising gets the bottom shelf. Door and drawers are open territory. Anything on the first shelf is fair game, so help yourself to soda, water, whatever."

"You're kidding."

He nudges the fridge door shut and twists open his water. "I shit you not. Wars were fought. Interns were poisoned. It got messy."

"What about the freezer?" I shove the bottle of water into my bag, now almost overflowing with souvenirs from my journey thus far.

"Do *not* go in there."

Down the hallway that separates the Editorial and Ad sections of the floor is the main conference room.

"The Slaughterhouse," Addison tells me. We stop to spy on the pitch meeting through the glass walls. "Beware, all ye who enter."

Because the Slaughterhouse is where the animals are

butchered. Fitting. In my experience, pitch sessions are a brutal event in which writers let the happy, hopeful balloons of their precious dreams and ideas float into the air, only to have an editor shoot them out of the sky with a sniper rifle and take a piss all over the exploded, shriveled remains.

Ed and Cara sit at opposite ends of the rectangular table, flanked by half a dozen of the writing staff with iPads and open laptops. In the center, facing us, Ethan stabs at his phone. That deep, vexed crease between his eyebrows slices down the center of his face. Whatever has him so upset, I fear for the person on the receiving end of his angry texting.

"Ethan wanted to show you around, but Ed pulled him in," Addison says.

"It's fine. I think I'm getting the more informative version of the tour." Somehow I doubt Ethan's would be as colorful.

"Stick with me, kid." Addison nudges my shoulder. "Speaking of which, where'd you and Ethan sneak off to after the bar?"

As if he's heard us, Ethan looks up. His crinkled face relaxes. He draws across the screen of his iPad with his index finger then holds it up for us to see, which catches the attention of Ed, Cara, and everyone else in the room. Great.

"Meet for lunch—15," the screen reads.

Addison nods and gives Ethan a thumbs-up, leading me down the hallway to continue the tour. It concludes in the Cave—a dark, stuffy room furnished with dilapidated desks that look like they were salvaged from a fire sale. The air is clogged with a vague smell of dirty carpet mixed with subtle hints of hot garbage, the latter stench emanating from the restaurant Dumpster in the alley below and creeping in through the window's cracked weather seal.

"Yeah," Addison says, his face warped by sympathy, "this is you."

The size of the room suggests it was designed as a conference room or storage space, but is now congested with shadow-dwelling writers all but sitting on top of each other in the glow of computer screens. Where overhead fluorescent tubes should be, only empty tracks.

Addison brings me over to a bearded guy in a tight pair of jorts. The kind of bony, leathery man whose social calendar revolves around Critical Mass meetups. He smells of WD-40 and wilted kale. Two desks arranged in an L shape in the center of the room create a small fort from which he oversees his modest territory.

"This is Cyle with a C, the associate web editor and keeper of the Cave." Addison's introduction carries a chipper-yet-sarcastic tinge to his voice. "Cyle, this is Avery."

I hold out my hand. "Nice to meet you."

He gives me a limp reciprocation and jerks his head toward a chipped, laminate desktop supported by two waist-high filing cabinets. A brown molded-plastic chair, like the ones in a school cafeteria, sits beside the makeshift desk.

"That's yours. You'll need to talk to IT about getting a laptop assigned."

"Yeah," I say, a polite smile slapped on my lips as I take in the sad little workspace shoved up against the wall. "Great. Thank you."

Any notions I had about the glamorous world of internet journalism? Cured.

"Better be worth it." Cyle wraps his headphones around his ears and slouches over his laptop. "We're losing three paid interns this summer for you."

So it isn't just apathy but outright hostility. Grand. Cyle and I are off to a great start.

Addison tosses me a pitying glance as I set my bag down on the warped, uneven surface of the desk top. A dip in the center leaves one corner raised off its cabinet. Which corner depends on where the weight is distributed. So that'll be fun.

No one else in the room even lifts their eyes from the hypnotic radiance of their computers. They all wear earbuds or headphones, jacked into the Matrix and unconcerned by my appearance. Until Ethan enters the room and takes a hard look at my desk.

"The fuck is this shit?" He darkens the doorway for a moment, snapping every pair of startled eyes in his direction, before stalking up to Cyle. "She needs a proper desk."

Cyle leans back in his adjustable, ergonomic throne, crossing his ankle over his knee. "New chick can deal until we get some money in the budget." Prick. "We're out of spares."

"I don't mind," I say. "I'm not picky." The last thing I need is to inspire a turf war over a stupid desk. Hell, I'll bring mine in from home if I have to.

"No," Ethan barks at me. "Fuck that." He glares down at Cyle, violent shadows across his face. "You've got two desks for what? Stop being an asshat and give her one."

"She's your pet." Cyle sends a snide glance at me over his shoulder. Super prick. "Feel free to find her better accommodations."

"I think that's lunch." Addison jerks his head toward the door.

I grab my bag, swallowing down the burning acid rising up the back of my throat, and slip along the wall toward the exit. I had hoped to blend in at first, slide into a comfortable rhythm, and allow my work to get me noticed. Instead, I've become a disturbance.

"How about you try not being such a miserable bastard, yeah?" Ethan's voice is coarse with restrained rage. Though he releases some of the tension from his jaw, his eyes still sting with hatred. "Little less time up your own ass."

"Goodbye, Cave people." Addison waves at the spectators caught in the darkness and pushes me into the hallway. "Let us know when you're ready to overthrow the fascist regime."

At the elevator, Ethan catches up to us. He punches the button with his fist and stares at his rigid reflection in the metallic doors. The obvious ire has evaporated from his expression, replaced by an eerie, implacable veneer.

"Let's get a drink."

\* \* \*

Out on the sidewalk, severe noon sun splits through the leafy branches of trees dotting the curb. The lunch rush clogs the street with passing cars. Addison and I appraise Ethan, both waiting for an eruption that doesn't come.

"So…" Addison says, swinging his arms in an uncertain gesture. "Taco stand?"

Ethan squints at the sun, glancing down the block. "It's too hot to sit outside." He looks to me. "It's your first day. Let me buy you a real lunch."

"Dude." Addison scoffs, almost offended at the thought. "Taco Tuesday."

"So I'll take her to El Centro." Ethan steps beside me, putting Addison on the other side of the invisible line drawn on the sidewalk. "We can get a drink and relax instead of standing in line for twenty minutes."

They become tangled in an exchange of unreadable stares. Silent messages pass between their unmoving lips. There's a story there, twisting in the air between them.

"Whatever you two want to do," I say. Because I'm not about to pick sides. "I'm just along for the ride."

The front doors open, releasing the hungry horde of the magazine staff onto the sidewalk. They hardly pause to shuffle around us, on their way down the block. Navid and C.J. wave, mid-conversation with each other, then move on.

"Yeah, have fun," Addison says to Ethan and me, his eyes skeptical. "Catch up with you later." And he turns to follow the stampede.

"Right then." Ethan holds his hand out to point the way in the opposite direction. "Let's go."

\* \* \*

Seated at a two-person booth in the noisy Mexican restaurant, smears of cheese sauce and sprinkles of rice are all that's left of my meal.

"You sure you don't want a drink?" Ethan finishes his first

tequila, neat, and waves down the waiter for a second. "It's on me."

I sip water and look past him toward the windows and line of patrons at the hostess stand waiting to be seated.

"What?" he asks, dipping a chip into his salsa.

"Nothing."

I'm plenty irritated with him, Cyle, the whole stupid tirade, but I don't have room for petty bullshit. I learned a long time ago to let go of the little stuff. Emptied a damn suitcase-load of little stuff and set it on fire. Felt much better ever since.

"That means *something*." His bland expression and patient eyes say he'll wait all day for an answer.

"It *means* I don't want to open a discussion on the *something*. I'm capable of keeping my thoughts to myself."

"You're mad at me." Ethan smirks and pushes his hair off his forehead. "I should let that little snot push you around?"

I stab my straw through the ice blockade inside my cup.

"Go on, then. Let it out."

Fine. Fuck it. "You embarrassed me back there with Cyle. You caused a whole confrontation that will probably have little or no effect on your daily life, but which creates a whole mess of uncomfortable problems for me."

"He's a jackass."

"I don't get the luxury of calling Cyle names to his face."

"Why not?" He slouches back in the booth, amused. "He's calling you a cunt behind your back."

Charming.

"Because I'm new. I'm new and have been plucked from

obscurity for the unfortunate and inequitable reason that the story of my upbringing was popular for a day. And then only because it ended in mass murder."

"That all?"

The waiter arrives with Ethan's drink, which he takes and holds to his smiling lips.

"And because I'm a woman in a newsroom dominated by men. I don't get to pitch a princess fit over the crappy desk they stick me with. Because then I'm needy and difficult. But you waltz in, defending my honor, and still all the negative repercussions will land on my shoulders. Because you're Ethan Ash, and Ethan Ash is just a hot temper who always has a 'fuck this' or 'fuck that' every time he enters a room."

"On occasion I've been known to enter a room without saying anything at all." He winks. Snarky shit.

"And you know what they're thinking." I slide my finished plate of food to the edge of the table to alert the waiter that we're ready for the check. "Everyone in the Cave and everyone they've told so far."

"That we're sleeping together," Ethan says, dry and without inflection. "Maybe you're sleeping with half the senior staff and that's why you have a job when there are more experienced and qualified candidates begging for scraps."

"Pretty much."

"Do you want to?"

"What?"

"Sleep together."

"Ethan..." Glad he's taking this seriously.

"Look." He sets down his glass and leans forward. "Nobody's handing out Brownie points for nobility in that place. If you want something, take it. If you don't like something, fix it. Cyle doesn't have his job because he's nice to people. Five years ago he was an intern who chased away everyone else who wanted his gig until he got to sit in that dark little hole and lord over his minions. If you want people to respect you, don't take any shit."

"That's you," I say, folding my straw wrapper into an accordion. "That's not me."

"It could be. This is your shot to define your identity. Don't waste it on being a shadow." Ethan sips his tequila like the world could explode around him and it'd barely ruffle a hair out of place. "Because whatever you were doing before, Avery, it wasn't working."

He's not wrong, and that bugs me more than it should. Ethan can't understand what it's like to have already shed one whole person from my psyche. To look back just ten years and barely recognize myself. As if the memories were of a past life, of a stranger. Echo was a failed attempt at being. Not viable once removed from the controlled environment in which she was created. She wasn't equipped for the outside world. Delicate, unable to withstand the stimulation and disorder, pain and loneliness. Echo was shriveling, breaking down. She became destructive. So I killed her. A very late term abortion.

But it's like fragments of her survived, implanted so deep I can't claw them out. I see afterimages that flash and flicker behind my eyes. Hear her inflection in my voice. Sometimes I still taste her cravings on my tongue.

Becoming who you want to be requires conviction and stamina.

Ethan will never get that.

\* \* \*

When we get back to the office, Ethan tows me around the Farm from desk to desk like it's the first day of school all over again and I'm today's show-and-tell. Arts and Culture girls with thick black glasses, and cardigans over striped shirts like they live in a perpetual French film festival. Econ boys in pressed button-downs and skinny ties, laptop screens an ordered frenzy of charts and decimals. The crime-and-punishment crew, all haggard and going to or coming from their smoke breaks on the roof. There's a permanent stench of tobacco in the air around them. Traversing the landscape, doing the grip-and-grin, I'm regarded by the staff with about as much enthusiasm as a flyer handed out on a street corner.

"Every one of them assumes you're out to take their job," Ethan says. "The better you are, the more they'll hate you."

"Is that supposed to make me feel better?"

"No."

Seems the group I met Friday night were selected as the more-welcoming face of *Riot Street* and Ethan was saving the less-savory personalities for after I signed the contract.

Once we've made the rounds, he takes me to IT on the third floor to pick up my laptop, after which we sit at his desk while he escorts me through the process of setting up log-in credentials for the magazine's intranet, email, publishing platform, and a few other sites and services I'll need access to.

"Getting settled in?" Ed leans over the side wall of Ethan's cubicle. His eyes are a bit droopy from a Taco Tuesday food coma and his faux hawk is a smidge off-center.

"All good," I say, sitting up straight. "Got a tour, I'm all plugged in…"

"Uh-huh."

"I just want to thank you, again, for giving me a chance. I know my interview wasn't—"

Ethan shoots me a chastising glance as Ed swats at the air in a dismissive gesture. Not much of a talker, Ed. Seems his visit is more a formality than genuine interest.

"I'm not sending her back to the Cave." Ethan reclines in his chair and folds his arms behind his head, like he's issuing a decree and his word is final. Now I send him a glare, because I thought we'd come to an understanding on the matter.

Ed looks away. At the wall or at dust moats floating through the air. "I heard."

Undeterred by my silent thought waves begging him to back off, Ethan grabs my bag from the floor and drops it over the front wall of his cube to the adjacent empty desk. "Take that one."

Ed's lips stretch to a thin line, brow furrowed. "Vee's desk?"

"She's not coming back," Ethan says, harsh and clipped.

"Who's Vee?"

Ethan stares past me like he's pretending really hard not to hear her name. Ed just taps the top of the wall and nods before walking away. The man has no fucks left to give about shit like this.

"Seriously?" I say, once Ed is out of earshot. "Will you stop?"

"Quit apologizing. If you walk around like a charity case, that's how people will treat you."

"Then stop acting like my chaperone."

"I'm not going to let you get absorbed and disappear. So you might try a little gratitude."

"And a touch of humility wouldn't kill you."

"I tried it once. Didn't suit me."

No kidding.

## 8

# THE SLAUGHTERHOUSE SIX

As a child, I was raised to assimilate. *Don't ask questions. Don't talk out of turn. Don't think too much.* Because an isolationist system built on the shaky foundation of a man as a conduit for the spiritual energy of the world doesn't survive on diversity and free expression. It requires the sort of harmony found only through totalitarian authority. *This is the line; walk it or perish.* The talent is in convincing people they like it.

In the newsroom, the editor's word is law. It is final and absolute. Quite often this power is wielded with ruthless disregard for petty, fragile ideas like compassion, ego, or sympathy. This is illustrated as, one by one, the five other writers in this pitch meeting step into the arena and are quickly struck down by the vicious ponytailed lion that is Cara tearing at their muddy flesh. I now feel privileged that she went so easy on me during our interview. And I realize that Ethan's brief warning this morning, before I walked into the Slaughterhouse for my first taste of the Wednesday Whipping, fell short of preparing me for the visceral carnage of it all.

"Stop talking." Sitting at the head of the conference table, Cara takes a deep inhale through her nose, manicured fingers pressed to her temples, and breathes out like a baby's whisper through pursed lips. "Amy, from a place of love," she says, eyes closed, "I need you to get an ice pick and stab that thirteen-year-old girl who lives in your head right in the eye. Can you do that for me?" She looks up. "Just—" Cara jabs at the air. "Right in her little sparkly pubescent eyeball. Okay?"

Amy nods, eyes liquid and lips clamped shut. Her pen slices frantic lines over the bulleted list of eviscerated story ideas.

"What's next?" Cara's steely eyes slide to another victim.

"I have a source," says the CPAC disciple in the mint poplin Dockers shirt, "who's offering photos of three congressional aides at a DCCC fund-raiser in Malibu with a gay male porn star."

Cara's shoulders tense before he's finished the sentence.

"New rule." She slaps her laptop shut with a force that tightens every ass in the room. "I don't give a shit about reality-show divas, hunting for secret gays, or dogs that look like dead celebrities. Any of you want to write that garbage, go work for the *New York Post*. We are not a dumping ground for your vapid listicles because you got too drunk last night to develop an authentic idea. We are not going to race every lazy BuzzFeed wannabe to the bottom of the media shit pile. Show your colleagues some respect and don't walk into this room without something you're willing to get arrested for. Clear?"

I'm so hard for Cara right now. Like I could climb across this table and grab her by the ponytail to lay one on her. But that would inappropriate. So I smother an aroused smile and give only a tight nod of agreement. I admit now that I pegged her wrong. Sure, she might be a bit too cozy with the business side of the magazine, but she isn't the soulless sellout I first thought.

"Avery." Cara's arctic eyes flash to mine and I'm reminded that I'm not just an invisible spectator. "What have you got?"

That's a damn good question. In light of the last several minutes, my scribbled pitches appear dead on the vine. Not that I would classify any of them as vapid or tabloid fodder, but neither do they comply with the one criterion I know will make Cara happy—they're not about Echo. And while I admire Cara's attempts to keep the magazine from getting sucked into the sewer, she scares the shit out of me. If I let her down, if I push back against the only reason I was invited to this table, I might watch my career wither before it's bloomed.

I've already wasted ten seconds on this existential crisis while the room narrows and every pair of eyes around the table turns away in embarrassment. Except for Cara's laser gaze. My blood drains into my feet and my shoes become two sizes too small. I can't feel my face. I'm aware of every excruciating second that ticks by while she waits, staring, and I blink, blink, blink in silence like doing so will change the image before my eyes until I'm no longer trapped in the chaos spiral unfolding around me.

"Anything else?" Cara glances at her phone then sweeps her eyes around the table of broken, defeated faces. "We're done here."

An anvil drops to the hard bottom of my gut, shaking organs and sending vibrations through my limbs. This is the lonely, silent sensation of utter failure. I'm not even worth mauling for sport.

We all gather our things and shuffle toward the door.

"Avery?" Cara calls from behind me. "A minute."

My breath stalls in my throat and my skin tingles. I let the others pass, catching a disparaging glance from Cyle, then turn to Cara standing beside her chair.

Her narrow, pristine face is vacant of expression. "I hear there was a disagreement yesterday."

Shit. "I—"

"I don't care. I'm not concerned with where you sit as long as your copy comes in on deadline. Understood?"

"Yes," I say, regaining sensation in my fingers.

Her posture shifts, shoulders relax. "Cyle suffers from a malignant case of Mediocre White Man Syndrome, but he does his job. You don't have to like each other, but you do have to work together. That going to be a problem?"

"No."

Cara likes short answers, so I keep them succinct. She's not interested in how Ethan took it upon himself to throw down the gauntlet or how I would be happy to fester in the dank recesses of the Cave with the other Morlocks. She just wants compliance.

"Good. Now the next time we meet, I expect you to contribute."

I think that's about as close as it gets to a pep talk with her. Not quite a womance, but it's a start.

Ethan is waiting for me when I get back to my desk. Reclined in his chair, office phone wedged against his ear, he wears an expectant smile until the hollow darkness of my expression sits him upright.

"How'd it go?" he asks, scooting forward with a hand covering the phone's mic.

"Oh, brilliant." I drop my notepad on my desk and yank my chair out.

"Okay…" I hate that smirk. "Care to elaborate?"

"It was a total burn-in, all right?" I flop down in my chair and stare at the drop-tile ceiling. "No survivors."

His phone clicks into its cradle. "What did you pitch her?" Then he rolls into the aisle beside our cubes.

"Who'd you just hang up on?"

"Director of Health and Human Services." He shrugs. "I was on hold."

Ethan stares then pops his eyebrows, still waiting for an answer.

"Nothing. I froze. Sat there like an idiot with nothing to say."

This is the shit that killed Echo. The anxiety and desperation. A shy little girl hiding in the shadows, afraid to be seen and longing for attention. But no matter how many ways I try to excise that part of her, it burrows deeper, only to resurface when it's most detrimental.

"Hey." He slides into my cube and yanks my chair forward to demand I look at him. "Relax. You're being too hard on yourself."

"No, I'm not. I had one job, and I failed. I've wanted this for so long, and when I finally have the chance to prove…" A

sick, nauseated feeling seeps through my stomach. "I humiliated myself."

"So what?" Ethan leans in, lowering his voice. "Are you going to give up?"

"No." I don't have an escape plan. There is no backup.

"Are you sure? Sounds like an end-of-the-world scenario.
Wouldn't you rather run away and find something easier, less
demanding to do? Somewhere your biggest responsibility is
counting back correct change?"

I have a sudden urge to throw something at his face. "No."

"Then quit your bitching, love, and get to work."

Great. Good talk.

\* \* \*

I spend the next two hours at my desk staring into the white
abyss of a blank screen. I try listening to music. Chew gum
and twirl a pencil between my fingers. Cross my eyes until
the tiny pixels become large and excited like static on a television. Drink three cups of coffee and eat two stale doughnuts
from the snack room. None of which produces a thought that
doesn't sound like something that would inspire Cara to homicidal rage.

"I can hear you thinking," Ethan says through the wall that
separates our cubicles. "Stop trying so hard."

"Of course. Why didn't I think of that? Just sit back and
wait for divine intervention. For the magical sprite of inspiration to land on my shoulder and fart an idea in my ear."

"You're mean when you're cranky."

"Stop talking."

"I can help. You want to bounce some pitches off me, brainstorm?"

"You want to write it for me, too?"

It's not that I don't appreciate Ethan's willingness to help, but I can't let his constant need to intervene become a crutch. If I can't even pitch one solid story on my own, what the hell am I doing here? Besides, it would only be a matter of time before his goodwill turned to resentment and I became a burden rather than a project.

No, it'll come. Eventually. Until then...I have to stave off the creeping sense of terror crawling up my neck. Maybe it's just me, but there's a strange disquiet rippling through the newsroom. Nothing material, per se, but rather an indistinct energy like someone sneaking up behind me. Whether morbid curiosity or something more, lingering stares and furtive glances hang on me while I sit frozen in stasis at my desk. But I'm accustomed to the attention—eyes that dart in the other direction when they catch my gaze, conversations that cease when I approach—and I can't let it distract me from...

Hell, I got nothing. A big, white, empty void of nothing.

I flinch when Addison taps me on the shoulder. "Lunch?"

My savior. "Yes."

"Ethan?" Addison asks, leaning over the cubicle wall.

"Go on ahead." He picks up his desk phone and wedges it between his ear and shoulder. "Careful with that one. She bites."

* * *

For some baffling reason, the staff doesn't observe an official Wednesday lunch alliteration.

"This seems like a grievous oversight," I say, as I wait in line with Addison and C.J. at the pita place down the street. We got here at 11:50 and still have fifteen people ahead of us. The line snakes through the room of tables and out the doors to the sidewalk. Better be a damn good pita.

"For a while there was a diner nearby that served chicken and waffles," Addison says. He wears his sunglasses inside to block the bright glare of sunlight that skips off passing car windshields and cuts through the restaurant. And because they go with the outfit. "Then a brief campaign was made for adopting Wing Wednesday, but a salmonella outbreak had half the staff on the toilet for two days, so…"

"We're about to eat." C.J. grimaces and shoves Addison's shoulder. "Is Ethan still at the office?"

"He had some calls to make," I say, and turn away from an aspiring hedge fund type with a date rapist smile waiting for his order. "Why, should we see if he wants us to bring back something?"

"Don't do it." C.J. shakes her head.

For someone who takes senators and pundits to task with the pitiless wit of a George Carlin and Samantha Bee love child, she's more approachable than I expected. And shorter. But then I had envisioned Serena Williams with a tape recorder and pencils in her hair.

"What, does he stiff you on the check?"

Addison takes off his sunglasses and looks at C.J. as if trying to parse out how best to phrase a response. "Ethan tends to be very *popular* with new girls. Usually interns," he qualifies, like I might take offense otherwise. "Before you know it, they're picking up his lunch orders, spending their weekends fact-checking his manuscripts, and devoting three weeks buried in the city hall archives of some tiny municipality in West Virginia."

"Oh, wow, yeah," C.J. says, taking a few steps forward as the line inches closer to the register. "I forgot about…"

"Brandy? Brittany?" Addison shrugs. "Something like that. She was never seen or heard from again."

"Is that what happened to Vee?"

A pause. C.J. and Addison stare at me like I just farted at a funeral.

"Persona non grata, sweetheart." Flippant, almost joking. Even I recognize Vee is a sore subject Addison would rather hurry past. "Let's call it creative differences."

"So Ethan is a prima donna." Which comes as a shock not at all. I wouldn't describe Ethan as the preening-peacock type, but neither is he oblivious to his professional stature or the influence he can exert over a room.

"I ain't mad at him," Addison says, quite happy to elaborate as long as I agree to ignore the tension around Vee's name. "Hell, I'd take a few doting interns who wanted to pick up my dry cleaning and walk my dog, but Ethan tends to horde the eager-to-please. Don't fall for the mysterious eyes and gorgeous hair—he's a crafty one."

I like to think I'm a pretty good judge of character. At least so far as picking out the dangerous types: liars, manipulators, users, abusers. Ethan may have a few personality flaws, but he doesn't trip my alarms.

"Don't get suckered into being nice to him as a gateway drug to washing his car," I say. "Got it."

* * *

Back at the office, Addison and I eat lunch at his desk while I get part two of my orientation to the newsroom landscape.

"The eastern block is critic territory. You can't play with them unless you like obscure bands from Sweden, eating foods you can't pronounce, or only watching films with subtitles."

Addison keeps a bottle of sriracha in his desk drawer. Squeezes long ribbons of it on his pita and makes a pool for dipping chips. It's more food group than condiment. Even puts the stuff in coffee. I'm getting a contact high just smelling it—sinuses cleared right up.

"But that little poser"—Addison throws a surreptitious nod toward a short guy with a man bun and something written in French across his T-shirt—"blasts Fall Out Boy in his head-phones like no one notices, so don't let him fool you."

Next Addison points to the far south corner of the Farm. There two perfectly flat-ironed heads of hair sit among col-orful mountains of cosmetic boxes. The fashion and beauty writers, in coordinating summer patterns and matching statement jewelry. I've never been that put-together in my life.

"Don't ever let them draft you as a test subject," Addison says. "Those two go after fresh meat and virgin hair like rabid hyenas. Last year Legal banned any further testing on interns after one suffered a severe allergic reaction to lip balm."

"I'm starting to see a pattern. Interns have a short shelf life here."

"True story."

Cara struts down the aisle between two rows of cubicles. She could be no one, but that self-assured gait, her raised chin—they say she knows exactly where she's going. She knows what she wants and she's come to take it. The sight of her renews the sense of dread and anxiety I'd held on Pause until now. It's not that I don't think I can meet this assignment, I just don't know where to start. Everything I was willing to divulge about Echo and Massasauga is in the essay. There's nothing left to say. So how do I spin that story into a series with legs? How do I get the stink of failure off me?

"Can I ask you something?" I say to Addison.

He balls up his pita wrapper and tosses it in the trash under the desk. "Sure."

"How do you keep writing your essays? I mean, how do you find the inspiration to discuss the same topic week after week? Doesn't it ever feel like you're repeating yourself?"

Addison's lips part like he's going to speak, then snap shut. A moment passes as he leans back in his chair and taps his fingers on the desk. Everything about him, his mannerisms, feels like a performance. Not in an affected, artificial sense, but like he's aware at all times he's starring in his own scripted series, cameras rolling.

"I was in a very different situation," Addison says. "When I started my column, I'd only recently come to terms with my gender identity. I was still exploring what it meant. I had this feeling of"—his eyes search my face, the wall behind me, the ceiling for the word until—"incongruity. Most of my life, feeling like everyone hears music when all I'm getting is static. I had more questions than answers. In my case, I fought to write those first essays. I needled Cara and Ed to give me the space to talk about this—without a format or a clear vision. Just to put my thoughts out there and see what the response might be and where it'd lead. It was an experiment that might not have lasted this long if the country hadn't arrived at the same conversation at roughly the same time." Addison sits forward and smiles in a sort of empathetic gesture. "But you're a different story. I know you sort of got the bait-and-switch on this gig. I feel you, believe me."

"So what should I do?" Short of banging my head against a wall until the internal hemorrhaging sparks an idea or kills me, I don't have a strategy.

"The best advice I can give," Addison says, "is to consider who you're speaking to. Think of an essay as more of a conversation than a statement."

It's good advice. If only I knew what to do with it. I take that thought back to my desk.

Before I can wake my laptop, Ethan is hovering behind me.

"Yeah?" I spin around in my chair to ask.

What I'm met with sends a cold sting down my back. Ethan's eyes are impassive in that eerie way a violent storm leaves silence in its wake. The first thought that comes to mind is that I've already been fired.

"What?" I ask. "What's wrong?"

My brain jogs from one worst-case scenario to the next. My apartment blew up. Aster was nuked. Kumi threw herself off the Brooklyn Bridge. No, really, I've just been fired thirteen hours into this job. I wait for an answer, but nothing happens. Ethan just stares at me like I should read his mind. His motionless lips make we want to pry open his mouth and yank the answer out.

"Ethan"—I get to my feet—"you're freaking me out. Say something."

"Follow me." He puts his hand behind my shoulder to push me down the aisle between the row of cubicles toward the hallway. Once we're out of sight from the Farm, he stops me.

"I got a phone call," he says, tentative and slow. The way one tiptoes through a darkened house when a noise wakes them in the middle of the night.

"Okay…"

"They didn't know how to find you."

So I'm not fired. "Spit it out."

"Your father died last night."

"Oh."

Barely a sound. *Oh.* It's all I can muster before my throat closes and my chest constricts. This hasn't happened in a long time. Years. The nearing rumble that shakes the ground beneath my feet. A building roar of thick white noise. A wave crashes over me, heavy and concussive. Pressure fills my head. Tumbling under the surf, weightless, everything blurs. Ethan keeps talking, but I hear only fragments.

"…my source at the prison contacted me…"

My eyes can't focus on anything more than his hands clenching, flexing, gesturing through the air at his sides because no one ever knows what to do with their hands at a time like this. I'd reach for them if I could, anchor myself to something grounded and sturdy. I know what happens next. But I'm pulled down, down, lungs empty. The light on the surface dims.

"…next of kin, so once they track down your forwarding address…"

I blink, and it's black.

*Gunshots. Quick succession of pops, impossible and unmistakable. Blood splatter on the walls and bodies sprawled in the mud. Breaking glass and shattered screams. Just run, and don't look back. Shots snapping off trees. My mother, keys jingling in her hand. The metal-on-metal groan as I yank open the rusted door of the pickup truck. The engine grunting to life. Tires whirring in search of traction. Then she grinds the stick shift into gear and it's all in the rearview mirror, bathed in the red glow of taillights.*

"Avery."

Blink again. Under the waves, climbing to the surface. White, wobbling circle of light just beyond my fingertips.

Ten, nine, eight, seven…

Breathe.

Six, five, four…

"Listen." Ethan bends to meet my eyes. "They'll need to know if you want to claim the body."

Breathe.

I open my mouth to speak, but nothing comes out. I'm not in my body. It's a limp, lifeless thing over which I have no control—disconnected and getting farther away.

"Are you hearing me?"

Three, two, one…

"Hey, *there* you are." Cyle comes charging down the hallway from the Cave. "Check your damn email."

Breathe.

Ethan snaps upright. "Not now, Cyle."

"Hit on the new girl later," he says. "I need her."

I plummet back inside myself. Can't let Cyle see me flinch.

"Yeah." I cough and clear my throat. "What can I help with?"

"No." Ethan puts himself between Cyle and me, claiming the center of the hallway. "Now's not a good time. She—"

"It's fine," I say.

Cyle shakes his head, like he's already had this argument in his mind. "She's been here for two days and done fuck-all. She needs to pull her weight."

Ethan steps forward until he's all but standing on Cyle's toes. "Fuck off, Cyle. Turn around."

Without making the decision to do so, I'm backing away. Toward the Farm and farther from these men. Somewhere else, dark and quiet. Because something's going to come out of me, and I'm not sure what.

"Dude, what is your deal?" Cyle takes two steps back, face turning red. His eyes dart to me, puzzled and angered. "What—"

"Ethan. Avery." Ed's at my back. He stands a few feet outside his open office door. "My office. Now."

It's the most volume or emotion I've heard out of Ed, and it isn't good. I go inside and stand in the center of the room. Ethan storms in with Ed on his heels, who shuts the door behind them.

"What's going—"

"Do you hear the shit that comes out of Cyle's mouth?" Ethan says, trampling over Ed's question. "That guy is a walking lawsuit. Why the fuck is here still here?"

"I heard *you*," Ed says. "The entire building heard you."

"She shouldn't have to put—"

"It isn't your place to—"

"—up with his condescension and—"

"—interfere with other sections—"

They go on like that so long I'm not sure I'm even in the room. And somewhere Cyle has already cornered Cara to spin another yarn about the slacker new girl. How he found me practically on my knees sucking Ethan's dick. How I've got him fighting my battles, dodging work on my hunt for my MRS. I think I'd like to jump out the window now, thanks.

"Her father died."

The hot spotlight of attention slaps me across the face. Ed stands arms crossed and mouth open, then his expression is something like contemplation. I glance at Ethan. He's a big wet blanket of sympathy and sad eyes, and I don't want to be in this room anymore.

"I'd like to go back to work now," I say.

"Avery." Ethan speaks my name in that delicate way you coddle a child who's scraped their knee or ripped the ear off their favorite stuffed animal. Makes me want to rip *his* ear off. "You need—"

"You have no idea *what* I need." Then fixing my steady gaze on Ed: "I'm fine. I want no part of his pissing contest with Cyle, and I'd just really like to go back to my desk, please."

Sighing, Ed wipes his hands over his face of sagging clay. "Sit down. Both of you."

"Ed," I say, "please, I—"

"Sit."

It isn't optional. Ethan and I plant ourselves in the chairs in front of Ed's desk and he perches on a stool. A calmness comes over him. An ease a man like Ed earns after so many years. In a way, it calms me, too.

"Avery," he says. "Are you okay? Is there anything we can do for you?"

I wouldn't know how to answer that question if there was. So I bury my hands in the pockets of my cardigan sweater and nod my head. "I'm fine. Thank you."

"Here's the situation," he says. "We can't ignore the story."

I feel Ethan staring at the side of my face, feel the words clawing at the tip of his tongue, but I can't look.

"Patrick Turner Murphy died in prison—that's news. We can't avoid the subject because a member of our staff is personally connected."

No, he's right. If Ethan's just the first to get wind of this, it is only a matter of time before every other outlet jumps on it. Good enough for a slow, midweek news cycle. Trot out the old archive photos from the trial and whatnot. It'll play till the end of the week unless the president unloads on another Twitter tirade to threaten war with China.

"Ethan," he says, "you've got the lead on that. Give me cause of death, his last days, and a brief historical recap. I want quotes from prison personnel and his attorney, if he still had one." He pauses on a breath. There's something more he wants to say, but not in front of me. If I didn't work here, they'd want my reaction on the record. My mother, perhaps. See if Ethan could track down any survivors or victims' families willing to talk. Ethan knows the drill. Ed doesn't have to say it out loud.

"Got it." But Ethan's tone is almost regretful.

I still can't look.

"Now, Avery…"

What I like about Ed, I think, is his commitment to indifference. He isn't rude, exactly. Not unkind or curt. Simply…dispassionate. I can appreciate that from a man in his position. At the moment, perhaps it's exactly what I need.

"Your affairs are your business," Ed tells me. "I don't need to know, and neither does Ethan. That said, I want you to take a couple of days off. If you need more time, just say so. But as of now, you're off the clock. Go home."

My instinct is to argue. To insist that the best medicine is to stay occupied. That I can't imagine being two days on the job and already taking time off. But Ed's demeanor says I don't have a choice. That this is the nice version of his offer. If I press, I might not get to come back at all. So I take it gracefully.

"Thank you. I appreciate it."

Ed stands, and so do we.

"That's all," he says, meaning, *Now get the hell out of my office.*

I'm up and out of my seat, out the door. Ethan's footsteps pound the floor at my heels. His presence presses against my back until I'm at my cubicle and he's got me cornered in the tight little box. Storm-weather eyes, narrow and accusing; all six unyielding feet of the man, towering over me.

"What are you going to do?" he asks.

"Go home." I turn away from him and wake up my laptop; start closing windows and quitting programs. "A couple means two, right? I'll be back Friday. If Cara asks, I'll check my email from home and see what Cyle needed."

"The prison—"

I unplug my laptop and shove it in my messenger bag. "I won't get in your way. Write whatever you want. Ed's right."

"Do you want the phone number?"

My bag slung over my shoulder, I squeeze past Ethan and head for the elevator, conscious of everyone conspicuously not looking at us. Not far behind, Ethan's got his bag by the handle. I stab the Call button three times. Yeah, it won't get here any faster, but it feels right.

"For what?" I ask. It's a rhetorical question and I don't need the answer.

"You have to speak with them. Tell them what you want to do with his body and personal effects."

The doors open and he follows me inside.

"I couldn't care less."

Ethan's finger beats me to the button for the first floor. He stands just behind me as the doors shut. We talk to each other in the wavy, hazy reflection of the brushed metal inner door.

"If you're not going to claim the body—"

"I'm not."

"You don't have to, but—"

"Didn't Ed say something about not having to include you in this decision?"

The doors part. I slip sideways out of that suffocating container and get a good ten feet between us, quick short-person stepping to the lobby and front doors. Ethan's soles clap double-time on the stone tiles to catch up, on my flank again as we pass Banana Republic Andrew waving behind the reception desk.

On the sidewalk outside, the city noise is reassuring. Cars surging through traffic, cutting off cyclists, and changing lanes blind around metro buses. Distant sirens, and millions of passing pedestrian conversations. Big and busy and unconcerned with one girl.

"Avery," he says, sharp and scolding.

"What?"

"Stop. Just…" He huffs out a frustrated breath. "Take a minute."

"I don't need a minute. I'm fine. You're the one getting all worked up about this."

"You're doing it again."

"Doing what?"

"Lying to me. To both of us."

For fuck's sake. "What do you want from me? Like, seriously, Ethan. What could you possibly expect from me, and why do you need to be part of it so damn badly?"

He says nothing for a moment. So long that I almost walk away. Long enough that I watch the first, second, third way he considers answering my question play across his face. Then he glances down the street and sucks in a full, warm breath of the viscid air.

"I want to help, Avery. Because I don't think you have anyone else."

"That's a real dick thing to say."

"Then tell me I'm wrong."

"Fine. You're wrong."

Ethan whips a quarter turn away from me. His fist rises to his waist like wants to punch a wall, then thinks better of it. Now he knows how I feel.

"Just…" Both hands weave through his hair. They grip the back of his neck while he closes his eyes to the sky. "Consider for a moment that this is a day you're never going to get back. Take some time to think about it before you—"

"Listen to me." With all the composure I can muster, I calm the heat of adrenaline stinging through my blood. This man is impossible, and I don't have the time or inclination to sort through his issues. "I don't know what I've done to give you the impression that I need a savior or a big brother, or whatever role you've imagined for yourself here, but I don't need your help. I don't want it. Please, just leave me alone."

"Avery…"

"Don't follow me."

I turn into the afternoon glare and leave him behind.

# 9

# THE BUTCHER

Enderly's father, my father, stands over the carcass of a slaughtered pig laid out on a wooden table. He dissects it with skilled precision, cutting slabs of meat while Enderly stands in the kitchen doorway, breathing through her mouth and staring at the floor. He does this on purpose. To intimidate and unsettle her. All part of his manipulative mastery to keep the people around him off balance. A means of control. And as he does this, brutalizing his daughter with the sight of this dead animal, he speaks about loyalty and questions her about the newcomer—the undercover journalist hiding in their ranks. Blade in hand, carving, he dares her to lie to him. Everything about the man is a carefully crafted threat.

I don't know what motivated me to pick up Ethan's book again. When I got home, the apartment empty, I put on my pajamas and tried three times to call my mother. Couldn't do it. There was, is, no part of that conversation I want to have with her. Over the years, she's mastered the art of avoidance.

A hint of the topic arises, and suddenly it's "The strawberries are coming in nicely this year" or "I'm thinking of taking up pastels."

Or maybe I'm afraid she'll care too much.

I've never asked what drove her to Massasauga in the first place. What catastrophe of a life she left behind to confine herself inside the forest walls that rimmed that compound. She was my age when she stepped through the wooden gates, down the long dirt drive. Arrived on foot, hitchhiking with a bag full of everything that mattered. Somewhere, somehow, her life took a sharp left turn straight toward Patrick Turner Murphy, his vision for a perfect tax haven, and a little girl a year later. At least once, and often more, every year of my life, I've wondered if my greatest mistake was being born.

Now sitting in the bathtub, steam creasing the pages of the book, Ethan's words instigate a strange sense of déjà vu. Almost as if Enderly's life is more real now, more tangible, than Echo's memories. Though the conversation he describes never took place, its essence is familiar. There's a level of authenticity that is both remarkable and unsettling. I can't shake the feeling that, though his version of events is quite different, Ethan was there. Like he was always part of the story, observing and unseen. His words know me. They see the truth of my father. Even as fiction, they are perhaps the truest rendition of that life that has thus far emerged. I admit, my essay wasn't as honest. I edited. I curtailed. In telling Echo's story, I protected the most vulnerable parts of her. What I still can't put into words, Ethan has managed to identify and distill.

Perhaps it is because Enderly was created to be approachable. To feel, on an emotional and psychological level, as real as any person walking around in the world today. Whereas Echo was always a fantasy. Conceived in a bubble, it was never the intention to make her fit for society at large. I don't share a last name with either of my parents. Avalon is just an idea, a lofty ambition. Fictitious. And what sort of name is Echo but a feedback loop that dissipates into nothing? A decaying, distorted copy.

Ethan has always seen that. Even before we met, and every day since, he's seen the blank, empty canvas of my identity. Not even unfinished, I'm not yet begun.

Three loud knocks shake me from the thought. Water sloshes in the tub around me. I stand and reach for a towel, dripping as I get out of the bath to dry off. Three more knocks.

"Yeah, just a second!"

With the towel wrapped around me and tucked under my arms, I navigate through the scattered stacks of moving boxes clogging our living room and go to the front door. I try to peer through the peephole, but the fisheye lens is dirty and crusted. All I see is a dark outline of a person.

Three more knocks.

"Who is it?"

"Ethan."

Shit.

"What do you want?"

"Are you going to make me do this through the door?"

"Yes."

There's a swollen pause, and I imagine him raking his hands

through his hair in that way he does when he's met with resistance.

"Look, I'm sorry. I came at you a little strong back there. That was insensitive, I know. I wasn't trying to maneuver you, I just—Avery, can you please open the door? I feel stupid shouting in the hallway."

"I'm not dressed," I say, standing in a puddle collecting on the floor.

"You're what?"

"I'm not *dressed*."

"Oh, uhh…"

Yeah. Bad timing there, buddy.

"Here." I take the chain off the door and unlock the deadbolt. "Wait thirty seconds, then you can let yourself in. If I see you before that, I'm coming after you with a baseball bat."

"Thirty seconds," he repeats, and I swear I hear a smile in his voice. "Got it."

I unlock the doorknob then scurry across the apartment to my bedroom and slam the door shut. Most of my clothes are still in trash bags from the move, so I dash around digging for the clean jeans and a shirt not too wrinkled. When I come out, Ethan's standing with his back to me.

"How do you know where I live?"

He turns to face me, not the least bit contrite. "Your father's attorney found your Syracuse address, the apartment manager gave me your forwarding address."

"That's a little creepy."

Ethan shrugs. "It's what we do."

True. A person has to go pretty far off the grid to hide from an investigative reporter. If you're motivated to find a person, there's always a way.

"So…" Kumi will lose her shit when I tell her Ethan Ash was standing in her living room, boxes and packing paper strewn all over the place. One of her bras hanging off the back of a chair at the kitchen table. "Is there something else you wanted to say, or…"

He walks past me to lean against the arm of the couch and stare at the floor. Ethan looks exhausted. Like his whole life's just caught up with him.

"I do think you should come with me to the prison," he says, and holds his hand up to stop me from interrupting. "And I understand that you have good reason not to. So let me explain."

Ethan is in a unique position, occupied by only one other person in my life: he's met my father. I can't explain the surreal, irrational fascination that holds, except to say I imagine it must be like traveling to a foreign country, some far-flung exotic location, and finding yourself sitting at a bar next to someone from your hometown. That sense of connection and security. Of kinship and familiarity. It's both attractive and unnerving.

But the conclusion I've come to is that, whatever his motivations, Ethan is honest. His intentions are good, if misguided. He is not like my father, and I have to let him out from under that burden of association. So I take a seat at the kitchen table and listen to what he has to say.

"My brother died last year." He tucks his hands in his pockets. I don't respond, because the solemnness in his voice is more ire than sadness, and I've never been good at consoling people. "He was three years older. When I was a kid, I wanted so badly to be like him. He played soccer, so I wanted to play. He liked Nirvana and Soundgarden, so those were my favorite bands, too. I idolized him, always following Evan and his friends around, being the butt of their jokes, just to get my brother's attention. I thought if I mimicked him in every way, did everything he said, he'd like me."

Hero worship is an alluring and dangerous affliction. Some never recover from the addiction, even as it corrodes and corrupts them. Such a destructive thing born of simple admiration. It's hard to imagine Ethan as ever so young or impressionable.

"But by the time we were teenagers, I realized my brother was just born an asshole. Evan went from ignoring to outright tormenting me. I'd come home from school and he and his friends would have pissed all over my bed. He cut a hole in my pillow and took a shit in it then put the cover back on. Broke my arm—twice. My freshman year of high school he started a rumor that I was having sex with the teacher who led the student newspaper. Almost got the guy fired. No girl would go near me for two years. When we got older, it just got worse. He conned our parents out of thousands of dollars for whatever bullshit new business plan he'd concocted that year. He was always on the verge of a major payday with some new startup. Always a venture capital investor *this close* to handing over a windfall. He took out credit cards in my name and racked up insane debts. The guy didn't have a fucking conscience. He never apologized or admitted guilt for anything is his life. And our parents never saw it, or they chose to ignore what was staring them right in the face—constantly making excuses for him. I can't tell you how maddening it was to watch him get away with torching everything he touched over and over again and coming out unscathed."

Ethan takes a deep breath, like he's been holding this in for years and now there's all this extra room in his body that wants to be filled. He rubs his hands up the back of his head then lets them fall at his sides.

"The last thing he did was skip out on our mother's sixtieth birthday party. It was this big affair, friends of hers from way back to preschool, practically everyone she'd ever met getting together. Dad flew people in from all over the country, put them up in hotels, hired caterers and a band—all that shit. But it's time to sing 'Happy Birthday,' and where's Evan? On some mountain in Big Sky."

He laughs to himself, one of those humorless, inaudible huffs. His tempest-blue eyes meet mine, and in them I see years of repressed hatred. The stain that so much unresolved rage leaves on a person.

"If I believed in such things, I'd think I killed him. Because every time he screwed us over, every time he betrayed us, I wished he'd just hurry up and die. Evan was a waste of a human being, and nothing anyone could do would ever change him." Then Ethan stands. He approaches and pulls out another chair at the kitchen table to sit beside me. As in our first encounter, he squeezes the space between us until he's the only thing in the room. "I didn't go to the funeral. My mom wanted flowers and a big service and people getting up to say nice things about a man who hadn't helped a single person a day in his life. I couldn't fucking do it. I couldn't sit there and play a part in his farce, even for her."

"And now," I say, searching for the moral of this story, "what? You realize you should have honored your mother, and your brother's memory, because family is family and—"

"Hell no." Ethan slouches back in his seat and crosses his arms, defiant and unapologetic. "It took a few months, then one day I started to wonder. What if I'd gone? Just to see him in that casket and made peace with all the shit he put us through. Maybe I wouldn't still be this angry. Maybe I could have let it go back then, instead of having a dead man wake me up in the middle of the night."

Even after I stopped dreaming of the blood, after the anxiety attacks became less frequent, I still had recurring nightmares about my father. One in particular that still wakes me in a cold sweat. In it, I'm maybe fifteen, and asleep in my bed. In the middle of the night I wake up to use the bathroom, but as I'm washing my hands, I hear voices coming from my mother's bedroom. I go to her door, and through the opening I see her standing in his arms. They're hugging, happy, and smiling in the dark. He tells me we're going to be a family again. That he's come back for us, and he's taking us away. I try to run, but the doors are locked. I beg my mother, yank her hand and try to drag her from his arms, pleading and screaming, but she just smiles in a hypnotic trance.

Reaching his hand across the table, stopping just short of touching my arm, Ethan says, "Avery, I don't think I'm ever going to forgive my brother. I don't even think I want to.

But he's dead, and I'm still walking around with shit I wish had died with him. Now maybe going to the funeral wouldn't have made a difference. I won't ever know that. My point is, if there's even a small part of you that is hung up on anger and resentment for your father, don't let yourself ask, What if? No one's telling you to bury the man if you don't want to, but if you think you can stomach it, come up there with me. It might be your only chance to find some kind of closure. Endings are important, Avery. You should have the one you deserve."

I've always thought of closure as a decision rather than something to seek and attain. Simply choose to shut the door. Pack it up, put it away, and have no further use for whatever business has been done. And it's worked, for the most part. Except with my father. His influence pervades me. It's malignant, multiplying with time. The longer it's been left to fester, the stronger it becomes, reinforcing its position. I concluded some time ago that it was a condition I would learn to live with. My new reality.

"How did he die? Your brother."

"Snowboarding accident that weekend in Big Sky. Went off a jump and missed the landing. Snapped his neck. Evan was always convinced of his own invincibility, so gravity smacked him back to Earth."

This might be a terrible mistake. What I think of now as a minor illness might become a debilitating disease if I allow myself any closer to my father and his memory. But what if it works? Even a slight remission would be an improvement. One less nightmare. One less anxiety attack. Isn't that what we're all seeking? Better quality of life, no matter how small.

Perhaps I could put this part of me to rest at last. And I don't have to do it alone.

"You're leaving now?"

"My truck's parked outside. Last I checked, the news still hasn't hit the wire. If you want to get in before the press is crawling all over the prison, we need to hurry."

If it were anyone else asking, I might not have let them through the door. But Ethan's different. Compelling, yes. More than that, though, he might be exactly what I need.

# 10

# THE ILLUSIVE DAUGHTER

I've seen dead bodies before. People I'd known my entire life. Some of them had held me as an infant, changed my diapers. There was one woman, Loraine, a former advertising executive who, I would only learn once her life prior to Massasauga was made public during my father's trial, had faked her own death in the autumn of '91. She taught me to play gin rummy and how to do that bridge trick for shuffling cards. Loraine was a beast at Pictionary and Scrabble. At Halloween, she told ghost stories. In the winter, we made snowmen.

The authorities concluded, after her body was identified among the victims of the massacre, she had deliberately wandered away from a campsite while on vacation in the Finger Lakes National Forest, leaving behind bloody clothing and her wedding ring along the way, in an effort to escape her abusive husband. The reports revealed, upon her supposed death, she had accumulated considerable savings, stocks, and other wealth—a nest egg she had hidden from her husband in preparation for her departure, and she willed it to a close friend with whom she had orchestrated the ruse. My father managed to swindle the money out of her, as he did to others who had any wealth to speak of, when Loraine eventually found herself among the inhabitants at Massasauga. But how or why she fell into my father's sphere of corruption was never determined. Like the other victims, she took the secret to her grave.

I cried for her the night my mother and I escaped, and many more nights thereafter.

Standing in a hallway outside the morgue of the Sing Sing Correctional Facility, I look through the glass of a reinforced window at the pale, lifeless body of Patrick Turner Murphy on a metal slab—and I feel nothing. A white sheet covers him from chest to ankles. His skin is the color of cinderblocks, the deathly hue darkening to shades of purple that peer around the backs of his shoulders and feet.

"Lividity," Ethan says beside me. "His blood is pooling to the bottom."

My father has a woolly gray beard that absorbs much of his face—somewhere underneath must be the scar from his suicide attempt—and a receded hairline exposing a mole off-center on top of his head. He's massive on the table. A fat, hulking brute with arms like ship canons and a whiskey-barrel stomach. This man must have eaten three of my father.

"Are they sure it's him?" I ask. "I don't even recognize him."

"I do," Ethan says. "He's maybe twenty, thirty pounds heavier than the last time I saw him, and the beard is longer, but that's Patrick."

And yet, it's not. That cold corpse is not the man whose face

Echo sees when she closes her eyes. He's a stranger. Some distorted, disfigured imposter. I realize, studying the disturbing stillness of the cadaver, that my father withered away years ago. Unbeknownst to anyone outside these walls, he grew slovenly and obese. His interests stunted, activities curtailed by incarceration, he simply sat down to collect moss, becoming embedded in the floor, rotting away.

The staff physician told us he suspected a heart attack as the cause of death based on a preliminary exam. As a matter of procedure, the body will be transferred to the coroner's office for a complete autopsy, a requirement for all inmate deaths.

"Why do you think he never gave an interview until you?" I ask.

Ethan watches the body. Hands tucked in his pockets, he absorbs the scene he'll describe later in his article. The flickering fluorescent light tubes. The stench of bleach and ammonia. The almost abandoned austerity of the morgue's interior visible through the window. Or maybe he's just trying to imprint on his mind the idea that the man who launched Ethan's career no longer exists.

"I asked him that question—several times. Rather than answer, he usually had a segue ready about the grand media monopoly and how the freedom of the press died in the bloom of the blogosphere. When anyone can call themselves a journalist, no one is. More than once he suggested I give it up, move out to Hollywood, and become a television writer. I'll admit, there are days I wonder if he was right."

"I think you might have picked up the same habit of dodging questions."

He gives me a chastising side eye. "If I had to guess, I'd say he was ashamed. Getting caught, I think, is the greatest embarrassment of his life. Patrick never felt remorse for his petty crimes, much less for the murders. But being mocked and humiliated through the course of the trial, getting locked in a cell where he shits in full view of another man, I think it left him in a deep depression. When his arrogance met with the reality of imprisonment for the rest of his life, he crawled deep inside himself."

If I'd never seen what had become of my father, I wouldn't have believed he was capable of anything nearing shame, embarrassment, or depression. His lack of humility was arguably what made him such an effective con man. He approached his prey with intellect, appealing to their sense of longing, confusion, dissatisfaction, or malaise through academic calculation rather than true empathy. I'm not sure he ever considered another person as a living thing. We were pawns on a chessboard. A means to an end.

"How'd you get him to agree?" I ask.

An abashed smile cuts across his lips. He scratches his fingers through his hair like he needs the time to decide if he'll give me an answer.

"Patrick was writing a book," he says.

Of course he was.

"It was more of a manifesto, really. He'd already spent hundreds of hours scribbling it by hand on loose sheets of paper. He wanted someone to read it and give him feedback, teach him how to be a writer. So I made him a deal: five pages for two hours; as long as he answered my questions, I'd read his stuff." He offers me a reassuring glance. "It was garbage, of course. Meandering and inarticulate. It was like he tried to shove a dozen thoughts into every sentence. Mostly, it was a last-ditch effort to defend himself to history."

"And then?"

"I don't know." Ethan shrugs one shoulder, indifferent. "After eight weeks I had everything I needed, so I stopped coming. That was it. Not sure if Patrick ever finished it."

That must have infuriated my father. Used up and tossed aside by some young, arrogant upstart. When he realized Ethan was never coming back. That this *kid* could just walk away without a second thought. My father had shared something material and sacred of himself, only to find he'd been the victim of Ethan's con. Discarded.

I admit it makes me feel a little better.

"Miss?" A guard approaches us from the end of the hall. "The superintendent can see you now, if you'll both follow me."

"Let's go," I say, and turn my back to the body. "I'm done here."

\* \* \*

During a perfunctory meeting, I sign the forms necessary to release my father's body, and I refuse his personal effects. His lawyer can deal with whatever's left of the man. A guard then escorts me to the visitors' waiting area while Ethan hangs back to conduct a few interviews for his article. I'm ten pages into a three-year-old magazine when the first reporter arrives, then another and another. Reuters, AP, *New York Times*—they've all come to pick over what's left of my father's legacy. Behind the cage that houses the reception desk, the guard's eyes flick to me as each new press badge is flashed in his face with an inquiry about Patrick Turner Murphy. A second and third guard are called to corral the growing number of reporters milling about.

"Ash is already here," one of the reporters says to another. They stand below a TV mounted to the wall, both staring at their phones. "Saw his truck in the parking lot."

Ethan drives a Land Rover Defender. It's an absurd green thing meant to carry tourists on safari or UN peacekeepers through Eastern Europe. Not exactly a commuter's car, but he loves it. So do I. When I saw it sitting along the curb outside my apartment, big and conspicuous on a Manhattan street, the truck became my favorite thing about him. Before that, it was his eyes. Like crashing waves on a black-sand beach. But everyone has eyes. Not many people still drive Defenders.

It suits him. On our drive up here this afternoon, I caught a momentary image of him as I glanced out the window at New Jersey across the Hudson. Like something Loraine in her first life might have pitched in a Madison Avenue conference room. Wearing a pair of Aviator sunglasses, V-neck shirt hugging his athletic frame, wavy hair swept back from his face and afternoon stubble along his jaw, Ethan was a living television ad. The camera finds him cruising down the highway, Manhattan skyline in the background, then cut to mud flying under the tires as he traverses rocky forest terrain. Cut to an orange dust cloud, the truck and its handsome, rugged pilot racing across the desert. Next, he's slicing through the surf on the shore of a white sand beach. Finally, it's dusk, and our hero arrives in the pristine paved drive of his modern mountain mansion.

Hell, I'd buy one.

No matter how savvy the consumer, there's always that voice that says, *Hey, maybe that guy knows something I don't. If I had that car, that watch, that suit, people would look at me the way I'm looking at him.* It's the art of the con. The optimism of aspirational consumerism. Telling ourselves, *Once I own this thing, I'll have attained some secret knowledge reserved for a select few.* The mystique of the In Crowd.

It's always a lie.

But on Ethan, it just fits. Classic, but not pretentious. An analog man born in the digital age. Ethan is the scent of fresh hardcover books. He's the Oxford comma.

Two more reporters enter and mingle with their competition. They take no notice of me. All the same, the waiting area is getting a little crowded, so I take my cue to slip out to the parking lot. As I'm walking to Ethan's truck, I see a man in a pressed dress shirt and creased slacks standing beside it. He's on his cell phone, squinting into the low sun dipping toward the horizon. There's nowhere else to go. It's either this or back inside. So I erase all trepidation from my face and approach the truck. When the man notices my shadow stretching toward him, he looks up. There's a moment of confusion on his face as he realizes I'm not Ethan.

"Who else is in there?" he asks.

"Wire services and the *Times*," I say. "Local NBC and Fox affiliates."

He nods and slides his phone into his pants pocket. "I guess Ash beat us to it. This is his truck, right? I'm guessing you're his new intern."

The man makes no attempt to hide his coded smile. The one that says, *It's okay, sweetheart. We both know you're screwing him.*

"Yep," I lie. Better to let people underestimate you at their own expense. "Ethan's inside wrapping up."

He's in his late twenties, maybe, with an artificial tan that makes him look mid-thirties. Short cropped hair and a clean shave. I'd guess cable news. A junior segment producer, maybe. His bosses figure there's nothing about this story he can screw up. Just get the cause of death, a couple of sound bites from the superintendent, and roll the archive reel while the on-camera reporter does a voice-over. Throw in some B-roll footage outside the gates, and call it a day.

"My crew's stuck on the parkway," he says, fishing his phone from his pocket to type out a text. "What do you hear?"

I don't know where it comes from. An expulsion of spite just flies off my tongue before I consider my words. "Murphy got fat. They think it was a heart attack."

The man's head jerks up. "You saw the body?"

Shit. Fuck me.

"Um…well, I—"

"Is the body still in there? Have they contacted next of kin? Has the daughter been here?"

The questions come rapid fire, one on top of the other before he's finished the last syllable. I start backing away, but he's following me step-for-step, getting closer.

"Wait. You look—" The suspicious gaze of a journalist scrutinizes me up and down. He catalogues the curly red hair and green eyes—just like Enderly. Like Echo. He takes a guess at my age and does the math in his head. "What's your name?"

Then I see the pieces click into place.

"Are you the daughter of Patrick Turner Murphy? You're her, aren't you?"

He holds up his phone like he's trying to get a picture. I cover my face, turning away, shrinking from his onslaught, but I'm trapped. There's nowhere to hide under the guard towers armed by officers with rifles. Inside, more reporters. Hot, rushing panic burns through my body.

"And you came here with Ethan Ash? Will there be a funeral? Are you planning to—"

I flinch and nearly scream when I feel Ethan's arm wrap around my shoulder. The man's questions come in a relentless barrage as Ethan shields me with his body while he unlocks the passenger door and shoves me inside. I'm out of breath, heart racing. Once the door's closed, he turns to the man and pushes him, both hands against his chest, back, back, several feet before pointing a finger in his face and issuing a threat I don't hear. Then Ethan stalks back to the truck and climbs in. Engine started, he peels out of the parking lot.

"Fuck him," Ethan says. "Brian's an asshole."

Everywhere, my skin turns hot and excited. The way it feels when you almost miss the next step going down a flight of stairs and grasp for the handrail in the split second you see your own death.

"It's my fault," he says, hands tight on the steering wheel. "I shouldn't have left you by yourself."

Noise like a train speeding through a tunnel fills my ears. A lump of air sticks in my throat as my eyes sting and blur, colors beyond the windshield washing into streaks.

"...to prepare yourself. He's going to run with the 'elusive daughter' story."

Tears trickle down my face. I try to stifle the quiet eruption, but they come unbidden down my cheeks to splatter dark spots on my shirt.

"Hey, are you okay? Did he touch you?"

It's mostly anger at being accosted, and a release of the stress that's been building not only today but maybe all of my life. Like when a runner finally limps and crawls their way to the marathon finish line. A boxer's hand raised at the end of a fight. The outburst of pent-up emotion when a victim's family hears the jury say *guilty*. That's what my father's death means to me.

Brian will take his pound of flesh, but it's nothing I can't live without.

From the corner of my eye, I see Ethan glance at me, and I turn toward the window to shield my face. He says nothing, sliding one hand to cover mine on the armrest. It's unexpected, the sudden contact, crossing the line between colleagues and...what? Have we tripped over ourselves and become friends? Would that be so bad? His hand is warm and comforting, like it's always been there.

Unlikely as it is, Ethan's become the one person with whom I feel most myself. He knows who I am, understands where I come from. There's no pretense or pressure to maintain a discreet distance between him and who I was. I can be honest without fear of exposure. Even with Kumi I perform a choreographed attempt at normalcy. Not because I think one day she might write a tell-all, but because I've heard it in her voice that my past makes her uneasy. She doesn't know how to relate to that person. Echo is alien and off-putting the way a cancer patient makes people nervous. Or how there's always an empty seat on the bus next to the guy with the tracheostomy.

I suppose the idea of Ethan is growing on me.

\* \* \*

"Thank you," I say, unbuckling my seat belt as Ethan parks along the curb outside my apartment building around eight. "For the ride, and everything."

He tilts his head toward me but his eyes remain fixed toward the street ahead. "Are you sorry you went?"

"No." Patrick Turner Murphy was pronounced dead today, but my father died a long time ago. Maybe now I can make peace with that. In any case, that's not what he meant. "You were right. Not going was just an excuse to ignore the issue, and it's not like I wouldn't have been sitting at home thinking about it anyway. At least now I feel like I accomplished something."

His response is a sad smile. A slight lift to the corner of his lips. I don't know if it's the thought of his brother that's grabbed him by the ankles, pulling him down, but he's only half-here.

"Are you sure you're okay? Brian—what exactly happened back there?"

Nothing I haven't experienced before. But it's that sensation of someone piercing the veil, thinking they have some right to me with no regard for my privacy or basic human dignity. All my life, other people have tried to own me.

"In college," I say, looking out the window. "My first roommate was a film student. She imagined herself the next Werner Herzog or something. She hid cameras in our dorm room to record me with the intention of putting together some stupid documentary. Kept a journal about me."

If you've ever been robbed, you know the feeling. Someone's violated the sanctity of your home, defiled it. Nothing can take away that sting of invasion. From that moment, nothing feels safe anymore.

"Two months of every moment of my life inside that room saved on a hard drive before I discovered what she'd been up to. I don't how she figured out who I was. I guess it doesn't matter."

Because I was a minor when my father's trial convened, my name was redacted from case files. The police and prosecutors went to great lengths to protect my identity. It was the only thing that gave me any chance at a normal life.

"She was expelled and made to turn over everything she'd collected on me. In exchange, I didn't press charges. I wasn't mad at her, you know? Just…hurt. All I wanted was an apology, but I never got one."

"People are assholes," he says.

"I don't mind talking about it. If she'd asked, said she was curious, I probably would have talked to her. But it was the *way* she did it. People read about you, and they get this idea that you belong to them somehow. You're not a person anymore."

"I wish I could say that guys like Brian are the exception in this business, but it seems like there are more of them coming up every day."

"If their audience wasn't drooling over shit like that, they wouldn't run it. Guys like Brian just give them what they want."

"Still," he says, "I'm sorry."

"No," I say, realizing this a bit late. "I apologize. I was awful to you earlier. I've been in a shit mood since the day we met. That hasn't been fair to you."

"Don't sweat it. I've been told I have that effect on people."

"Nevertheless, I appreciate everything you've done for me. So, yeah, I'm sorry."

"Avery…" His eyes shift to mine. In profile, illuminated by the streetlamps and neon signs of restaurant windows, he is quite striking. Yet there's a darkness in him, deep and quiet. Something that dulls the shine on the world he observes. "You don't ever have to apologize to me for being who you are."

His statement takes me off guard. How do I respond to such spontaneous generosity of what might be among the nicest things anyone has ever said to another human being? Because isn't that what we all want? Acceptance. The reassurance that we're enough. Not just despite our flaws but because of the sum of who we are as people, dismissing all caveats and mitigations.

Silence builds between us, tight and compact. A star collapsing in on itself. I notice for the first time he smells faintly of eucalyptus and mint. And that he has a small birthmark under his left eye and an indentation of a scar under his chin. It makes me wonder, what does he notice about me?

Which are thoughts better left unexplored.

"Well, thank you again," I say, climbing out of the truck. "Good night."

There's more he wants to say, written in the tension of his jaw. "Good night, Avery."

But he settles for getting me home in one piece.

\*\*\*

The apartment is dark and empty when I get inside. Kumi's got a job for the summer, interning at her uncle's law firm. Being the boss's niece, she can't leave the office until he does, lest there be any appearance of favoritism. He made her apply and sit through three interviews before she was hired, squashing any notions she had about quickly making partner once she graduates from law school.

After I've showered the prison stink off me, I change into my pajamas and order a pizza for dinner. With the TV on for background noise, I sit on the couch in the living room with my laptop to look through my work emails. There are five from Cyle, two sent after Ed kicked me out of the office. His demands amount to grunt work. Fact-checking, light copyediting—the kind of stuff he would otherwise assign to his beloved interns if some tabloid Dumpster fire who fancies herself a writer hadn't come along and stolen his budget. But it's work, and since I haven't produced anything else of value this week, I'm not above spending my exile catering to his spiteful needs.

There is something in the final email that catches my attention. The *Riot Street* website has an obscure, almost hidden section that's become quite popular over the years among the site's most loyal readership. According to lore, the page began in response to a phenomenon that occurred not long after the site's launch in the late nineties. At the bottom of the original FAQ page was an email address that allowed readers to send questions—intended for queries about subscriptions, circulation, and other pertinent information about the magazine. Instead, in the infancy of magazine websites, readers used the address to send in news tips, complain about articles, and occasionally, ask questions entirely unrelated to the magazine or its coverage. These questions ranged from minor borough concerns like road construction or subway delays, to general questions like "Is Y2K a hoax?" and "What's a google?"

No one would have blamed the poor soul on the receiving end of that email address for simply ignoring and deleting the messages. Instead, something remarkable happened. The questions were answered, first via email responses directly to the reader, and later in an expanded and continually updated FAQ list. The page gained a sort of cult following as a place the *Riot Street* diehards went to see what absurd questions were posted that week, or maybe learn something new. Like what's the difference between a road, a street, and an avenue. Eventually, the library of responses grew so large it was moved from the FAQ page, which still had a legitimate job to do for those who just wanted to know what day the new issue came out or whom to call about a billing discrepancy, to its new home under the heading of "Infrequently Asked Questions," where it remains to this day.

According to Cyle's email, he's designated me as the new IAQ elf. No byline. No credit. Just looking up inane facts for people too lazy to Google it themselves. Out of curiosity, I use the log-in credentials he sent me to check the IAQ email account. Three hundred and fourteen unread emails. If I drank, I'd be about ready to jump knee-deep into a bottle about now.

In any case, I've had a long day, so I find the least brain-intensive assignment on Cyle's list and start with that. I'm not ten minutes into fact-checking a movie review of the first summer box office bomb when there's a knock at my door. Either pizza delivery around here is on point, or Kumi's already lost her keys.

"Yeah," I say, uncurling myself from the couch, "coming."

In my haste, I catch my foot on the coffee table and fall on a stack of boxes we still haven't unpacked. Dishes, from the sound of it. We've got to get on that. It's starting to feel like we're squatting. I then hobble through the kitchen with a bruised toe.

Opening the door, I forget all about the pain.

"Uh, hi," I say, wearing an old T-shirt too big for my body and pajama pants too long for my legs. I suddenly feel like a fucking four-year-old, and now I understand why people on TV are always fully dressed at home, even when just sitting around the house. "What are you doing here?"

"Rats?" Ethan says, peering around me into the apartment. "What?"

"I heard a noise. Sounded like you were killing something in there."

"Oh, no." I cross my arms over my chest like that'll hide the rest of me. "Just, uh, tripped. Too many damn boxes."

"Hey, so, listen…" He combs his fingers through his hair, pensive, his eyes on the floor. "I'm sorry to wake you up—"

"I wasn't asleep." That comes out quicker than necessary. "Catching up on Cyle's to-do list."

"Ah, okay. Well…" His hands adjust the strap of his messenger bag, then they brace against the doorjamb. "See, the reason I came by—I should have called, now that I think about it. I'm not really sure why that didn't occur to me."

He fidgets, unsure what to do with his hands or where to look. Ethan's nervous, which is sort of making me nervous. My father already died today, what else could he have to tell me that even approaches that level of uncomfortable conversation?

"Ethan?"

He looks up. "Yeah?"

"Spit it out."

"Right." He clears his throat and stands up straight, now determined to at least make an attempt at getting to the point. "I came back because I lied to you earlier, and I couldn't leave it like that."

His nervous shuffling is less cute now. "Okay…"

"The reason Patrick agreed to the interview," he says. "He also asked me to find you."

Once it's out of his mouth, Ethan finds his sturdy footing again. He leans in against the frame. I don't miss that he nudges his foot across the threshold, in case I try to slam the door in his face.

"I agreed because, hell, I would have agreed to anything back then. As long as it got me the interview. But I swear, Avery, I never gave him anything. I spent eight weeks convincing him you might have changed your name and left the country. Frankly, if I'd told him you were still in the state, he might not have believed me."

"But you did look for me, didn't you?"

"Yes." This part he isn't contrite about. "He made me curious."

"And you found me."

"I did."

Ernest, unrepentant. Ethan has the kind of self-assured confidence my father must have recognized and admired. I guess I do, too. Though I haven't yet decided what to do with this new information. On the one hand, I appreciate that he respects me enough to turn around and knock on my door, not content to let the omission stand. On the other, had I not asked the question, he might never have revealed the truth. That for the better part of two years, he's been following my ghost.

"But what I saw," he says, like he senses the door closing, "was a normal, bright young woman trying to move on with her life. I never had any intention of taking that away from you. I think, like the rest of the country, I wanted to know you'd turned out okay. You'd survived."

What would he think if he knew what really became of

Echo? Detox isn't pretty. Ravaged by drug addition, she died kicking and screaming and shitting herself on a bare cot in a state-funded rehab facility. I'm what's left when she emerged.

Yet, painful as that experience was, I learned a few things about forgiveness. They're big on that in rehab. Making amends to those we've hurt isn't worth attempting if *we* can't forgive *ourselves* first.

"Answer me one thing," I say, "and I'll let you off the hook."

"Okay. Shoot."

"Was it Cara's idea to offer me the job, or yours?"

"It was Ed's."

He's fucking with me. "You're fucking with me."

"Ed read your essay, called me into his office, and said, 'Get me that girl.' Cara was indifferent until she saw the viral lift it had after only a few hours. I had nothing to do with it."

This time I believe him. Though it does make me look at Ed in a new light. Was he so absent in our interview because he'd already made up his mind? I suppose he's just a distant person. In any case, with one notable exception, I don't make it a habit to hold grudges, so Ethan was never in any real danger. And now that he's here, I don't entirely want him to leave. I admit, there was the slightest sting of excitement when I answered the door. Like Enderly said, he's new. And new is interesting.

"Hey," I say, "if you haven't eaten yet, I've got a pizza coming. My roommate's out, and I'm not going to finish it by myself, so…"

"I still have to write this article. Ed's going to be waiting up for it. He'll start calling every fifteen minutes until I send it in."

"Oh, right. Yeah, no problem." I start pushing the door closed to shield myself from the embarrassment of being a dumb-ass. "Good—"

"But—" He stops the door with his foot. "I'm starving. If you don't mind me working while…"

"Sure, yeah." Stepping back from the door, I let him in. "I was just working on the couch. But, uh, sit wherever. Sorry about the mess."

"I've lived in my place for a year." He follows me to the living room and sits on the couch beside me to pull his laptop out of his bag. "I still haven't unpacked everything."

Propping my feet up on the coffee table, I wake up my laptop and return to Cyle's to-do list. We fall into a comfortable silence together, not unlike at the office. Except now there isn't a fabric-padded wall between us. And like his hand covering mine while I cried, it feels familiar. Like we've been here a hundred times.

A few minutes later we get up when the pizza arrives and pause to eat and watch a little TV, skipping over the news channels.

"Christ," Ethan says, opening the box in the kitchen while I get us some paper plates. "Is there anything you don't put on your pizza?"

"Meat." My signature order is mushrooms, onions, tomatoes, goat cheese, spinach, basil, black olives, and green olives. "But I feel like you already knew that."

It isn't stated outright, but Enderly reads as a vegetarian.

"Patrick told me a story about how you cried and went on a hunger strike the first time they slaughtered a cow." He takes the box back to the coffee table and pulls out a slice. "I extrapolated from there for the book."

"No, it's fine." I curl up beside him on the couch with my plate in my lap. "You're like my own polite stalker. It's only a little creepy."

"There it is." Taking a bite, he reclines and stares up at the ceiling. "She said the S-word."

"Really. I mean, I get it. I'm fascinating. You're obsessed with me. Just as long as you don't let it interfere with doing our jobs."

He laughs, shaking his head. "You're such a brat."

"Creeper."

Later, I mention the IAQ duty, to which Ethan explains that it isn't so much Cyle's attempt at torture but more a rite of passage. Every new member of the staff, even Banana Republic Andrew, takes a turn manning the helm. It does make me feel better, like part of the team rather than the redheaded stepchild, even though the sheer number of emails is a bit overwhelming.

"You don't have to answer every one," he tells me. "Just pick a few every week, only what you can comfortably handle, and write up a paragraph or two at most. Some only need a short answer. Just be sure to search through the archive to see if it's a question that's been answered before. The fun part, really, is that everyone who runs the IAQ has their own sort of flair. They pick different sorts of questions. Have fun with it."

Fun. I can do that.

By ten we're both engrossed in our laptops when his phone rings. The sudden noise startles me from my productivity trance. Ethan yanks his phone out of his pocket to look at the screen, then he jumps to his feet.

"Sorry. I've got to take this."

"No problem," I say, and point toward my room.

He's been in there for ten, fifteen minutes, by the time Kumi gets home.

"Hey," she says, coming through the front door with two arms full of grocery bags. I get up to help her and move boxes from the counter to give her a place to set them down. "I just grabbed some essentials. How was work?"

"Got sent home early. You?" I unpack sodas and iced tea from a bag and line them up in the fridge while Kumi puts stuff away in the pantry.

"What, why? Something happen?"

We hear "What the hell does that mean?" come from my bedroom. Kumi's eyes perk up.

"You have a guy over?" she asks.

"Ethan. He doesn't count."

She drops a loaf of bread on the counter and corners me against the kitchen table. "Ethan Ash is in your bedroom?"

"He was sitting at this table earlier. Next to your bra."

I hold it up and twirl it at her. She snatches it and tosses it aimlessly across the room. The woman has no shame.

"So..." Her eyes get big and excited. "Fill me in."

"My father died. The boss sent me home early, and Ethan took me to the prison."

"Whoa. Okay." All humor leaves her face, and she grabs me by the wrist to drag me to the couch. "Serious time. How are you feeling? Is this an ice cream thing or a—well, you don't drink, so—or a smash some plates then sit alone in the dark thing?"

"I'm fine."

Her response is a dubious frown.

"Really. I made my peace and cried it out. I'd like to move on. Now, if possible."

Sure, I admit, the topic of him and all the ways he ruined my life will never be fully resolved. If not tomorrow or the next day, then at some point sooner or later I'll still feel the occasional pang of resentment and anger. I'll probably still have a nightmare that seems brought on by nothing in particular. When I haven't thought of him in days, something will trigger an anxiety attack and I'll count back from ten and breathe through my nose and tell myself it's all in the past. But for today, I'm just tired.

"Okay," she says. "No more daddy issues tonight."

I sort of love her tactlessness.

"And that being the case…" Kumi brings both knees up to her chest like a kid ready for story time. "Tell me more about why you've got Ethan Ash locked up in your bedroom. Are you going to do sexy times to him?"

She needs a therapist.

"No."

"Can I?"

"Settle down, kitty." This is how she ends up falling in love with the first rebound that comes along. She's ruled by her libido. "We're working. I invited him to stay for pizza after he dropped me off."

Well, dropped me off, drove around, came back…not important.

"Oh, see…" Her lips screw to the left in a second-place-Olympic-gymnast sort of way. "You don't do pizza on a date if you're planning to hook up. Nobody wants garlic breath and bloated pizza farts in bed. That's not hot."

Though her logic is sound, I can't have her using Ethan as a scratching post or making winking insinuations every time he comes over. Because I guess I've decided that this doesn't have to be a one-time occurrence.

"Promise me you won't—"

Her attention darts over my shoulder. I turn to see Ethan walking out of my bedroom. He pauses, noticing Kumi.

"You must be the roommate," he says, and comes to the coffee table to grab his laptop and shove it in his bag. There's tension in his shoulders, in his hurried steps. With the bag slung over his shoulder, he holds out his hand to Kumi. "Ethan, nice to meet you." Then to me: "Thanks for dinner. Sorry, but I've got to head out."

"Everything okay?" I get up to see him to the door.

"Yeah, yeah." But he's practically running ahead of me. "Just something I've got to take care of."

He opens the door and only pauses on the other side as an afterthought. "I'll see you."

I lock up behind him and turn to see Kumi's puzzled expression staring at me from across the room.

"What was that about?"

"No idea."

Whatever it was, Ethan looked spooked.

# 11

# The Ingénue

I couldn't sleep. Was wide awake this morning at six when Kumi left for work. The first thing I did was roll over in bed and reach for my phone on the nightstand. I had texted Ethan last night, just to make sure he was okay, but he hasn't replied. Not that I expected him to after I went to bed at three without a response. Maybe he was already asleep by then. And he probably hasn't woken up yet. Or he *is* an early riser, but replying to my messages isn't the most pressing part of his morning routine. Now I just feel stupid. Ethan's a big boy. If he wants my help, he'll ask for it. Unlike me, he probably isn't suffering from a dearth of available friendships that have lasted longer than the two weeks we've officially known each other.

By seven I'm caffeinated, showered, dressed, and out the door. My father's affairs have been settled as far as my involvement is concerned, so there's no reason I can't go back to work. Now that I know Ed was my secret admirer, I'm less hesitant to stand my ground on this one. Not like he's going to fire me for cutting short my bereavement leave. Without bereavement, it's just leave.

Whether it's the three cups of coffee or my morning meds kicking in, I even find the courage to call my mother while I'm walking to the subway.

"Echo," she says, like we've spotted each other across a crowded room. "Good morning, sweetheart. You're up early."

"On my way to work."

"Where are you? It's so loud."

I don't even notice it. The car horns and screeching brakes. Timing belts squealing and storefront roll gates clanging open. That's something else Ethan got right about Massasauga. It was too quiet. So much silence has a way of driving a person mad. Without the commotion of society, you spend too much time absorbed in your own head.

"I'm walking," I say.

"Echo, no." It's like I'm five again, and she's smacking my hand before I pluck a big cluster of poison oak. "You shouldn't be on your phone while you're out in the city. You've got to keep your attention on your surroundings. You could get mugged or hit by a bus."

"Mom, that could happen whether I'm on my phone or not."

"Don't say that. Oh, God, don't say something like that. You put thoughts like that into the universe and they have a way of coming back to you."

I walked right into that one.

"Listen, Mom, I called because I need to tell you something."

"How's the new apartment?" Her voice rises to that artificial octave of pleasantness. "You girls getting settled in okay? Use your dead bolt, Echo."

"Mom, please, I—"

"And keep the chain on the door. You have a chain, right? I worry about you two by yourselves."

I knew this was going to happen. Why I entertained even for a moment that she'd let me get it out, I have no idea. There's only one way to combat her avoidance tactics, and that's with a brutal assault.

"Mom, he's dead. I went to the prison and left him to the state."

"You know, I'd really like to meet your roommate one of these days. You should bring her up here soon, before she starts school again."

Like she doesn't even hear me.

"I'll talk to you later, Mom. Bye."

\* \* \*

At the office, no one says anything when I walk through the Farm. Eyes follow me from the elevator and down the aisle between cubicles. Addison gives me a tentative hello nod. C.J., a hesitant wave. Navid has his headphones on and is too consumed by his screen to notice me walk by. I don't think he even takes bathroom breaks. Probably just has a Gatorade bottle under his desk, or a rigged-up catheter-condom situation. It's not until I've got my laptop on and bring up my news feed that I see the headlines. In big bold type: INFAMOUS CULT

LEADER DEAD AT 68, DAUGHTER EMERGES FROM HIDING. PATRICK TURNER MURPHY DIES IN PRISON, DAUGHTER SIGHTED. CULT KID MOURNS CONVICTED MURDERER.

Mortified, I glance around me. From all directions they watch me then turn away startled when our eyes meet. I'm a head-on collision and they have to look, but no one admits to gawking at the mangled wreckage. No one wants to be caught finding entertainment in the carnage. There's nothing I can do but close the browser and choose to ignore the red, violent heat building in my chest. It'll pass. It always does. Some other poor soul will have their life ripped from their fingers, and this will all be forgotten by the weekend. There's no use dwelling on it. So I put on my headphones and tune out the world.

Except Ethan's desk is empty.

He's not here by the time I send Cyle an email with the first batch of my completed assignments from last night. He's not in when I take my first coffee break at nine, and then a foraging trip back to the snack room at ten when I hear someone mention bagels. It's almost noon when Ed walks by, glances in my direction, then doubles back to my cubicle.

"I told you to take the day off," he says, holding a clear plastic cup of some bog-green smoothie.

"I took care of it. I'm good to go."

He considers me with skeptical eyes, searching for a crack in my armor. "Have you heard from Ethan?"

As a reflex, my attention darts to my phone on the desk. "Not today. I rode with him to the prison yesterday..."

Ed doesn't need to know the rest.

"He said he was going to get you a draft of the article last night," I say, hoping Ed might give me a hint. He only produces a noncommittal nod and walks off.

Now I'm a little worried. If Ed hasn't heard from Ethan, that's got to mean something, right? I last ten minutes combing through IAQ emails before I can't stand the uncertainty any longer.

Avery Avalon
12:05 PM
Ed's asking about you.
Coming in today?

Rather than wait for an answer, I go find Addison for lunch. It's Thai Thursday, after all. I was promised spring rolls. And if anyone's got the skinny on Ethan's disappearance, it's my all-knowing Sherpa.

* * *

"It's like explaining thermodynamics to a caveman before the discovery of fire," Navid says, flicking his hand through the air with a hunk of green bell pepper between his chopsticks. "They think they're after some criminal mastermind, but I'm trying to explain that any ten-year-old with a computer and a rudimentary grasp of phishing tactics can hack an email account."

"Please let me quote you on that," C.J. says, grinning.

We're gathered around a table at the Thai place down the street, everything gilded gold and tangy melodies of soft plucked string music playing through the room. Navid tells us about his deposition for the Justice Department this week. Or at least the parts he's allowed to talk about. I glance down at my phone in my lap. Still nothing.

"You're trying to get me sent to Gitmo, aren't you?" He shoves the pepper in his mouth and talks around it. "You *know* what they do to 'uncooperative' brown people from desert climates."

"Well," C.J. says, "the ones without a wealthy monarchy and a rich tourism economy, at least."

I'm thankful that they seem to have come to a silent agreement not to ask about my father. The last thing I want is to spend the day telling everyone how fine I am.

"All right." Addison puts down his chopsticks and cocks his head to the side with an impatient scowl. "What is going on down there?"

"What?" I say, startled. "Me?"

"You keep looking down at your phone every five seconds. Tell me you're not reading those articles."

"No."

I was going to ask anyway, I just wanted to do it less…awkwardly.

"Ed asked me if I'd heard from Ethan today," I say. "Is it normal for him not to show up without telling anybody?"

Addison doesn't react at first, then shrugs. But it's the way C.J. and Navid become fascinated by their meals that sends up warning flags.

"What? What am I missing?"

Taking pity on me, Addison sighs and pushes his plate

aside. "He sometimes has a habit of…wandering off. It's not unheard of that he goes off the reservation for a day or two—"

"A week or two," Navid interjects.

"—without checking in first."

"Has he said—I mean, is there something going on with him?"

Taking off from work without letting his boss know isn't a normal thing to do. Yeah, a journalist isn't chained to their desk, and someone of Ethan's status has more leeway than most, but it's still a job. He's still accountable.

"We don't worry anymore," C.J. says. "The first time, Ed was sending out the search party. After Vee—" She coughs, choking on the name as she seems to remember I'm not of the pre-Vee era. "Yeah, we don't worry anymore. Eventually he'll call Ed and tell him he's taking a few vacation days. I wouldn't stress about it."

But I was there. They didn't see the way his demeanor turned on a dime when he got that phone call. How he rushed out of my apartment, barely saying goodbye. More than that, it's the fact that he hasn't returned my texts that's got me on edge. This is a guy who went through the trouble of tracking down my address just to convince me to face my father's death. The guy who drove halfway, maybe all the way home, just to turn around and knock on my door because he had to tell me in person that he was sorry he'd lied to me. This man, whose life for the last two years has been engrossed in my family, and who protected me from my father's prying curiosity rather than disrupt the smallest shred of normalcy I'd managed to attain.

No, I don't buy it. Something's wrong.

* * *

Back at my desk after lunch, I dig into the magazine's website for answers. I find only one Vee in the online archive: Vivian Mott. Most of her dozen or so articles dated during an eight-month period cover environmental issues, climate change, and related policy matters. There's a particular series, however, that catches my eye. For five weeks she reported on an armed stand-off at a visitors' center on the national bison range in Montana. In the sixth week, she traveled to Moiese as the situation intensified and a resolution appeared imminent. What's interesting is in that week her updates included credit to Ethan for additional reporting. Then in the next print issue of the magazine following the end of the standoff, Ethan penned a full run-down of the ordeal. Vivian's name was left off the article. She has nothing published for *Riot Street* after the Moiese series. That was ten months ago.

A Google search turns up nothing dated after Montana. No staff positions since leaving the magazine. Either she's dropped out of the news business, or she's working under a new pen name. I find five Vivian Motts spread out across various social media profiles, but all are either the wrong age or show no matching work history and interests. Wherever she is, Vivian went to some trouble to scrub herself from the internet.

Still, none of this gives me any insight into why Ethan's dropped off the grid. All I have are coincidences, vague conjecture, and a building sense of dread. That feeling is multiplied when I notice Ed's written up a brief, bare-bones summary on my father's death and pushed it to the front page of the website. There's no way Ethan would give up the final word on Patrick Turner Murphy without a fight—unless he didn't have a choice.

* * *

Storm clouds roll in around seven that evening. The office has thinned out a bit, people taking their work home with them to avoid getting stuck in the rain. I've been sifting through IAQ emails for the better part of the day, but as I peek up from my cubicle and see another full elevator headed downstairs, I figure I'd better take their lead before I'm stuck walking to the subway in a full-on downpour.

Turns out, I make that decision too late. Just as I'm closing applications on my laptop, Cyle comes cruising down the aisle straight toward me.

Deep breath.

"Hey, Cyle," I say, like we aren't sworn office enemies. "Did you get the assignments I sent back?"

"Uh-huh." He stands behind my chair to hover over me, staring at my screen. "You started on the IAQ questions?"

I want to tell him that's a redundant phrase. The Q stands for Questions, and thus he's asking if I've started on the Question questions. But it's not polite to one-up your boss and shine a glaring spotlight on his shortcomings, so I smile and nod.

"Yep. Figured I'd start by clearing out the backlog of repeat questions that have already been answered, getting rid of random nutters, before I narrow down which questions to answer."

"Uh-huh."

I don't get what's so interesting on my screen that he's transfixed, but I feel his hand brace against the back of my chair, his fingers brushing my shoulder. It sends a shudder of revulsion down my spine.

"One other thing," he says. "Jeremy's out sick. You've done TV reviews before, right?"

Really? "Uh, yeah, on my blog. I did a little entertainment reporting at—"

"Yeah, great." He doesn't look at me. "We've got a show premiere I need a write-up on. I'll send you the link for the screener. If you could bang that out tonight, that'd be great."

"Sure," I say, taken aback. Getting to write anything I can put my real name on that isn't about Echo or my father is a step in the right direction. "Thank you."

"And I'm going to need you to cover the assignment desk tonight. Melissa will be in at midnight to relieve you."

That vindictive little prick. Now I get it. Give her the carrot then smack her with a stick. There's no use telling him I've already put in eleven hours, I barely got an hour of sleep last night, and that if Manhattan does burn down or Word War III breaks out on my watch, I'm liable to snooze through the whole thing. None of it matters. My guess: Cyle wants to make my experience working here so unpleasant I'll quit. Well, he'll have to try a lot harder than that.

"Sure thing," I say. "I'm happy to help."

"Good."

He puts his hand on my shoulder and squeezes. Like we're pals now. Golfing buddies or some shit. It takes all my restraint not to spin around and punch him in the scrotum. This is what happens when Ethan isn't here to fire warning shots.

"I'll send you an email with the link for the show screener and instructions for the assignment desk. See you tomorrow."

Fuck Cyle. To hell with him and whatever unholy union from which he spawned.

\* \* \*

At nine I go rummaging in the snack room for whatever's been left behind. I have to settle for a soda and a bag of dehydrated vegetable chips discarded by the food writers from a sample shipment. As I'm walking out, Addison comes in with his coffee cup.

"Hey," I say. "Thought you'd left already."

He opens one of the overhead cabinets and pulls down a canister of coffee grounds to make a fresh pot. "Nah, I've got to do a Skype interview at ten. Internet's been dodgy at my place for a couple of days, so I'm sticking around." He scoops a few spoonfuls into the paper filter then fills the pot with water from the sink. "Still clawing your way through the IAQ?"

"Yeah." I lean against the counter to milk Addison for all the distraction he can provide. This place will get real boring once the last of the staff goes home for the night. "And Cyle's got me pulling assignment desk duty until midnight, so that's fun."

"In that case…" Addison tosses in three more scoops of grounds into the filter. "You'll need extra-strength."

He loads the basin then pushes the button to start the hissing, gurgling percolation. There's a brief silence between Addison and me. Both watching each other for an indication to segue from polite chatter to real talk. He knows what I'm going to ask, he's just waiting for the words.

"Vivian," I say. "She never came back from Montana."

A dramatic sigh covers his walk to the round table in the center of the room, where Addison sits and pushes out a chair for me with his foot.

"Officially," he says, as I join him at the table, "no one knows what happened. Ed, maybe. But only Ethan and Vee know what really went down out there."

"And unofficially?"

"Before Montana, they were thick as mud."

There's a dose of Carolina twang in Addison's voice tonight. A product of exhaustion, I suspect. Like his tongue's too tired to fake it. I knew a Brazilian girl in college; after too many drinks she only spoke Portuguese.

"Ethan was all about her from day one. I don't know if they were sleeping together—they'd say it wasn't like that—but that was the vibe they gave off. Then the Montana story, and Vee convinced Ed to let her go out there. Whether Ethan volunteered or Ed didn't want the rookie out there alone—that's a matter of speculation. All I know is, he got on the plane home and she didn't. Ethan didn't talk to anyone for days. He turned in his copy on deadline, left one night, and disappeared for two weeks. I broke into his loft just to make sure he hadn't hung himself in there or something."

There's more sympathy than fascination in Addison's voice. While he's maybe a little jaded about Ethan's penchant for vanishing into thin air, there is a level of concern that whatever the motivating factor, Ethan's antics are more a symptom of distress than willful negligence. Ethan isn't doing it because he's an unreliable dick who just jets off to Tahiti on a whim—he's hiding.

"And?" I ask.

"Well, not dead, obviously. He wasn't there. Looked like he hadn't been there in days. Then one morning he shows up like nothing happened. All better, back to work."

"Did anyone ask why?"

"Sure, but he just brushed it off. Said he was exhausted and needed some time off. He put out two books in two years, plus press and publicity tours while still working full-time. Hadn't taken a day off in months. Everybody burns out at some point, and this was it all catching up to him. So, yeah, we bought it. The first time. Then we stopped asking."

Ed has to know. I don't care how popular Ethan is, there's no way Ed tolerates a reporter who's perpetually taking off without explanation. At some point, he has to have sat Ethan down and given him an ultimatum: *Give me a good reason or you're fired.* Ed must have been satisfied with the answer.

"What about that intern you mentioned before. Brittany?"

Addison shakes his head. "Nah, that girl just quit. Had a total nervous breakdown in the middle of the office. Cops had to escort her out of the building after she locked herself in the bathroom and refused to leave."

"Oh."

"Yeah, you'd be surprised how often that kind of thing happens around here. Like, no one ever just quits quietly. They all want to be the guy who pulls the emergency exit lever on the plane, sliding out with two giant middle fingers in the air. But we didn't want to scare you off your first day."

Somehow, I'm not surprised.

"Avery, let me be real with you for a minute." Addison leans toward me across the table. "Ethan is addictive. He's smart, and charming, and most of the time a lot of fun to be around. But the guy's always got one foot out the door. We used to be tight. But little by little, he drifts away. I don't think he means to, it's who he is. Easily distracted and forever absorbed in his own mind. If he doesn't have constant stimulation, he gets bored. Once someone's lost that luster of a shiny new toy, he loses interest."

"Why are you telling me this?"

Addison raises a sarcastic eyebrow. "You seem like a good girl. I get that you and Ethan meet at this weird sort of tragic intersection, but when the novelty of it wears off, I don't want you to be another cynical victim of his short attention span. One bright new ingénue didn't come back, and he drove the other one to madness. Just once, I'd like the new girl to make it through her first year unscathed."

Addison means well, even if his advice is a bit insulting. I have no intention of letting Ethan or anyone else distract me from the reason I took this job. All the same, when I get back to my desk, I can't escape the notion that the office feels empty without Ethan. His presence has a way of filling the room, even when he isn't doing anything at all. Ethan doesn't have to pull focus—it finds him. In his absence, it's too quiet. Dullness permeates the air. Now he's run off.

I know this preoccupation isn't healthy—becoming too entangled in the messy affairs of others is a quick way to drown in their troubles—but I have a bit of a soft spot for people who are in a perpetual state of disarray. And I know, if our places were reversed, Ethan would look for me.

* * *

I get out of work at midnight and catch the subway up to the East Village. There were only two addresses online for an Ethan Ash in the five boroughs. The first was an apartment building reserved for senior citizens. The other, it turns out, is a single-story structure that looks like it had a previous life as an auto shop. Three gooseneck lamps hang across the face of the building, illuminating the matte façade of painted white brick with huge, irregular swaths of primary colors, red, yellow, green, and blue, cutting across the entire wall. In the center, a ten-foot anatomical heart carefully rendered to resemble a pencil sketch. Something like a spear pierces through the heart at an angle. For this mural alone the trip was worth it, but I remind myself this isn't a sightseeing excursion.

On either side of the heart are identical metal doors. I take a guess at the one on the left and knock. After a few seconds, I knock again. Nothing. Doubt seeps in. What if this isn't Ethan's place and I'm some crazy woman pounding on a stranger's door in the middle of the night? Sure, the thought occurred to me before I came out here, but on the way I convinced myself that it had to be his. Addison said he had a loft. I guess this counts, right?

Once more, just to be sure, I knock again. This time, I hear movement on the other side. It takes several seconds before the scraping sound of metal on metal, then the door whips open.

"Avery?"

Ethan stands shirtless in the doorway. I'm met eye-level by the kind of body you see on Olympic swimmers. His hair looks like someone's been tugging at it. Lines like pillow creases cut across one side of his face. He wears only a loose pair of black pajama bottoms hanging low on his hips. I've just made a horrible mistake.

"What are you doing here?"

He pokes his head out the door just a fraction, looking behind me like he expects someone to jump out from the shadows. I wish I had a good answer, but now everything that made perfect sense an hour ago seems completely mental.

"You weren't at work," I say, blood pumping fast and heat flaring across my face. "And you never returned my messages."

He sighs and runs one hand through his hair. If he'd slammed the door in my face, I wouldn't feel as small as I do right now.

"You shouldn't be here," he says. "It's, what, almost one in the morning."

"Right, no, I know." That part didn't seem so egregious when I was thinking about his penchant for texting me in the middle of the night. How he insisted he kept late hours. Now that seems like ages ago. A different person. "Ed was asking about you, and I was concerned, so…"

"Go home, Avery."

Cold, detached, his voice is almost unrecognizable and it

cuts right to the bone. Framed in the doorway, arms braced on either side, he's a wall that reads, *Do not enter.*

"Is there something wrong? After you got that phone call last night—"

"Christ, Avery. I can't do this right now, okay?"

"I'm sorry, I only wanted—"

"I'm fine. Please, just go home."

Something cracks open inside of me. Broken by the hard, impassive expression on Ethan's face. I don't recognize him. It leaves me disoriented, stranded in the dark. My hands shake as I turn my back to him and walk away to the sound of the metal door shutting behind me.

Addison was right. Ethan is dangerous.

# 12

# THE FRAUD

Navid Kirmani has a secret identity. By day he's the mild-mannered senior tech reporter for *Riot Street*. At night he descends into a secret underbelly of Manhattan that few ever see. It's a dangerous, unforgiving world of cutthroats and renegades where only the most calloused dare enter. They are the outermost fringes of society. The nameless. The sleepers biding their time for that one moment of glory where fame is the ultimate reward. But fail, and it's a fate worse than death.

"And now," says the disembodied voice coming through the crackling speakers overhead, "please welcome to the stage a favorite here at the Hired Gun and recently added to the no-fly list, the very mediocre Navid Kirmani."

Friday night, after spending the day at work in a sleep-deprived daze, I sit in a darkened basement comedy club in Brooklyn with Addison and C.J. I also managed to convince Kumi to come along once I told her a brilliant MIT grad had made a point of inviting her to his show. Or she's expecting an Ethan sighting. I'm hoping he never comes back.

He wasn't at work today, which was for the best. I don't think I could have survived the embarrassment. Nor did I tell anyone about going to his place last night. If there's any mercy in the world, he'll let us both pretend it never happened. Better yet, maybe he'll finally take my father's advice and move to the West Coast, where there is no chance of us ever having to be in the same room together. But I suppose I should thank him. When I got home last night, I couldn't sit still. Too much hostility pulsing through my veins. Mostly, though, it was the pain and sadness of trying to be someone's friend only to be scornfully rejected. So I found something useful to do: I wrote an essay about my father's death. About the strange, nebulous experience of death without grief and the difference between choosing to love your parents and complying with the expectation that you do so. I emailed it to Cara at three this morning. When I walked into the office today, it was already up on the website. I guess I should be proud of myself.

Against the backdrop of a brick wall with the club's crosshairs logo, Navid takes the stage and is hit with the blinding glow of a single spotlight. There's a decent turnout here, spectators wrapped around the bar and occupying several tables on the main floor. Thus far, they've made enough noise for a packed house. I'm terrified for Navid after the reaction one of the earlier acts received—he was booed off the stage with people flinging french fries at him—but Navid looks completely at ease, a big smile on his face.

"Thank you," Navid says, and pulls the microphone from

its stand. "Thank you, I'm Navid Kirmani, and welcome to my first suicide bombing."

The audience erupts with laughter. C.J. damn near falls out of her chair and Addison's already got tears in his eyes.

"All right, that joke killed." He chuckles to himself and the line gets another big laugh. "This is a good room. Okay, we're going to have fun together. But first, let's clear this up, white folks. People are always coming up to me and asking where I'm from. In the proud tradition of my hometown, I tell them, I'm from Brooklyn, asshole. What's it to ya?" Loud whistles and cheers fill the room in response. "But seriously, though, my heritage is Iranian. You might remember us as that country America was totally cool with, you sold us a bunch of weapons, and then we're like, you know what? Fuck it. Death to America! So basically every Middle Eastern country you've ever heard of."

Addison's choking on his drink, coughing like a coal miner.

"He's good," Kumi says beside me, leaning in. "Kind of cute, in that mathletes sort of way."

"And a member of Mensa," I tell her as Navid segues into a bit about the difference between Arabs and Persians. "So you'd never have to do your own taxes again."

"Good point."

Kumi is an absolute encyclopedia of legal knowledge. She hasn't even started her first semester of law school and she can already rattle off New York statutes like she's reading them from a book printed in her head. But every year right around April, she has a complete meltdown. I don't know if it's fear of the IRS or an aversion to numbers, but she always ends up coming to me an hour before the deadline begging me to make it go away.

"...but I get it, white people. We can't tell you apart, either..."

Something stands looming behind me. A warm, thrumming, energetic sensation. Kumi looks over my head, eyes big and impressed. Shit.

"...When really we should all blame the English." Navid walks the stage, holding the audience on the edge of their seats. "Think about it..."

I'm afraid to turn around. In the last twenty-four hours, I've realized that I put more emphasis than he did on whatever supposed connection I felt with Ethan. Spun out of loneliness and a desperate need to fit in at the magazine, I tricked myself into seeing something that was never there. It's Echo all over again, seizing on to anything to make herself feel whole.

Too bad I figured that out *after* I showed up at his door like a crazed stalker. Worse, one of his doting interns.

"...They're history's version of that kid on the playground running around licking everything they see. Like, ooh, monkey bars, those are mine. Slide—that's mine. Swings, mine. Just licking fucking everything. Because if there's one thing I think America and its adversaries have ever agreed on, it's fuck the English."

"Hey!" Addison turns and glances at the dark shadow hovering behind me. "He lives! Glad you made it. Navid's opener was vicious."

Ethan stands there, daunting and silent, like he's waiting to see how long I'm capable of ignoring him. But I'm not going to turn my back on Navid's set just because Ethan Ash walks into a room.

"Hi, I'm Kumi."

My roommate, on the other hand…

She stands to shake his hand over my head. "I didn't get a chance to introduce myself the other night."

For just a bright, fleeting moment, I sort of hate her.

"Sorry about that," he says. "It's nice to meet you."

The ringing in my ears that is their polite chattering overtakes Navid's voice until the high-pitched peal becomes color and texture behind my eyes.

"…Thank you, you've been a terrific crowd. My name is Navid Kirmani. Good night, and remember to tip your waiters."

He's cheered off the stage and comes straight to our table. I didn't even hear the closer.

"Ah, Ethan, man, you made it," Navid says, sweating and out of breath. He takes a big swig from the bottle of beer he left on the table. "What'd you guys think?"

"Not even exaggerating," Addison says, "I almost peed."

C.J. takes off her glasses to wipe her eyes, residual giggles still bubbling up from her belly. "Your best set yet. By far."

"Having a good time?" Navid asks me. He wipes sweat from his face with a handful of napkins.

I was until Ethan walked in. Now I've got a knot twisting my stomach and a fever-hot rush burning my face.

"Absolutely. You were really great up there."

"I was worried the bombing line wouldn't land well on a New York crowd." He takes a seat between Addison and C.J.

across the table. "Before I went on, I was trying to prep myself to dodge bottles if they started throwing them at my head."

"Avery." Something like sparks struck from flint shoot down my neck as Ethan bends to speak in my ear. "May I talk to you?"

I'd rather slit my own throat.

However, I can't say no with everyone looking at us. Refusing would create a scene. I don't want to steal the attention away from Navid, and I'm not going to give Ethan the satisfaction of seeing me humiliated twice. So I push back from the table and stand, first meeting Kumi's eyes. She flashes a secret smile that's far more obvious than she knows.

"I'll be right back," I tell her, then I walk in the opposite direction from Ethan.

A wall of thick humidity and car exhaust accosts me as I climb the stairs from the basement club up to the sidewalk. My back to the entrance, I hear Ethan's footsteps stop behind me.

"You're mad at me," he says.

I watch my reflection appear in the windows of passing cars. "What does it matter?"

"Quite a bit, actually."

"You don't owe me anything."

We both fell into a trap of artificial association. The threads connecting us formed a thin bridge built on nothing more than coincidence and anecdotes. A weak basis for a friendship. Now I see it didn't need much to snap the strings. The truth is, Ethan knows no more about the person I am than I know about him. We're familiar strangers. Colleagues, at best. That's how it should be.

"And yet," he says, stepping closer until I feel him like a closing storm, "I do."

"Let's not do this, okay? You made your point clear. I'll leave you alone."

"Avery…" Impatient, he expels a breath. "Will you please look at me?"

With some effort, I steel myself and turn, raking my gaze up the length of him to reach his face. The image of him half-naked in his doorway last night flashes behind my eyes. And the hurt I carried home when he shut me out. I can't erase it.

"I was an incredible asshole last night. I'm sorry." Hands in his pockets, he stands with slumped shoulders. It doesn't fit him, the contrite posture. Like wearing someone else's clothes. "You just took me by surprise. Which is no excuse, I know. I was—it's been a rough forty-eight hours. I am so sorry."

I don't want to be mad at him. This feeling of distance and embarrassment pushing us apart, when from the moment we met, I've only felt the pull.

"I was worried about you." I shrug in an effort to make the statement sound less sincere than it is. "When you didn't turn in the article, and then Addison told me you do this sometimes…"

His jaw tenses. Aggression creases his brow. "Addison doesn't—"

"Will you tell me what happened?"

"I'd rather not."

He's still closing me out, slamming doors. A few days ago there were no barriers. Now I understand I simply hadn't reached them yet.

"You can't tell me everything's fine. I'll admit I made a mistake going over there, but you—"

"Can't it be enough to trust me?" he says. "Please."

There's fear in the way his voice strains, rough and tired. Fear of what happens when someone pushes too hard on the door. He's got his back against it, braced and weakening. I know that feeling. If our roles were reversed, I wouldn't react any better to being cornered with a sudden inquisition. There are whole swaths of my past I'm not eager to share. Even with Ethan. Maybe especially him.

"Yeah," I say, backing off. "Okay."

A slow, grateful smile crosses his lips. His shoulders relax, and he pulls his hands from his pockets. "It is nice to know you missed me."

"I wouldn't go that far."

"No, no." Ethan crosses his arms, chest big and confident. The smile turns playful. "You missed me."

"Don't flatter yourself."

Sensing my demeanor softening, he closes the space between us. "This might sound crazy…" Ethan licks his lips, and I see the idea forming in his mind. He studies me with narrow eyes, alive with mischief. "But I'm in the mood for a drive. Come with me."

"Another road trip?"

"No prisons this time, I promise."

There's something different about him tonight. Yes, his mood has improved since the last time we spoke, but it's more than that.

"It's almost midnight," I say.

"I don't see your point."

"You don't think it's a little late?"

"Not for me."

I've yet to see him so excited until now. Full of energy like his Ritalin's just kicked in. But if this is a response to whatever kept him out of the office for the last two days…

"I can't just leave," I say. "Kumi's here, and Navid—"

"His set's over. After a few more drinks he'll barely remember we were here."

"Kumi—"

"Yeah, I don't think we should bring her with us." He pops one eyebrow the way he does when he's amusing himself. "She seems nice, but I'm pretty sure she wants to sleep with me, and I think that'd be an awkward dynamic between the three of us."

"Funny."

Impulse control has always been an issue for me. Spontaneity and the allure of not knowing exactly what will happen next. It's also gotten me into trouble.

"I don't think—"

"Please."

Expression sobering, Ethan takes a step toward me. He has an aura that's enveloping. The closer he gets, the more potent it becomes, intense and persuasive.

"I only came out tonight because I hoped I'd see you. I feel horrible about the way I acted. Haven't been able to think about anything else." He reaches out and takes my hand, squeezing. "Let me make it up to you. Come with me. Give me a chance to get back on your good side."

It is impossible to say no to Ethan when he's staring me in the face. Which I suppose explains his entire career. And while there's a small voice whispering *caution* in the back of my mind, the larger part of me wants to be wherever he is. The hole in my chest closed the minute I looked into his eyes tonight. The emptiness that hadn't been there until he wasn't. I'm afraid where it's leading me, but more scared to miss it.

\* \* \*

After we've said good night to the others and Kumi assures me she is in good hands with Navid—those two got cozy real quick—we get in Ethan's truck headed east. He won't tell me where we're going, if he has a plan at all, but I'm content to watch him behind the wheel, city lights around us.

"I read your essay about Patrick," he says, pulling up to a red light.

"Yeah." My hand falls to my lap to trace the outline of the shell casing in my pocket through my jeans. "I, uh, got restless last night."

"How are you doing?"

"Fine, I guess. I emailed it to Cara in a close-your-eyes-and-jump state of mind. Just hit Send and don't think about it, you know? So now I'm trying to forget about it. It'll be easier when they stop calling me 'Cult Kid' on TV."

"For what it's worth…" The light changes. Ethan wrestles the truck into gear and follows the traffic ahead of him. "I'm proud of you. I know how hard it was to dig all that out of your head. I hope you can be proud of yourself."

"I'll work up to that. Right now I'm somewhere between indifferent and relieved."

Now that my father's dead and I have the essay out of the way, I'd prefer never to think of him again. I've been waiting my whole life to get out from under his shadow. To be my own person, whoever that is, without him as my defining characteristic.

"Vivian," I say, in the interest of changing the subject. "What's the story there?"

He flinches, surprised for a moment, then recovers his composure while running a hand through his hair.

"What do you mean?"

"Tell me about her."

Leaning his elbow against the door, he takes a breath. His lips thin to a hard line.

"She was a magnificent catastrophe."

I can only believe there's fondness in such a poetic insult. A person must leave a profound impression on another to earn such an epithet. It reveals a level of respect, and perhaps even regret. Whatever her tragic flaw, she was almost perfect. Enough so that losing her drove Ethan into seclusion for two weeks.

"Please," I say, "elaborate."

"She was like a lot of eager rookies. You remind me a little of her, in fact."

Not the comparison I want to hear right now, considering Addison's warning about Ethan's body count.

"Smart, tenacious. She had a ton of energy and wanted to hit the ground running. Did pretty well for herself."

"Until Montana."

Something passes across his face. A memory that sucks the color from his skin.

"Why does everyone go a little wiggy at the mention of her name?"

"Vee didn't have many friends at the magazine."

"Why's that?"

"I can't speak for anyone else." He glances out the window like the right answer might pass by on the side of a bus. "But I think it boils down to a fundamental difference of philosophy. She believed in absolute truths and the necessity for unfiltered honesty, which meant she found herself at odds with anyone who tried to temper her voice. She'd get into shouting matches with associate editors for sneaking contrasting quotes into her articles or cutting something that sounded too much like commentary. But in her mind, it wasn't our job to present both sides of an argument if one of them was total bullshit."

"I have a hard time believing that made her an outcast."

*Riot Street* is far from stodgy. It built its reputation on experimentation and a radical commitment to questioning authority. In every era of major American conflict since the magazine's inception, it has been an outspoken proponent of progressivism and free expression. *Riot Street* is special for its contribution to the voice of the counterculture.

"Vee could be brash and abrasive. She had a habit of calling out her colleagues for what she perceived as weak journalistic integrity. Publicly, in some instances."

"Meaning?"

Ethan checks his mirrors, merging onto the parkway headed east toward Queens.

"Well, more than once she Tweeted rather blunt takedowns of other reporters' work. That's all well and good when you're taking the competition to task. It doesn't go over well when you do it to members of your own staff, though."

Shit. While it's a pretty dick move, I have to admire her conviction.

"But it sounds like you didn't share their opinion of her."

"I understood her."

Ethan drives the way he commands a room, the way he writes. With total authority. He's efficient, if also a bit impatient. I think he likes the idea of road trips more than he likes enduring other drivers.

"Vee was determined to change the world. By force, if necessary. She didn't give a shit what anyone thought of her. It was irrelevant to her mission. That kind of self-assuredness is infectious, you know? Being around a person like that, if you can get past the culture shock, can give you a sort of contact high. You start seeing the world through their lens. Minor bullshit doesn't get to you anymore. Things that used to ruin your day or drive you crazy—that petty garbage—it all becomes so small until you don't even notice it anymore. She saw life in simple terms: there's right and wrong, good and evil, and everything else is a lie."

For the first time in my life, I know what real jealousy is. Not the little pangs we feel when we see someone prettier, thinner, smarter, or richer. True, burning, aching jealousy. Because I don't think there's a soul in this world who would speak about me with such passionate admiration as the way Ethan describes Vivian. We should all be so fortunate to leave such witnesses in our wake.

"So you two were close."

Now I understand what Addison meant about their vibe. A straight man doesn't talk about a woman this way if there isn't at least some level of attraction. Which makes an ugly breakup the most likely scenario for why only one of them came back from Montana.

"She came around at a strange time in my life. Everything was happening, and I felt none of it. Every day someone was calling me up to do an appearance or give a talk. I'd never had so many people wanting to know me. If that's not making it, what is, right? I should have been thrilled, but it felt like it was happening to someone else and I was watching through their eyes. Like you said, my life wasn't my own anymore. Guess I lost touch with myself. Disconnected. Vee was like a jump start."

"Do you miss her?"

He laughs to himself, sharp and humorless. Then he glances at me like he's just remembered I'm sitting here.

"I used to," he says. "Not so much anymore. There was a lot of good about Vee, but she was also volatile and unpredictable. Didn't know how to back down from a fight or admit when she was wrong. When her temper came out, it'd bring down a whole city block. Sometimes I think she'd start a fight purely out of boredom. You never really felt like she cared if you lived or died. If you got hit by a car right in front of her, she'd just keep walking. Some people blamed it on using, but it was all her. She was wired differently than the rest of us."

"Using?"

Shame slithers under my skin. I become hyperaware of the muscles in my face, trying to maintain a neutral arrangement.

"Mm-hmm." He flicks his turn signal and changes lanes around a car crawling in the left lane. "Everyone's dropped a little acid at a party, sure. I don't know anyone who hasn't smoked pot or tried ecstasy at least once. But Vee's coke habit wasn't so cute when she started throwing kitchen knives at Cara's living room wall during a Halloween party. Like she was training for the fucking Hunger Games. Even less cute when she tells me right after I get stopped for a bad taillight in Queens that she's holding."

This is what's so difficult about staying clean. Using is easy. It's accepting what you are, and living with it, that's the hard part.

I feel like a fraud. Dressed up to appear presentable, but underneath is a place dark and cavernous where a shriveled, withering, grotesque abomination hides in the deepest black. Its bones warped and brittle. Body sunken and emaciated. Skin, like the burnt pages of a book that turn to dust in your hand, covers spindly limbs. Long, jagged, bleeding wounds where claws tear at the flesh, consuming it.

"Avery?"

My head snaps up. "What?"

"Where'd you go?"

Nowhere he's been.

## 13

# The Cliff and Other Hazards

Past three in the morning, Ethan turns down a dirt road off Old Montauk Highway. It's pitch-black but for the truck's headlights casting wide yellow beams at the walls of trees and shrubs on either side of us. The moon hidden behind threatening storm clouds. We drive another half mile and come to a dead end where the road empties into a dirt cul-de-sac carved out from the sylvan landscape.

"Are we lost?"

For the last hour or so we followed the same road through Long Island and into Montauk. I figured he'd drive until we hit water. Somehow we've managed to miss the ocean entirely. Which is impressive, I guess.

Ethan cuts the engine and drops us into total darkness.

"Don't you trust me?"

He gets out of the truck and comes around to my side. No lights come on when the doors open. It's just his hand helping me find the ground and the sound of the door slamming shut behind me.

"Ethan…"

He leads me forward, toward the wall of trees. My heart pounds in my chest, breath coming quick and shallow. He doesn't understand, or maybe he's forgotten; the last time I was dragged through the woods in the middle of the night, my father was shooting at us.

"Tell me where we're going."

In my pocket, I find the shell casing and roll it between my fingers.

"I've got you." He wraps an arm around my shoulders and pulls me against his body. "Just a little farther. You'll hear it soon."

We walk down a path, I think. There's nothing in front of us but space. No branches blocking our way or bushes scraping my legs. Wherever we are, he knows it well. There's no hesitation in his steps. We cover the length of a football field, maybe less. I can't judge the distance with the trees thick overhead and crowding out the sky.

Then I hear it. Enormous and powerful. Surging. We emerge from the trees to find the moon lighting our path, and walk through tall grass until we reach the edge of a sloped cliff. Twenty feet down, the ocean crashes against the shore. Out over the water, the moon is nearly full between the passing storm clouds—a brilliant silver orb casting white light rippling on the waves.

"What do you think?" he asks, still clutching me to his side. His body is warm and solid, and it makes me a little nervous that neither of us lets go. "Worth the drive?"

More than worth it. It's magnificent. "I've never seen the ocean." Not in person, anyway.

"You're kidding."

"No."

"Not even Brighton or—"

"Never had a reason to go to the beach. I burn under bright lamps, and Kumi is more the metropolitan type."

"Then I consider it an honor to be the first to show it to you."

Ethan takes my hand and helps me down the wooden steps to the beach below. It's only a narrow sliver of shoreline dotted by rocks that have slid down the eroding cliff. We sit at the bottom of the stairs to watch the waves rush in and retreat. Here in the darkness, there's something nurturing and amniotic about the beach. The sound of the water moving like a steady heart rhythm, the night encasing me. The air smells different out here. Pure and fortifying. I feel myself changing, the salt clinging to my skin and getting trapped in my hair. Tilting my head back, I inhale a deep breath, letting the breeze wash over me.

"I think this is my favorite place in the world," Ethan says. His voice is hushed, barely rising over the waves. As if he doesn't dare compete. "Because it's private, you know? Could spend hours out here and not see another person. Almost forget there are any."

"There are a lot of places to get lost in the world. Plenty more secluded than this."

"Yeah." He leans back on his palms. "But this one's mine. What business do I have staking out a secret hideout in Finland, right?"

"I guess you have a point there. The Finns should get first dibs in their own backyards."

"There you go. As a New Yorker, I've claimed this beach."

"How'd you find it?"

He glances over his shoulder and back where we came from.

"My parents' summer house is just up there."

"So you're saying we didn't *have* to go traipsing through the woods. That was just, what, for funsies?"

Ethan turns his head to face me, a coy smirk curving his lips.

"You have to respect theatrics. It's all about the reveal."

"Uh-huh. I see."

"Actually, the first time I broke my arm was falling off that cliff."

"You fell from up there?"

That's no small tumble. The height of a two-story building, at least.

"How old were you?"

"Eight, I think? Give or take a year. My brother and I were playing. We'd start, I don't know, twenty yards back, and race at a full sprint to the edge."

He pauses a moment, and his voice changes. The resentment and anger rise to the surface. Darkness envelops him.

"Except Evan thought it'd be more fun to stop short and push me over. Believe me, those were the longest seconds of my life. Landed right on my arm. Nearly snapped it in half."

"Shit, Ethan."

I'm not good at comfort. Never have been. But I know enough to see that the memories of his brother cut deep.

"I'm sorry."

"After that, this is where I'd come to get away from him and be alone. As a kid, I kind of thought this place gave me superpowers, right. Because I'd lived. This was the one place I *knew* couldn't hurt me."

Ethan doesn't have to say it out loud. This beach is his apology. He took me here to share a piece of himself because, whatever it is, he couldn't tell me why he missed work and reacted the way he did when I went to his loft. This is his trade for my forgiveness.

"That's the sweetest, saddest thing I've ever heard."

"You're the only person I've brought here. I guess it was getting a little too lonely."

He can't know how much this means to me. Feeling like I've been at a disadvantage against him since the day we met. While that score may never be even, he's made an effort to let me know him. To share something I would never have thought to ask for. It's all the more meaningful because I hear in his voice the hurt that still lingers in his mind.

"Hold out your hand." I dig into my pocket and pull out the shell casing. Dubious, he complies, and I place the casing in the center of his palm. For a moment, he doesn't quite know what to do or what it is—expecting it to do a trick, maybe. Then he holds it up in the moonlight to inspect the brass cylinder. Brow furrowed, he regards me with curiosity and perhaps mild alarm.

"This is a shell casing. Avery, why are you carrying this?"

"I have it on me at all times. Whenever I leave home. That," I say, nodding, "is *my* superpower. Because I lived."

Ethan brings the casing closer, turning it in his hand

and running his finger over the stamped indentation on the bottom.

"This is from that night. The night your father killed all those people. It should be in evidence in a warehouse somewhere. How do you have this?"

"The prosecutor asked my mother and me to go back out there, do a re-creation of that night, and explain how it happened. They wanted this whole map and video layout for the trial to show where and how each victim died. Brought all of the survivors at various points. Well," I say, shrugging when Ethan questions me with a look, "all the ones they managed to subpoena. But it was just us that day. Did a step-by-step walk-through of the entire ordeal." The parts we remembered clearly, anyway. "I was standing there while the lawyers were talking to my mother, and I saw something shiny on the ground. It was this, just lying there in the grass months later. So I put it in my pocket and never told anyone. When I get nervous or anxious—whatever—I rub it between my fingers and remind myself that if I could survive that night, I can survive this, too."

"Christ."

He hands the casing back to me and wraps his hands behind his head, staring up at the sky.

"That's the saddest, coolest thing I've ever heard."

I tuck the casing back in my pocket.

"Just don't tell anyone I stole evidence from a murder trial."

"Strictly off the record. Secret's safe with me."

For several minutes neither of us speaks as we sit and watch the waves. He's easy to share the silence with. I don't know why, we hardly know each other at all, and yet being with him feels natural. Perhaps more familiar than anyone else who's passed through my life. It's just something in his presence that relaxes me, takes the anxiety away.

"Why did you want to know about Vee?" he asks.

"No reason."

If I could go back, I'd have let the mystery stay in the past where it belongs. At least I could have remained blissfully ignorant that someday soon I'm going to leave Ethan disappointed. Again, I consider telling him. About Jenny and rehab and my little collection of NA chips in the bottom of the jar where I keep loose change. But this place is too nice to spoil. The moment is too perfect.

"Hey," he says, sitting up. "Forget what I said before. Truth is, you two are nothing alike."

"Yeah, no, I get it."

"I mean it. With everything you've been through in your life, no one would blame you for being a total mess, but you're not. Avery, you're probably one of the most well-adjusted people I've ever met. Prep school kids from Connecticut have more disorders."

"Trust me," I say, staring at the ground. "I'm not that together."

He reaches out, fingers pushing the hair off my face.

"You're remarkable."

"Ethan..." A feeling like my stomach being pulled through a funnel overwhelms me. "Don't do that."

"Do what?"

"Say nice things to me."

Leaning closer, he studies my face. I feel exposed, being under his scrutiny. Naked and nowhere to hide.

"Why not?"

I'm not sure this is real anymore. The ocean and the stars, moon watching us from above. These moments don't happen to me. Any minute I'll wake up and Ethan, Manhattan, and the magazine will all have been a dream. I'm strapped to a hospital bed somewhere, hallucinating through another round of detox.

Unable to sit still any longer, I jump to my feet.

"Because."

"That's an awful reason."

He's up right after me, keeping pace as I walk down the shore.

"I wonder if you might let me try something," he says.

Static reaches through me, right down to my fingertips.

"Like what?"

"I think I should I kiss you."

"You think?"

"I'd like to."

My pulse quickens, throbbing in my neck.

"That's a terrible idea," I say.

Ethan is the kind of attraction that ruins people. The one you don't come back from. He's got *relapse* written all over him.

"And yet…" Reaching out, he catches my hand to stop me walking away. Ethan turns me toward him as his other hand rises to cup the side of my face and brush his thumb under the ridge of my bottom lip. My skin is bright and alive, thrumming, everywhere his touch makes contact. It's waking up in pitch black, for a split second uncertain which way is up. He leans in. Ethan's hand slides to the back of my neck and pulls me toward him as he says, "I don't care."

I blink, and in the darkness his lips press to mine, warm and comforting. Like they've always been there.

Have you ever crashed your car in a dream? Or had the sensation of falling that jolts you awake? That's Ethan. He's a sudden impact that flares across every nerve. My mind stutters and halts. Instincts take over. Physical, tactile desire prevails and I kiss him back, hands finding the soft cotton of his T-shirt. Beneath my palms the muscles of his stomach contract as he breathes in and deepens the kiss, slow and gentle. Passionate, yet restrained. When he pulls away, his forehead pressed to mine, my hands slide up his chest, and I feel his heart pounding hard and quick.

"I dreamt about this last night," he says, voice a low rasp. One hand cradles my head, tangled in my hair, the other pressed to the small of my back. "Kissing you on this beach. I don't know where it came from, but I woke up, and it was the worst happiness I've ever felt. Because I didn't know if you'd let me and I might not get that feeling back. It would just be a memory of something that never happened."

They're beautiful words. It's easy to be seduced by them. In his arms, feeling his body, solid and strong, holding me tight, I can almost pretend we're alone in the world. Nothing can intrude. Until thought creeps in.

It's not this easy. I never asked to feel this way: inside out and turned around. But it's like trying to walk away from the horizon. It was always going to be impossible to avoid him, even before I knew his name.

"Ethan…" I close my eyes, fighting the ache tearing my head in two. "We can't do this. You know that."

"I know no such thing." Untangling his hand from my hair, he lifts my chin. "Give me a reason."

"We work together, for one."

Vivian is a perfect indication of how wrong that can go.

"There's no rule against it," he says. "We're both adults. Why should I deprive myself of the one person I want because we're inconveniently employed? Give me a better reason."

"Where is this coming from? You just woke up this morning and…"

"I was attracted to you the moment we met. I mean, fuck, Avery. You're beautiful and clever and you make me *feel* something. Every day since then, there's been this…*noise* in my head. I woke up this morning, and it was clear. It was you."

"We barely know each other."

"That's not even half-true."

"There are things about me you wouldn't like."

I step out of his arms, turning toward the moon overhead and the tide crawling up the sand. Out in the distance, lightning bursts through the clouds.

"You don't know everything."

"Avery." Ethan stands behind me, thunder rolling in. "I'm not going to go riffling through your past if you don't want to tell me. You're entitled to your privacy, and I can respect that. But I'm not going to let you scare me off, either. If you don't want me in your life, tell me. I won't force myself on you. But if you think you're trying to protect me from something, stop. Whatever it is, I don't care."

"You wouldn't say that if you knew."

It's easy to pretend without enough sense to know better. If I'd never asked about Vivian, maybe I would have told him already. Bitten the bullet and exposed the last of my ugly secrets. Now it's too late for that.

"If you want to send me off, say the word. I won't bother you again." Behind me, Ethan wraps his arms around my stomach and holds me against his chest. Another brilliant, electric flash lights up the sky. "Just understand I'm past the point of forgetting. There's nothing you can tell me that'll change the way this feels."

Every instinct I've developed over the years screams at me to push him away, to find any excuse to drive him off. If I let this happen, it only gets more complicated from here. Trouble is, I don't *want* to push him away. I didn't *want* him to stop wanting me. Addicts are inherently selfish.

"I think you might be good for me," he says with wistful gravity. "Give me a chance to be good for you."

"Ethan…"

I don't have a single notion in my mind of what to say to him. Words turn to disjointed emotions that I can't explain, even to myself.

The thunder becomes louder, more violent overhead.

"Have you really thought about this?"

"I don't need to. If you feel nothing, Avery, say so. Tell me I'm wrong and there's nothing here." His lips move against my neck, a whisper. "Stop me, if that's what you want."

It isn't *nothing*. I don't have a name for it—attraction, yes, physical. More than that it's…the person you want to see waiting when you step off a plane. The one you call first when something great happens, and the last one standing there when you've lost everything. The one you don't have to say anything to at all, because they've already read your mind.

I turn to face him, plant my hands against his chest. Looking up into his churning tempest eyes reflecting the moonlight, I know the right answer. It's clear, simple. And yet…

Few times in our lives are we aware of these moments when they occur. The intersections where one decision has a definite and discernible effect on the course of our lives. This is that place. The farther I drift toward Ethan, the more uncertain my future becomes. I give up what little control I have. I've just gotten my life together. I'm finally seeing tangible progress toward my goals. If I risk that now on all the ways Ethan could wreck everything that's just begun to take shape, I might never fit the pieces back together.

But attraction isn't rational. I can't help that looking at him makes me forget where I am. Or how his smile ties my stomach in knots and his voice makes my blood pump faster. He's addictive. That's the thing about recovery, though: every day is a choice. Sometimes, we make the wrong ones.

"I don't want you to stop."

An elated smile spreads across Ethan's face. With both hands he cups my jaw and bends to bring his lips to mine. I expect him to be forceful, urgent, the way he bursts into a room. Just the opposite. He's deliberate the way his mouth moves with mine. Unhurried. As far as he's concerned, this moment can last forever. Until lightning cracks somewhere above us. Close enough that every hair on my body stands taut and my muscles clench.

Suddenly, I'm hauled off my feet and upside down. Ethan tosses me over his shoulder, my ass in the air, and he jogs toward the stairs.

"What the hell are you doing?" I shout.

He climbs the steps two at a time like I weigh nothing at all.

"We have to get out of the storm."

As he says it, the sky opens up. Torrential rain beats down on my back and soaks through my clothes.

"I want to show you the house."

"I can walk!"

And there's water draining out of my hair and into my mouth, so if I don't get upright soon, I might drown.

"No, this is way more fun."

"Ethan!"

We reach the top of the stairs and he sets me on my feet. Then he grabs my hand and darts off, dragging me behind him. As we approach, the house comes into view. This isn't some quaint summer home, it's an estate. The massive structure is like a cottage that ate five other houses and kept growing. The entire rear is lined by white framed windows and glass doors. A covered patio stretches the length of the house. Under the shelter of the patio's roof, breathing heavily, I wipe the water from my arms and ring out my hair. Ethan disappears for a moment. Flames burst to life from a fireplace at the near end of the patio.

"Stay here," he says, "I'm going to run around to the front and open the door."

While I wait, I stand by the fire, my back to the heat, watching the lightning travel across the sky. Thunder shakes the windows and rattles my chest. There's nothing like a storm on the ocean. Fierce and monstrous. Like it's alive. Behind me, lights coming on in the house illuminate the backyard and a pool. Ethan steps out through one of the sliding glass doors and hands me a towel.

"Go ahead and kick off your shoes," he says, doing the same. "We'll let them dry by the fire."

Ethan then peels his shirt over his head and drapes it on the back of a lounge chair. His chest, lit by flickering orange flames, is slick and dripping. The shadows play tricks across his lean abdomen, accentuating the indentations. I can't get tired of looking. When he catches me, he gets a crooked, self-satisfied smirk.

"Whatever." I place my shoes and socks next to his in front of the fire. "Shut up."

He just laughs and unfolds a second towel to wipe himself down.

Once I've dried myself off as well as I can, I rub the towel through my hair. A long silence ensues, and I get this feeling like I've just walked out of the movie theater, the fictional world slowly falling away. I'm not sure what I'm supposed to do now or what happens next.

"Hey." Ethan pulls the towel away from me and tosses it at a chair. "This isn't that awkward moment where you have to wonder if I'm going to kiss you good night or call you tomorrow," he says. "Don't look so pensive."

Ethan grabs me around my ribs. Rubbing his thumbs in gentle strokes against my torso, his eyes smolder. I want to say something witty, but his stare saps the words from my lips. He lowers his face to mine, hovering just over my lips. When he lingers too long, I take it. I pull his bottom lip between mine. He groans, a soft rumble in the back of his throat. The vibration rolls through both of us as he clutches me tighter and pulls me against his firm body.

"Stay here with me," he breathes against my lips. "I don't think I can let you go."

As if to prove his point, Ethan grips me tighter.

This is the point of no return. I wake up tomorrow, and there's no changing my mind. No going back and agreeing to forget tonight ever happened. And I want to say yes. I really want to. I also promised myself a long time ago I wouldn't do this again. Be so enamored I jump without looking. What I remember most isn't the fall, but how much it hurt when I hit bottom. His arms around me, his kiss fresh on my lips, he feels like home. And that's a scary thought, because I've been here before.

There was a guy in college. A grad student and teaching assistant for English 102 the spring semester of my freshman year. Mark wore cardigans and horn-rimmed glasses like he was trying to hide the obvious fact that he'd been an athlete in high school—if a reluctant one. I think he liked me because I was so easily impressed. By him. By literature and poetry. Everything. Books had been my escape in Massasauga. They were a world all my own, private, into which I could disappear for hours or days at a time. Mark was a writer, and in my fascination with college and living on my own, and the great bewildering power and mystery of words, I poured into him all my amazement and wonder. When he talked about Kerouac or Ginsberg or Kesey, he became them, their embodiment. He recited poetry barefoot in his living room, glass of brandy in his hand. We lay beneath his bedroom window, my head in his lap, while he read to me. He graded papers by the fireplace while I did homework on the couch. Anything to be close to him. Mark was an editor at the campus literary journal, so I volunteered there, too. For four months, we lived in a perpetual nineties coming-of-age movie starring Moira Kelly and Ethan Hawke.

Mark became the first thing I ever adored. I lived and breathed by the sound of his voice. Slept in his shirt just to keep him close. No one had ever made me feel as wanted as Mark could when he glanced at me across a room or ran his fingertips down my arm. I was the happiest I'd ever been. Until the semester ended, and so did we.

The breakup was short and brutal. Mark had lost interest in the awkward, dull freshman. He needed someone who could challenge him intellectually and rise to his level of worldly experience. Someone he didn't have to hide from his friends, or his professors. A better lay.

That summer, I lost fifteen pounds. I barely ate. Didn't get out of bed for weeks. I lost all contact with anyone I had forged even the thinnest friendship with during my first year of college. Every day, all day, I thought about using. I'd tell myself, *If you can get out of bed, you can have a hit.* Just enough to get me moving again. Just enough to take away the deep, hollow aching in my chest. Then one day, I got up. Took my meds and a shower. Brushed my teeth and got dressed and found the NA meeting in the basement of the school library. Still, once I'd crawled out of my hole, there was damage to survey. I couldn't go back to the lit journal. Going anywhere near the English Department at all was out of the question. So sophomore year, I declared my journalism major.

Mark, Jenny—they're my cautionary tales. My teaching moments. Both represent the same innate flaw in my nature: I want to be loved too much. There I am, chasing the crumbs, unaware I've strayed off the path and deeper into the forest. Darker. I lose myself in there, consumed. Because as long as the love is strong, or it could be, almost enough, even when it isn't, it's okay that it gets harder to tell where they end and I begin. It's all right that I can't remember when I agreed to give up the things I once thought made me an individual. Until the love gets snatched away, then all I'm left with is empty space and a realization that it was never okay. A person can only rebuild herself so many times before parts go missing.

I don't want to add Ethan to that list. I don't want him to be a memory I can't stand to think about. A name that becomes shorthand for another mistake and another place I'll never return to.

"Just come to bed with me," Ethan says. "Let me fall asleep with you in my arms."

This is how it starts. A little taste, then a little more. The first one's always free. Euphoria, like there is a god and you're held in the great cosmic harmony of the divine embrace. At one with the universe and all living things. You feel every cell in your body slowing down, at peace. All sight and sound becomes a warm, vital glow of perfect light. Nothing matters. The world exactly as it should be. Mind free and limitless. There is no pain, only pleasure.

It never lasts, of course. It can't. The more you have, the less you feel it. That's why they call it chasing.

Addicts are reliable people. We always come back for more. Ethan is my drug now.

"Okay. I'll stay."

* * *

The house is bigger on the inside. Tall ceilings and huge living spaces artfully decorated like a Restoration Hardware catalogue. Everything is gray distressed wood and powder-coated black metal. Oversized brown leather couches, black-and-white photos hung on the walls. Ethan leads me into the enormous kitchen equipped with stainless steel appliances. I don't know what his parents do for a living, but I'm in the wrong career.

"Thirsty?" Ethan opens the fridge. It's fully stocked, everything lined up in perfect order.

"Sure. Water would be great."

He pulls out two bottles and passes one to me.

"Would you like to shower?"

Ethan leans back against the counter, his wet jeans hanging from his hips. I raise a questioning eyebrow.

"Alone. There are three of them."

"Thank you."

He pushes off the counter and escorts me upstairs past a series of closed doors. I count five bedrooms, at least. What I guess is his bedroom is at the end of the hall. It's decorated much like the rest of the house, with a dark wood sleigh bed and matching furniture. From the dresser on the near wall he pulls a pair of boxers, a T-shirt, and black pajama pants, offering them to me.

"To sleep in," he says. "What do you prefer?"

I opt for the shirt and shorts.

"Right through there." He nods to the door on the left, the en suite bathroom. "Feel free to use anything you need. I'll go after you're done."

The bathroom is tiled in slate gray with white marble counters. I feel almost, I don't know, intrusive, stepping into the shower under the rain faucet. Like it's a showroom model that isn't supposed to get wet. When I'm done, I find several new, packaged toothbrushes in a drawer along with toothpaste and little bottles of mouthwash. I assume they must rent this place out or lend it to friends. It's stocked like a hotel.

After I'm done in the bathroom and have changed clothes, I step out to see Ethan wrapped in nothing but a towel.

"You're shameless."

Ethan saunters over to wrap his arms around my waist.

"I've only just begun to seduce you." He kisses the top of my head. "I left a comb out for you, if you'd like. Sorry, I couldn't find a brush."

"No, that's perfect."

"You smell good," he says against my damp hair.

I slide my arms to his shoulders.

"I smell like you."

The bottle of shampoo in the shower was the same scent of mint and eucalyptus that I've noticed on Ethan before.

"Exactly."

Maybe it's a girl thing, but wearing a man's clothes, smelling like his products, is like being wrapped in a warm blanket of intimate security. I guess it's a man thing to mark his territory with his body wash.

"Feel free to dig around for anything you need," he says. "Go ahead and get comfortable."

I find the comb and tug it through the tangles in my hair, then wrap my head in the towel. I then chug the bottle of water and climb onto the bed to check my phone. By now Kumi is asleep. Still, I don't want her to worry tomorrow that I'm not home when she wakes up, so I send her a quick text. She's going to be impossible to live with now. I'm going to have to move out or I'll never hear the end of her gloating.

Soon enough, Ethan reappears wearing the black pajama pants he offered me. It's unfair how the sight of him, naked from the hip up, makes me a little nervous. His eyes narrow, staring at me for a long moment before he shakes his head and cocks a crooked grin. He sighs as he runs his hand through his damp hair.

"What's that about?" I ask.

He approaches the bed in a few long strides, stopping to sit on the edge. I pull the towel out of my hair.

"I like looking at you in my bed." His eyes turn from pleased amusement to something darker. "And you're making it difficult for me to behave myself."

"I am? What about you?" I wave my hand up and down between us. "What am I supposed to do about all this?"

"Anything you want. I'm at your mercy."

"Uh-huh. Take it easy, sport."

"Come here."

Ethan scoops me into his lap, burying his face against my neck. His fingers play against my ribs, soft and teasing.

"Hey." I shove at his shoulder until he meets my eyes. "If you want me to stay here, we should sleep before the sun comes up. I'm cranky in the morning if I don't sleep well."

Ethan nods with a look of mock seriousness, pursing his lips.

"Were you under the impression I was going to let you leave?"

"Watch it, buster."

I crawl off his lap to scoot over to the far side of the bed.

"I might be small, but I'm scrappy."

"I'm not a man to be trifled with." He stands up from the bed to turn off the lights and regards me with menace. "If you're thinking of taming me, you'll be left disappointed."

"Oh," I say, "I wouldn't dare."

In darkness, Ethan comes back to the bed and holds the comforter back for both of us to slip underneath. I rest against the pillows, rolling onto my side to face him. Settled in, Ethan brings one of my hands up to his lips and kisses the pads of my fingers.

"I had a wonderful night," he says.

It's best when it's new. That bursting, overwhelming need to be closer. To become part of him.

He places my hand on his chest and pulls my leg across his hips. When it's new, you don't want space. Doesn't matter that you'll wake up with a stiff neck and your arm numb.

"Me, too."

After a moment of silence and listening to Ethan's heart beat a steady, strong rhythm, something occurs to me.

"What do we tell people?"

"Nothing, if you don't want to. Or the truth: you're mine and I'm not giving you back."

"And what are you?"

"Infatuated."

# 14

# THE ABSENT HOST

Sunlight warms my face as I lie in bed. Blinking, I open my eyes, for a moment confused by my surroundings until I become aware of Ethan's arm draped over my stomach and his body pressed against my back. The night filters through my head, a little hazy and out of order. What I remember most, though, is the high. The elated, terrifying weightlessness of leaving my own body. That's how it feels when Ethan kisses me. A little scary—like taking your hands off the wheel driving down a long dark road at ninety miles an hour. And a lot like walking away from the wreck.

Though I'm still not certain any of this was a good idea, I can't deny that, right now, right here, is exactly where I want to be.

"You're awake." His hand flexes against my stomach to hold me closer as he kisses my shoulder. "Sleep well?"

"Mm-hmm." I roll over to face him. "Time is it?"

"Almost eleven. I wanted to let you rest."

He's been awake for some time, eyes clear and bright. His hair's still bed-messed, though. Wild and erratic. I reach up and run my fingers through it, fascinated. Ethan closes his eyes and exhales.

"I've wanted to do this for a while now," I say.

"Don't stop."

He grabs the back of my knee and hitches my leg over his hip. His hand slides down my calf and back up to my thigh. With just the lightest touch, every nerve in my body wakes and blood rushes hot through my veins.

"What's this?" Ethan's fingers trace the scar on the back of my calf. Around the stippled, disfigured skin that is nearly invisible but for the indentation beneath it.

"It's, um, from the night we left," I say, tracing my fingers across his collarbone.

"You were shot?"

"No, uh, not exactly."

Faint freckles dot Ethan's shoulders. Barely there. Forming constellations across his skin. I draw shapes in their patterns.

"The first four, you know, died in bed. He stood in the room and shot them, one after the other. They never had time to react. But the others, he chased them. Nobody knew where to go, where the shots were coming from."

You can't imagine how dark it gets in the middle of nowhere when you're terrified and running. He picked them off, as they were scattered and screaming.

"He saw us. My mother and me. All I could think was *Keep running and don't look back*. Then something hot stung my leg.

I think I was so scared, so much adrenaline pumping, I didn't understand what happened until later when I looked at it and saw all the blood. Doctor at the hospital said it was probably a ricochet."

"See." Ethan covers my scar with his hand, massaging my leg. "I learn something exceptional about you every day."

"There's nothing exceptional about sort of getting shot."

"Face it, ace, you're a badass." He leans in, lips brushing against mine, gentle and teasing. His hand slides up the back of my thigh as my fingers trail down his chest, the ridges of his stomach. His muscles clench beneath my touch.

"Christ," he hisses. "You were right. This is never going to work."

"What? Why?"

His eyes peel open, barely seeing me through thick lashes. "How am I supposed to spend all day sitting beside you in an office and get any work done?"

Charming men who know they're charming are the worst.

"I guess you'll just have to suffer through it."

"You know…" Ethan brings his hand up to wrap behind my neck, running his thumb along the bottom of my jaw. "There are rooms in that building where no one ever goes."

"Yeah, I'm actually trying to avoid the label of *office slut*. So maybe we keep this confined to appropriate spaces."

"Hey…" He rolls onto his back, bringing me with him to lay my head on his shoulder. "There's no shame in your game. When a woman wants some D—"

"Shut up." Laughing, I smother his mouth with my hand.

Teeth nip at my fingers as he pries my hand away.

"Come on." He tilts my chin up to give me a kiss, brief and sweet. "I'll make you breakfast."

"Out of curiosity," I say as we both climb out of bed. "What's the plan? We are going home today, right?"

On the other side of the bed, Ethan stands shirtless, scratching his hand through his hair.

"Well, I was going to mention this after breakfast..."

"What, that you've actually kidnapped me, told Kumi I'm dead, and plan to keep me locked in this house forever? Wait, is this even your house? Did we break into some random celebrity's summer home last night? I don't want to end up on TMZ."

"Fuck, what gave me away?"

I follow him out to the kitchen and take a seat on a stool at the island.

"Seriously, though. Clue me in."

He goes to the refrigerator and pulls out fruit, milk, and a tub of butter.

"Actually, my parents will be here later this afternoon."

"What?" I say too loudly. Then, lowering my voice, "Your *parents* are coming?"

"They're having an anniversary party tonight."

Ethan goes to the pantry and pulls out a loaf of bread and a bag of powdered sugar.

"Caterers and whatnot will start showing up at one."

"You didn't think to mention this earlier? I can't meet your parents like this. I don't have any clothes. You're going to introduce me to your mother while I'm wearing your underwear?"

He turns around, hands braced on the counter as he surveys me with a crooked grin.

"I don't know, Avery, you look adorable as hell."

"Stop it. Be serious."

Stepping away from the counter, he comes to stand behind me and wraps his arms around my stomach.

"I was up at eight this morning. I've already washed our clothes and made sure your shoes were dry. If you don't want to stay, I'll drive you home. If you do," he says, pressing his lips to my temple, "and I hope you will, we can go find a shop in town and get you something to wear."

I don't know what's gotten into Ethan, or if this is his normal resting position and everything until last night was a passing phase, but I think I like it.

"You're nuts, you know that?" I tilt my head back to look up at him. "Like, you need adult supervision."

He kisses my forehead. "And now I have you."

\* \* \*

Ethan figures out pretty quickly that I hate shopping for clothes. A few miles west of his parents' house, near the tip of the island, we stop in a busy shopping district full of boutique stores and little mom-and-pop restaurants. After watching me wander aimlessly through the clothing racks at first one and then a second shop, Ethan takes over. With the same sort of commanding, impatient efficiency he applies to most tasks, he whips through the store grabbing dresses and piles them up in my arms. Five try-ons later, we fight over who gets to pay until

I look at the price tag of the navy linen wrap dress and give up the argument. Throw in a pair of sandals on top of that, and I'm going to need a second job to pay him back.

"It's a gift," he insists as he hands the clerk his credit card. "I'm the one who kidnapped you and talked you into staying for this party. At least make me pay for it."

I'd like to say I have too much pride to accept expensive presents the morning after spending the night in a man's bed, but I'm poor. If it makes Ethan feel better to blow his money on a dress, so be it.

We wander the town for a while, then visit the Montauk Point Lighthouse and the state park at the tip of the island. There's a gorgeous view from the high grassy hill. Nothing but ocean and clouds straight out to the horizon. The wind kicks up, lashing my hair around my face as I watch seagulls hang suspended in the air.

"I've always wanted to do something," he tells me as we make our way to the lighthouse museum.

The museum is the old keeper's house, essentially. Three bedrooms and a parlor that connect to the communications and oil rooms through a hallway.

"Do what?"

The answer requires we climb 128 steps, 86 feet, to the top of the tower. There, in front of the big lantern and half a dozen other tourists with their children, he grabs me in his arms and dips me halfway to the floor. Deep and assertive, he kisses me like a man who's just found out he's got a week left to live. Finishes with a big, dumb smile as he pulls me upright.

"You've lost your mind," I tell him, laughing and shielding my face from the confused spectators.

"No." He stares into my eyes and brushes his fingers along my temple to tuck my hair behind my ear. "I've only just found it."

But there's something wanting in his voice. Something subtle hiding in his inflection. Desperate to show me yet terrified to reveal himself. It's a puzzle that occupies me for much of the day.

Around four that afternoon, we arrive at the house to find a convoy of box trucks and cargo vans parked in the circular driveway. I also spot a black Range Rover, which I guess to be his parents'. Several platoons uniformed in black-and-white formal wear pass us going back and forth through the front door. Caterers with coolers and big rolling racks, decorators rearranging furniture and carrying tall cocktail tables to the backyard. So many people running around in so many different directions, it's like the house itself is alive and moving.

"This is going to be some party," I say to Ethan as we stand in the living room dodging traffic.

"It's their thirtieth anniversary. And my dad likes to go big."

A hint of disapproval tinges his voice as he surveys the activity. I don't know if it's parties that put him off, or his parents in general. He seemed happy enough to support them in celebrating this milestone, but in telling me the story of his brother, he expressed some resentment toward them. As with most families, I suppose it's complicated.

"Dad?" he calls into the void.

A voice answers back from the kitchen. "In here."

We find Ethan's father standing at the island, making a sandwich, among several men and women in chefs' coats all unpacking bins and containers to spread out on the counter. In khakis and a white button-down with the sleeves rolled up, Ethan's father is the spitting image of his son. Or the other way around. Shorter hair, a distinguished level of salt-and-pepper, and a longer nose, but he's Ethan thirty years older.

"You just getting in?" his dad asks, not looking up from the cutting board, where he rips leaves of lettuce and slices tomato.

"We drove up last night."

Ethan puts his arm around my shoulder. It's the *we* part that catches his dad's attention. He looks up, first to his son. Then his gray-blue eyes slide to me. If you've ever met someone and known in an instant that they already despised you, before you even opened your mouth, then you can understand how I feel at the bitter contempt that flashes across this man's face. It's quite subtle and only lasts a second, but the look is potent and unmistakable. He puts down the knife and wipes his hands on a dishrag, taking a moment to appraise me, if only to confirm his initial reaction.

"Who's this?" he asks.

"This is Avery. She writes for the magazine. Avery," Ethan says, voice tight and attention fixed on his dad, "this is my father, Paul."

"It's nice to meet you. Happy anniversary."

"Uh-huh," is his dismissive reply. "Son, may I have a word?"

I try to step out of his grasp, but Ethan holds me in place.

"Where's Mom?"

"Upstairs."

"I want to introduce her to Avery."

"She's resting," Paul says. He has the same tells as his son. Subtle gestures of his jaw. The inflection of his voice. These men are having an argument in subtext. "Later, perhaps."

Conceding, if only for the moment, Ethan looks down at me with a poor approximation of a reassuring smile.

"Give me a minute," he says. "I'll come find you."

Ethan follows his dad through the kitchen toward the other side of the house, and I'm left in a beehive of activity buzzing all around. I turn and nearly bump into a woman carrying huge slabs of raw red meat. I turn again and there's a knife-wielding man in a floppy hat. Drifting through the house, dodging caravans of people carrying tables and linens and pieces of what looks like a dance floor, I'm in someone's way everywhere I go. It's too hectic. Anxiety begins to build as a numb sensation in my lips. Then a pulsing electricity through my limbs. This happens sometimes. A response to unfamiliar surroundings or a general feeling of disorientation. I just have to find some room to breathe.

In an effort to escape, I slip through one of the open sliding glass doors and make my way across the backyard toward the cliff, where I take the steps down to the beach. It doesn't occur to me until I'm sitting in the sand, counting back from ten with my eyes closed and my hands cramping into fists, that I didn't take my medication this morning. I don't have it with me.

Once a month I meet with a psychiatrist for an hour, read through my stress journal, talk about coping mechanisms and managing trigger scenarios, and stop by the pharmacy to refill my prescriptions for anxiety and depression. After rehab flushed everything out of my system, I attempted the drug-free approach to treating mental illness—exercise, change in diet, and other bullshit homeopathic remedies. Suffice it to say, it didn't work. So I got a new shrink and began the slow, grueling process of finding a regimen that worked. After nearly a year and more than a few setbacks, we arrived at a happy medium. I still have mild anxiety attacks, still tumble into the occasional bout of depression, but they're tolerable. They don't rule my life as they once did.

So I can do this. It's only one day. *Just grin and bear it.*

A few minutes later, as I'm watching a sailboat cut across the horizon, I hear Ethan walking down the steps behind me.

"Thought I might find you here," he says, and sits beside me on the sand. "It's a good hiding spot, isn't it?"

"Your dad doesn't like me."

"My dad's a prick."

He picks up a small rock and chucks it toward the surf.

"I shouldn't be here. That's what you two talked about, right?"

Ethan inhales a deep breath and runs both hands through his hair, propping his elbows on his knees. He's reverted. The energy and excitement that brought us here sucked dry. He sits behind an implacable shroud, cold and detached.

"I want you here. End of story."

The muscle in the side of his jaw flexes as he keeps his eyes trained on the waves.

"I'm just some random girl who spent the night in his house. Someone he's never heard of and—"

"Don't take his side."

"I'm not. I'm just saying—"

"Stop."

With one fierce, biting look, he shuts down and shuts me out. The door slams, and I'm left on the other side. This is his boundary. His father, or their friction—it's his barbwire fence. Now I understand why I'm here. Why Ethan absconded with me in the middle of the night and begged me to stay. He didn't want to endure this party alone.

"Hey." I run my fingers through his hair, combing along his temple then up the back of his scalp. "I am on your side. Talk to me."

Ethan's head drops forward, and his shoulders relax. He's quiet awhile, wandering in his own mind. It's like the day I started at the magazine: Ethan leaning against a wall, angrily typing on his phone, and a ten-pound weight slung around his neck.

"I'm sorry," he sighs. "I didn't mean to snap at you. He gets to me. We haven't gotten along since I was about thirteen. Frankly, I don't think he likes me very much."

"Why do you say that?"

He shrugs. "My dad's never understood me, and he doesn't want to."

Trying to imagine Ethan as a child is difficult. The way you can't see a blowhard politician or corporate CEO as ever having played in puddles or cried over a skinned knee. Some people you meet and it seems they must have come out of the womb a fully formed adult. Or hatched from an egg, in some cases. With Ethan, I can't envision the boy chasing his brother around in a desperate attempt to be liked. I can't see him sniffling, holding his breath, eyes red, while a doctor sets his arm in a cast. That the man next to me has ever spent a moment concerned about the opinions of others is almost inconceivable. There are glimpses, though. Of a kind, sensitive kid who every year layered on one more defense until he'd built himself a fortress. We're all just children, dressed up, walking around in a grown-up suit.

"Well, look at it this way: at least your father didn't keep you confined to a two-hundred-acre compound for half your life then murder nearly everyone you'd ever known."

Ethan turns his head to look at me.

"You are *dark*."

"Can't help it."

\* \* \*

When Ethan works a room, he has an almost unnatural ability to adapt to the energy of each person who enters the conversation. It's something to marvel at. Like watching it rain on only one side of the street. He switches from one topic to another, pivoting easily. It's dizzying. We haven't moved in an hour. We're stuck in one spot near the living room fireplace. Ethan doesn't make the rounds—he is the destination.

"My wife is waiting for your next book," says the commercial real estate developer who wears too much cologne. "I don't—where did she go? She's a big fan. Loved *The Cult of Silence*. Have you considered a sequel?"

A financial planner, with his business card aimed and ready, says, "I heard you walked away with a pretty nice advance. Are you investing? Give my office a call. We should talk about long-term growth."

Two hundred people, maybe more, all meander through the party, smiling and making polite small talk in scattered circles, and all with one eye on Ethan. He's the rare and elusive creature at the zoo, the last of his kind, and everyone's queued up for their turn to press their noses to the glass.

"I don't suspect we'll see Walter here tonight," says a man in Tommy Bahama who introduced himself only as Jim.

Jim strikes me as the guy who tells everyone he's Paul Ash's best friend, they go way back, but in reality Paul wouldn't recognize him if the two were the last men on Earth. He gestures with his glass of whiskey; a little wink-wink, nudge-nudge that makes the muscle in Ethan's jaw tick.

"After that hit piece you put out last month." Jim's hacking, black-lung laugh exposes the fillings in his molars. "Heads are *still* rolling at Kreight Industries, I bet. Waterboarding secretaries and junior executives in the basement."

Beside me, I feel the tension in Ethan's body that he keeps concealed behind a flat expression. Ethan's fingers around my waist twitch with the effort he exerts to endure this man.

"Which article was that?" I ask, because I'm tired of being an ornament. "I think I missed that one."

"Oh, well…" Jim tosses back another swig of his drink. A drop seeps from the corner of his mouth and traces his chin. "Ethan here claims Walter Kreight is secretly bankrolling some, what, neo-Nazi terrorists?"

"I don't claim anything," he says. "There are three credible sources and financial disclosures that suggest Walter Kreight is funneling money through an ultraconservative political action committee to an alt-right militia group."

Jim rolls his eyes, his whole head, because Ethan's details are getting in the way of his story. He leans too close to me with sour, tree-bark breath. "Ethan got up in front of three hundred million people and accused one of the most powerful men in American of sedition and treason, is what he did."

"Twenty million," he says.

Jim's face crinkles. "Huh?"

"The magazine's readership. Roughly twenty million. At most."

Ethan glances at me with a sardonic little glint in his eyes. Smart-ass.

"And Kreight Industries," I say. "What do they do?"

Jim swallows the rest of his drink. "They make your toothpaste, your laundry detergent, your paper plates—everything. Half the shit in every home in the country. Half the civilized world, for that matter. Every time you wipe your ass or blow your nose, Walter Kreight makes a nickel. And this motherfucker," he says, shaking one fat finger through the air and too close to Ethan's face, "took a big shit right in his lap. You've got a serious set of big, brass floor-draggers, my friend."

The vein in Ethan's neck is bulging, but thankfully Jim spots someone else he must accost, so we're spared his further attempts at banter.

"Why would Walter Kreight be here?" I ask Ethan as he presses his hand to the small of my back and diverts us outside toward one of the five bars set up around the party. "Are your parents' friends of his, or…?"

Ethan takes a glass of champagne from the bar and I wave off the one he offers to me.

"It's like living in a small town. Once you reach a certain tax bracket, everyone knows everyone. The people here tonight make up half the Fortune Five Hundred. The rest are lobbyists or would-be politicians. I'm sure if we looked around, we could find a senator or two."

"What do your parents do for a living?"

"My dad helps rich people get richer. These parties are an excuse to do business. You get everyone in a room for a circle jerk and tomorrow there's a new skyscraper going up and a merger announced and somewhere an inconvenient piece of legislation quietly dies in committee."

He makes no attempt to hide his disdain as he surveys the yard. Though he's impeccably dressed, khakis and a sapphire sports coat over a powder blue button-down, you don't have to look too closely to notice Ethan doesn't fit in here. He might have been bred from the same stock as these people, but his collar's unbuttoned and he hasn't shaved today. His hair's a bit too long. Ethan's the black sheep. The disruptive voice.

"Are you sure you don't want something to drink?" he asks, downing another glass of champagne because it's there and someone's got to drink it. "I can't handle these things sober."

"No, I'm good."

I don't know how long I can get away with not spelling it out that I don't drink. It isn't a conversation I enjoy having. You tell someone, and their reaction is usually a surprised *Oh* followed by a judgmental *Ohhh*. Because the first place their mind goes is that you're a raging alcoholic. Somewhere, not so far in your past, you were a sloppy, degenerate, booze-soaked pile of stumbling human waste getting tossed out of bars and waking up in your own vomit. They expect that right at this very moment, you're a rabid animal held back by a very thin leash, ready to swallow a gallon of hand sanitizer. Might just Hulk-out and go on a tear through the party, grabbing drinks off tables and draining every bottle in the building until you drown in liquor and self-loathing.

Fact is, no one expects to be an alcoholic. Like finding out you're allergic to shellfish when choking on your tongue with a piece of shrimp lodged in your throat—it's just bad fucking luck.

I don't know if I'm an alcoholic, but I could be. I'm an addict—same thing.

"And your mother? What does she do?"

This party's been going for three hours and I still haven't met Mrs. Ash.

"She was a thoracic surgeon. Until recently."

Darkness again falls over him like a shadow. That same saturnine vacancy creeps across his face. I expect him to elaborate, but instead he downs his third glass of champagne.

"Tell me you dance," he says.

"Not professionally."

"Good enough."

Taking my hand, he leads us to the center of the dance floor built on the lawn overlooking the beach. Huge white balloon lanterns illuminate the backyard. Strings of lights span the floor between posts driven into the grass. A band set up on a platform stage launches into the first chords of "Moondance" as Ethan takes me by the waist, my hand in his. He holds me flush against the length of his body and gives me not a moment to blink before he's driving me backward, making my feet move. The jazz beat and sensual bass guitar possess him, transform him. A smile spreads across his lips while I cling for dear life just to keep up.

"Don't you dare spin me," I tell him, feet barely touching the ground.

"Don't tempt me."

He moves like a man made of music and rhythm. Confident, his body talks directly to mine, my mind left standing on the edge of the dance floor. For a few too-brief minutes I'm aware of nothing but his hands and his steady shoulders and the way his eyes watch only me. I lose myself in them. In the reflection of what might be. A glimpse into a future that hasn't yet come to pass though I feel it as if it were yesterday.

The music ends too soon.

"You don't have any idea, do you?"

"What?" I ask.

Standing still, ignoring the chords of the next song, he runs his hand up my back and into my hair.

"What it does to a man when you look at him like that."

"Excuse me." A waiter comes up and taps Ethan on the shoulder. "Your father needs a moment."

Eyes fixed on mine, Ethan hardly reacts but for a regretful smile. His hand untangles from my hair as he leans in to speak against my ear.

"Don't wander off."

Then he kisses my cheek and follows the man to find Paul.

To wait for Ethan, I make my way back to the bar and ask for a club soda. As the bartender pours my drink, a woman in a conspicuous black dress steps up beside me. She's every movie's version of the Other Woman: a tall, thin, gorgeous twenty-something. She stands out even among the many second and third wives on the arms of much older men. The woman the first wives eye with suspicion should she come too near their husbands.

"Vodka tonic," she says to the bartender once he hands me my drink.

But she has an air about her. This woman's never been any man's *honey* or *sweetheart*. She doesn't get her ass pinched; she grabs men by the balls.

"He does have a thing for redheads," she says.

I glance over to see her staring at the side of my face.

"What?"

"Ethan. Like a moth to a flame."

And now I hate her.

"What an odd way to start a conversation."

She smiles. Like she thinks I'm cute. A cat impressed that the maimed mouse still has some fight left in it.

"But you never can get him to stay in one place very long."

Scanning the crowd, I sip my drink. At this point, I'd run into Jim's hairy arms if I spotted him.

"I wouldn't know."

The bartender sets her drink on the counter and she ignores it.

"Where'd you two meet, if you don't mind my asking?"

I mind, and she doesn't care. But if I walk away now, I might not find Ethan till morning.

"Mutual acquaintance."

In a manner of speaking.

"It is sort of odd, though, don't you think? A man who's forever chasing after a character from his own book? A character he based on a child, for that matter. Makes you wonder what sort of issues a guy like that keeps buried in his closet."

Setting my drink on the bar, I turn to face her. "If you'll excuse me, you're a spectacular bitch, and I don't want to talk to you anymore."

Then I walk back toward the house with my heart beating double-time and my fingers going numb. Rage swells in my chest and seeps into my blood. The kind that makes you envision grabbing a woman by her hair and dragging her across hot coals. Inside, I search for Ethan, but I can't find him. There are just too many people. My lips begin to tingle and curl in around my teeth. Cramps pull at my arms and clench my hands into fists. I've got to get somewhere quiet. Somewhere alone. I don't think I can make it all the way back to the beach without collapsing and causing a scene, so I head for the closest bathroom.

It's occupied.

And so is the next one.

I go upstairs but every door I try is locked.

My hand can barely grip the doorknob when I find one that's unlocked and stumble inside.

"Hello?"

Shit. My eyes snap up to see a woman in a bathrobe sitting up in bed among several pillows, blankets folded down at her lap. This is the master bedroom.

"I'm sorry. I'm sorry." I turn to run out. "I was just looking—"

"Don't go."

I stop in my tracks. My blood turns to acid, legs close to total paralysis.

"Oh, you're not okay at all," she says, climbing out of bed.

I stand there, frozen, my vision going black around the edges. I'm like a worm on a hot sidewalk, burning, curling in on itself to die.

"Come on," she says, taking me by the arms to bring me to the bed.

I sit down and close my eyes, trying to remember how to breathe and what comes after eight and thinking, *Please don't let Ethan find me like this.*

"It's all right. It's all right. Just take deep breaths." Standing in front of me, she holds my hands. "Nice and slow. Clear your mind. You're okay. I've got you."

*Seven, six, five…*

"That's it. You're doing well. In and out."

*Four, three…*

Feeling returns to my limbs. My muscles begin to relax.

"There you go. You're okay."

*Two, one.*

The worst part isn't the panic attack, it's the aftermath when someone's watched it happen. The overwhelming feeling of embarrassment that, for no good reason whatsoever, your brain simply turned on itself. In an act of spontaneous revolt, it's just tried to kill you.

"I'm so sorry," I say, unclenching and opening my eyes to stare at my ghostly pale legs and shaking feet. "I was—"

"Have you had panic attacks before?" the woman asks.

"Yes. I'll be fine. I should get—"

"Please." She sits on the bed beside me. "Stay. Take a minute. There's no rush."

"I was just looking for a bathroom or…"

"Somewhere to hide?"

I look up to see her empathetic smile. That's when I notice the scarf wrapped around her head and her missing eyebrows.

"Yeah."

"I used to get them in college. All through medical school and my residency, in fact. They got so bad I nearly dropped out. Twice."

"I take medication," I tell her. "I, uh, didn't expect to be here tonight, so I didn't bring it with me."

"Yes…" She scoots back on the bed to cross her legs. "I understand my impetuous son carted you off in the middle of the night. He can get a little carried away."

"You know who I am?"

She winks. "Educated guess."

Right now I might prefer death.

"Really, Mrs. Ash, I didn't mean to barge in on you like this."

"It's no bother at all. It was getting a little lonely up here anyway."

She doesn't look sick the way you imagine dying people should. Her skin is a bit pale, eyes a little sunken and tired, but there's life in her. She can still smile.

"Not much in the mood for a party, I take it."

"It's one of the perks of cancer." She shrugs, unconcerned. "You can stop doing everything you don't want to do, and no one can tell you otherwise."

Got a point there.

"My husband means well."

I guess I have to take her word for it.

"He hoped a party would lift my spirits. The truth is, I don't want to spend a minute more of my life making small talk with a bunch of pretentious assholes."

A loud, shotgun blast of laughter erupts from my throat. I can't stop it. The pressure valve is released, and it's like everything I've kept suppressed until now explodes out of me all at once. Ethan definitely takes after his mother.

"What brought you up here, if I may?"

The laughter leaves me.

"One of the pretentious assholes downstairs."

"You'll have to be more specific."

Staring down at my lap, I pick lint off my dress.

"This woman came up to me, talking about Ethan. She wasn't very pleasant to begin with, then she made a comment about…" I study her eyes—dark, deep-water blue like her son's. "You know who I am, right? Who I *really* am?"

She nods. "He told me."

"It's just that everyone who sees Ethan and me together,

they make the connection. That I look like Enderly. And they wonder."

"That's an unfortunate burden."

To say the least.

Standing next to him, I might as well wear a sign. All this time I've been trying to get away from Echo and my father, but Ethan's name will forever be linked to them. It's unavoidable. The difference is, he had a choice.

"But if I might offer an unsolicited opinion," she says.

"What kind of person would I be if I said no now, right?"

"He's worth it."

Not what I expected.

"Not because I'm his mother. From one woman to another. If you ever find yourself wondering. He's worth it. Don't let that be the reason it doesn't work out."

"Oh, well, I mean, we only just met, so—"

Mrs. Ash rests her fragile hand on my arm. She knows what I'm going to say, but she's already made up her mind.

"Just be good to each other."

The door opens. Paul stands at the threshold. A slight flicker of anxiety tightens my chest as he appraises me sitting with his wife. He has the same eerie presence his son exudes. The same gravity that sucks out all the oxygen in the room. He's surrounded by the empty vacuum of space. It makes me wonder if he was always like this, or if it was the death of his elder son that cast a pall over his being.

"Linda," he asks, "is there anything I can get for you?"

She shakes her head and climbs back up to the head of the bed to get in under the blankets.

"I'm fine. Just getting to know Avery. Maybe you better take her back to the party before Ethan gets himself into too much trouble down there."

She certainly knows her son.

As I'm walking out, Paul enters to give his wife a kiss. But I make it only to the bottom of the stairs before he's caught up to me. Unlike his wife, with her welcoming energy and a sincere, patient smile, Paul makes me nervous. He's the wolf you catch out of the corner of your eye, stalking just on the periphery. The predator might do nothing at all, might simply be curious. Or it's corralling you into an ambush.

"Avery?" he says, and comes up beside me. Paul gestures with his hand toward the hallway that leads to the other end of the house. "Join me for a moment."

Not like I have a choice, I suppose.

Paul leads me into a library with floor-to-ceiling bookshelves stocked on every wall. There are two high-back leather chairs in the center of the room and a desk near the far wall opposite the tall windows facing the beach.

"This is a gorgeous library," I say, scanning the room. "You have an amazing collection."

Clearing his throat, he takes a seat in one of the leather chairs and motions for me to sit.

"A renovation three years ago. The decorator insisted. After a certain price point, it improves resale value."

How sad and cynical. This man has everything and appreciates none of it. I'm beginning to see why he and his son don't get along.

"Look, Avery…" He crosses his legs, leaning to one side

against the chair's armrest. "You seem like a nice girl. I'm sure you have only good intentions."

It's something people say right before they're about to insult you. My hand reaches to where my pocket should be, but I don't have any in this dress. The shell casing isn't there. Instead it's sitting on the dresser in Ethan's bedroom.

"My family is going through a hard time right now. Linda's cancer has returned after a period of remission. I'm afraid the outlook isn't good and Ethan is having difficulty accepting the reality of his mother's condition."

A stone sinks in my stomach.

Now it makes sense. Ethan's disappearance and agitation. The reluctance to talk to me about why he wasn't at work. The reason he bit my head off and sent me away when I went to his house. The one person in his family he's closest to, the only one who has ever understood him, is leaving him. And he has no choice but to watch it happen. Slowly, painfully, he'll watch his mother slip away a little at a time. Until it's just Ethan and a father he doesn't love.

"I'm very sorry. I had no idea."

"As I'm aware, you have troubles of your own."

Now we're getting to it. The part where I'm not good enough for his only surviving progeny. Not fit to be seen on the arm of what will be left of the Ash legacy. I'm tainted goods. A tragedy celebrity who grabs all the wrong headlines. Even being at this party, I'm an embarrassment to Paul and the impression he would give his very important guests. He doesn't understand that I've had this conversation with myself a dozen times. When a boyfriend asks about my family and why he'll never meet them. Relationships don't last when you only know half the person you're with. I guess I thought Ethan could be different.

"Mr. Ash, I appreciate your trying to be delicate, but why not just say what's on your mind? If you're trying to spare my feelings—don't."

I've grown impatient with this night. Anesthetized. As I sit here, I feel the wet blanket dripping down my shoulders. The apathy soaking in. Colors gray. Sound and sensation dim. Frosted glass walls rise around me and everything else is just a hazy, muted image on the other side.

"All right," he says, uncrossing his legs. The pretense falls away and what's left is the austere severity of a man who holds nothing sacred that doesn't serve a purpose. "Ethan is prone to…instability. Stressful situations cause him to act out, behave erratically. The situation with his mother being what it is, I suspect that explains his sudden fascination with you. I do apologize for him, Avery. None of this is your fault. I simply think it best that you move on."

"Why would I do that?"

He takes a breath, jaw working back and forth.

"A time is going to come soon when he will have to accept a new painful reality. When that happens, you are not equipped to handle him. I'm afraid your presence in his life only does more harm than good."

He might be right. I'm not the one people turn to in search of comfort. I have no particular skills for consoling someone through tragedy. Maybe because I still haven't learned to evolve past my own. You don't go to a carpenter who has a broken sign on the door. But I'm willing to try. And I can listen. If I can at least be there for Ethan, hold his hand and let him lean on me—that's something, right? And if he doesn't want to talk, I can be someone to share the silence with. The darkness is a little less unbearable when you don't have to endure it alone. I've been there, and I know the way out.

Standing, I smooth the creases from my dress.

"Thank you for having me, Mr. Ash. It was a lovely party."

I turn around and stop dead. Ethan's standing in the doorway, a black figure cloaked in shadow. Even from across the room I feel the anger radiating out from his body.

"What's going on in here?"

"Nothing," I say, walking toward him. "Just a chat."

He stalks past me, his expression hard and impassive. I reach for his arm, but he yanks it away and keeps going toward his father.

"What did you say to her?"

Paul gets to his feet and sighs. "Ethan, there's no cause for dramatics."

"You don't talk to her." Inches from his father's face, Ethan is composed fury. "Ever. You understand me?"

"Ethan?" I say, standing in the doorway. "Please. Everything's fine."

Hurried and vicious, he turns and strides toward me. Ethan puts his hand on the small of my back, pushing, and doesn't say a word until we get to his truck outside.

"What about my stuff?" I ask.

He tosses me the keys and goes to the passenger side.

"It's in the truck. You drive. I've been drinking."

I climb in behind the wheel and watch Ethan buckle his seat belt then dig his phone out of his pocket.

"What's going on?"

"Ed needs us back at the office." He nods at me to start the engine. "Armed men have taken the Federal Reserve Bank on Liberty."

"Holy shit."

That's only a block from the magazine. I put the truck in gear and turn us around to head out of the driveway.

"Nothing yet on their identities or motives," he says. "Ed's bringing everyone in."

As I pull onto the main road, Ethan dials his phone and puts it on speaker. It rings through the cab.

"Ethan," the hushed male voice on the other end says, "now's not a good—"

"Carter," he says, "tell me what you know."

"I'm about to head into a briefing. Give me…three, four hours. I'll get you—"

"Not good enough. In two hours I'm going to be standing on your dick. Give me something to go on."

"Jesus, Ethan. We're still just gathering intelligence from—"

"'Special Agent Carter Grant indicates the FBI has *no* information on the unknown number of armed assailants who have now seized the largest Federal Reserve Bank in the United States.' That's the lead, Carter, if you don't give me something useful."

I glance at Ethan, then snap my eyes back to the road. I like this side of him. Hungry. Ravenous, even. There's tenacity in his voice and urgency in his eyes. What attracts me to this career field is perhaps what attracts me to people: drive, ambition, and never-ceasing curiosity. Put on a press badge, and you become the shark. You're the dark figure in the water. We prey on the predators.

"Fuck you, Ash."

"Hey, hey. Be nice and I'll let you blow me."

Out of the corner of my eye I see Ethan smirk. He's enjoying this.

"Look, I'm about to walk into a briefing. Right now we suspect seven men. Caucasian. We've got a lead on a possible motive, but I can't say anything until we've looked at it and determined the intel's credible."

"How'd they get in?"

"Based on CCTV footage, looks like they walked through the front door. Someone on the inside let them in. No shots fired, as far as we know."

"Any hostages inside? Have you made contact?"

"That's all I got. Two hours, and I'll let you know."

"You're my favorite, Carter."

"Yeah, die in a fire."

Ethan picks up the phone to end the call, but before he can, there's noise on the other end.

"Wait, Ethan?"

"Yeah?"

"I'm looking at something here. When was the last time you spoke to Patrick Turner Murphy?"

# 15

# THE BAIT

Ethan and I race into the office just after midnight, breathless and sweating. We had to dump his truck three blocks away when we couldn't get past the police barricades set up around the Federal Reserve building.

Stepping off the elevator, I'm still trying to get my head around what's happening. In a sudden vertigo, I feel like the ground is getting farther away but also somehow rushing up to meet me. It started with Carter's question about my father.

When Ethan told him it'd been years since they'd spoken, Carter tried to hang up without telling us why he'd asked. Ethan pressed but was only able to get out of him that he was looking at a memo generated through the FBI's Manhattan field office that no one had bothered to read until it became relevant. All we knew for certain: Patrick Turner Murphy was reaching out from the grave. Ethan's gears were spinning before he ended the call.

While I drove, he worked the phones. First to track down the warden from Sing Sing to find out if anyone had claimed my father's possessions. Then waking my father's attorney to demand he gather any papers retrieved from the prison and messenger them to me at the magazine. The pieces were coming together, and it wasn't a pretty picture.

"'Unknown number of armed assailants gained entry to the Federal Reserve Bank on Liberty at 8:47 p.m.,'" Ethan reads aloud from his phone as we jog to our desks.

Everyone in the Farm is running around, ragged, shouting at each other across the room. I open up my laptop and bring up the Messenger app to send a text to Navid. It's more efficient than trying to yell above the noise.

Avery Avalon
12:09 AM
What do you know about alt-right message boards on the deep web?

"No reports of shots fired." Ethan pulls off his sports coat and tosses it on the back of his chair then searches through his desk drawers. "Off-duty NYPD officer called it in after witnessing several suspects entering the building through a side door. Described as males wearing military-style uniforms and bandannas over their faces, armed with assault rifles. CCTV footage shows someone inside opened a door to allow the suspects to enter. No communication with the on-duty security detail working in the building."

My laptop chimes with a new message.

Navid Kirmani

12:09 AM

What do you need?

Avery Avalon

12:09 AM

Search for any mention of Patrick Turner Murphy.

"Here." Ethan pulls a folder from his drawer. "Photocopies of everything Patrick gave me during our interviews. Pages from his book."

"Navid's looking into it," I say, talking to Ethan over the wall of our cubes. "I'll read through—"

That's when Ed pops up like a vole from his burrow. The man must have an extensive tunnel system through the office, because I never see him until he's right on top of us.

"What've you got?" He spares me only a brief glance before turning his attention to Ethan.

"My source at the FBI gave us the preliminary details," Ethan answers. "We've been gathering some background on a possible lead."

Ed shoves his hands into his skinny jeans, which crinkle loose around toothpick legs. If he's pleased or at least satisfied, he doesn't show it. The man's face is a topography of permanent undulating hills and long, snaking valleys.

"Your source can confirm?" Ed asks.

"He will."

I feel someone behind me, like the sun at my back, before I notice Ethan looking over my shoulder. Cara's there in a T-shirt and jeans, hair tied up on top of her head. If

I saw her on the street, I wouldn't recognize her.

Phone to her ear, she says, "C.J. checked in from the scene. I've given her the Twitter feed and sent one of mine to get video. Hearing there still isn't any word from inside the building. She's trying to confirm if officials believe the target is the vault or—"

"It isn't," I say before I think better than to interject. "At least, we think we have a pretty good reason to assume it's not."

My laptop chimes again with a message from Navid. There's a link and a file attachment, so I let Ethan explain while I check it.

"Thursday evening a memo was generated from the FBI's Manhattan office warning about chatter it picked up from an alt-right message board. Specifically, it mentioned a series of posts where several members discussed staging a demonstration wherein they would seize a piece of federal property. One of the locations suggested was the Federal Reserve Bank."

Looking through Ethan's photocopies of my father's book, I start comparing them to the pages Navid's sent. It's eerie, seeing my father's handwriting, reading his words. I hear his voice in my head like he's standing right behind me, whispering in my ear.

"You're suggesting a link to domestic terrorists?" Ed asks.

"More like militia," Ethan says. I catch his eye and give him a nod. We've found what we're looking for. "They're a far-right group of sovereign-citizen types who contest the legality of the federal government. The Federal Reserve is one of their favorite boogeymen."

"Okay..." Ed scratches at the prickly white stubble along his sagging chin while he leans against the wall of an empty cubicle. "Get your source to confirm and find me evidence we can print—"

"There's more," Ethan says, turning to me. "Avery…"

Frantic heart beating against my ribs, I don't think, just speak and hope it comes out in English. I've always hated the spotlight. Strange for a journalist, I know. But even Adele gets stage fright.

"While he was in prison, my father began writing a book. A manifesto."

Ed and Cara share a glance. They stand up a little straighter, attentive.

"Sometime in the last two years, he managed to disseminate his writing outside the prison. Navid has found several references to Patrick and his writings on alt-right message boards. He's also mentioned numerous times on a website for a group like the one described in the FBI memo: Juris Christian Constitutional Assembly."

For more than a decade I've been running as fast as I can to get away from my father. Turns out I've been running in circles. I should have known better than to believe prison would silence him, or that he'd allow himself to fade into obscurity and become irrelevant. Legacy was always very important to him. Without a loyal child to carry on his message, he needed a new audience. Seems he found one.

"Put it together for me," Ed says.

"It seems this group has adopted Patrick's philosophy, if you will, into their anti-government agenda," Ethan says. "Patrick wrote about the illegitimacy of the federal government, the illegality of federal taxes, and a vast and convoluted conspiracy theory concerning central banking. It seems the men who have taken the building are members of this group, and that this demonstration is in response to Patrick Turner Murphy's death."

"There are hundreds of posts," I add, "on these message boards claiming my father's death was carried out by the government in a secret plot to silence him. They're using his death as a rallying cry to lure people to their cause."

Cara shakes her head, rubbing her eyes. "So they're insane, is what you're getting at."

"And armed," I say. "However absurd their beliefs, they're committed to them."

It's easy to dismiss people like these men, my father, as lunatics and ignore them. But I've seen one of them up close. They're far more dangerous than just some schizophrenic shouting at a lamppost or muttering to himself on the subway. What people mock as tinfoil-hat-wearers are organized, militarized, and growing in number every day. In every corner of the country there are people like Patrick Turner Murphy cultivating their flocks, feeding them lies and paranoia. I know better than most what happens when that paranoia hits a tipping point.

Ed clears his throat and checks his smartwatch. "Ethan, I want you down there. See what your source is willing to confirm and get a statement on the record."

"All right, here's how this works," Cara says to me. "C.J. and my guy can keep gathering updates from the scene. We'll put the feed up on the front page of the website and supplement with any additional details that come in. Avery, if you're up to it…"

"Yes." I asked for this. A chance at a real story. No way I'm backing down now. "I'm all over it."

"You're sending *her*?" Cyle appears behind Ed like the Ghost of Shitting in My Cereal.

"Problem?" Ethan's still itching for a fight. Doesn't matter who. Cyle's as good a target as any right now.

"Yeah." Cyle hacks his answer like he's got a pepper flake stuck on the back of his throat. "She's too green. Let me send one of my people."

The insinuation being that, despite my assignment to the online section, I am not one of *his* people. I'm the enemy in the cold war between print and digital.

"I can handle it." Looking Cara dead in her crisp blue eyes, I straighten my spine. "There's no one more qualified to report *this* story than me."

"Oh, come on." Cyle all but stomps his feet. "This chick's never covered something like this. She'll get railroaded out there, and that's only if she isn't trampled first."

"This *chick* ran three miles with a bullet in her leg."

The words are out of my mouth and snap off the walls before I know I've spoken. Then it's the absolute silence after a gunshot cracks through the air and everyone holds their breath and strains their ears. The phantom pain behind the scar on my leg throbs and burns as if it were still fresh.

"And the next time you call me a chick, you better be wearing a cup."

In my peripheral vision, I think I catch Ed's lips twitch.

"That settles it," Cara says. When I check her face to gauge the fallout of my outburst, she looks almost proud. "Go with Ethan. I want a write-up for the website by five a.m."

* * *

After the debate has ended and the others have dispersed, I go to the bathroom to change my outfit. I can't run around in this dress, so I've got no choice but to change back into the clothes I've been wearing since Friday night. As I'm walking back to my desk, Ed gets my attention and calls me into his office, then shuts the door behind us.

"Are you sure you're up to this?" he asks, standing in the center of the room.

"Would you ask a man the same question?"

"Under the circumstances, yes."

"I'm up to it."

Emotional detachment has never been my problem. I spent several years of my adolescence making an art of it. The hard part is pretending there's still something human left in the hollow places. For so long my father's been the reason anything good gets ripped out of my hands. I'm not letting him take this, too.

Ed crosses his arms, and I realize the uncomfortable part of this conversation hasn't started yet.

"You were with Ethan tonight," he says.

There's no point denying the obvious conclusion he's already drawn. Ed knows Ethan and I were together when he called him back to the office. That we were two hours away in

Montauk. It doesn't take a great deal of deduction to figure out what that means.

"Yes."

"Just keep it out of the office. What you do on your own time is your business. If it has to become my business, I won't hesitate to fire either one of you. Fair?"

"That's fair."

As much as I like the idea of what Ethan and I could have together, I'm not about to risk my career on a man. Escaping Massasauga, getting through rehab, I've used up my second and third chances. One thing I've learned: I have to look out for myself.

"One more thing," he says, taking a seat on the stool beside his desk. "How much has Ethan had to drink tonight?"

His question gives me pause. I stare at him, blinking, knowing every second I don't respond sews doubt in Ed's mind. He's not some frail, feeble old man. Despite his apparent age, Ed is sharp and incisive, and he's made a long career out of recognizing bullshit.

"I wasn't counting."

He doesn't even blink, but we both understand.

"Keep an eye on him."

With that, I'm dismissed. I don't know if it's just general concern that Ed doesn't want to send a drunk reporter out to the scene of a major story—with armed law enforcement no less—or that he is still worried over Ethan's two-day disappearance. But now understanding what Ethan's been going through with his mother, I can't fault him for needing a couple of days to himself. And I don't think having a couple of glasses of champagne at a party qualifies as excessive.

Ethan is waiting for me when I come out of Ed's office. He's found my press pass in my desk and hands it to me as we walk to the elevator.

"What was that about?" he asks.

"A pep talk," I say, hitting the Call button. "Ed wanted to make sure I've got my head on straight."

"Don't be mad at me..."

The doors open and we step inside the elevator.

"But you going off on Cyle like that..." Ethan runs both hands through his hair and slides me a look as the doors close. "I'm so turned on right now."

"Yeah. Me, too."

*  *  *

Outside, Ethan gets on the phone. It looks like the police have widened the perimeter from the Fed building; the barricades are now visible at the end of our block. Traffic is snarled with drivers trying to navigate around closed streets. Car horns trumpet and bray over the bleats and wails of sirens. Everything's talking.

"Carter's not answering," Ethan says, sweat gathering at his hairline.

New York summer nights, hot and thick, everything and everyone in the city lingers in the pungent air.

"What do you want to do?" I ask.

"He's likely still at his office."

"We're not going to the bank?"

"Quick detour," he says.

So we head uptown, thirteen blocks north to Federal Plaza. Once we pass through the metal detectors—and I get a curious stare from the guard when I put the shell casing in the plastic bowl with my cell phone—it's a short wait until Carter Grant is standing in the cold, gray lobby of the FBI Manhattan field office, arms crossed, giving Ethan and me a look like we're the mice that keep skipping the moldy cheese in the trap and going straight for the pantry.

"Let's go," Carter says, and jerks his head toward the elevator.

On the twenty-third floor he leads us to his office and two matching chairs from the lowest-bidder line of office furniture sets.

"I really regret knowing you." Carter dumps himself behind his laminate wood desk and loosens his tie.

He doesn't look at Ethan, instead training me with a skeptical gaze. He's plain in all the ways a man can be. No particular shade of brown hair. Terribly ordinary brown eyes. He's got the Midwestern bone structure of thirty million other American men. Standard issue, just like the furniture and his typical black suit.

"You know this doesn't look good for me, right?" Carter reclines in his pleather office chair. "People wondering why I've got two reporters sitting in my office during a major security situation. Wearing the badges was a nice touch, by the way."

I glance down at the press pass hanging around my neck. Ethan told me to leave it on.

"Makes it harder for you to get rid of us."

"So what's so important you have to ambush me?"

Carter can't help it; his eyes pull in my direction even as he speaks to Ethan. He feels the incongruity in the room. The stranger sitting right in front of him, somehow familiar. He's trying to place me, digging around in his mind for the switch that turns on the lights.

Ethan pulls his phone out of his back pocket, swipes, taps, and tosses it on Carter's desk. "Avery has some information pertinent to your situation."

With a darting, accusatory glance at me, Carter lurches forward in his seat and grabs the phone. His attention then falls to the screen as I question Ethan's profile. He won't look at me, though I know he senses my questions boring holes in the side of his face. This suddenly feels like a trap.

"What is this?" Carter asks, pushing the phone at Ethan across the desk. He grabs a notepad from his top drawer and pulls a pen from his shirt pocket. "Forward that to me with a screenshot of the originals."

Ethan hands me his phone to show me a series of comments on the *Riot Street* website signed by Juris Christian Constitutional Assembly. Each a declaration of support for Patrick, espousing more of their misguided doctrine. And an invitation for Echo to contact them.

"Where are these from?" I ask.

He doesn't respond but for heavy silence.

A chill slides down my spine, through my limbs. These are in response to my most recent essay.

"You didn't think to mention these earlier?" Carter asks.

"The site gets hundreds of comments a day," Ethan says.

"No one can read them all. I didn't think to look until you made the connection to Patrick's death."

"Fine." Carter scratches at the shadow of stubble creeping down his neck. "But how does this help us? We've already identified three of the possible suspects inside." A pause, as Carter gives Ethan a pointed look that I'm guessing is to remind him that we're off the record in here. "The domestic-terrorism task force lost track of two individuals it was monitoring in New Hampshire. The third is linked to the IP address used to post on the message board. We believe the suspects gained entry with the help of a member of the security detail sympathetic to their cause."

"You still haven't made contact. We can help with that."

Carter's cell phone rings. He glances at the screen then stands to take the call outside, closing the door behind him.

I don't like this. Ethan came here with a plan, but I'm not in on it. I get the sense I'm being maneuvered, manipulated, and it grates right to the bone. Hands fisted in my lap, my entire body shaking with anger, I'd punch a wall if I didn't think it'd get me arrested.

"What the hell are you doing?"

"Carter's a friend," Ethan tells me, impassioned plea in his eyes. "You can trust him."

Dread rolls down my spine.

"What does that mean?"

He leans in and lowers his voice. "There are half a dozen armed men, maybe more, inside that building with the largest stockpile of gold reserves in the world. This isn't going to end like Montana, with the feds sitting back and waiting them out for weeks. These men walked right inside the United States' impenetrable fortress without any resistance. For the last four hours, the world's watched us do nothing about it. Every minute that passes without a resolution emboldens the next guy and casts doubt on the government's ability to secure its assets. It's an embarrassment law enforcement can't tolerate. This thing ends before the sun comes up. If they can't get someone on the phone and talk them out, FBI and SWAT are going in. Then it's shoot first and let the coroner sort it out."

We're here to get the story. It's not my job to be partial about the outcome.

"You didn't tell me about those comments before we came down here. You're hiding things from me. Again."

I can let him off the hook for not telling me about his mother, but this is different. I thought after he'd come back to tell me the truth about why my father had agreed to the interview that I could trust him. Completely. There wouldn't be anything Ethan would lie to me about if he could admit that. Being wrong cuts to the core of what I liked most about him.

"You can still back out," he says, and reaches out to tuck my hair behind my ear. His fingertips skim my neck, and I hate that his touch is like rain dousing the blaze burning in my chest. "I won't ask you to do anything you don't want to."

"I don't understand what you expect from me."

"The only story worth telling is the one going on inside that building."

Behind us, Carter whips open his office door. As our eyes meet, I read it on his face. He's caught up, finally made the connection. In that instant, I see Ethan's plan spread out like an enormous pattern in the sand. Impossible to discern up close, but from a distance a clear image emerges.

"You," Carter says, pointing with his phone in his hand. "Tell me your name."

I'm the bait and the hook. Because I have something no one else does—my father's blood.

\* \* \*

Twenty minutes later and a harrowing ride speeding down Broadway with an FBI escort, Carter brings Ethan and me to the mobile command vehicle set up outside the Federal Reserve building. Police have the entire area cordoned off. Patrol cops and K-9 units man the barriers every ten feet. SWAT officers in bulletproof vests and helmets carry rifles, scanning the crowds pressed up against the metal rails lined along the sidewalks and blocking streets. Above our heads, snipers stand perched on rooftops.

We're brought inside the truck, no bigger than a large family camper, where Carter sits me down at a counter among several computer monitors and radios. Five other FBI agents stand around, watching, scrutinizing. It's more than a little unnerving being in the presence of so many badges and guns, even when you haven't done anything wrong.

"Here's how this is going to work…"

My role is simple, get the men inside to talk. The FBI negotiator was able to make contact about thirty minutes ago, but only long enough to gather that the suspects didn't want money or a jet fueled and waiting to take them to Fiji. They wanted total surrender of the federal government. So, basically, a nonstarter. Instead, I need to ease them into a conversation. Placate them, listen, until such time as they feel satisfied that their message has been heard and will start talking seriously about surrendering without anyone getting killed.

Just before we begin, Ethan pulls me aside.

Hands on my shoulders, he says, "You can still say no."

Though I am mad at him, Ethan has that unshakable confidence that somehow reaches right into my chest and slows my heart. It quiets the noise and focuses my vision.

"I can do this."

I have to do this. Not because Carter asked me to or Ethan steered me into this position. What would I tell Ed and Cara about why I refused? I was afraid? There are dozens of other reporters outside, hundreds all over the city, who would sell their own mothers to be in my position. They wouldn't hesitate to pick up that phone and say anything, be anything necessary to get the best story. Tomorrow morning, our article will be the authority on what took place here and the events that set this standoff in motion. My byline will circulate all over the world, people reading my words. What I do here, what I write, will shape opinion and impact debate. I have the opportunity to do something important, even if it is just through dumb luck.

Turns out, I am my father's daughter after all. Two heads of the same beast.

So I sit down in front of the phone with Carter, Ethan, and a half-dozen skeptics looking over my shoulder. The negotiator dials the number and hands me the phone, listening in through a headset as it rings.

"Who's this?" a voice says on the other end.

"My name is Echo. I'm Patrick Turner Murphy's daughter."

# 16

# AND SWITCH

They wanted legitimacy," I say. "To have their message vali-
dated. In their minds, speaking to me—rather, my listening to
them—was akin to, I mean, not to sound blasphemous or anything, but you could think of it like the way Catholics pray to
saints or confess to priests. They just wanted to feel closer to
my father through me."

Six a.m., Sunday morning, Ethan and I sit in Ed's office
with Cara. He's reading over our draft on the standoff, everyone having worked through the night. A grimy film covers us
all. Like our bodies are rapidly decaying and the only thing
keeping us alive is a constant infusion of caffeine. I've got a
headache splitting my skull open with a crowbar and I haven't
eaten solid food since a canapé at the party in Montauk. For
the past couple of hours, I've been hallucinating that I'm sitting in my bathtub, shower faucet raining down on me. The
way a pee dream is your body's gentle warning that you need
to use the restroom.

"She was brilliant," Ethan says, sitting in the chair beside me. "Gained their trust and worked them where she needed them to go. I'm telling you…" He slides me a glance, tired cooked grin across his lips. "Avery could talk the pope out of wearing white."

In the end, the gambit worked—mostly. For two hours, I stayed on the line with a man named Robert Phelps. I learned he had a wife, Annette, and an eight-year-old daughter named Alissa who liked to ride horses. They live on a small berry farm in Carroll County, New Hampshire. And thanks to Robert, their life is over. Maybe they'll start a new one, somewhere far away from the stain Robert has left behind. Or maybe they'll cling to the past with both hands and with fingertips and nails, until it's yanked out from under them an inch at a time. I know how that story ends, and I take no pleasure in writing it.

"The last man," Cara says, shoes off and legs curled beneath her on the small sofa against the wall. "What was his name?"

Carl Poole, twenty-six, from Aroostook County, Maine. Sometimes worked as a roofer, when he could find work at all. He was one of the people who read the call to arms on that message board and drove down to New Hampshire to join Phelps and his crew. But when the FBI's crisis negotiator convinced the men inside the bank to leave their weapons and surrender, Carl stayed behind. That's when SWAT and FBI moved in. First cutting the lights to the building. Then tossing a couple of flash-bangs through the front doors before charging inside with guns drawn. Whether out of a misguided commitment to the cause or fear of prison, Carl shot himself with a .9mm semiautomatic handgun before authorities had even breached the doors.

I'll know his name for the rest of my life.

Stupid, fucking Carl Poole.

"We're still waiting on a few quotes to wrap it up," Ethan says to Ed, rubbing his eyes. "My source promised something on the record by ten from the FBI, and Navid's helping us track down family and friends of the suspects. We can post the web version with the quotes from the White House press secretary and Fed chairman."

The quick and dirty version of our article will go up this morning on the front page of the *Riot Street* website. Just a rundown of the major facts and a time line of events with preliminary information. On the other hand, the process of publishing a print article is like something between bringing a pregnancy to term and applying for a mortgage. The easy part is compiling twenty pages of scribbled notes and ten pages of transcribed audio recordings into a coherent outline of half sentences and disjointed ideas typed out in bullet points over which Ethan and I will take turns writing in the margins and arguing about structure.

Once we have a draft that at least resembles an article, it will go to an associate editor and come back with dried feces on it and a note that says something like *Kill yourself* or *Die in a fire.*

Okay, not verbatim. I'm paraphrasing here. And it might be an ink smudge. But you get the idea: *You suck. Do it better.*

So we'll take another crack at it, and we'll do it better.

Then it goes to a team of fact-checkers who verify every

date, name, location, etc. Each minute detail is circled and referenced. After that it goes to the ~~Grammar Nazis~~ copy editors who ~~spew a pint of blood~~ thoughtfully point out our comma splices and nonsensical use of semicolons. And then—assuming we've not yet taken the associate editor's advice and carried out a murder-suicide pact—well then, we'll go back to the beginning and run through the gauntlet of shame and humiliation twice more until the perfect, polished pearl of brilliance is ready for Ed's stamp of approval and final layout. The entire process takes about two weeks. We have one.

No wonder print magazines are dying.

"Excellent work." Ed pounds a cup of coffee like a shot of tequila and wipes his wrinkled mouth. Eyes drooping like they might slide right off his face, he looks to me. "One thing we have to discuss."

"Yeah?"

"You need to make a decision on who my reporter is. We've got to disclose your relationship to Patrick, so either you stick with calling yourself Echo and we go with that, or…"

Or I out myself. Cram Echo and Avery back into the same body and forever give up the notion that they can be separate people.

My eyes drift toward Ethan, searching for confirmation or encouragement, as I have done since before I knew why. Despite his withholding information that sat me smack in the middle of this incident, I'm still drifting toward him. It's unconscious, subliminal. No more within my control than the directive that tells my hair to grow or my skin to heal. It's both comforting and terrifying. Because there's something here, real and tangible. But it's also an affliction. If I'm not in control, it's controlling me.

Ethan reaches across the space between us to lay his hand on my arm. Too tired to conceal his affection or having no intention of doing so.

"You don't have to hide who you are," he says. "You have nothing to be afraid of."

Men with blue eyes are dangerous. They make you believe in miracles.

"Never liked Echo anyway. Think I'll stick with Avery."

\* \* \*

Before we can leave for the day, Ethan and I go back to the Slaughterhouse to gather our notes and laptops. All that's left of the war room are scattered pages of my father's writings, notepads, and empty coffee cups littering the conference table. Going around the room with a waste bin, I pick up trash while Ethan collates the loose sheets of Patrick's book into file folders.

"Are you okay?" he asks.

All things considered, sure. But no, not really.

"We need to talk." I set the bin on the table.

"All right." On the other side of the room, Ethan steps back to lean against the wall.

"You used me."

He crosses his arms, a flat, impassive expression staring back at me.

"I managed you."

"How is that different?"

"It's my job to—"

"I'm not your responsibility," I snap back. "I didn't ask for a mentor."

"You need one."

My hands clench, nails digging into the tabletop.

"Why is it so hard for you to let me make my own decisions?"

"You want to be a reporter? This is the job. Work your sources. Kick the doors down. Do whatever's necessary to get the story."

"By manipulating me? What happened to right and wrong and everything else is a lie?"

"Like you manipulated the men inside that building?" He pushes off the wall to place both hands on the back of a chair, leaning over the table. "You made a lot of promises to them about telling their side of the story, getting their message heard. Tell me with a straight face you meant every word of it."

"Of course not," I shout. "But that's—"

"Different? How? You were just trying to help because you're such a patriotic American? Or because the longer you kept them on the phone, the better *your* version of the story?"

"That's not fair."

"Welcome to the real world, Avery." Sarcastic and smiling, his arms gesture wide through the air. "If you thought it was all noble quests for truth and justice, getting a goddamn medal hung around your neck, you should have joined the fucking Peace Corps. Most of the time, the news is a dirty business.

You either hike up your skirt and jump in the mud, or you wash out."

"Fuck you. I'm not a child."

I don't understand where this side of Ethan is coming from, but it makes me want to hurl furniture at him. Condescension isn't a turn-on, and neither is having my integrity questioned by a man who, lately, has a complicated relationship with the truth.

"No," he says. "You're not. So grow up."

"Oh, is it time for my maturity lesson from a man who can't go one day without throwing a tantrum in the office?"

"You are such a fucking brat."

"Suck my dick."

He flinches and stands upright. Then a smirk creeps across his lips.

"Excuse me? Did you tell me to suck your dick?"

A snort escapes me, and I slap my hand over my mouth.

"Jesus Christ." He shakes his head, laughing. "This girl just told me to suck her dick. I have nothing to say to that. I'm honestly impressed."

The giggles set in like a bad infection.

"Shut up."

"Also a little appalled."

It must be fatigue, or my brain chemistry is out of balance, as I head into day two without my medication, because I double over. Almost collapse to the floor. Hysterical laughter bursts out of me, so convulsive and painful I can barely breathe. He comes to stand over me as I clutch a chair to stay on my feet, dry laughing with no sound able to escape my chest.

"We're delirious," he says and rubs my back. "I'm an asshole, and you need a nap."

I get myself under control, standing upright and wiping tears from my eyes. The release feels good, cleansing. Like yanking off your bra and popping open the button of your jeans that has held in your gut like a finger plugging a dam.

"I'm still mad at you."

He tucks my hair behind my ear. "I know. I'm sorry. I was trying not to overwhelm you all at once."

Turning away, I grab the waste bin and set it back in the corner. "Don't make those decisions for me. Let me be over-whelmed. If I'm going to react, if I'm going freak out and have a meltdown, let me. At least I'll know you respect me enough to let me be my own person."

"You're right," he says, coming toward me. "I made a mistake, but I can do better. Don't write me off yet."

"Well, I didn't say that." I look up into his eyes, still enamored by their vivid depth. "I can be attracted to you and mad at you at the same time. I'm great at multitasking."

"I see." Licking his lips, Ethan smirks. "So I'm forgiven?"

"You kidding? You called me a brat. Start with groveling and we'll see where it goes."

"Oh, I can grovel." He brushes past me to grab his laptop and folders, then whispering in my ear: "I'll give new meaning to the word."

* * *

Sitting in Ethan's truck outside my apartment, my vision plays tricks on me. I could have sworn the door to my building was brown, or a dark shade of green, maybe. Now it's red. This place just doesn't feel like home yet. Not permanent or stable. There's a blade hanging over my head, twisting on a thin, unraveling thread, like all of this is one tug away from coming to an end. It's the consequence of never quite feeling like I had a home. Not since the only one I'd ever known went up in flames. The last decade spent as a visitor in my own life.

"Hey." Ethan takes my hand. "I did hear you, okay? I'll stop being such an overbearing jackass."

"Yeah, I know."

"What's bothering you?"

Exhaustion, mostly. And the cold, dark cloud that slides in when I'm off my meds. But there's one other thing we haven't resolved.

"I met your mom."

He lets go of my hand to run his through his hair.

"When did this happen?"

"After our dance. I found her by accident."

"Yeah, well…" He stares out the windshield. "Let's not get into to it today, yeah?"

"If you want to talk…"

"What's to talk about, right?"

If he doesn't want to share this with me, there's nothing I can do to make him.

I gather up my stuff and open the door. Ethan catches my arm just before I climb out. Conflict and uncertainty color his face. There's more he wants to say, maybe too much at once, all crowded and confused on his tongue. He leans in and presses his lips to mine. Barely there but no less stirring. He exhales, tension in his jaw. I wish I knew how to take his pain away. To quell the turmoil inside him. But, so far, the only solutions I've found come with a prescription.

"Call me later," he says, and strokes his thumb under my bottom lip. "Get some rest."

I watch him pull away from the curb. Then I head inside. When I enter the apartment, I find Kumi on the couch watching TV. She leaps to her feet as I toss my stuff on the kitchen table and make a beeline to the bathroom.

"Oh my God! You look like shit. Where have you been? Did you see what happened?"

I head straight for the shower, to be followed by a deep hibernation.

"I was there."

\* \* \*

Best I can recall, I closed my eyes sometime around eight Sunday morning. When they open again, splinter of sunlight shooting across my face, it feels like only minutes later. Then I feel something slide across my forehead. The scent of coffee, fried dough, and sugar tickle my nose.

"Good morning," he says.

I roll over in bed, blinking and blind, to the blurry image of Ethan standing there.

"What?" I scrub my eyes but the image doesn't get any clearer. "What are you doing here?"

The bed dips as he sits beside me.

"I caught Kumi as she was leaving. She let me in."

Of course she did.

"Time is it?"

"Seven thirty. I brought you breakfast."

It takes several seconds while I lick the dry ash from my tongue and scrape the crust out of my eyes before his words sink in.

"In the morning? What day is it?"

"Monday. I came to start my groveling."

Monday. Fuck. We've got to get to work.

"Yeah. Yeah, okay." I sit up and toss the covers off. "Just need to…"

"Take your time. I'll wait in the living room."

He places a kiss on my forehead and walks out, shutting the door behind him. When my brain catches up to the rest of me, I take a look around the room. He's left coffee on the nightstand. A box of doughnuts on my desk. And a truckload of flowers everywhere else. Roses and tulips and gardenias. And other flowers I can't name. Flowers I've never seen before. Maybe a few that only grow in the darkest of the deepest of Chilean caves. On my dresser and chair and lined up against the walls. On top of still-unpacked boxes at the foot of my bed.

Groveling.

Ethan doesn't do anything halfway.

Out of bed, I stuff half a doughnut in my mouth and chug the coffee. Then I find Ethan in the living room watching TV on the couch. Like he's always been here.

"You're too much," I say, taking a moment to appreciate the sight of him.

Even in worn jeans and a faded T-shirt, he's impressive. Broad shoulders and long legs—almost too big for the room, he swallows it. I sometimes forget he's only a few years older than I am. Ethan has the confidence and quiet gravity that defy his age. But then there are glimpses of a young man. In his wavy, tousled hair pushed back from his face. A few chestnut strands falling over his forehead. And his vivid marine eyes that stand out in Technicolor from across a gray room.

He gives me a little beckoning nod to bring me over, then takes my hand to yank me down on his lap. One hand braces against my back, the other tangled in my hair. He takes my lips like he hasn't seen me in weeks. Starving and ravenous, sighing in satisfaction as he exhales. As if I'd forgotten. As though it were possible. The way his body fits with mine like a missing limb reattached. How every time he touches me, an empty space is filled that I didn't know was there. That being in his arms reminds me what it is to feel at all.

"So you like the flowers?" he says against my lips.

"Eh, I'm not big on flowers. But that doughnut was on *point*."

Ethan smiles, licking his lips in that predatory way he has.

"Such a brat."

"See?" I squirm out of his arms and back away. "That's going to cost you double."

Lunging forward, he catches my wrist to pull me toward him and in a flurry I'm lying on the couch beneath him. Ethan pins me with the solid length of his body. Air leaves my lungs.

"You're not getting away that easy," he rasps at my ear.

His voice is like a switch that awakens every repressed urge I've ignored since the last time we were this close. All the urgent, fierce desire that erupted to the surface the first time he held me in his arms on the beach and made me want him. My fingers tug at his hair, needing an anchor as his lips go to my neck, teeth nipping at my flesh. He does something to me on an instinctual level. Like I'm only half-alive when he isn't with me.

"Yesterday was torture," he groans, kissing my throat as his hand pushes my legs apart to accommodate him then hooks the back of my knee up around his hip. Ethan's erection presses against my core. "I was going mad at home, alone, thinking about the next time I could touch you."

My back arches, an involuntary response to him, his fervent passion, as his hand slides up from my leg to cup my breast and brush his thumb over my nipple through my tank top. I wrench my head back, straining for breath. We don't have time for this now, but I can't make myself stop. Dragging my nails down his back, I can't let go. With Ethan, absorbing and magnetic as he is, I lose all sense of control. And when you've trained yourself to avoid anything too potent, too satisfying, a man like him is dangerous.

"I want you," he says, his voice ragged and wild eyes staring into mine. "All the time. I can barely concentrate on anything else because now I know how soft your lips are and the way your back arches when I kiss you and how fucking great it feels when you're scratching your nails down the back of my neck."

He grinds himself between my legs, as if to accentuate his

words. He then yanks down the neck of my tank top, almost ripping the fabric to expose my breast.

"Ethan."

He freezes. "Do you want me to stop?"

No, and that's the problem. I want more. All of him. Now and for hours, forsaking responsibilities. This is how it happens: the sudden infusion of the drug into my bloodstream that renders other concerns irrelevant. I know my heart and its tendencies. I can't do casual sex. I'm not wired that way. And yet...

"Don't stop."

His mouth wraps around the hard peak, licking and tugging with his teeth. Ethan's restrained power, the gentle violence of it, fills my head with primal images. Of shredding clothes and sweat-slick skin and the hard, firm planes of his naked body. Then his hand glides down my ribs to dip below the waistband of my pajama pants and cup my sex.

"I want to make you come, Avery." Soft and tender, his fingers caress me as my eyes close. "I want to show you how it can be with us."

One slow, deliberate finger pushes inside. I bite my lip to suppress a moan, clawing the couch cushion. He's almost too much. The scent of his skin, the forceful intensity of his passion. Ethan is a man who overwhelms as a matter of course. He couldn't temper himself if he tried.

"You're so tight," he whispers in my ear. He draws his finger out then back inside. "So beautiful."

"Ethan, I..."

A second finger enters me, and I can barely stay still. My

hips rise to meet him, greedy. But he forces me down with the full weight of his body pressing on his hand—into me.

"Let me give this to you," he says, lips brushing against mine. "You deserve pleasure, Avery. And I think it's been too long since a man's given you any without expecting something in return."

I don't know how he came to that conclusion, but he isn't wrong. And it's so very typical of Ethan to see even that which I'd never show him. The phase in which I thought being a good girlfriend, loving someone, meant giving and giving until they'd taken it all for granted. So I surrender to him. Eyes closed, I think only of his touch, his kiss, and the building ache as Ethan brings me toward release with patient determination.

* * *

When we get to the office, Ethan's still walking around with a rather self-satisfied grin on his face. We're up against a deadline to finalize our article and don't have much time to finish, but you wouldn't know it to look at him. As far as Ethan's concerned, it's just another sunny day in paradise. He follows me into the snack room for coffee, standing too close beside me as I pour a cup and add cream and sugar.

"Stop it," I say, feeling his stare.

"I'm not doing anything."

"You're being positively obscene."

"What's obscene about looking at you?"

"It's the way you're doing it. It's graphic."

"Only in my head."

I turn toward him, biting back a smile. "We don't do that here. That's the rule."

"Come over tonight." Beside me, he leans against the counter. "I want to cook you dinner."

I take my mug and head back to my desk, Ethan glued to my shoulder.

"That sounds harmless enough."

"I'm anything but harmless," he says, lowering his voice as we reach our cubicles. "This way I have you behind closed doors, all to myself."

"Keep it in your pants, sport." I grab my notepad from my desk. "We've got a meeting."

As much as I'd love to bask in the warm fuzzies and innuendo, the constant sexual tension and hyperexcitement when everything is new and unexplored, this isn't the week to lose focus. Minutes later, we step into Ed's office, where he and Cara are waiting for us. Seems the morning shows are calling. Radio stations and cable news. Now that our first article on the standoff has circulated, everyone wants a piece of us. Well, they want Echo.

"You two are part of the story now," Ed says, sucking on a bright orange smoothie.

"Hang on." Ethan takes a combative posture standing in the center of the room. "We're not forcing Avery into—"

"No one's saying—"

"Sure sounds like—"

"Bottom line," Cara says over the bickering men, "we're in the business of selling magazines."

"Really?" Ethan slides into that blistering sarcastic tone.

"Because I thought we were in the business of reporting the news."

"Not all of us can live on sanctimony alone."

"No, just the blood of the innocent and small, furry creatures. Right, Cara? How do you tolerate the daylight?"

I clearly didn't need to be here for this. Ed slides me a sympathetic glance as Ethan and Cara engage in their favorite pastime. If I slipped out now, it could be days before either of them noticed.

"Unless you're volunteering to take your salary in good thoughts and wishes, we have to turn a profit. A little publicity can double our ad revenue and—"

"So now we're whoring out our reporters for—"

"Okay," I say, putting my hands up. "I think I'm drawing the line at being called a whore."

"Avery, no." Ethan turns to me, a genuine look of panic draining the color from his face. "That's not what I—"

"I know. I get it. But all the same…" I say to Ed, who figured out before this argument began how it would end. "I don't do interviews. Period. I just want to do good work."

"That's all I needed to hear," he says.

"But Cara's right," I tell Ethan. "Doing some press helps the magazine. And it helps you, too. So you should do the interviews."

The damage is done. I knew it the minute Carter said my father's name. Before I ever walked into that truck and picked up the phone. If I'm honest with myself, Ethan was right when he said this *thing* has been clawing its way to the surface for a long time. Writing that first essay opened this door, and there's no going back now. So I can't act all surprised or indignant when the natural course of it unfolds.

"Are you sure you're ready for this?" He steps toward me and leans in as if this could be a private conversation. "We can keep our heads down, let it blow over. If I do this, they're not just going to ask about the standoff and Patrick. People have been itching for a glimpse of you for years. Your name is out there now. Fuck the book or anything else, I'm not going on camera if it makes you uncomfortable."

He promised I wouldn't have to do this alone. The night he convinced me to take this job. Ethan made me believe in a life where I didn't have to hide or feel ashamed of who I am. There is no career in which I remain anonymous and succeed. I realize that now. So while mugging for the camera or enduring melodramatic sit-downs might be a step too far, it isn't realistic to think I can keep a lid on everyone and everything around me. People can't live in hermetically sealed cases. There's only so much oxygen in tight, confined spaces. And while we're hiding, safe and secure in our protected containers, the whole world is happening around us. I didn't escape Massasauga just to build a new fence somewhere else.

"I'm sure."

## 17

# THE EXTRAORDINARY
# MACHINE

I'm breaking all my rules now. Sitting in the Slaughterhouse, waiting for the pitch meeting Wednesday morning as the other online writers file in, I watch the clips of Ethan's interviews. Seven appearances in all, regurgitating the same generic version of the story. The camera loves him. On the bright living room sets of the morning shows, behind the shiny glass desks on cable news panels, he eats the audience. Ethan has that charisma you can't teach. Even when the anchor pivots to a question about me, digging for some of that juicy tabloid gossip, Ethan is unflappable.

"Leave it to your boyfriend to make it all about him," Cyle says, two seats down.

Cyle shovels chips into his mouth, licking the salt from his fingers, and I remind myself not to touch the door handle after him.

Ethan and I haven't gotten much time alone over the last two days. He had to give me a rain check on dinner Monday night. Between taping his interviews and working twelve-hour days at the office, we haven't spent more than a couple of hours together without witnesses. I admit, there's a building sexual tension clouding my head. I keep thinking about Monday morning on the couch. His hands and his voice tearing down my hesitation. I'm a little edgy.

"Okay." Cara walks in, cream silk shirt and a neutral pencil skirt. Every day in her life is a page out of *Vogue*. She opens her laptop and takes a seat at the head of the table. "Let's get started. Avery, you're up first."

I've been itching for this. The last two days, reading the nonsense trotted out to prop up Phelps's agenda. Totally ignoring the fact that he takes his philosophy from a convicted murderer who didn't even believe his own dogma.

"Have you looked at the crowdfunding campaigns set up for Robert Phelps's defense fund?" I begin. "The first one started five hours into the standoff. It raised nine thousand dollars before he'd even been arrested. As of this morning there are four more set up for Phelps and his accomplices. A combined seven hundred thousand dollars and counting. I can't help wondering if, after the men who seized the bison range in Montana were acquitted, this supposed call to arms isn't just a dangerous scheme to bilk gullible saps out of their money."

"Isn't everyone entitled to a defense?" Cyle says, chip dust in his beard. "What kind of representation is an anti-government activist going to get with a public defender?"

"That's a pretty loose application of the term *activist*, but okay," I say.

We go back and forth, the arrogant prick doing his best to

shoot me down. I'm not sure where the fervor comes from; I can't make myself shut up. Something about his face inspires rage.

"Cara, come on." Cyle leans over the table to look past me. Around us, the other Cave dwellers stare down at their notes or laptops. He's got them so whipped into submission they can't even bare to look at him. "She shouldn't have been on this story in the first place. We can't let her use our magazine as her bully pulpit to sort out her daddy issues."

"Shove it up your ass, Cyle." I slap my laptop shut. "It is exactly this magazine's job to aim a big bright spotlight on a con artist like Phelps and call bullshit. That is the chief purpose of the press. Not only to report what's happening but to put it into context. Strip back every layer until only the naked facts are left. To stand by and let people like Phelps, people who want to follow in Patrick Turner Murphy's footsteps, write their own undisputed narrative—it isn't just negligent; it's fucking criminal."

Cyle stands from the table and pushes his chair in. "Cara, you need to send her home. Then we should have a talk about whether or not this experiment is working."

Her icy blue eyes cut to me. For a moment, I hold my breath, ready to turn in my badge and walk out should she say the word. If this is the hill I have to die on, so be it. But I couldn't live with myself if I sat back, watched this happen, and stayed silent.

"This is your next essay?" she asks me.

"Yes."

"Fifteen hundred words on my desk by five."

*Suck it, Cyle.*

* * *

When lunch rolls around, Ethan is out of the office and most everyone is up to their eyeballs in crunch time, so Addison and I pop over to the deli next door to grab a couple of to-go orders.

"I need to start going to these pitch meetings," Addison says when I tell him about my not-so-private contretemps with Cyle.

"Not sure I'll get away with too many more of those. But he had it coming."

It felt pretty damn good to shut him down. Even better that it didn't result in my being escorted from the premises with a restraining order. While we wait for our orders to come up, I check my phone and see I have a missed text from Ethan.

Ethan Ash
12:21 PM
How'd it go?
Avery Avalon
12:44 PM
Nailed it.
Ethan Ash
12:44 PM
That's my girl.
Avery Avalon
12:44 PM
And Cyle tried to have me fired.
Ethan Ash

12:45 PM

Want me to kick his teeth in?

Avery Avalon

12:45 PM

I handled it.

Ethan Ash

12:46 PM

Tell him to suck your dick?

Avery Avalon

12:46 PM

No, that's our special thing.

I put him in his place, though.

Ethan Ash

12:47 PM

Wish I'd been there to see it.

Avery Avalon

12:47 PM

It was pretty hot.

Ethan Ash

12:48 PM

You can't say things like that.

Avery Avalon

12:48 PM

Why not?

Ethan Ash

12:49 PM

Because I'm sitting in Carter's office trying not to get a hard-on.

And now he's looking at me funny.

Avery Avalon

12:49 PM

On that note…

Ethan Ash

12:50 PM

Too much?

Avery Avalon

12:50

You've got to warn a girl before you decide we've reached the conspicuous public boner phase of the relationship.

Ethan Ash

12:51 PM

Noted.

"Care to share with the class?" Addison says.

I look up to see him staring at me much the way I suspect Carter is looking at Ethan.

"Sorry," I say, sliding my phone back in my pocket. "Checking in with Ethan. He's meeting with his FBI source to gather some more background for the article."

"Mm-hmm." Addison's lips screw to one side of his face as he turns to watch the men in aprons behind the counter build our orders.

"What?"

A dramatic sigh escapes Addison as he crosses his arms, pointedly giving me the cold shoulder. "I couldn't help overhearing that you two ran off to Montauk for the weekend."

"It was sort of a spontaneous road trip. We weren't sipping cocktails on the beach or anything."

"So you two are a thing now."

"What constitutes a thing?"

Honestly, I don't know what we are. Ethan and I haven't had much time to discuss what this is or where it's going. If it's anything at all. For the moment, what I know is I prefer being around him more than not. And when we're in the same room, it's difficult not to touch him. To not think about how it feels when he touches me.

"Are you sleeping with him?"

No. But also technically yes.

"We like each other," I say. "What's so awful about that?"

"Hey, I get it. I warned you it'd be like this. Getting involved with Ethan is like a *Jurassic Park* movie. Like the man said: it's all *ooh* and *ahh*, then comes the running and screaming."

"What do you have against him? What could Ethan possibly have done to make you want to sabotage him every chance you get?"

"Oh, all right." Addison takes a step back. "That was uncalled for."

I'm not sure what sets me off. Whether the residual angst of going another round with Cyle or the fact that Addison won't let me have this, but it gets me riled. I'm already fending off daily phone calls from my mother asking me to quit and move in with her. I'm so sick of everyone pulling me in different directions.

"Look, I didn't ask for your advice," I say, grabbing my salad from the counter. "From now on, keep it to yourself."

"Sure, girl. You do you."

I leave Addison behind and take my food to my desk to

bury myself in work. I've got to finish this essay for Cara, Ethan and I still have the print article to revise, plus I've got IAQ emails to sift through. That's all on top of Cyle sending me bullshit fact-checking and research every fifteen minutes with URGENT in the subject line. Passive-aggressive little prick.

It's not until I hit Send, emailing my essay to Cara at 4:55, that I realize I never touched my salad. That tends to happen when I go back on my meds. A sudden influx of chemicals soaking my bloodstream like mainlining the drugs. Getting snapped back on a bungee cord. They're non-narcotic, but I still get the subtle rush of using. That artificial clarity and focus I've become addicted to. A gentle lift. Some find it in choco-late or cheese. But mine can send me into a four-hour trance, after which I barely remember what I've done.

"Hey there, gorgeous." Ethan comes up behind me and rests two warm, firm hands on my shoulders. "You ready for a break?"

The clock on my screen now reads 5:17. Where the hell did twenty-two minutes go?

"Yeah."

We grab some coffee from the snack room then go up to the roof. The smokers have put together a nice little patio with mismatched chairs lifted from the office and maybe Dumpster dives. A piece of artificial turf laid out like a rug and a metal bucket in the center where they dump their cigarette butts. There's probably a month's worth in there.

Ethan and I go to the side overlooking Liberty Street. It really isn't much of a view; we're surrounded and shadowed on all sides by taller buildings. But if you lean out over the north-east corner, you can glimpse the Federal Reserve building. The police tape is gone now. The barricades removed. Like it never happened. This city gets bored easily.

From the southeast corner, we peer into the windows of a high-rise apartment building. The kind where junior execu-tives and new stockbrokers start inching their way up toward the penthouse suite.

"I don't think I've said this since…everything"—Ethan catches my hair flying across my face and tucks it behind my ear—"but I am so proud of you."

"Do you ever notice how you can't say those words without sounding like someone's parent after a grade school recital?"

"No, not until now. That makes me feel kind of creepy when you put it that way."

"Right?"

Ethan looks good on a Manhattan rooftop. A magazine ad of a handsome, fashionable male contemplating his empire with the breeze blowing through his hair. If he were wearing a scarf and a camel coat, I might get the sudden urge to buy a Rolex or something.

"Attend a lot of grade school recitals, did you?" he asks with a smirk.

"Only on TV."

"I can't even imagine." Shaking his head, he gazes out at the walls of glass, steel, and stone. "So many things the rest of us take for granted. All those stupid coming-of-age moments, and where you were when Ross and Rachel kissed."

"Weren't you like five years old?"

"Yeah, but I saw the reruns."

He shouldn't make me laugh when I'm standing at the edge of a building five stories up.

"But you did imagine it," I say. "You wrote the book about it."

"It's not the same thing. Enderly walks off the page before she must grapple with the true, devastating reality of entering a world she doesn't recognize. And she's an adult by then. You were just a kid, shoved out into society, no idea what's been going on around you."

"I have to tell you, space travel came as a real shock."

He freezes, eyes wide until he catches on.

"Ah, I see. That was a joke. I deserve that."

"We did have books. I did have what you'd consider homeschooling, to a certain extent. It wasn't that I was kept completely ignorant of the outside world, just taught that it was awful and corrupt and not a place that I should ever want to go."

"Well, maybe Patrick wasn't entirely wrong."

In the apartment across the street, a woman is undressing a man in front of the floor-to-ceiling window. She pulls his tie from his neck, tugs his shirttails from his waistband. Apparently with no concern that anyone might be watching.

"There are times I miss it. The simplicity. My father built a beautiful world. But he was made of poison, and he tainted everything he touched."

She pushes his shirt down his arms and lets it drop to the floor. Next, his belt is ripped from its loops. Then her fingers pull at the button on his pants while he stands there, watching, breathless with anticipation.

We put so much trust in each other. All of us. Trust that the guy standing next to you on the subway platform isn't going to shove you in front of the train. Trust that the driver of the car in the next lane isn't going to suddenly yank the wheel to the left and run you off the road. That when you order a plate of spaghetti, it isn't laced with arsenic. What is that intangible quality? How are we born so trusting? Even when someone is crushed on the tracks, is sent careening into oncoming traffic, or chokes on the blood filling their lungs, we go on. We keep trusting.

"I want to take you on a real date," he says. "Tonight. Dinner and a show. Give you the authentic Manhattan night-on-the-town experience."

"You know, I've heard rumors there are cheaper ways to get me into bed."

"Sue me. I'm a romantic."

\* \* \*

Kumi meets me at the apartment that night after work to help me get ready for Ethan's version of a *real* date. Once she deems my entire wardrobe hopeless, she lends me a dress and spends the next half hour speeding through my hair and makeup. Right on time, Ethan knocks on our door. My lips tingle as I slide on a pair of Kumi's shoes and she fusses with my hair. A knot forms in my gut. It's not anxiety, exactly, but the rush of peering out over a very long drop. That nervous, mortal fear you get watching that guy jump out of the capsule in Earth's stratosphere, freefalling toward certain death until the big, brilliant plume of a parachute jerks him upright and slows his fall.

"Remember..." Kumi hands me a clutch purse and wipes a lipstick smudge from my mouth. "Don't get anything on the dress."

"Thanks, Mom."

When I open the door, the trepidation evaporates. Electricity and want, his soft lips and gentle hands—it all comes rushing back. The sight of Ethan now, with his hair swept back like he's just hopped off a boat, ocean eyes peering at me from under thick, dark lashes—I start to forget why I ever thought we were a bad idea, or why I agreed to it at all.

"You clean up nice," I tell him as I step into the hall to close the door because I'm pretty sure Kumi's behind me making lewd hand gestures.

Ethan smiles, sort of. Regarding me, his hand goes to his jaw and fingers rub across his mouth. "You look incredible."

"Yes, I put on a dress, and I'm transformed from a grotesque swamp monster."

"No, no." He gestures for me to walk ahead of him toward the stairs. "Just...Wow, that's all. Very nice."

We sort of match, too. He wears a tailored charcoal suit and crisp white shirt with a muted turquoise tie almost the same shade as my dress. We're already fucking obnoxious.

Outside, Ethan opens the door of his truck for me and offers me his hand as I climb in. He pauses for a moment, staring at me. The muscle in his jaw flexes as he swallows. Something animal and instinctive skitters through my limbs. A creature that knows it's been spotted by something vicious and hungry.

"You have to stop doing that," I tell him.

He blinks and licks his lips.

"I have no idea what you're talking about."

\* \* \*

Ethan knows everyone. A guy on Broadway who stands wait-ing to park his truck and actually brings it back. The usher at the theater who escorts us to our seats before doors open to the hundreds waiting outside. The producer of the show who meets us after curtain call to give us a backstage tour and get my program signed by the cast. The chef-owner at the new Vietnamese restaurant our magazine's food critics are raving about. Ethan shows up, and people drop what they're doing to shake his hand, share a laugh. They look me in the eyes when they greet me and treat me like I'm someone, not just an orna-ment on Ethan's arm.

"Please tell me you're not blackmailing all these people," I say, scraping the last bite off my plate.

He pauses, glass of wine at his lips, and tempers a subtle grin. "Not all of them, no."

We sit in a corner booth, quiet and secluded from the ca-pacity crowd. Dinner was delicious, the show spectacular. But it's Ethan, the atmosphere he brings to a room; he walks in, and everything shines a little brighter. Colors more vivid. You didn't know it till now, but you've been looking at the world through dirty, crusted glass. Ethan smashes out the window.

"How do you know all these people?"

"Mutual friends, mostly. Parties. That kind of thing." Beside me, he shrugs, unimpressed with himself. "At one point it was very popular to know me."

"Still is, I'd say."

"It's a particularly good week."

The light fixture above our heads, woven wicker ball around a warm yellow bulb, casts tiny shards of light like fireflies across Ethan's face that seem to dance as he talks.

"I had to call in some old favors. Bodies I helped dump. Couches I carried up four flights of stairs."

"So don't get used to it, is what you're saying."

"Avery, if this was the life you wanted, you'd have it."

Heat rises over my face as I look down at my empty plate and reach for my water instead.

"But you're not that girl."

"Oh?" I say, propping my elbow on the table to rest my chin in my hand. "And what kind of girl am I?"

"You're the Met on Sunday afternoon. The beach in winter. Jazz in the park and playing cards by candlelight during a storm." His hand slides over my knee, fingertips skimming my skin with just the lightest teasing touch that sends static rolling through my body. "You are the woman men see in their dreams while they're wondering how their lives became so empty and meaningless."

"Ethan…"

"What?"

Looking into his eyes is like observing the Earth from space. And you think, how I can ever set foot on the ground again?

"You have this odd habit of speaking in wedding vows."

"Do I?"

Back and forth, fingers tracing the curves of my knee, sowing madness.

"What would you say?" he asks.

"To marriage?"

"If I were to propose to you right now."

His palm lies flat on my knee. Glancing over his shoulder, toward the dining room of tables and well-dressed people, he says, "If I told you that man there"—he nods toward a waiter across the room carrying a tray with two glasses of champagne—"was given a box, and in that box was a ring. That this man"—getting closer, coming toward us—"was instructed to put the ring in a glass"—eyes dead ahead, weaving through tables with expert balance, tray held high—"to fill that glass with the most expensive champagne money can buy"—Ethan's hand slides to the inside of my knee—"and awaiting my signal"—he grips the back of my knee, firm and startling—"deliver it to you."

My heart throbs against my ribs, anxious and terrified, the waiter coming closer.

Five feet.

Four feet.

"What would you say?"

He veers to the left, to the couple two tables away.

Air leaves my lungs in desperate relief.

"Christ, Avery." Ethan smiles and takes his hand away.

*Asshole.*

"You have a deep, profound fear of commitment."

"No." I chug the rest of my water, pulse returning to normal.

"I have a rational fear of being proposed to on a first date by a man I barely know."

The humor leaves his face. He furrows his brow. "You keep saying that, but it isn't true. You do know me."

"Everything I know could fit on a Post-it Note."

"Then ask me something." He pushes our plates away, moves the utensils and glasses crowding the table between us. "Anything you want."

"Is your mother the reason you weren't at work last week?"

Ethan must have guessed I'd ask this question. It's the one topic between us he's thus far been unwilling to talk about. If the question affects him at all, he doesn't show it. His perfect cheekbones and angular jaw stay steady, in place.

"Yes."

"Tell me about it. Why?"

Leaning back, he grabs his wineglass and swigs the last of it. A sort of preparation happens: he runs his fingers through his hair, exhales, slides his gaze around the room before staring at his fingers drumming on the table.

"You met her," he says, "so you know she's sick."

"Your dad said she had gone into remission, but now it's back."

The muscle in his jaw ticks.

"He smoked a pack a day. As long as I can remember, half the time my father was home, he spent it on the porch with a cigarette in his hand. Since he was a teenager. Then just before my brother died, my mother was diagnosed with lung cancer. Never smoked a day in her life, but you spend thirty years with a smoker and their lungs become yours."

Ethan twists the stem of his empty wineglass between his fingers, drawing little circles on the table with the base.

"She was a brilliant surgeon. Loved to sail. Before cancer, my mother was full of energy. She'd put in twelve, fifteen hours at the hospital and still manage a smile when my father dragged her out for a dinner party for some asshole client. He quit smoking after they found out, as if it made a difference at that point."

He clears his throat, eyes glassy. I reach out and take his hand in both of mine.

"Is that why you and your dad don't get along?"

"One on a long list of reasons."

"I'm sure he's just as heartbroken as you are. He—"

Ethan snatches his hand from mine. "Please, don't defend him. That man has smoked for two-thirds of his life, and he's healthier than I am. Instead, he killed his wife."

"Ethan—"

"Let's not talk about this anymore, okay?" The darkness in his eyes recedes, voice softens. He trails his fingers along my temple and down my neck. "I don't want to spoil the evening for you."

I'd tell him he isn't spoiling anything, that I'd rather he'd be honest and grim than pretend, but our waiter returns with a tray of desserts and a bottle of wine.

"Compliments of the chef," he says, placing two dishes in front of us. "Here we have almond jelly with lychees, jackfruit, and strawberries, as well as mandarin sorbet with currant cookies."

The waiter then sets out two new wineglasses and proceeds

to pull the cork from the bottle. He offers to fill mine, but I put my hand over it.

"Thank you, no. I'm okay."

"Are you sure?" Ethan asks, holding out his glass to the waiter. "I promise not to think less of you if I have to carry you home."

"No, really, I'm good."

Looking a bit offended, the waiter sets the bottle on the table and walks away. Before I can decide which dessert to try first, I notice Ethan studying me.

"Do you have a preference?" I ask.

"You don't drink."

Shit.

"Any particular reason?" he asks.

My hands go to my lap, fingers twisting until Ethan places his hand over mine. He closes in, arm across the table in front of me, shielding us.

"Avery, whatever it is, just say it."

I wish it were that simple. But the answer isn't an easy box to open. It's boxes inside of boxes, unpacking and assembling a whole person. An entire life and the people and places that made her this way. How do I explain it to him when he can't see Jenny's nose ring or smell the ammonia soaked into her clothes? Can't watch my shrink's glass eye linger on the other side of the room, like it was watching a ghost in the corner. Echo, sweating and thrashing, screaming for mercy and ripping at her hair.

"Hey, hey," he says, wiping his thumb across my cheek. "What's wrong?"

"I don't think I can stay here."

My breath comes shorter, quicker. Fingers tingle.

"Okay. We can go."

Pulling out his wallet, Ethan leaves cash on the table and takes my hand as we slide out of the booth. He takes off his jacket and places it over my shoulders, leading me through the restaurant and outside to the noise and throbbing activity.

"Tell me what you need," he says, both hands cupping my face. Urgency forms creases at the corners of his eyes. "What can I do?"

This isn't fair to him. Quiet mysteries and hiding in dark corners. I can't expect total, unfettered honesty when I'm still concealing locked rooms behind mirrors and curtains. It's about more than trust. It comes down to whether or not I want Ethan to know me. Not his imagined ideal or the character he pieced together with parts of himself. Beneath the person I've tried to portray since I got sober and dropped my first name. Me, and everyone that used to be.

So I make a choice, and hold out my hand.

"Take a walk with me."

# 18

# SOBER

$M$y name is Echo, and I'm an addict."

In a room of Saint Francis of Assisi Church on Thirty-First Street, a room like a dozen others I've seen, I stand up from the metal folding chair. Beside me, Ethan watches, silent, concealing any reaction to me or the nine other people sipping coffee and eating doughnuts.

"I've been clean for eight years, and I still think about using every day. I miss it like you miss sleep when you're working a twelve-hour shift and it feels like you haven't seen your bed in days. I miss it the way people talk about their childhoods, the good old days, all golden hues."

Then again, that's the thing about the good old days: they were never so pretty as we remember. Even the memories we regret, the ones that keep us up at night when our mind wanders and we relive our mistakes over and over in the dark—they're a little less painful than the real thing. The sounds have muted. The sting of embarrassment has all but faded, and only the red, swollen mark remains.

"Today someone asked me why I don't drink, and I didn't know how to answer. How do you explain that you're a toy Mom took the batteries out of because the first time the kid played with you, you nearly burned the house down? That you have to stay broken because what you are is destructive. I know we're not supposed to think of ourselves that way, but let's face it, we were built for chaos. Not because we want to destroy—we're not malicious—it's just the way we were made. I don't drink not because I'm afraid of what might happen, but because I *know* what can happen. And I might like it. That's the sword we live under. Denying our nature. Withholding from ourselves the one thing we want most. Because our true selves aren't meant for this world. We'd swallow it hole if we could—stick it in a needle and straight in our veins."

They're all looking at me. The gangly woman, all tendons and bone, flesh like socks after the elastic's worn out. Big, bald, beach ball man with sweat stains under his arms and a second doughnut on his lap. Sweet, blonde yogi in a long-sleeved silk cardigan, no doubt covering her track marks. They're all me. They're some of you. They're anyone at all.

"Anyway…"

I needed Ethan to see this. There's no other way to understand it.

"Today makes it eight years, five months, and twenty-three days. I miss it, but it gets a little easier every day."

As I sit, Ethan takes my hand, clasping it tight in his. He

never lets go as we stay through another hour, listening to the stories and confessions, the readings and recitations. I think about nothing. Let my mind clear and wander into empty space. It's been weeks trapped under this clutter, the layers thickening, hardening above my head. Tonight, it's cracked, crumbling around my shoulders. Whatever Ethan sees of me now, at least it's the truth.

When the meeting ends and we emerge from the bowels of the church, I tell Ethan about Jenny. About getting kicked out of school and my first shrink with the glass eye. He says nothing. To the sidewalk, the end of the block. Waiting at the corner for the cars to pass and the light to change. Then we just keep walking, his jacket over my shoulders and my hand in his. Back to his truck while I tell him about rehab and Maureen. His silence persists, impassive shadows across his face, to my apartment and upstairs to my front door. Every step, every minute, dread soaking into my bones.

I wouldn't blame him now, as I put my key in the door, if this were the end. A cold good night and uncomfortable glances at the office. Stilted conversation as we both try to forget. I slide his jacket off my shoulders and hold it out to him.

"Invite me in," he says.

"You don't have to say anything. I'm sorry if I made this awkward."

Ethan takes the jacket and drapes it over his arm.

"Invite me in."

Intensity flares behind his eyes, in the tight restraint of his voice. His entire body radiating tension. I unlock the door and let us inside. The apartment is dark except for the light over the stove. Kumi's in bed already and left me a night light. I turn to lock up and hear Ethan go straight to my room.

I'm not ready for the talk. Maybe he's too noble, too kind to let this end without an explanation, but I'm not ready to hear it. I'd prefer the unspoken agreement to avoid each other and understand that when "everyone" is going out for lunch or to catch Navid's next show, that doesn't mean me. So I let him wait while I go to the bathroom to hang up the dress and slip back into my pajamas. I wash the makeup from my face and pull down my hair. Brush my teeth and sit on the edge of the tub, hoping he might give up and leave. But there isn't a sound. Just the two of us on separate sides of the same wall, each waiting for the other to make the first move.

*Fine. Let's get this over with.*

Ethan stands in the middle of my bedroom, his back to me, among the piles of clothes and unpacked boxes. Some of the flowers are still where he left them, others are scattered around the apartment, and a few that didn't last are gone. I watch him until I can't stand it any longer.

"Ethan."

He turns, and in two strides he's caught me in his arms. His body, his lips, press to mine. Deep, desperate. Holding me to him as if I might be ripped away. Sudden fever engulfs me as my hands find their way into his hair and tug, my feet pushing him toward the bed. Ethan sits on the edge, pulling me to stand between his legs. Hands slide to my ribs, up and down, skimming his thumbs over my stomach.

Inhaling, he breaks away. In his eyes I see the same fury and desire heating my blood, teasing my nerves like touching live wires.

"Christ, Avery." Ethan licks his lips and looks me up and down. "What are you wearing?"

"Umm...pajamas?"

A tank top and lounge pants, to be precise. The same ones I slept in last night, and the night before. Because I hate going to the laundry and it's impossible to find anything when all my clothes are strewn across the floor or stuffed in garbage bags. I'm lucky I find underwear in the mornings.

"You don't even know," he says, shaking his head.

"What?"

"How fucking sexy you are."

Gripping my ribs, his hands slide up, just below my breasts, and I have to stop myself from shivering.

"I thought..."

"You were hiding in the bathroom because you thought I was dumping you."

"Pretty much."

"No. Not even a little." He slides back onto the bed. "Come here." And brings me with him to sit propped up against my pillows. "I'm glad you brought me there. I just needed some time to process, that's all. And I wanted you to have space to decompress."

"You're not, I don't know, mad at me or freaked out?"

"No." Ethan wraps his arm behind my back and encourages me to rest my head on his chest.

Idly, my fingers trace the buttons on his shirt, up and over the tiny valleys of the fabric.

"I think you're extraordinary. You don't understand how rare it is to have that kind of willpower and persevere through the kind of shit you've been through. Fuck, Avery. I couldn't do it. I'd have given up and shot myself a long time ago."

My hand fists his shirt. "Don't say things like that."

He places a kiss on my forehead and lays his hand over mine. "I'm sorry. But my point's the same. Everything I learn about you makes me more convinced that you're my hero."

"Wow, that *is* depressing."

"You don't give yourself enough credit."

"I give the minimal amount of credit for being alive. There are people out there who have it much worse. I'm not under any illusions that my circumstances approach anything nearing extreme."

"Fair enough," he says. "But that changes nothing. I'm still a fan."

"I do feel better, now that you know."

"Great, because I feel like a jackass. I promise to stop dragging you to bars and—"

"No," I say, looking up at him. "That's exactly why I don't tell people. I got clean before I was ever old enough to drink, so it isn't like I know what I'm missing. It's precautionary. And anyway, I don't want to change your life."

"You already have." Soft and tender, he brushes the back of his hand across my cheek and weaves his hand into my hair. "You've been changing me since the moment we met. I'm not the same person I was, and I never will be."

And that's the moment it happens.

Ethan hooks the back of my knee to drape my leg across his and reaches for the lamp on my nightstand, plunging us into night.

"Are you staying?"

"I wouldn't be anywhere else."

The moment I fall in love with him.

# 19

# THE AGITATOR

Thursday morning, I wake to the tender, teasing ministrations of Ethan's fingers trailing up and down my arm. I lie draped across his chest in nearly the same position as when I fell asleep.

"Morning," I mumble into his bare skin.

Not sure when he took his shirt off last night, but he's still wearing his dress pants.

"I like this," he says, "waking up with you. I missed it when you weren't the first thing I saw in the morning."

One of the best parts about Ethan: he doesn't even know how unusually sweet he is. His words aren't flattery aimed at a purpose, they're simple and kind and spoken with honesty. Like it wouldn't even occur to him to merely talk a woman into bed. I don't think he could be that disingenuous.

I kiss the hollow place beneath his collarbone, and my hand roams his chest and down his stomach. Muscles squeeze and flex beneath my palm.

"Fuck, Avery." He hisses the words then sucks in a sharp breath. "How do you do that?"

"What?"

He reaches for my leg and hitches it up across his lap. I feel his erection hard beneath my thigh and it sends a shiver of want coursing hot through my limbs. An ache building deep inside as flashes of memory play behind my eyes.

"You barely touch me and I get so fucking hard it hurts."

"Is that bad?" I say, dragging my thigh up and down, nails skimming the ridges of his abs.

"No." Voice hoarse, his heart beats faster. His chest rises and falls on slow, ragged breaths. Both of his hands rise to weave through his hair, then hug the pillow. "Just different."

"Different than what?"

"Anything. Anyone."

His hips rise off the bed just a fraction but immediately fall, pressed into the bed as he attempts to restrain himself.

"I want you to know," I say, and unbuckle his leather belt. "I appreciate how well you took things last night. And that you stayed with me." Next I undo the button of his pants. "And that you understood what I needed most was not to be alone." Then slide down the zipper. "I also want you to know that I don't take your generosity for granted." Slipping my hand inside his boxers, I free his long, hard length.

"Avery," he says, almost choking on the word. "You don't have to."

"I know I don't." I stroke him from base to tip, slow and deliberate, the way he did with me. "That's the point. You never ask for anything. You give because you want to."

"Because I care," he says, swallowing thick. "Because you're special to me."

"And so are you to me."

Against all my better judgment, I've fallen for Ethan. Deep and fast in a way I'd promised myself never to do again. But even if I'd seen him coming, I don't think I'd have had the will to avoid him. Ethan is a life-altering event. The kind of man who marks a place in time in which all else is referred to as before and after. Pre-Ethan and post-. And though there are three words on my tongue I'm desperate to express, I don't want to put him under the gun. Right now, there's nothing more I need from him than what he gives. So I show him. Taking my time, I give him the pleasure he's shown me. Not just my body, but every aspect of my life that's become brighter, richer because of him.

"Avery…" Ethan's hand tangles in my hair. His stomach clenches, and his penis jerks in my palm. "Fuck, baby, I'm gonna come."

He pulls me up to reach his lips, kissing me, desperate and frantic as I pump him to completion. Then his entire body goes slack, exhausted and satisfied.

"Goddamn, Avery." Ethan exhales against my lips. "You're fucking amazing."

\* \* \*

Once Ethan's cleaned up and dressed again, he heads home to change for work. I'm digging through the bags of clean clothes on my floor before getting in the shower when I hear the front door open and slam shut. I jump, startled at the sound, and barely step out of my bedroom when I see Ethan standing in the living room with his phone to his ear. He's gone pale. Ghostly. But I see the rage register on his face and the tension straining his neck.

"Carter, I'm at Avery's. You need to get down here. No, fuck the cops. You need to see this."

"Ethan?"

His head jerks up. In a few quick strides, he's right in front of me and pushing me back in my room, kicking the door shut behind him. He rattles off my address to Carter as my legs hit the bed and I sit on the edge. Ethan stands above me, hand on my shoulder, like he's shielding me from something. Nervous energy chokes me, fingers buzz with anxiety. Then he ends the call and shoves his phone in his pocket.

"Ethan, what's wrong?"

"Avery?" Before he can answer, Kumi calls my name. All the slamming doors have woken her up.

"In here," I call.

Ethan goes to the door and lets her in. She flinches at the sight of him, not used to finding a man in a suit standing in my bedroom at six in the morning. But then I suspect it's the harried look in his eyes that sends her gaze shooting past his shoulder to question me.

"You two should both stay here," he says, stepping back to urge Kumi inside. "Carter's on his way."

"Who's that?" Kumi's still in her pajamas. An oversized SU T-shirt and a pair of Batman lounge pants she stole from an ex. "What was all that slamming?"

"Carter is Ethan's friend," I answer cautiously. "And FBI."

"The hell?"

Kumi whips around to stare at Ethan, who stands completely composed, hands shoved in his pockets. The only sign of concern is buried in his eyes and the deep crease through his brow. The tightness bunching his shoulders.

"Ethan," I say, "what is it?"

"There was a note on your door."

"Okay…"

"A death threat."

* * *

An hour later, NYPD show up to take a statement. Carter throws his weight around to get a look at security camera footage from the bodega and the restaurant downstairs, checking for any angles that might have caught who came and went from our building last night. Out of an abundance of caution, I suggested Kumi stay with her uncle for a few days. Though the note is probably just an idle threat meant to intimidate me, Carter doesn't want us taking any chances. I hadn't bothered to check social media lately until Ethan looked at my phone. My Twitter feed has been flooded with threats and vile hatred in response to my essay on Phelps.

Now Ethan sits with me in my bedroom as I stare at the floor, trying to piece together a plan. The worst part: Carter had agents contact my mother to be on the lookout in case anyone suspicious starts creeping around Aster.

"My mom is freaking out," I tell him. "She wants me to quit and move in with her."

"She's worried about you," he says, rubbing my back. "She's your mom. It's what they do."

"Maybe she's right. Maybe this is a failed experiment and I had no business trying to make a career in news. It's too visible."

"Fuck that. If anything, this bullshit proves you're doing something right. People wouldn't be trying to intimidate you, shut you up, if you hadn't struck a nerve. Far as I'm concerned, you're exactly where you're supposed to be."

"But look what I've done to Kumi. It's one thing to accept that deranged assholes come with the job, but she didn't have a choice. If I were in her place…"

"She'll be fine. It's a disruption, sure, but nothing insurmountable. Don't take it as evidence that you've done anything wrong. This isn't your fault."

"Isn't it, though? I brought this on myself. I can't put something out there and not expect consequences."

"Listen to me." Ethan lifts my chin to make me look at him. "It is *not* your fault. Speaking your mind is not an invitation for death threats. People want to disagree, call you names, boycott the magazine—fine. It's a free country. But that freedom stops at violence. Don't you dare blame yourself, Avery. I won't let you."

There's a knock on my door, and I look up to see Carter standing at the threshold.

"Just want to let you know we've wrapped up here."

"Thank you," Ethan says pointedly. "I appreciate you handling this yourself."

Carter nods as he slides a sympathetic glance toward me. "Avery, you might want to consider staying somewhere else for a couple of days. As a precaution." He takes out a business card and leaves it on my desk near the door. "My cell number is on the back. Anything you need. Don't hesitate."

Once he's left and I hear the front door shut behind him, I stand up from the bed to start packing up some clothes.

"Stay with me," Ethan says.

"I don't know if that's such a good idea."

"Why not?" Sitting on the edge of the bed, Ethan reaches for me and pulls me to stand between his legs. "Give me a good reason."

"Because. We're…"

"Dating," he says, smiling. "Engaged in a monogamous relationship. Are very good at sharing a bed together. Madly attracted to each other. Please, stop me when I get to the problem."

"Ethan, come on." My fingers comb through his hair, rising against the grain at the back of his neck. "It's been one date. You don't want me crashing."

"Why, do you pee with the door open?"

"Be serious, please."

"I am serious. Stay with me."

His hands move to my ribs, holding firm while his thumbs glide up and down my stomach. He knows what that does to me, and it isn't fighting fair.

"At least I'll know you're safe. It's that, or let me get us a hotel together. I'm not letting you out of my sight until this thing blows over."

"Doesn't sound like I have a choice."

"You do," he says, eyes soft and pleading. "But I'm hoping you'll take pity on me. I won't be able to function if you're alone and I'm not there to protect you. Give me some peace of mind. Please."

I can appreciate his desire to swoop in and save me. Play the hero and reap the rewards. Of course I want to say yes. There's nowhere I'd rather be than with Ethan. Going to bed beside him. Waking up to his face in the morning. Just lying on the couch, watching TV, my head in his lap while his fingers trace patterns down my arm. But too much too soon is an easy way to ruin a relationship before it begins. Even two people who are otherwise compatible can crumble under the stress of co-habitation. Some people just aren't meant to live together.

Then again, it isn't permanent. This state of emergency can't last forever. A few days. A couple of weeks, at most. Things will go back to normal—Ethan in his space and me in mine. If we can't survive that, perhaps it's better to know now. Because the longer Ethan is in my life, the harder it gets to imagine it without him.

"Okay," I tell him. "But this is just temporary."

\* \* \*

We don't bother going into the office today. When Ethan calls Ed from my apartment, we're warned to lie low until Monday. Seems a crowd of protesters has gathered outside the building, and the phones have been ringing all morning with crackpots calling for my head. Just as well. I'd rather not have to face Cyle and his inevitable *I told you so*.

Instead, I gather up my stuff, and we head to Ethan's place to work from there. When he lets us inside, I'm struck by its austerity. Ethan's loft is empty. Not just sparse—bare. Surrounded by exposed brick and cement floors, nothing hangs on the walls. On one end, the shiny stainless steel kitchen with a long marble island. At the other, his king-sized bed and single chest of drawers. There are two rolling racks of clothes equating to a closet. Dividing the two areas is a worn leather sectional couch facing a TV on a short entertainment center filled with books and vinyl records. There's a small desk off to the side next to a huge standing lamp. But otherwise, the sprawling layout is uninhabited. Against the wall beside the front door are several stacked cardboard boxes, the unpacked remnants of his move a year ago. He owns just enough furniture to make the place livable.

"Not much for decorating," I say, tossing my duffle bag on his bed as I walk the space.

"Clutter gets distracting. I make it a point not to keep too much stuff around me."

Physically, maybe, but inside the rooms of his mind, he's climbing over piles of debris.

For most of the day we sit on his couch, music playing in the background, while we put the finishing touches on our article. But every few minutes I peek over at Ethan's laptop screen to see him combing through pages of message board threads about Phelps and all the ways his supporters would like to see me publicly debased. He's obsessed, torturing himself with the vitriolic tirades of sad, impotent people.

"Ignore it," I say, because it's impossible for me to tune it out when he's sitting right beside me. "There's no point subjecting yourself to it."

"Someone leaked your address. I want to know who."

There's no reasoning with Ethan once he's set his mind on a project. Fact is, we both know the answer. Either someone I know leaked my address, which pretty much narrows it down to a neighbor or someone at the magazine, or I was followed.

"Don't worry." Ethan glances at me. Whatever he reads on my face prompts him to shut his laptop and lean over to kiss my forehead. "Carter knows what he's doing. This will be over soon."

"I know." Faces flick behind my eyes, a catalogue of potential traitors. A scrapbook of liars. "I'm not worried."

If only I could make myself believe that.

"How about a bath?" Ethan weaves his fingers through my hair, stroking my cheek with his thumb. "Relax, unwind. I'll make us dinner."

"Yeah, okay."

Though I try to quiet the suspicion circulating through my head, I can't get past the question of who. A deep sense of betrayal wraps itself around my neck, squeezing, choking off everything else until only the paranoia remains. This must have been how my father felt, fearing the FBI closing in on him. Knowing that one of us, the people closest to him, had sold him out. The people he ate breakfast with, the people he built homes and cultivated a life with. Sometimes it was even good. But he had pressed us too far. Years of authoritarian rule, starving people of their individuality and free thought. He held on too tight. And if his life was over, he wasn't going alone.

While Ethan gets to work in the kitchen, I grab my copy of his book and soak in a warm tub. Maybe it seems silly, I already know how it ends, but the more I read of Enderly, the more I understand the man who wrote her. Ethan is a romantic, concerned with spirit and expression. With fairness and truth. If he could stop the world long enough to fix it, move the pieces around, he's certain he could create something wondrous and beautiful. But he's chained by pain and pessimism. Like a penned whale swimming circles in a tank, a magnificent creature dulled and stunted, he has only vague primal instincts that whisper fantasies of what life could be. Great open spaces and miles unhindered. Ethan wants that for Enderly. In every word, he imagines for her a place where she runs toward the horizon just because she can.

It's a lovely notion. One I think I even constructed for myself when I answered Ethan's email and accepted the interview at the magazine. I had imagined a reality where who I was, who my father was, didn't matter. Like I could outlive his memory and what it meant to people. But it was an illusion. We can't cut out pieces of our past and pretend we're a whole person without those artifacts in place. Without our history, we're incomplete. We're flat facsimiles—no depth or dimension. I understand that now. Though the question remains, Where do I go from here? What are dreams worth if they hurt the people around you?

Later that night, lying in bed with Ethan asleep beside me, I stare across the darkened room still unable to quiet my mind. Too much noise and activity colliding inside my head.

"You awake?" Ethan shifts next to me in bed beneath the blankets. "Something wrong?"

"I'm fine. Go back to sleep."

He rolls to his side, wrapping his arm around my waist. "Talk to me."

"Really, it's nothing. I'm just restless."

"You're safe with me." His fingers slide under the hem of my tank top to lightly brush bare skin. "I won't let anything happen to you."

"No, I know. It isn't that, I'm just…"

I don't have the words to articulate it. Even if I could, I'm not sure it'd make sense.

"What can I do?" he asks, trying to understand.

Ethan needs a problem he can fix. Something with bolts and buttons. Something he can take apart, reassemble, or knock with a hammer. People aren't as easy.

Instead, I kiss him. My lips against his, it isn't a solution, but it makes me feel better. Wrapped in blankets, secluded in darkness, he overwhelms my senses. The taste of mint on his tongue, the clean, rich scent of his skin—they drive all other thoughts from my mind. I feel only his mouth, his tongue teasing mine, and his heart beating under my palm.

"Avery," he hums against my lips. "Wait a minute."

My fingers comb into his hair, tugging. I don't want him to speak. To let words break the illusion. I just want him, everywhere, all at once and nothing else.

"Listen to me." He breaks away. "I want you to hear this."

Hand caressing the side of my face, he runs his thumb under my bottom lip until I settle.

"I mean it. Whenever you're scared or hurting, I want you to feel safe with me. I want to be the person you talk to, not the one you hide from. Anything at all, or nothing, whatever it is that gets inside your head and makes you want to run, give it to me. I'll take it away. I'll bury it in the ground, and never let it hurt you again. I promise, Avery, with all my heart. You never have to be afraid of anything when you're with me."

The darkness turns liquid and my chest clenches.

"Why do you say things like that?" I barely whisper.

"Because they're true. And because I love you."

Wiping a tear from my cheek, he kisses me. Ethan imbues such a small gesture with so much meaning—breaks my heart like tearing muscles helps them grow. More than his handsome face or enticing body, it's his words that seduce me. Since the day we met, he's talked his way under my skin. Like he's known me my whole life—and I guess he has. Like we've always been here. Anxious with need, I wrap my leg over his hip. He's hard against my thigh. The thick, rigid length of his erection evidence of our connection. That I have no less an effect on him than he has on me.

"Fuck, Avery." He sighs the words and grabs my ass to press himself between my legs.

Kissing his way down my neck, Ethan moves his hand beneath my shirt to run his flat palm up my stomach and between my breasts. His touch, so warm and enlivening, sets my pulse racing. He cups my breast and brushes his thumb over my nipple. It's excruciating how precisely he can unravel me. How exact his attention pierces the center of everything I am. Nothing else exists when our bodies meet. I peel my shirt over my head and toss it into the darkness. Then I push his pants down his legs to palm him in my hand, stroking.

"Tell me what you want," Ethan groans. His hand slides down my body and between my legs. "Tell me how you want me to make you come."

Patient and deliberate, he stokes the ache burning inside me. One finger pushes into me and already I'm close to collapse.

"Tell me," he demands, pushing a second finger through my entrance.

I have to let go of him to brace my hand against his hip, nails digging into his skin at the beautiful severity of his intrusion. Clenching around him, spasms riot through my muscles. I'm almost there, and he isn't even trying yet.

"Avery," he says, now a sharp bite in his hushed voice. "Say the words."

"I want you inside me."

He licks across my lips, his fingers pushing deeper. A startled sound escapes me as my legs begin to tremble.

"Avery…"

Ethan presses his thumb against my clitoris and my eyes snap shut, breath hitches in my throat. I've never experienced such subdued eroticism the way Ethan plays my body. Methodical and intoxicating. He's a long, slow burn. A consuming fire. I meet his mouth, hungry for him, then whisper against his lips.

"Make love to me."

Withdrawing his fingers, he pulls my panties free of my legs then reaches into his nightstand for a condom and slides it on.

Positioning himself on top of me, he pries my legs apart with his knee and aligns himself at my entrance. The wide head of his penis slides up and down my sex, teasing me to the point of frustration.

"Tell me," he says again, massaging my breasts in both hands.

I don't know what he's asking for this time. When I raise my hips to seek him, he pins me down. Just a fraction, a torturous inch, he enters me. I arch my back, anticipating and needy.

"Avery, I'm not fucking around with you." All seduction leaves his voice. There's only flat honesty. "I don't make it a habit to mess around with the women I work with, and I didn't bring you into my home for easy access. The last time I introduced a girl to my parents was in high school. So please, for fuck's sake, stop hedging your bets and just give me three words."

He rips my heart right out of my chest. I've never met a man who's needed to be loved as much as Ethan craves it. And I wonder if he's ever truly been loved at all. Reaching up, I drag my fingers down the side of his face and swipe my thumb under his bottom lip.

"I love you." More than I thought I could. More than I've ever wanted to love anyone. "Maybe too much."

His lips crash to mine as his entire body covers me and his hips flex, pushing inside in one long, wonderful, agonizing penetration.

"We're going to be very good for each other," he whispers. "I promise you."

Together in the darkness, he bares himself to me. All his

adoration and kindness—his body speaking to mine. What it can be when you find someone you trust, who trusts you. When you've broken down the barriers and find the honesty in each other.

Maybe, even when you make every wrong decision, sometimes you still end up in exactly the right place.

# 20

# THE SPY

Over the next three days, while Ethan and I play house for the weekend, we barely make it out of bed, and then only so far as the couch. We watch old movies, Ethan chastising me for not having caught up on an eternity of popular culture.

"*The Sandlot*? You never seen *The Sandlot*? Have you been living under a rock?"

"For the first twelve years, yes."

"You're killing me, Smalls!"

"See, that means nothing to me."

And when TV gets boring, we play cards and board games. As it turns out, Ethan is a terrible loser.

"What was that?" he says, pointing at my leg as we play Scrabble in bed.

"What?"

"That." He jabs at the air. "What you just did."

"Uh, scratching an itch."

I rearrange my tiles on my shelf then lay out *zeaxanthin*

across two of Ethan's words to land on a triple word score.

"Fuck off," he says, swiping his hand through the air. "That's not a word."

"Is so."

"Then what is it?"

"Something in our retinas. I don't remember exactly, but it's a real thing."

"Bullshit."

"Fine, look it up."

"Uh-huh." He shakes his head, indignant. "Pull up your pant leg."

"No. Why?"

"Just do it. If you've nothing to hide, you have nothing to fear."

"McCarthy said the same thing."

His eyes grow wide, mouth dropping open. "You filthy little cheater."

A gasp fills my lungs. "How dare you. I would never sully the sacred game of Scrabble by resorting to nefarious—"

Ethan lunges across the bed, crushing the board and sending little wooden tiles scattering across the floor. He tackles me backward before I can jump out of the way, holding me down with all his weight. I try to squirm, break free, but he's too heavy and too strong on top of me. His hand reaches for my ankle and yanks down my sock. Three tiles fall out.

"You're a goddamn thief," he says, smiling with a sort of awe in his eyes. "I don't even know who you are anymore."

"Whatever." I blow hair out of my face. "Cheating is just a strategy if you don't get caught."

But by Monday our playhouse is interrupted by responsibility and we must rejoin the rest of the working stiffs. Leaving Ethan's place, we see the black sedan with government plates parked at the end of the block. It's a stark reminder that despite our best attempts to ignore it, the real world was waiting just outside the door. A fact that hasn't escaped Ethan as he keeps his arm around my shoulder, eyes roving and head on a swivel. I try not to think about it, instead choosing to believe that the threats are nothing more than talk, and that Carter has it under control. Anything else would drive me mad.

"We'll have the investigation and the trial to cover," Ethan says as we cut through Louise Nevelson Plaza a block from the office. "But you should give some thought to the next story you want to pitch for a feature. After all the work you put in on the standoff piece, I know Ed will listen."

"I think I have a topic in mind, actually. I watched this documentary last month about—"

My phone vibrates in my pocket.

"It's Kumi," I say, staring at her name flashing across the screen. We haven't spoken all weekend. A knot twists in my gut. "It could be—"

"Answer it."

We stop at a bench in the busy plaza while I take the call.

"Hello?"

"Avery, hi," she says. "How are you?"

There's a reluctant tremble in her voice. This isn't a call she wants to make.

"I'm good. Everything okay?"

"Um...well..."

"What? What is it?"

She inhales, then it all comes rushing out in one hurried breath. "I didn't mean for him to find out but my uncle told my dad and my dad freaked out and now he's talking about getting a new apartment, and I told him there was no way, it's not fair, but…"

In the back of my mind, I knew this was coming. Her father's never met me. I'm no one to him. If I were in his position, I wouldn't want me around his daughter, either.

"He wants me to move out," I say.

"I told him he was being unreasonable. It's not like you can control what people do."

"But it's me or the apartment, right?"

She sighs, both out of regret and relief, I suspect. "Right. Really, Avery, I don't want you to go. I'll tell him to stick it up his ass and we'll find somewhere else. I don't need—"

"No, don't do that." I appreciate that Kumi's willing to blow up a good thing to stay loyal, but I'm not letting her forsake a free apartment just to accommodate me. "He's just doing what he thinks is best to protect you. Can't blame him for that. I don't want you fighting with him again because of me."

"Avery, I'm so sorry. I really did try, but he's being a stubborn ass about it. He told my mom, and now she's losing her mind…"

"It's okay. I'll give you a call later. We'll figure it out."

Once I've ended the call, Ethan wraps his arms around me, hugging me to his chest.

"She's kicking you out?" he says.

"No, her father. He pays for the apartment. Kumi feels awful about it, but there isn't much she can do. Without her father's help, there's no way she can afford to live in the city and go to law school. I can't ruin that for her."

"Hey," he says, holding my shoulders. "You know what? Fuck him. This is a good thing. You'll move in with me. Maybe a little sooner than planned, but what the hell, right?"

"That's different, though. It's one thing to play sleepover for a few nights, but do you really want—"

"Yes." He brushes his fingers against my cheek and tucks my hair behind my ear. "Absolutely. Unequivocally. Wholeheartedly, yes. That's exactly what I want."

A wide, almost painful smile spreads across my lips as I stare into his bright, emphatic eyes. I love this man. So much it hurts.

"Okay," I tell him. "But you've lost your adverb privileges."

Ethan winks and kisses my forehead.

"Deal."

For better or worse, this is happening. All that's left to do is hang on tight and hope I don't get thrown from the ride.

When we get to the office and step off the elevator on our floor, it's obvious right away that something is amiss. It's too quiet. No talking, no one shouting at each other across the Farm. The TVs on the wall are on Mute, and not even the keyboards are clicking. If it weren't for the few heads poking up from their cubicles, I'd think the place was empty.

"Uh…is it your birthday?" I ask Ethan, imagining a sudden eruption when two-dozen people jump out to scream *Surprise!* and toss a pie in his face.

"No." He scans the room, sensing the same unsettling atmosphere. "Yours?"

"Nope."

"All right."

We go to our desks and put our stuff down. At that point I see half the editorial staff crowded around Ed's office with their ears pressed to the wall.

"So that's odd."

Ethan turns to question me and I nod toward the scene.

"It is."

Wheels spin behind his eyes as he again glances around the room. We see Navid pop up from his cubicle and, spotting us, come rushing over.

"What's happening?" Ethan asks him, eyes glued to Ed's office door.

"Hey, guys." Navid leans in, sort of crouching down like he's expecting enemy fire. "Have a good weekend?"

"Yeah, great, splendid," I say. "What's going on in Ed's office?"

"Ah, yes." He looks over his shoulder then lowers his voice. "Well, this weekend I did a little looking around. What with the death threats and whatnot." He offers a sympathetic smile, but I'd prefer he get on with it. "So, yeah, I was able to track down the thread where your address was posted. Actually, it wasn't that hard to trace the username back to a few other sites where he used the same one, then find an email associated with one of them. Yelp, if you can believe it. Like, bro, if you're going to secret message boards to circlejerk with the other meninist fuckboys, at least get a dummy email account."

"Christ, Navid." Ethan drags his hands through his hair. "What the fuck are you getting at?"

"Oh, yeah. I figured out who doxxed Avery. Dumb-ass used his work email to create his profile."

So I was right. It was one of them.

"Who?" A switch flips in Ethan. Something rabid and vicious. "Who's in there?"

"Well, I told Ed first and he called the FBI guys who were here on—"

Ethan tears away, stalking down the row of cubicles. Heads pop up like prairie dogs from their burrows to watch him. When I realize what's about to happen, I chase after him. The staff crowded around the door scatter as Ethan throws it open, slamming it off the wall.

"You motherfucker!"

He charges at Cyle sitting in front of Ed's desk. The guy barely has enough time to turn his head before Ethan grabs the back of his shirt and snaps him backward, yanking him to the floor and out of his overturned chair. I lunge toward him, certain Ethan is about to break Cyle's face, but Carter gets there first. Like you only see in movies, he reacts in a blink to jerk Ethan's arm behind his back then restrain him in a choke. Cyle's left startled and shaking on the ground. Then his eyes meet mine. It takes all my restraint not to spit on him and kick him in the nuts.

"You're a spineless little shit!" Ethan continues to shout as Carter pulls him out of the office. "Fuck you, worthless bastard!"

I follow them all the way to the stairwell, where Carter shoves Ethan through the door and up against the cement wall.

"Enough," Carter shouts. His voice cracks off the walls, echoing in the narrow chamber. "Get yourself under control."

"Why isn't he under arrest?" Ethan pushes off the wall, fire in his eyes. For a moment I think he might take a swing at Carter. "That dickless fuck—"

"Calm the fuck down." Carter gets in Ethan's face, nose to nose. "You want to get slapped with an assault charge over him? Get your shit together."

That seems to get through to him as Ethan takes a breath and backs up against the wall, scrubbing his hands through his hair.

"Carter?" I say. Both men look at me like they'd forgotten I'm here. "Can you fill me in?"

He casts one last cautionary look at Ethan, then adjusts his stance, sliding on the professional persona.

"Your editor called me this morning to let me know they'd identified a member of the staff as having leaked your home address. Specifically, they discovered he improperly accessed the human resources database of employee records. I only arrived a few minutes before you." He cuts a glare at Ethan. "And was in the process of confronting the individual with the information. He's admitted to his actions."

"What does that mean now?"

"He can be charged under New York State law as well as the Computer Fraud and Abuse Act. So yes," he says to Ethan, "he will be arrested."

Carter straightens his tie, then adjusts his gun holster inside his jacket. Everything back in place, uniform and precise, he tells Ethan, "Stay here until I have him out of the building. If you're incredibly lucky, he won't press charges."

"Hurry," he says.

Carter leaves us as Ethan and I take a seat at the top of the stairs to wait. His hands shake, full of unextinguished rage. I know the feeling.

"Don't tell Carter I said this…" I reach up and run my fingers through Ethan's hair, which gets him to exhale and close his eyes. "Because you're a very bad boy and must sit in time-out…"

He peeks up, a smirk tugging at his lips.

"But that was kind of hot how you ran in there to vanquish my dragon."

Grabbing my knee and squeezing, Ethan groans and drops his head. "Don't do that to me."

"What?"

His hand slides up my thigh.

"You know what."

"I don't know what you're talking about."

He lifts his head, eyes narrowed and mean. "So help me, Avery, I would put you up against that wall right now."

"Promises, promises."

"Christ, woman." Ethan sprawls backward to lie on the ground, arms out wide. "You're going to make my dick fall off."

"Eh." I shrug and pat his leg. "You'll live. It's not even my favorite part of you."

"I hate you so much right now."

"Love you, too."

Together we wait in the stairwell for about twenty minutes to allow Carter plenty of time to get Cyle out and prevent Ethan from deciding jail is worth breaking his nose. If Ed or Cara have anything to say about Ethan's violent outburst, they're saving it for later, as no one looks at us when we walk back to our desks. But when we approach, I realize there's a woman sitting in my chair. She has short, pixie-cut, pink hair, the kind that could signal a ship at night, and a narrow face that comes to a sharp point at her chin. It's her eyes that bother me most, though. Big, alien gray crystals in her head. Anime eyes on cartoon schoolgirls. I don't know how, but I know who she is before she ever opens her mouth.

"What the hell are you doing here?" Ethan stops dead in the aisle, as if he's afraid to get closer.

"Hello, Ethan. Did you miss me?"

"No. Why are you here?"

She smiles, coy in the way only a woman can be when she's luring a man over the trapdoor beneath his feet.

"I've been following the news. Looks like you could use my help."

"Why would you think that?"

"Because I've spent the last ten months living on Phelps's farm, and I know where all the bodies are buried."

# 21

# THE FOURTH ESTATE

Forty-five minutes ago Ethan pulled Vivian into the conference room while I've been left to stew at my desk. I don't much care for the feeling crawling around in my gut, slithering up into my head and building its nest. In my experience, no one ever comes strolling back into your life with good intentions. There's always a scheme, some complex machination to take what they've come for and leave you naked and stranded in the middle of the desert. She's got con artist written all over her.

Right about the time I'm ready to pull an Ethan and go barging in there, Cara comes strutting toward me. I don't even try to look busy.

"Cyle's been fired," she says, short and to the point. I like that about her. "I'm cleaning out his desk and will have his belongings mailed to him."

"Thank you. I figured as much."

Relaxing her posture, Cara pulls the chair from Ethan's desk to sit in front of my cubicle.

"I want to apologize to you," she says. Crossing her legs, iPad on her lap, she leans toward me.

For the first time since we've met, I see the other side of Cara. The person she is with friends or at home with her family. When she visits her parents and spends the night in her childhood bed. Despite the persona she puts on at work, there's warmth behind her chilling blue eyes. She's not just the robot or the ballbuster; she's human.

"What he did was inexcusable. I take full responsibility for allowing this to happen on my watch."

"I don't blame you. Cyle's a petty asshole. I blame him."

"All the same, I want you to know that I've spoken to HR about developing better security practices to prevent something like this from happening again. And Ed and I both want to make clear that any retaliatory behavior among the staff will not be tolerated. You have our word."

"Thank you, but I'm not concerned. Far as I've seen, he was the bad apple. Otherwise, I'm really happy here."

I think I get her now. She's not so dissimilar from Ethan, in a way. Both carrying a heavy load of armor accumulated over the years. Blonde, beautiful, no one ever wanted to take her seriously. They weren't interested in her mind or what she had to say, only how she looked in a dress. So through her life she battled men like Cyle. Men who would put her down, minimize her talents, because they feared a strong, intelligent, fierce woman and the ways she could surpass them as she changed the world. Now she has the power and the respect she's spent so long clawing to acquire, but it isn't enough to break through the glass ceiling—she'll spend the rest of her life trying not to get pushed down the hole she climbed out of.

"You've done excellent work for us," she says. "I have every confidence you'll continue to do so. Which is why Ed and I want you to know that the magazine stands behind you. This place is a family, and you're part of it."

She wakes up her iPad and hands it to me. On screen is the front page of the *Riot Street* website. But under the main title and navigation bar, the other sections are missing. In their place, a full-page article fills the screen. Rather, it's a letter.

*On behalf of Riot Street magazine, its staff and ownership, we condemn the deplorable attacks committed against our reporter. Avery Avalon is a valued member of our team and a talented journalist devoted to our profession, upholding its standards in the highest regard. We stand against all those who would use violence, and the threat of violence, to intimidate or silence a member of the free press. An attack on one reporter is an attack on the very institution of journalism, and we invite our colleagues to join us in denouncing those who would seek to tear down the foundation that stands at the core of our free society. The Fourth Estate is not only a result of a stable and functioning democracy, it is necessary to its very survival. We at Riot Street do not cave to intimidation. We will not surrender to violence. We stand in solidarity with Ms. Avalon, proud to call her one of our own.*

*—Riot Street Staff*

Below the signature, every member of the magazine is listed by name. By the time I've read them all, my eyes are stinging and my breath is caught behind the stone lodged in my throat. Never have I received such a sincere outpouring of support. I spent most of my life getting kicked in the stomach, chased out, and ridiculed. Always bracing for the next door to slam in my face. Never feeling as though I fit in. I wish I knew how to tell them. How to express how much this means to me and my deep sense of gratitude. But anything I could say seems somehow insufficient.

"Cara, thank you. I—thank you so much."

She smiles, a knowing glint in her eyes. Maybe she and I aren't so different, either.

"It was Ethan's idea. He organized it with Ed."

Of course he did. Ethan would move planets if he thought it would make me smile.

"I'm glad you're with us, Avery."

I hand back her iPad as she stands and pushes Ethan's chair back to his desk.

"You're doing fine. Just keep it up."

Not long after she leaves, Ethan returns. He comes to lean against the wall of my cubicle, concern etched across his face.

"What's wrong?" he says, brow furrowed. "You look like you've been crying."

"No. Nothing's wrong." I reach for his hand, too in need of his touch to care about the rules. "I read the letter."

A sweet, beautiful smile pulls at his lips. He squeezes my hand.

"It was the least we could do. For you, I'd burn buildings

if you asked me to. But that letter would get printed for any person in this building. They wanted to do it. I didn't have to push."

"Just the same, thank you."

He pulls out his chair and slides into my cubicle. A shift takes place as I watch him take off the boyfriend hat and slip back into work mode.

"Vivian," I say, anticipating the segue.

"She's in talking to Ed. I told her she had to go explain herself to him. All he got was an email when she didn't come back from Montana and not a word since. She owes him something."

"So what's the deal? Is she back?"

I'll knife-fight her for this desk if she has any bright ideas about reclaiming it.

"No. I told her in no uncertain terms she isn't welcome here."

I'm not sure that decision is up to him, though I'm glad to know we're on the same page.

"Then what does she really want?"

"Vee says she can help us prove that Robert Phelps has been taking money off the books from politicians and corporations who are funding his movement and even encouraging actions like the standoff at the Fed and in Montana to advance their political agenda."

"But how so? How is anyone benefiting from Phelps? Doesn't it hurt their cause every time one of these guys goes too far and gets arrested?"

"Not anymore. Research I've seen says for every Montana

or Fed incident the number of people flocking to groups like Phelps's jumps. The more headlines they grab, the more guys like Phelps play the martyr and claim they're political prisoners of an overreaching government, the more those on the far right run into fringe territory. A shift is happening, and it's being bought and paid for by rich men hiding behind farmers and cattle ranchers. Ultimately, these corporations are after deregulation or access to public lands to drive an oil pipeline through it. Shrinking the federal government is the first step to privatizing it, which means more power and higher profits for corporations ready to benefit."

Just when my faith in humanity spikes, there's something waiting to smack it down again. There are some days, and lately more often than not, I think humanity is a failed experiment. Time to surrender the planet to the cats and whales and fuck off.

"So we're going to chase the story," I say.

"Yes. If Vee's right, Walter Kreight might be indicative of a much larger problem."

"And Vivian's going to help."

Ethan inhales, looking away. He scratches his hand through his hair, face drawn and tired.

"She's a source. She'll help us research, tell us what she knows and where to look. But that's it. If she wanted the story for herself, she could have it. But I told her, if she wants me to follow up on it, she does it our way."

Wonderful. This'll be super fun.

\* \* \*

That afternoon the three of us meet with Ed to pitch the story and get his approval to move forward. He sets a tentative deadline for three months from now, pinning the article as the cover feature if we can get our ducks in a row by then. Everything we bring in must be vetted by the magazine's lawyers, and we won't be able to attribute any evidence or background to Vivian, since the veracity of anything she gathered can be challenged on the grounds that she misrepresented herself when she joined Phelps. So that means tracking down new sources willing to go on the record. But Ethan's right, it's the kind of story you build a career on. If we nail it, I'll never have to write another essay as long as I live.

After we leave Ed's office, we assemble our war room in one of the smaller offices that has lately been used for storing old issues of the magazine. It's cramped, windowless, and doesn't have an air duct, so it's fifteen degrees warmer than the rest of the building, but it affords us space to work where we can keep our research contained.

Of course, Vivian's here. Sitting on the corner of the rectangular table, kicking her legs, generally being a spectacular annoyance. Any woman over the age of thirteen who dangles their legs, kicking air, does a disservice to the entire institution of feminism.

"How 'bout lunch?" she says, like she just invented the concept.

Ethan slides me a glance, waiting for my reaction before offering an answer. He may continue to live.

"Come on. A peace offering. My treat. For both of you." She tilts her head, a tight-lipped smile aimed at me. "We can catch up and you can ask me all your burning questions about Robert."

If a ceiling tile fell on her head right now, I'd devote my life to whichever deity claimed credit.

"Sure," I say, when the roof doesn't cave in. Because I'm a great big person with great big patience and *so much* tolerance for this obnoxious little sprite. "Sounds like fun."

First Vivian tries to take us to a barbecue place, but Ethan informs her I don't eat meat. Then we wind up at a bar, by which time I don't have the energy or inclination to argue. If I'm going to win this war of attrition, I can't get myself painted as the difficult one on the first day. So we take a seat at a booth and stare at the meager menus while Vivian orders a pitcher of beer for the table and I assure Ethan with a look that I'm not going to have a meltdown. He does earn points for seeing and subsequently showing sympathy for how willing I am to cooperate.

"I went by your place earlier," she says. "Saw the mural's still there."

While I pick at the brown-leaf salad in front of me, Vivian finishes her second beer. I don't know if it's the stress of seeing her again or an unconscious attempt to keep up, but Ethan's halfway through his second as well.

"Uh-huh." He stares past her toward the door or at his hamburger, anywhere but her face.

"I half-expected you to paint over it by now."

"Seemed like a lot of effort."

A renewed pang of territorial jealousy flares through my chest. "You painted it?"

Vivian flashes a self-satisfied smile. "Mm-hmm. A house-warming present when Ethan bought the place." Then she shoots a pointed look at him. "I knew it'd grow on you."

"I hardly notice it anymore."

Ethan gets a gold star for throwing out the stop sticks in all directions.

"So," she says, hot-pink eyebrow raised, "are you two an item?"

Ethan's hand slides to my knee under the table. "Avery's my girlfriend. We live together."

I could maul him to the floor right now. Rip off his clothes and do very good things to him.

"That was quick, huh? You only started at the magazine, like, a couple of weeks ago, right?"

It's been a rather strange couple of weeks. Though, if she thinks pointing out that she's done her research on me will put me at a disadvantage, she's sorely mistaken.

"But then, Ethan, you must feel like you've known her for years. Strange how that worked out."

Nothing in that sounded like it warrants a response, so neither of us produces one. Ethan swigs his beer.

"So there must be quite a story in how you snuck out of Montana and wound up at Phelps's farm," I say, shifting the focus.

Ethan squeezes my knee under the table. Though I'm not sure if that's a *Back off* squeeze or a *You're so damn adorable I could fuck you on this table* gesture. We're still working out the subtleties of under-the-table language.

Vivian clears her throat and pours herself a third glass of

beer. "I always say, work with what you're given. Our last night in Montana I wandered into a bar and got to talking with some of the guys who had come out in support of the men who were occupying the bison range. I was playing the part. You know, one of them. They hinted that the 'real movement' was in New Hampshire. That there was a guy there who was talking about taking real action. So I convinced these guys to take me with them. Figured there'd be a story in it sooner or later."

I don't care how Lois Lane you are, taking off in the middle of the night, halfway across the country, with strange men who admit they're total crackpots bent on overthrowing the government, is straight-up nuts. Going undercover for a story is one thing; what Vivian did was reckless.

"But you didn't tell anyone you where you were going."

"That'd sort of spoil the surprise, wouldn't it?"

She says it like I'm daft for suggesting otherwise. As if her actions are so obvious as to not require explanation. I'm starting to see why Vivian wasn't so popular on the staff.

"And it worked." She winks at Ethan, who remains steadfast in his devotion to silence. "Didn't it?"

"Then why not write the story yourself and take the credit?" I ask. "You'd have no problem selling a freelance piece anywhere you wanted."

"True," she says with an affected sigh. "But I don't have the resources to do the necessary research on my own. Plus, there is the issue of culpability."

"Meaning what, exactly?"

"Well, not everything I did down there was strictly within the bounds of the law. I put my name on this, I open myself up to retaliation. But you two don't have that problem." Her eyes land on me like we share a secret. "You've got nothing left to hide."

This time when Ethan squeezes my knee, there's nothing lost in translation. It says, *Settle, tiger.* At this point, he's just trying to keep me in my seat.

* * *

After spending a day locked in a small, confined space with Vivian, Ethan doing his best to pretend he's somewhere else, I was about ready to chew off my own arm if it'd get me away from her. Sure, there's the lingering jealousy of how Ethan first described her. Larger than life and too big to contain. How she swooped in and altered his life, changing him on a fundamental level. A neon-bright ball of space dust. The manic pixie nightmare. But I've never met a woman in real life who actually is that person. Beneath the hair dye and knee-high combat boots, there's either an unloved child or a career sociopath. Sometimes both. Though what I hate about her, I think, is that she reminds me of Jenny. She reminds me of the person I was and who I might have become. What I hate about her, then, is everything I hate about myself.

It's a hard pill to swallow, and I hate her more for sticking it on my tongue.

Rinsing dishes in the sink after dinner at his place, Ethan watches me. He's been doing it most of the day, now into evening. I get it. He's waiting for something to happen. I'm the firecracker whose fuse fizzled out and is waiting to go off as soon as someone picks it up. He's afraid to dip his toe in the pool because there is definitely a shark prowling the deep end.

"Tell me I have nothing to worry about," I say, handing him plates to load in the dishwasher. "Just tell me that, and I'll believe you."

"You have nothing to worry about." Then he watches me. "Why would you think you should worry?"

"Well, I got the impression you and Vivian were, you know, involved at one point."

Ethan grabs the plate out of my hand and drops it on the counter. "Who told you that?"

"It doesn't matter."

"It matters a hell of a lot to me." He takes me by my hips, pressing my back to the sink, his body powerful and flush against mine. "Listen to me. I never slept with her. I never dated her. I never had any interest in doing so. I'd have preferred she stayed gone, but that's not the case."

"Okay," I say, stunned by his sudden ferocity. The veins in his arms strain against the skin, his eyes electric. "I believe you. I'm sorry."

"I love you, Avery. I'm with you because I want to be, not because I couldn't be with someone else."

Now I feel like an asshole. Ethan didn't do anything wrong, and it's out of line for me to accuse him before the fact of something he might do in one of my paranoid delusions. I guess the idea of losing him, of having him snatched away, makes me a little crazy.

Sliding my hands up his chest, combing through his hair, I

try to find comfort in touching him, knowing, tangibly, he's here.

"I'm sorry. I won't bring it up again."

His eyes soften, head lowering to press against mine. Ethan's hands move up my hips to stroke up my ribs with thumbs grazing my breasts.

"I want you to bring it up. Whatever bothers you, say it. I'd rather you tell me than keep it bottled up. There's nothing I can do about it if I don't know what you're thinking."

Licking my lips, I drag my hands down his chest, his stomach, feeling his abs clench under my touch.

"Can you guess what I'm thinking now?"

He brings his lips to mine and pulls me from the counter. "You're insatiable."

## 22

# THE ENEMY

Over the next several weeks, Ethan and I wade through miles of sewage pipe. The truth is, most of the time, investigative journalism is nothing like the sexy, death-defying heroism you see in the movies. It's gathering and sifting through mountains of paper, scouring hundreds, thousands, of innocuous pages for that one relevant item. It's spending days with a phone glued to your ear, and getting hung up on. Reading transcripts and data charts until your eyes bleed. Getting jerked around by people who must take pleasure in being difficult. Hitting dead ends at every turn until you can't remember anymore where you are or how you got here. And it's coffee—obscene amounts of coffee to stimulate just enough of your brain to form words and sometimes cogent thought.

Six weeks, and we do it all with Vivian watching over our shoulders.

Mostly, I've learned to tolerate her. Now that the initial irritation with her existence has worn off, she isn't such a distraction in the office. I've even come to see why she had a job here to begin with. She does know what she's doing, and it's incredible the amount of information she was able to collect and piece together while under the constant threat of being discovered as a spy.

If there is one positive to Vivian's sudden reappearance, it's that working on this story seems to have kept Ethan's mind off his mother's illness. They talk on the phone a few times a week, which always leaves him in a dark temper, but once his mind refocuses on work, the tension leaves his shoulders and the darkness recedes. Until today.

His mother has invited us over for dinner at their house, meaning Ethan's been in a shit mood since he woke up this morning. I understand the contradiction clashing inside him; Ethan loves his mother, but he's angry that once again he's faced with losing her after he thought they'd escaped. Seeing her only reminds him that he has one less day than he did yesterday, and seeing his father means staring into the face of the man Ethan blames for killing her. Because he knows, no matter how much he grasps for optimism, that his mother isn't getting any better.

We pull up to a townhouse on East Sixty-Second Street just before seven. Actually, his parents' house is two adjoining townhomes between Fifth and Madison Avenues, five stories high with a terrace on the roof. Bigger than my entire apartment building. Staring out the window of Ethan's truck, raking my eyes up the elegant stone façade and two-dozen shiny windows, it's a bit intimidating. I'm almost afraid to ask how many properties his family owns.

"Is this where you grew up?"

"Somewhat." Ethan's voice is rueful. A distant, detached melancholy has settled over him. "Evan and I went to private school in the city until I reached ninth grade. They sent me to boarding school at Exeter after that. To separate us."

He doesn't talk about his brother often, but when he does, I understand better why he carries so much resentment. Though Evan was the troublemaker, the instigator, it was Ethan who was banished from his home and family most of the year. The seclusion he must have felt, that's something I can identify with. And I suppose it explains the wide berth Ethan enforces around himself. In the months we've known each other, Carter is the only real friend of his I've met outside the office. I don't think Ethan has many at all. Yet another reason we seem to understand each other.

"Thank you for doing this," Ethan says, wrapping his hand over mine as I turn to face him. "I promise, we'll make it quick. Dinner, skip coffee, and we're out."

He's dressed for the occasion: charcoal sports coat over a crisp bone button-down, black pants, and shoes to match. Despite his apparent reluctance to be here, Ethan puts forth an effort. He takes dinner with the parents seriously. I, however, feel rather inadequate in the silk blouse and pencil skirt I bought when I was interviewing for internships during my senior year of college. Like I'm a kid wearing her mom's clothes. Dressing up just doesn't suit me.

"Try not to fight with your dad, okay?"

Ethan's jaw tightens in response.

"I know," I say, "but for your mother's sake, behave."

Relaxing his expression, Ethan skims his fingertips across my temple to tuck my hair behind my ear. He cups the side of my face to run the pad of his thumb under the ridge of my bottom lip. Every time he does that, those modest little gestures, I feel his affection. The deep, pure endearment of the gentle act. And I love him even more.

"No wandering off this time," he says with a teasing grin.

We get out of the truck and go to the door to ring the bell. A moment later his father answers. Paul's gray-blue eyes cut straight to us as a tight frown creases the corners of his mouth. Stepping back, he invites us inside. We make it only a few steps into the foyer.

"Avery, it is a pleasure to see you again. I wasn't aware you would be joining us."

Paul tucks his hands into the pockets of his navy pants. The impassive, solitary posture is one I recognize. A hereditary trait passed on to his son.

"I invited her." Holding my hand, Ethan squeezes. Almost painfully tight.

"And of course you're always welcome," Paul says to me with a sort of polite enmity. His focus then rises to Ethan. "Though tonight isn't the best time. Your mother asked you here because there are family matters to discuss."

Ethan tucks my arm under his, possessive and protective. "She is my family."

"Avery, sweetheart." Linda appears at the opposite end of the foyer. She's a petite woman dressed simply in a cotton blouse and loose ankle pants that were probably tighter on her a few months ago. The scarf is absent today, revealing her pale, bald scalp. Still, she's a beautiful woman. "What a lovely surprise. I'm so happy you're here."

She comes to offer me a hug, her embrace genuine and welcoming. Despite her bright energy, I sense the weakness in her muscles as she pulls away. Her eyes have dimmed since we first met.

"Don't you look nice," she says, holding my hands out to appraise me. "Ethan, you two didn't have to get dressed up. It's just a casual dinner at home."

"Hi, Mom." He smiles indulgently and kisses her cheek. "How are you feeling?"

"Oh, fine, fine." Linda cuts a subtle glare at her husband. I suspect it refers to a similar warning that Paul not allow this evening to descend into another argument. "Come in, get settled. Dinner's almost ready."

As she escorts us, I'm overwhelmed at the size and rich elegance of their home. Everything decorated in warm cream and other neutrals. Marble floors and high ceilings. This must have required a massive renovation to convert the original structures, knocking out walls to create an open floorplan.

"Mom," Ethan says as we pass the kitchen toward the living room, "you're not cooking, are you? That's too much work by yourself."

"Nonsense." She drifts away, gesturing for us to make ourselves comfortable. "I'm plenty capable of operating an oven."

Paul wanders off somewhere, and Ethan and I stand awkwardly in the center of the room. Edgy and radiating tension, he behaves almost as if he'd never been here before. The way you feel trapped in place when entering a stranger's home, afraid to touch anything or drift too far from the spot where they left you. Already he's thinking of making a quick exit.

"Maybe I should go," I say, concerned that I've overstepped a boundary of privacy. Being the party crasher is becoming a tired recurrence. "I don't want to intrude."

"No." He trails his fingers down my arms, eliciting a slight shiver that travels to my toes. "I want you here. I meant what I said, Avery. You're my family; he needs to get used to the idea."

Something desperate in the quiet force of his voice pleads with me, the emphatic honesty behind his eyes. He didn't bring me here to soften the edges or rub his rebellion in his father's face—I'm a crutch. Ethan perhaps wouldn't have made it past the door if I hadn't been there to prop him up. For as strong a performance as he's put on over the past weeks, inside he's coming apart.

By the time we're all seated in the formal dining room, Ethan's retreated behind two glasses of scotch and half a glass of red wine. Beside me, he exudes a quiet hostility growing more pervasive as the meal wears on. That Paul does most of the talking doesn't help matters.

"Seems you've created quite a stir," he says, cutting into his chicken breast. "My office has been fielding calls for the last month. People anxious to move assets."

"Get ready for the subpoenas." Ethan swallows another urgent mouthful of wine.

"I think you're overestimating the fallout." Paul composes himself in that mannered way moneyed people do. A delicate grip on his utensils, back straight and chin high. He's a man who comes from wealth and has never known anything else.

"There's considerable gray territory between strategic self-interest and fraud."

"You would know," is Ethan's curt response.

I keep my head down, attempting to blend into my chair as I diligently cut sautéed vegetables into manageable bites. There's no part of this conversation that requires my input. Not when Ethan and his father are pissing at each other from either side of a fence. This must be a pastime of theirs. An example of everything that separates them. Ethan on a mission to topple the pillars of power constructed by men like his father; Paul concerned with building them taller.

"Let's not talk business at the table," Linda gently chides them.

I can't imagine what life was like when she had three of them to wrangle.

"Avery." Topping off my glass of water, Paul fixes his attention on me. Much like his son, he has a way of pinning a person with his eyes. "I understand you had something of a scare recently. Must be quite troubling for a young woman who—"

Ethan drops his silverware on his plate, a stinging noise piercing the room. "Don't do that. Don't condescend to her."

"Ethan." I slide my hand to his leg. "It's fine. He didn't mean—"

"No, he did mean." Glaring at his father, his shoulders tense. "This is what he does."

"Son, your father wasn't implying anything," Linda says with soft reassurance. "We were both simply concerned to hear Avery had experienced some unwanted attention."

No arrest was ever made in regard to the note on my door, but after a couple of weeks the outrage wore off and the messages stopped flooding my work email and the magazine's comment sections. I suppose it's a badge of honor now. A rite of passage.

"Death threats," Ethan bites out through clenched teeth. "People threatening to kill her."

"Really"—plastering on something like a smile, I squeeze Ethan's leg to insist he shut the hell up—"it wasn't anything serious. People with too much time on their hands."

"There, see?" Paul picks up his glass of wine and gestures toward me. "Avery can manage some perspective. Comes with the territory, right?"

A snide remark or perhaps a full-scale tirade is on the tip of Ethan's tongue, but his mother speaks before he can make the decision to utter it. She steers the conversation to more polite territory, asking how I'm enjoying living in the city and what sights I've yet to explore. We talk about museums and architecture while Ethan and his father engage in wordless combat beside us. But as the evening winds down and we finish our meals, I watch a resigned shadow cast itself over Linda's face. She's less engaged, only half-listening, and her attention seems to drift elsewhere.

"What's the latest from the doctors?" Ethan asks when his father mentions that he and Linda are considering a vacation next month. "How's the chemo going?"

Silence, as Paul stares at his wife.

"What? What's wrong?"

"Perhaps this conversation is best left to another time," Paul says, clearing his throat. He wipes a cloth napkin over his mouth.

That is a not-so-subtle reference to my unexpected presence.

Ethan stiffens beside me. "Someone fucking tell me what's going on."

"Well…" Linda pushes her plate away. It's evident in the downward curve of her mouth, the slope of her eyes, that exhaustion is setting in. "I'm no longer receiving chemo treatments."

"Meaning what?"

Oh, no. I hear the tires screeching in the distance. Swerving headlights cutting quickly and erratically through the darkness. The moment you tense right before the horror of impact. My hand goes to Ethan's resting on the table. He doesn't look at me, but tightens his fingers around mine more out of reflex.

"Just that," Linda says from behind a sturdy wall of armor. "I've decided to stop seeking treatment. The cancer has spread to a point where remission is no longer a probable outcome. At this stage, the responsible course of action is pain management rather than aggressive treatment."

"You can't be serious." He's trembling in my hand. Ethan's entire body is nearly vibrating beside me. "You're giving up?"

"I'm afraid it isn't much of a choice. The prognosis—"

"Fuck the prognosis!" he shouts. "Fight it. There are alternatives. You can't—"

"Ethan, stop it." Paul raises his voice. Contained fury lashes out across the table. "This isn't a matter open for debate. Your mother has made a decision in consultation with her doctors, and we will support her choice. That's it."

"Jesus Christ, Dad. Did you even try? Or are you in such a hurry to absolve yourself of the guilt."

"Ethan—"

"That's enough—"

"No, forget it." Ethan pushes back from the table and stands, grabbing my hand to pull me to my feet. "I clearly didn't need to be here for this. We're leaving."

"Hey, hey." I implore Ethan to stop as he drags me toward the foyer. At the door, I finally get him to pause long enough to focus his attention on me. "You can't storm out of here like this. She's your mother and she needs you to understand."

"What's to understand? She's giving up, and he apparently can't wait to get rid of her."

"You don't mean that. He's just trying to respect his wife's wishes and support her decision. That's what you do when you love someone."

"Goddammit, Avery." He recoils from me, pure rage sparking behind his eyes. "Would it kill you to take my side? Why are you always fighting me?"

"I'm not," I say, reaching for his hand. He yanks it away. Like he's disgusted. "I'm trying to keep you from running out on your family. They need you. Just go back in there and—"

"I can't deal with this shit. Any of you."

"Ethan—"

But he's gone. Out the door. Slamming it in my face. Leaving me behind as he drives away. I stand there, stunned for a moment, until Paul walks up beside me.

"Shall I call you a car?" he asks, completely unaffected by the explosive encounter.

Staring out the narrow window beside the door, I take a deep breath. My hand slides to where my pocket should be and where the shell casing isn't.

"No, I can find my own way home."

"I did try to warn you," he says. "Ethan has always had volatile tendencies."

I didn't doubt Paul's assertion the first time, but I was certain whatever might come, Ethan would let me bear it with him. That he'd trust me that much. Seems I made a gross miscalculation.

* * *

Ethan isn't home when I get back to the loft. I call and text him but get no response. It's after midnight when I shower and get in bed. I turn up the volume on my phone's ringer and leave it on Ethan's pillow beside me. Sometime later, a noise jerks me awake.

"Ethan?"

Rubbing my eyes, a bit disoriented, I see him standing in front of the open refrigerator. Bright white light casts him in a black silhouette.

"What time is it?"

He doesn't answer. The fridge door shuts and the space is black again. Cabinet doors clap shut. Glass clinks. I throw back the blankets and climb out of bed to tentatively make my way to the kitchen. The clock on the microwave reads 3:47 a.m.

"Ethan," I say, when my eyes adjust and I see him standing at the island. "Where have you been?"

"Out."

I hear a plastic cap unscrew then the solid *thunk* of a heavy glass bottle hitting the granite counter. When I find the stove, I flick on the range light. Ethan stands with a glass of dark liquor at his lips. His eyes are bloodshot, hair a dizzy mess. A thin sheen of sweat covers his face. He's discarded the jacket he was wearing earlier this evening, shirtsleeves rolled up to his elbows.

"Out where?"

"Christ, could you wait like five seconds before you pounce on me?"

He tosses back a heavy mouthful then pours himself another.

Standing on the opposite side of the island, I cross my arms over my stomach, relieved that he's home but disturbed by the state in which he's returned. I can't even begin to wonder how the hell he managed to drive home tonight, assuming he didn't ditch his truck somewhere. That's a fight for another time.

"I was worried about you. I tried calling."

"Shut off my phone."

He doesn't look at me, preoccupied with the glass in his hand. Again he takes a swig and pours.

"You left me there."

"Funny," he says, nose curled and brow furrowed. "The way I remember it, you left me."

"That's not fair."

"Nope, I didn't think so, either."

I hate this person. Whoever he is, I don't recognize him.

Curt and sarcastic, callous to the point of cruelty. It leaves a cold, empty space inside me that Ethan once filled.

"So that's it, then. I'm the enemy now."

"I'm not the one siding against you."

"Fine."

I shut off the light, unable to look at him any longer. There's a fire building in my gut, a sharp, shooting impulse threatening in the back of my head. If I stand here much longer, I'll say something I can't take back. As I come around the island, I brush past him and pause.

"You smell like the floor of a bar and cheap perfume," I tell him, catching a whiff of sweat, liquor, and something noxious. "Take a shower."

His hand captures mine as I turn away. In the darkness, I feel his stare boring into me. Tension travels through his arm and into mine. He's silent, still. I try to yank my hand away but he holds tight.

"Ethan…" I warn.

"Do I?" The bite is gone. No trace of his simmering temper. "Honestly."

"Yes." This time he lets go when I tug against his hold.

"I didn't do anything," he says, hushed and timid. "Avery, I swear."

"Fine. Whatever."

I go back to bed and do my best to ignore the big black hole on the other side of the room, but it's impossible not to notice him. I listen as he puts the bottle back in the cabinet and rinses the glass in the sink. I turn away from the light that briefly pierces the darkness as he goes into the bathroom and turns on the shower faucet. And I'm awake when he eventually slips into bed beside me, refreshed and smelling rich and clean. Like himself again. A scent that teases every nerve as I feel the warmth of his body inches from mine.

"Avery…" Searching and cautious, he wraps his arm across my stomach and presses himself flush to my back. "Hey, I wouldn't do that to you, okay? I'd never cheat on you."

I hate that I can't pull away from him. That his skin against mine is like a blade of sunlight slicing through the chill on a cloudy winter day. My body so attuned to his that it awakens with desire and anticipation when he holds me in his arms. That it doesn't matter if I'm mad at him, I still want him.

"You believe me, don't you?"

He's an asshole, but he's not a liar. Angry as I am, I can't find any part of me that believes the first thing he'd do after a night like this is go out and screw some random woman in a bar. Despite the rumors around the office, I've seen no evidence of that man.

"Yes," I tell him.

"I'd never betray you. Whatever else happens, I love you."

Fucking asshole.

"You can't just say you love me and make the rest of it go away." Clutching my pillow under my head, it's all I can do to keep from rolling over and smacking him in the head. "I was mortified back there. You turned on me so fast—"

"So you do know how I felt."

"Stop it." I throw his arm off me. "I wasn't the one being unreasonable. You can't call me a traitor every time I don't agree with you. Ethan, you were a spectacular jackass tonight. More so to your parents."

"It'd be nice," he says, speaking low and calm behind me, "if just once you didn't jump at the chance to agree with my father."

"Then I guess we're at an impasse, Ethan." Painful as it is—agonizing, in fact—I throw the blankets off me and sit up to get out of bed. "I'm done arguing with you."

"Wait." He shoots up beside me. "Where are you going?"

"Somewhere else."

"No." He grabs my face between both strong, firm hands. "Don't leave. Please."

"You've made up your mind that you can't trust me." I tear his hands from my face, steeling myself for what I'm about to suffer. "What's the point?"

I stand and go to the dresser for my clothes.

"You're not leaving," he says. More a demand than a question.

"I can't stay here." Not if he's unwilling to apologize or even acknowledge that ditching me at his parents' house, embarrassing all of us, was a shit thing to do.

"Don't." He crushes into me. Sudden and fierce. Arms wrapped around my chest and stomach, he cages me against his hard, powerful body. It's only then I realize he's naked, his skin feverish and heart slamming in his chest. "Don't go."

"I'm not going to do this, Ethan. I'm not going to be the girl who nags and argues."

"So don't be."

"But I can't let you take shots at me because you're pissed off at your dad or scared about your mom. I'm not going to play the easy target and just shut up and take it."

"I'm sorry," he breathes against my ear. A gust of air escapes his lungs. "Fuck, baby, I'm sorry. Please don't hate me."

"That's the problem. I don't think I can." Even if it kills me.

The longer he keeps me here, encased in his arms, engulfed in the heat of his embrace, the harder it is to maintain the anger. His touch is the antidote to everything that wounds me.

"Stay." He turns me to face him. "I need you. Don't let me ruin us. I'm sorry I fucked up. Just…"

His lips crash to mine, kissing me in an anguished appeal where words fail him. I have only a brief thought of pushing him away before my lips part and my hands go to his hair, tugging and holding him to me.

"Fuck, Avery." The sound is hoarse and full of want.

He grabs the backs of my thighs and hoists me up, legs wrapped around his hips and arms gripping his shoulders. His hips flex, pressing his thick erection against my core and defeating the last of the notion I had about walking away from him.

"I have to be inside you," he groans.

Ethan lays me down on the edge of the bed, standing between my legs and covering me with his body. Ripping away my underwear, he pushes inside me with barely a warning. The sudden sting of intrusion flares through my body, replaced just as quickly with the warm, wonderful ache of being reconnected.

"I love you," he says, voice ragged and strained. He entwines our fingers to stretch both of my arms above my head.

Lying like this, completely open and vulnerable to him, I've never felt so safe or protected with another man. Despite the arguments and unresolved strain between us, I recognize he only lashed out at me out of pain. He's terrified of being abandoned. Spent his entire life feeling betrayed by his family. He wants just one person in the world who chooses him first. And in return, he offers unconditional love. For that, I can forgive him. That, I understand.

"Please," he breaths against my lips as he pulls out just a fraction and pushes inside again, nearly all his weight focused on the place where we connect. "Tell me."

"I love you, too."

* * *

The next morning, I can't get Ethan out of bed. He's barely lucid, and no matter what I say, he won't budge. After last night, I just don't have the energy to fight him. Given how much he likely had to drink, maybe it's just as well. It's probably better that he not show up at work with a hangover.

At the office, I settle into the war room. I've got some calls scheduled for today, and I have to get through typing up a couple of audio transcripts before a check-in meeting with Ed to catch him up on our progress. Around eleven, Vivian wanders in. She's dressed like it's laundry day, downscaled from her usual cry-for-attention wardrobe to a faded T-shirt and worn jeans; wearing dark sunglasses and carrying a cardboard tray with three enormous cups of coffee.

"You like dark roast, right?" she says, and sets a cup in front of me.

"Uh, yeah. Thank you." A brief notion that it might be poisoned crosses my mind, but I figure if Vivian were to attempt homicide, she'd do it with fewer witnesses nearby.

Setting the tray down on the table, she pulls up a chair across from me and opens her laptop.

"I take it Ethan's sleeping it off?"

My head snaps up. "What?"

"Last night. He was on some bender."

Face flushing red, pulse racing, I damn near lunge across the table.

"You were with him?"

Vivian takes a long, leisurely sip from her coffee. "Met him for a drink. Kinda turned into several. You two didn't have a fight, did you?"

Like I'd tell her. "Family thing."

"Ah." She nods, knowing and smug. "His mother, I'm guessing. Unless his father finally dropped dead."

"What do you know about his mother?"

"I was there when she first got sick. He spent more than a few nights sleeping it off at my place."

Hot, scorching ire flames through my skull, tightening my shoulders. If I could get away with it, I'd toss my coffee in her face. Because I know what she's doing. Every woman can recognize it. Teasing me, baiting. Vivian's chumming the waters. I believe Ethan when he says he never had any interest in her, but that doesn't mean she felt the same. There's no doubt in my mind that if given the chance, she'd pounce on him. Which makes her my mortal enemy.

"But don't worry," she says, cloying smile on her thin lips. "I took good care of him. He was very well behaved."

Uh-huh.

\* \* \*

Whatever professional respect I had accumulated for Vivian is obliterated right there, and fully paved over by the growing contempt she elicits when she finds a way to spend all night drinking on Ethan's couch with increasing frequency over the following two weeks. These at-home sessions began as a means of working through the night in a more comfortable environment, Ethan cooking dinner while Vivian and I kept at it. But as the days have worn on, less work gets done once we've cleared our plates, and more of the evening becomes dedicated to swapping old war stories and getting to the bottom of a bottle. At first I told myself this was preferable to having him roam the city with her, but now I regret not speaking up weeks ago.

Coming out of the shower one night, in my pajamas and making it quite evident that I'm one yawn away from passing out, I find them still sitting in the kitchen with a bottle of whiskey between them.

"Ethan?" I say, standing across the room beside the bed. "Can I have a minute?"

"Yeah, yeah." He pushes himself up from the stool and saunters over, a little wobbly and listing to the left. "Hey, you going to bed? What time is it?"

"Almost three," I say pointedly. "I can't stay up. I'm exhausted."

"Yeah, baby, get some sleep." He wraps his arms around me, leaning down to kiss my forehead with harsh whiskey breath. "We're just talking. I'll get rid of her and be there in a minute."

I stare into his red, glassy eyes, wishing I didn't know that in an hour when I'm still awake, staring at the ceiling, they'll still be sitting at the island in the kitchen, still drinking.

"Okay," I tell him, running my hands down his stomach. His muscles don't move, too numb to feel me. "I love you."

His fingers push my hair behind my ear, trailing down my neck. At least I know, somewhere in there, he hasn't forgotten me.

"Love you."

And it goes on like that, days and nights. Everywhere I turn, Vivian's face. We're so close to the end—wrap up this story, make deadline, and be rid of her. Just a few more weeks, and things will get back to normal. It's what I tell myself. But every day it gets harder to believe it. Every day, I'm watching him unravel. He won't talk about his mother. Not sure he's talking to her, either. The only thing he wants to do is drink and sleep and I don't know how to break him out of the cycle. Half the time he's too sloshed when he does come to bed to even notice I'm there. It doesn't help that Vivian is feeding all of his worst instincts. I'd hide the liquor, but he'd go elsewhere. I'd kick her out, but it isn't my house.

Another day, and again I find myself standing over Ethan in the morning. Lying in bed, he's half-unconscious and surly as fuck.

"You can't call out again this week," I insist, ripping the blanket from his body. He groans and turns away. "Every time you ditch work, I've got to smooth it over with Ed. He's getting tired of the excuses."

"He'll deal. Tell him I'm working from home."

"That's what you always say, but I keep getting stuck picking up your slack."

"Christ, Avery, get off my case. Let me get a few hours, and I'll be in later."

"Forget it." I never win this argument, so why do I keep trying? "I'm going to be late."

When I step off the elevator at the office, I hurry straight for the war room to avoid being spotted, but Ed catches me at the door like a parent sitting in the dark waiting for their kid to sneak in after curfew.

"Ethan?" he asks without preamble. We both already know the answer.

"He's tying up some work, and he'll be in later," I say.

Neither of us is impressed with my lackluster performance.

"Uh-huh." Ed crosses his arms and I can't escape the gnawing feeling that I'm burning through any capital I'd earned with him. "I sent you the edits on Ethan's other pending articles. His work has turned to shit lately. Maybe you can fix it before he writes himself out of a job."

That's no idle threat.

## 23

# THE LIBERTINE

There's a tavern in Tribeca, a homey spot with exposed pipes crossing the water-stained ceiling. It's got cheap beer and comfy pleather barstools worn in by decades of asses. The bartenders are friendly, which almost makes up for the trauma of walking into the blue-ribbon winner for worst bathroom in Manhattan. The cozy dive is lit by blue lanterns and red pin spots; drink specials are scrawled on chalkboards. At first glance, there's nothing much remarkable about the almost-decrepit hole in the wall. But within its exposed brick walls, a cold war rages. One that has divided the New York publishing community since the first Bush administration.

"If I may have everyone's attention." Addison stands in front of a worn-out pool table with scratches and drink stains on the felt. About forty people crowd in around him. Above his head, a hanging exposed bulb casts bright orange light on his narrow shoulders. "This is the twenty-sixth annual tournament of champions for the right to claim The Table…"

As it goes, this crusty bar has been a popular hangout among the several magazines that reside in Lower Manhattan. As the publications traded staff over the years, more magazines began calling this place home. Until scuffles and even a few bar brawls broke out over who had claimed the territory first and to whom dibs on The Table—at perfect equidistance to the billiards and bar—belonged. One night those present nominated a champion from each magazine to play a tournament to settle the matter. And since then, for nearly three decades, we still gather to uphold the tradition. Really, at this point, it's more about pride and bragging rights. And it's an excuse to heckle the fancy kids from *Vogue* and the *New Yorker*.

*Riot Street* has entrusted our fate to Cara's hands for the last several years, I'm told. So the rest of us stand back to watch and jeer while the champions battle it out.

"Where's Ethan?"

That is the question that's recently come to define my life. Tonight, it's Kumi asking. We sit at a high-top table listening to Addison read the rules to the participants gathered around the pool table.

"I left him at home," I tell her. "He wasn't feeling up to it."

A phrase Ethan uses a lot these days. About the only thing he gets up to is a bottle of whiskey, or whatever's handy. It's gotten to the point that I don't bother waking him for work in the morning. Some days he comes in; some he doesn't. Barely skating by on his assignments, while I do my best to cover for him. The tedium is getting to me, but nothing I say seems to make a difference. Not when Vivian's always right there, enabling. Tonight, I'm almost happy to get away from him for a few hours.

"Are you two doing okay?" she asks.

Her hair has grown out a little, almost to her shoulders. It reminds me how long it's been since I've seen her, and how much of my life I've ignored under Ethan's influence.

"The problem isn't really us, you know?" Considering her deep brown eyes, I inwardly cringe at the pity behind them. I know how I sound. "He just won't face this thing with his mom. Like if he ignores it long enough, it'll go away. He's in pain and he won't talk to me. All Ethan wants to do is get shit-faced with *her* and stay numb."

"Vee?" Kumi's attention wanders toward Navid across the room. "Navi's mentioned her. Sounds *super*."

"Pretty much."

I've missed their entire relationship—Navid and Kumi. From the night they met at his show, I've been completely out of the loop. There was a time I couldn't make a friend if I paid them. Somehow, it's gotten too easy to forget the ones I have.

"You know…" she says, reaching across the table to cover my hand with hers. "You can always move back in with me."

"I—"

"No, I know. You love him, and you want to make it work. But if at some point you decide it doesn't, I'm here for you. I miss having my roommate. Besides, the new apartment is way nicer." She winks and tips back whatever cherry-red con-coction she's drinking. "My dad felt so bad about kicking you out—well, I laid the guilt on thick—he sprang for better digs and new furniture. And this one has a doorman."

"Doesn't really change the fact that he thinks I'm a bad influence or a dangerous omen or something."

"Eh." Kumi shrugs and rolls her eyes. "When you need me, I'll be there. He can deal."

I've taken her for granted. A mistake I intend to put right. Same goes for Addison. Once he's wrapped up his spiel, I corner him near the rack of pool cues.

"Hey," I say, sliding up next to him as the first two players start their game.

He eyes me skeptically. "Hi."

I deserve that. We've barely talked since our spat. Well, since I acted like a total jackass. Without the Ethan blinders obscuring my vision, I realize the apology we've been waiting on is mine.

"Can I buy you a drink?"

"Nah, I'm good. Got to pace myself." He leans against the wall, arms crossed. Addison's not going to make this easy on me, and I guess I deserve that, too.

"Look, I'm sorry. That day at lunch, I was way out of line. You were just trying to help, and I threw it back in your face. That was a shit thing to do, and I apologize."

"Yeah, well..." Staring off into space, at the crowded bar thrumming with music and sweaty bodies, his expression warms. "Maybe it wasn't my place to tell you your business. I probably wouldn't have appreciated someone sticking their nose in, either."

He smiles, a coy little grin. Enough to say there are no hard feelings. Enough that it puts me in a better mood as the night ramps up. Navid gets Kumi lubricated to the point she even takes a couple of turns at the microphone for karaoke. It isn't pretty, but the crowd's too drunk to care. For the first time in weeks, I'm actually enjoying myself.

As we all cheer on the face-off between a guy from *Gotham* and Cara, C.J. pulls up a stool beside me at the high-top. Of everyone I first met when I started at the magazine, she's the person I got to know the least. Lately, though, we've become better acquainted since she was promoted into Cyle's old job. Everyone's started to notice the writing on the wall: Ed's certain to retire soon—another few years, five at most—and Cara's next in line to be the editor-in-chief. With C.J., Cara's grooming her replacement to head the online section. And with Ethan being unreliable these days, I've found myself going to C.J. more often for advice on how to approach an interview or how to cut through bureaucratic red tape when requesting public records. She's a good teacher, and she's a great editor.

"I think that guy's in over his head," I say to her, raising my voice over the jukebox music and conversations around us.

We watch Cara sink three shots in a row and round the table to line up the next one.

"There's something I wanted to mention." C.J. leans in, pushing the discarded beer bottles and empty glasses out of the way. "I had a talk with her and Ed today."

"Yeah?"

"I've been asked to name my replacement in the Features section. They want to promote in-house rather than bringing in someone new."

"Oh." My fingers go a little numb. Anxious, excited energy

skitters through my limbs as I try to keep a neutral expression. "I didn't realize they were going to fill the spot."

It's been weeks since C.J. moved to online. She's been pulling double duty, editing and still pushing out articles for the print side. I figured it'd stay that way.

"There's an argument to be made for seniority," she says, with the same intimidating gaze that makes her so powerful to watch on the cable news panels, "but I'm more interested in drive. We've all been watching you pull this story together with, let's face it, almost no help."

C.J. doesn't mince words. It's not in her nature, I've learned. The dig at Ethan isn't malice—though it hurts me that he's pissing away his reputation—but simply an honest assessment. I just wish I weren't making my bones on his failures.

"It'd mean a bump in pay and a better title," she says. "It also comes with more responsibility."

Her pointed tone isn't lost on me. I'm a teenager again, back in rehab with Maureen telling me sobriety is a journey, not a destination, and every day, several times a day, we have to make a choice to take responsibility for our own recovery.

"I don't want an answer now," she says. "Take some time to think it over. If you accept, Ed will expect even more from you. It only gets harder from here. You'll need to consider if you can apply the proper focus to handle the job. Consider if there are any distractions you can afford to lose."

And there it is. The summation of the last month of my life. And further proof that Ethan, and our off-hours association, has started to taint the milk, so to speak. Everyone's past the point of looking the other way and ignoring the glaring empty space in the office. They've moved well beyond accepting Ethan's erratic behavior as the price of doing business with an otherwise-brilliant writer. He's one spark away from burning his career to the ground. And if I'm not careful, I might find myself trapped in the flames.

As I'm about to thank her for considering me, I notice C.J. looking over my shoulder, her lips thinning to a hard line. I don't have to turn around.

"Hey, gorgeous," he purrs at my ear. Ethan wraps his arms around my waist. "I missed you."

C.J. peels away with a parting glance at me that is none too subtle.

"I thought you were staying home," I say, pulling away as he kisses my neck.

He turns me on the stool to face him. Eyes dilated and red, unfocused, he wears a smirk that reminds me I used to hate that look.

"Changed my mind." Ethan pushes my legs apart to stand between them, hands on my hips. "I don't like being home when you're not there. It's lonely."

"Funny." I look away, toward the pool table surrounded by spectators for the next set in the tournament about to begin. Cara's made it past the first round in quick order. "I was starting to think you didn't notice anymore."

"What's that supposed to mean?"

"Nothing." It's not worth another argument.

Licking his lips, he runs his hands up the outside of my thighs. It's almost painful, the ache in my heart, when I realize his touch only leaves me numb.

"Come home. I want to take you to bed."

"This is important." Sure, it's just stupid bar games, but these little traditions are the difference between an office and a family. I push his hands from my legs. "I want to stay."

"What's with the fucking attitude?"

Ethan backs away. I close my legs.

"You're already drunk, Ethan. I'm not getting baited into a fight with you here."

"And there it is." He makes a big show with his arms, voice rising. "Every fucking day, Avery. When you are going to cut me a break?"

Now they're looking. Ed and Navid, peering over their shoulders. Kumi questioning if I need a rescue. It's humiliating.

I look him straight in his dead, vacant eyes. The frustration from his voice, any feeling or light at all, left them weeks ago.

"When you sober up."

"Uh-oh." Vivian appears beside him, shock of pink hair blinding under red lights, holding three shots of something dark and pungent. Her thin lips and inhuman gray eyes offer a saccharine smile that makes me want to vomit. "Someone's wound a little tight."

She holds out one shot glass to me but Ethan snatches it from her. "She doesn't drink."

"Well." Vivian winks and gives him the second shot, too. "More for us."

"Avery!" Kumi comes bouncing over, her affected act she puts on when trying to cover a strategic rescue. "Someone I want you to meet. They graduated from SU, too."

"Yeah." I hop off my stool to join her and leave Ethan and Vivian to their vices. "Have fun with that."

For the next two hours, though I try to keep my mind only on the tournament and listening to Kumi talk about life at her uncle's law firm, I can't help watching Ethan knock back drinks, or Vivian handing them to him. Her voice carries, the high-pitched, cloying whine. She lays into one writer after another, offering her unsolicited opinions on everything wrong with their publication and all the ways she's so philosophically superior. I admire their fortitude to stand there absorbing her drunken rants as long as they do before slipping away and passing her off to the next victim.

Ethan, for his part, is all but absent. He medicates, staring at nothing and speaking to no one. He's furniture at this point. A marble bust on a pedestal. Every part of me wants to run my fingers through his hair, hold his face in my hands, and tell him to snap out of it. Take him home, get him in bed, and make him remember who he used to be. But I've tried, and there's no getting through to him. I'm at a loss, drifting rudderless. At the mercy of his tide swelling higher with each day.

I can't look at it anymore.

Just as Cara slays another victim, I head to the restroom. It's a filthy closet with one stall. Holes in the wall and mold creeping up from the baseboards. The toilet is basically the fifth circle of hell. I have to wipe the seat and build a nest of toilet paper, then still sort of hover above it as I half-sit. Outside the stall, the bathroom door squeals with someone entering. Now I'm in a semi-squat with someone listening as I'm about to pee. I fucking hate that.

"Avery?"

Oh, for fuck's sake.

"Sorry," Vivian says. "Didn't mean to interrupt."

*Seriously, die in fire.*

My bladder is at maximum capacity and the overflow backing up into my kidneys, so I have no choice but to let it go.

"Listen…"

Like I have a choice.

"I want us to be friends. I think I'm going to be sticking around, and it'd really be best for everyone if you and I could get along."

By "everyone," she means Ethan. To which my answer is an emphatic *Fuck off*.

When I'm done and walk out of the stall, she's waiting beside the sink.

"We don't have to be enemies, Avery."

Vivian stares at the side of my face while I wash my hands. I have zero intention of humoring this bullshit performance. Ripping a couple of paper towels from the dispenser, I watch in the mirror as she pulls a tiny vial from her pocket and spoons out a bump of white powder to snort up her nose. I'm frozen, our eyes meeting in the reflection. A stinging, sour taste pricks my tongue and my mouth fills with saliva. My fingertips go cold. I blink, and I see the vivid, spectacular color of the first time Jenny and I snorted heroin together. The blissful, serene silence. Total comfort and perfect peace. I'd never been so content in all my life.

See, that's the thing about heroin: it isn't scary. Sure, everyone knows the horror stories. We're all scared straight—now.

But for me, back then, ignorant as a newborn, it was a way out of a cycle of nightmares and depression. It doesn't fuck you up or freak you out. It just makes you happy. The rest we do to ourselves. We imbue this wonder drug with all meaning and joy in the world. And we need it. To wake up. To function. To breathe. Then we need more of it. There's no such thing as enough, like it's impossible to quantify the oxygen you need for a lifetime.

"Want a hit?"

She sees it. The desire heating my face. The monster, decrepit and clawing to the surface. Vivian finds me doused in gasoline and offers to light the match.

"No," I say, balling up the paper towels and tossing them in the trash. "I'm straight."

It's all I can do to keep from grabbing it, all of it, whatever it is, and getting it inside me as quickly as possible.

"Suit yourself," she says with a shrug. "More for us."

To hell with this. All of it. To babysitting a grown man, watching a brilliant, beautiful person I love waste away to a torpid shell of his former self. I'm not built for this. Never have been. Just taking care of myself is almost more than I can handle, and I'm not even very good at that. I've spent last several years in a straitjacket, muzzled and sedated. Walking a thin white line on the floor painted there to keep me out of trouble. When do I get to relax? When is it my turn to misbehave?

That's when I realize there's no one stopping me.

From the bathroom, I head straight for the bar and climb up on a stool. The balding bartender spots me in the mirror framed by bottles and turns to me with a nod.

"Tequila," I say. "Neat. Top shelf."

He sets a short glass in front of me and pulls down the bottle to pour my drink, setting a lime wedge on the rim. I sniff it first. The sour, salty tinge stings my nose and makes my eyes water.

"Having second thoughts?" Beside me, a thirty-something blond guy in a plaid button-down, sleeves pushed up to his elbows. He smiles, looking at me over his shoulder.

No. I down the drink in one gulp and nod at the bartender for another. My throat flames and the scorched trail burns all the way to my gut. But it's a good pain, soothing. Like plucking your eyebrows. The bartender pushes my refill at me and I brace for a second hit, but the blond makes me pause.

"Maybe go easy," he says. He turns on his stool, elbow propped on the bar top. "An awful lot of nosy witnesses here tonight."

Well, I suppose he has a point there.

"Marshall West." He holds out his hand to shake mine. His grip is firm, deliberate. Not one of those insipid men who limp-wrist a woman. "*New Yorker.*"

"Nice to meet you." I bring my drink to my lips and try sipping this time.

"You're Avery Avalon, correct?"

"What gave me away?"

Marshall smirks, because we both know I can't hide in here. The secret's out now. All that's left to do is get used to it.

"I read your last essay."

"You're not armed, are you?"

Leaning toward me, he breathes out a subdued laugh. "Actually, I found it sharp and incisive. Not everyone can excel at a first-person essay, but I think you have a certain knack for it."

"Funny you should say that," I bring my drink to my lips, "I—"

"The fuck is this?" Ethan comes up beside me and grabs my wrist. He stands there, brow creased and eyes narrowed. His jaw set tight. "You're drinking?"

I rip my arms from his grasp and take another sip. "Just following your lead, ace."

"Enough." Grabbing the glass from my hand, he sets it down and wraps his arm around my waist to pull me from the stool. "You're coming with me."

"Uh, no." I look up into his tempest eyes and for the first time in weeks see some semblance of life. But too little, too late. "I'm good here. Thanks."

Ethan bends to speak in my ear, his fingers digging into my hip. "Avery, don't be difficult."

"Ash, lay off." Marshall stands, both men tall and hovering over me. "She said no."

"Mind your fucking business, asshole."

"Ethan, stop it." Pulling his hand from my hip, I take a step back. "I'm fine here. Leave it alone."

"See? She said no."

"Has he offered to show you his office yet?" Ethan spits out. "Take in the view while he's bending you over his desk."

"Screw off, Ash."

"Hey." I shove at Ethan's stomach. "Don't be crass. You're embarrassing yourself."

"Time to go." Marshall puts his hand on Ethan's chest and he smacks it away.

They shove, shouting at each other. The scuffle quickly gathers a crowd as staff from both sides jump in to break them up. It isn't until a man pulls Marshall away and Ed gets in Ethan's face that he finally relents. Breathing heavily, face red, he charges out of the bar and leaves me standing there, mortified in front of everyone I know and a few dozen people who already have suspect notions about me. I'm trembling with rage when Kumi comes up, her eyes wide with concern when she smells the alcohol on my breath.

"Come home with me," she says, hands rubbing my upper arms. "Stay a few nights to clear your head."

I would. I want to. But there's the lingering fear of what Ethan might do if I'm gone. He's at a dangerous precipice, and it seems I'm not ready to abandon him to the fall. Not yet.

## 24

# UNTOUCHABLE FACE

Ethan's asleep when I get home. He doesn't wake up as I slip in bed. The next morning, we go about our routine in silence. I don't know if I should take his getting up for work as a sign of progress or remorse for last night, and I'm not ready to talk about it, so we hardly acknowledge each other on our way to the office.

For my part, I'm not proud of the way I behaved. Breaking my rules and letting a guy flirt with me because it was nice to have the attention. Because I hoped Ethan would see it. I wanted him to be jealous, angry. I wanted him to rush up, put a possessive arm around my shoulder, and demand I come home with him. If only to know he still cared. It was petty and ugly and I want to smack myself for letting it happen. I don't like the person I'm becoming. Our relationship is deteriorating into shouting matches punctuated by prolonged silences—I don't want to be one of those couples who stay together because neither will take the first step to end it. Living out of fear of being alone or disrupting the status quo. A person can get used to anything if they tolerate it long enough.

When we get to the office, I dump my bag at my desk and go to the snack room for coffee. Addison's there, and he straightens up when I walk in and pour myself a cup.

"So…" He leans against the counter, watching me from the corner of his eye. "Last night was fun."

Sighing, I take my mug to the round table in the center of the room and sit. In a manner of speaking, I'm still holding my breath. There will be consequences. I'm bracing for the fallout.

"How bad is it?"

Addison takes a seat beside me, reclining in his chair with his long legs sprawled out.

"Not good," he says with a shrug. "People are pissed. It's one thing when Ethan takes it out on himself. Starting bar fights is a whole new level."

"It's my fault. I provoked him."

"Uh-uh." He sits up to lean forward. "You can't hold yourself responsible for that mess. Ethan is a grown-ass man. This train's been coming for a long time. He's had plenty of chances to get out of the way."

"I don't know what to do." My gaze falls to my mug, staring into the black and watching the steam rise and curl. "Everything I say, he either ignores me or he flies off the handle. I want to help, but he won't let me."

"Then there's your answer." Addison reaches out to put his hand on my arm, empathy in his eyes. "I get you don't want to hear this, but we can't save everyone. Some people have to be left to their own devices."

It'd be easier if Vivian weren't in the way. The moment she showed up, she began spinning her web around him, invading every part of our lives. She's the harbinger of death. A vile, malicious wraith. And I have no idea how to get rid of her.

Later, as I'm sitting at my desk, I feel Ethan standing behind me. He looms, casting a long shadow that chills the air around me. I've begun to dread him. These moments when the static rushing up my arms means there's a fight about to erupt.

"When are you going to talk to me?" he says, voice hoarse and tired.

I stare at my screen, scrolling through the latest edits from Ed on another one of Ethan's past-due articles. He's all but abandoned them in favor of what little effort he does put in on this Phelps story.

"Not here," I say. That's the rule.

"I can't spend an entire day with you ignoring me."

"Well, I'm not ignoring you. I'm working. Try it."

He expels a loud, frustrated breath. "You went too far last night, Avery."

"Me?" I spin around in my chair to look up into his bloodshot eyes. "You were about to rip some guy's head off. Do you have any idea how much you had to drink last night?"

"Because he was trying to pick up my girlfriend," he snaps back. He steps into my cubicle and braces his hands against both walls to cage me in. "And what the fuck were you doing with a drink in your hand?"

"I'm not even going to start on the hypocrisy of that statement."

"Christ, Avery." His hands roughly comb through his hair

as he clenches his eyes shut, jaw locked. "I was looking out for you. Am I supposed to stand there and watch some asshole hit on you? When should I step in, when he's calling a cab, or wait until he pulls his dick out?"

I laugh. Not because it's funny, but because I have nothing left. "You know what? You lost your right to have a say in the men I talk to when you started bringing Vivian home every night. Do you know she offered me coke in the bathroom? Seemed to imply you two had done a little pre-partying. Anything you want to tell me?"

He flinches, brow furrowed. "So this is revenge? You're planning to go fuck half of Manhattan to get back at me?"

I get to my feet, fists balled at my sides. The urge to take a swing at him burns through my arms. "Fuck you, you impossible jackass."

"Ethan! Avery!" Ed shouts across the room. "My office. Now."

*Fuck.*

This is exactly the bullshit I've tried to avoid since Ethan began his plunge into self-destruction. But bravo for him, he's managed to suck me down with him.

We go to Ed's office to stand at opposite sides of the room as Ed slams his door shut.

"This shit stops now," he barks out. His wrinkled face is pink and getting angrier. Gone is the mild-mannered, implacable façade. "I've let this go hoping you two would sort out your business, but that's over. What happened last night was an embarrassment for this magazine and I won't have you two dragging down our good reputation."

"Ed," I say, fearing where this conversation is headed, "I'm sorry. You're absolutely right, and it won't happen again."

"Goddamn right it won't." He crosses his arms, leaning back against his desk. "You're on notice. Another outburst or incident, I'll send your ass out on the street."

"Hey." Ethan turns, shoulders high and tight around his neck. "Don't fucking talk to her like that. She's done nothing but bust her ass for you and take more shit than anyone else in this office just for doing her damn job. You should be glad she didn't sue and liquidate this publication for the way Cyle harassed her."

"You," Ed says, stabbing his finger in the air. "Have run out of rope, my friend. I've been more than patient, but this is it. You've burned the last bridge you had."

"The hell's that supposed to mean?" he shouts back. "Even on a bad day I'm still the best reporter you've got. I'm turning my stuff in on time. What do—"

"Your work's been garbage for weeks. Avery's been doing your rewrites just to cover your ass."

*Thanks, Ed. Thanks for that.*

Ethan jerks toward me. He stares, dumbfounded. "You've been lying to me?"

"I've been helping you keep your job!" I shout back, unable to restrain myself.

He shakes his head, stepping back. I watch the hurt, the shock, emerge in his eyes.

"I would never, ever do that to you. Lie right to your face. For weeks, Avery. Christ!"

"Ethan," Ed says, lowering his voice as he sees the betrayal sink in. "You're off the Phelps story. I'm handing it over to Avery and suspending you for a month without pay. Take the time to decide if you still want a job here and what you're going to do to convince me you should still have one."

"No, you what? Don't bother." Stalking toward the door, he leaves a last glance on me. If he'd smacked me, it wouldn't have stung this much. "I quit."

My blood runs cold. For several seconds I stand there, staring at the door after Ethan slams it shut behind him. The concussion reverberates in my chest and rings in my ears. How did it come to this? Not even three months ago we met in this office and he all but begged me to take the job. Now he's gone, and it's like he took all the air in the room with him.

"It was bound to happen," Ed says. He takes a seat on his stool, feet propped up on the top rung.

The sword falls, and it splits me in half.

I don't know what else to do, so I take a seat facing his desk.

"Talk to me," he says. "What's really been going on with him?"

It all comes out in a rush. The weeks of pent-up frustration and worry.

"I don't know what Vivian does to him, but from the moment she came back, he's been a different person. He's drinking constantly, he's snapping at me, and half the time we don't even talk to each other at home if it isn't about work. He's changed, and I don't know how to get him back."

Ed unfolds from his perch and pulls up another chair beside me. He's quiet for a moment, studying the floor. Without the implacable, disinterested veneer, suddenly Ed looks like someone's dad, or grandfather. Concern creases his brow and age creeps over his face. His thin, spotted arms prop up his chin then fall between his knees.

"You and me both, kid."

I don't know exactly what that means, or if he'll elaborate, so I sit, silent, until he speaks again.

"Same time Vee took off on us," he says, "Ethan went MIA, too."

"Yeah, I, uh, heard as much."

"Ethan looked a lot then like he looks now."

"It's his mother's illness. She's been battling cancer, and I guess for a while it went into remission, but now it's back and he isn't taking it well, and…"

My heart aches for him. I know a day is coming when he'll have to face the harsh reality of his mother's condition, and I can't bear the idea of his having to do it alone.

"Avery, Ethan's an alcoholic. He doesn't need an excuse."

My brain stops dead. I stare at Ed, blinking, unable to process what he's just said.

"No. No, he's not. I mean, lately isn't a good example. He's self-medicating, I get that, but he's not an alcoholic. I've been out with him. I've seen him have a couple of glasses of wine and walk away."

"He got better at it for a while, but he's still an alcoholic. Ethan's a bargainer. He tells himself, Okay, if I can go three days, four days, without a drink, I can have two, three, four drinks the next day. He survives by spreading them out, always living for the next one. Until now."

I can't wrap my head around that. It's like Ed's talking about a different person I've never met.

"I know it's hard to hear," he says, "but that's how it is. We've had a lot of long conversations in this office. I tried to get him to a meeting at one point."

Eyes snapping to Ed's, I realize the piece of him I've never understood. The gray area where the missing matter should go.

"You're an alcoholic."

"Thirty-five years sober this month." He pulls a silver chain from around his neck to show me the medallion tucked inside his shirt. "There are more of us than you'd guess in this office."

He says "us" and for a moment I'm not sure if he knows what that means. Then it's there, in his all-knowing, all-seeing eyes. He's had me pegged from the start.

"What do I do?" I beg him.

At this point, I just want someone to give me the right answer and point me in a direction.

"Talk to him," he tells me, the sympathy on his face saying he knows what a futile effort that can be. "You've got to get him sober. Then he needs to get to rehab."

"I don't know if I can convince him of all that. I want to—don't get me wrong—I'll do whatever it takes to help him, but he hasn't listened to me so far. I don't see how that's going to change."

"I don't have a simple solution for you. I've got to worry about the magazine. If it were anyone else, he'd have been fired a long time ago. I care about that guy, I really do, but there's only so much you can do for them before they've got to want to do it for themselves. Get him cleaned up. Get him to rehab. Where he's headed right now, it gets worse pretty fast."

\* \* \*

I try calling Ethan, but he won't answer his phone or return my texts. All I can do right now is wait and hope he's home when I get there tonight because rushing off to chase him isn't an option today. With Ethan gone, I'm solely responsible for getting the Phelps article wrapped up. I've got about three weeks to deadline, and two months' worth of work left to accomplish.

Later, when I pop out to grab lunch, I see Vivian walking into the building. Like a good career user, she's bright-eyed and wide awake. It's the careful ones you have to watch out for. The people who keep it all neat and tidy and so well hidden.

"Morning, Avery," she says, passing me in the lobby.

"Afternoon."

I make it to the front doors when the ire stops me. There's no reason to play nice anymore. We're past the point of civility. The chains are off, and I've got plenty to say. So I whip around and jog down the hallway to catch her at the elevator. We step inside together, heading up to the fifth floor.

"We need to talk."

I stab the Emergency button and the elevator jerks to a halt. Ethan taught me that trick, back when he still had a hard time keeping his hands to himself whenever we were out of sight of other people. No sirens or alarms, just privacy.

"Okay," she says, too-cheery smile on her lips. "What's on your mind?"

"From now on, you're not welcome here. Ethan quit, and I don't want your help."

"Good for Ethan. This place was stifling him anyway."

"And you can't come over anymore. No more late-night drinks, no more dinners, no more sitting on our couch watching cartoons at two in the morning."

"Is this Ethan talking, or you? Because I'm pretty sure it's his home."

"I'm speaking for him because lately he's too drunk to know better. You're killing him, Vivian. He is barely keeping it together, and you just keep shoving the liquor down his throat. I don't want you near him. You're poison."

She cocks her head to the side, lips pressed to a thin line. "Ethan is a big boy. He doesn't do anything he doesn't want to. Maybe he just got bored playing Scrabble and watching TV every night. He's still a young man, why should he live like he's got one foot in the grave?"

There's a big, raging, furious violence in me that wants to bounce her little pink head off a wall. But I'm not that person. So I take a breath and push the image out of my mind.

"This is your only warning," I tell her. "Leave him alone, don't set foot inside our home again, or I swear on my life I will find a way to get you locked up."

She laughs. Until she doesn't.

"So now you're a snitch?"

"I'll be whatever I have to be to protect him. I'll lie, cheat, and steal. I'll break into your apartment and leave a kilo of coke hidden somewhere only the drug dogs will find it. Trust me, Vivian. You don't want to test me."

I never would have imagined those words coming out of my mouth. The inflection, the cold, hard, flat earnestness in my voice. It's my father speaking through me. His detachment and blade-sharp cruelty. And I mean every word of it.

When she has nothing to say in response, I hit the Emergency button again to send the elevator up to the fifth floor. After I step out, I watch the elevator doors close on Vivian to carry her back down.

\* \* \*

Fear choked me the entire way home that night, terrified I'd get home to find Ethan's truck missing and half his clothes gone. If he left now, wouldn't talk to me, I don't know what I'd do. Those two days he was gone, when he ran out of my apartment after the phone call, I was so twisted up I couldn't think about anything else. I can't go through that again. Not now. Not when I know he's suffering and my entire life is wrapped up in his.

But as I walk up to the building, I see his truck parked on the street. I let out a breath and practically sprint through the door.

"Ethan?" I call out.

The place looks empty until I see him on the floor beside the bed, knees pulled up and his head in his hands. I drop my bag and rush over to crouch in front of him.

"Ethan, babe, what's wrong?"

He doesn't speak, but his chest convulses. His back rises on heaving, jerking breaths. Arms straining, his fingers are white. His face bright red.

"Ethan, please, babe. Look at me. Tell me what's wrong."

He lets me pry his hands from his face and I see the tears

streaming down his cheeks. His ocean eyes, so bright and vivid, are stung red. The sight of him breaks my heart, cracks it open.

"What's wrong? Please tell me. Let me help."

"She wants to die," he stutters out, so choked and choppy I almost don't understand him until I rattle the words around and realize what he's saying.

"Your mom? What do you mean?"

He scrubs his eyes then tugs at his hair.

"She wants to die. She's going to kill herself."

Grabbing his hands, I hold them in mine.

"I don't understand, Ethan. What happened?"

Deep, gasping, he inhales and drops his head back on the edge of the bed.

"She's stage four. There's nothing left to do. Even if she wanted to, it'd be pointless. The cancer has spread to her brain and—"

He can't do it. Can't push out another word. I have no better idea what to do than crawl into his lap and hold him, let him cry against my shoulder. I wish I was better at this. That I had that special gift for knowing the right thing to say or how to take the sting away, but I'm hopeless at it. I was born without the gene for consoling people.

"I'm so sorry, Ethan. I'm so, so sorry."

Running my fingers through his hair, I try simply to show him I love him. That he is loved. And that as insufficient as I am, I want to be here for him.

"She doesn't want to live with it anymore," he mutters against my neck, a little calmer now. "She's talking about assisted suicide."

Fuck. What the hell do I say that makes this any better?

"And my dad's just letting her do it. He's just going to stand there and watch her kill herself."

"Ethan, that's not what he's doing. This is—"

"Yes," he bites back, pulling away. "It is. I'd never stand by and watch you die if I could stop it. I'd fight for you. I'd make you fight. That's what love is, isn't it? Living for someone else. How can he do that to her?"

"Ethan, believe me, I understand how painful this is for you, but it is her choice. Your dad does love her, and that's why he's respecting her decision no matter how much it breaks his heart."

"Christ, Avery." He pushes me off his lap and gets to his feet, pacing the floor. "Why? Why do you take his side every time? I swear it's like you do it just to drive me insane."

"That's not true. I'm not taking his side. I'm always on your side, Ethan. I just think you're missing the point. She doesn't want to spend whatever time she has left in pain and misery. You can't blame her for that. She'd rather go on her own terms, while she's still herself."

He stops, turning to stare at me. In all my life, not since my father have I ever seen such raw hatred in a person's eyes. Everything I love in Ethan drains away. What's left is pure contempt bottled up inside him, pointed right at me.

"I don't understand what's happened to you," he says, "but I think maybe we need some time apart."

"Ethan, don't do that. This isn't you. Please."

I try to go to him, but he yanks his arms away and dodges past me.

"Ethan, talk to me. Don't leave."

He's out the door, slamming it behind him.

That night, he doesn't come home.

Or the next.

Or the next.

## 25

# THE EXTERMINATING ANGEL

This place doesn't feel like home without him. Too big, too empty. It doesn't smell like him anymore. I've spent so many nights on his side of the bed, even his pillow has turned dull. Every time I hear a car pass outside or park at the curb, I rush to the door and look outside. But it isn't him. For two weeks, it hasn't been him.

So I bury myself in work. I've accepted C.J.'s offer to move into her old job in the Features section once I've wrapped up this Phelps article. Alone now on the story, I work fifteen hours a day pulling it together. It's almost there, and I guess I should be proud of myself, but it's a hollow victory when the one person I want most to share it with isn't here. After the first week, I was certain he'd be back by Monday. Now closing out the second, I'm starting to wonder if he's ever coming back.

It's the nights, though, that are the hardest. Alone in bed, in the dark and restless. I feel adrift on the water with no wind and no stars to navigate by. Loneliness is my new normal. I've started leaving messes around the house, just to make it feel like someone else has been here. Dishes in the sink and laundry on the floor. Sometimes I leave the TV on all night just to hear the voices. Leave it on when I go to work so I come home to someone.

I hate this. Hate that he won't at least tell me he's okay. Hate that he's capable of ignoring me this long when I'm crumbling inside. It isn't fair that every day I pack my bags and put them by the door, tell myself it's been long enough and I'm not doing it anymore. Then I hate myself some more for putting my clothes back in the dresser and kicking the bag under the bed.

His father says he hasn't heard from him, but I don't think he'd tell me if he had. Six times a day I consider showing up at their townhouse in the city, taking the bus out to their home in Greenwich, or hopping the train to Montauk. Then I think about his mother, and I remember that the last thing that poor woman needs is the crazy girlfriend showing up to rain drama and unholy hellfire down on her dying days. That woman's been through enough. The least she deserves is some privacy. Every day I check the obituaries, dreading the day Mrs. Ash's name shows up and uncertain what it will mean when it does.

Carter's no help. He must know where Ethan is, or at least that he's alive, because his only answer is that an adult isn't missing if they left on their own. Clearly not concerned that Ethan's lying facedown in a ditch or floating in the East River. If there's something Carter doesn't want to tell me, there's no dragging it out of him. Anything more would require a car battery and methods prohibited by the Geneva convention.

So I wait.

And I work.

Trapped in a cycle of doubt and fear.

If I knew how to get in touch with Vivian, I'd try, but no one at the magazine has a working number for her, and online searches for an address only bring up the old apartment she had in Brooklyn before she took off to New Hampshire. She's a ghost, dropped off the map.

By the third week, Ethan's phone goes straight to voicemail, telling me the mailbox is full. So I text him. Every morning and every night. A few lines to say I miss him, I love him, please come home.

My mom calls every day now. To make sure I'm alive. She begs me to move in with her. Leave the city and all traces of Ethan behind. But I can't. Because I know, deep in my bones like I know my hair is red, the minute I leave, he'll walk through the door and wonder how long ago I left him. He'll see the first day I packed a bag and set it by the door, and he'll watch me walk out, think I'm gone for good. I can't do that to him. Not until I know. I just want to hear it from his lips. That we're over, have been for weeks, and I should have taken the hint by now. Then at least I'll know I tried. Did everything I could to stick it out, be strong. He'd do the same for me.

That sounds stupid, I know. The level of pathetic to which I have sunk doesn't escape me. One week I put on five pounds, the next I drop ten. My meds do nothing for me anymore. My brain chemistry is too disrupted to use them like it should. I can't explain it other than to say that I know, in my soul, that if our positions were reversed, Ethan would be waiting.

No, that's not true.

If our places were reversed, Ethan would have found me by now. He'd have searched every building and basement in the city. He'd have scoured every tunnel and sewer. Because though it was brief, our love was real. I felt it. In his touch, in his kiss, in the sound of his voice and the beating of his heart. It was real. And right now, I'd do anything to get it back.

# 26

# THE SHARPEST LIVES

Something wakes me. A sound that produces a fleeting dream of walking down the street when a garbage truck passes. Then I'm standing on a subway platform. In pitch black, the noise persists. I ignore it, rolling over in bed to the big empty space beside me. Then my brain catches up and I realize my phone is vibrating somewhere. I reach to the nightstand, but I can't find it. Buzzing, skittering. I crawl around on the bed then drop to the floor. Finally, I see the light and reach for it. Carter's name flashes on the screen.

"Carter? Hey, you there?"

"Yeah, Avery."

"What's wrong? Did you find him? Where is he? Is he okay?"

"Listen. I need you to take a breath, all right?"

"Tell me, dammit!"

Sitting on the cold cement floor, my heart races. My head is filled with the sound of a beating bass drum and blood rushing between my ears. I brace for impact, eyes clenched shut. If it's bad news, if he's hurt or worse, I don't know if I can take it.

"Ethan's been arrested. He's okay, but—"

"What? What for?"

Air fills my lungs, big and heavy.

"Avery, listen to me. He was arrested outside his parents' house uptown. Police found him with a baseball bat smashing out the windows of his father's car."

*Christ, Ethan.*

"Paul isn't pressing charges—"

"So he's being released?" I jump to my feet and dart around in the dark for the first pair of jeans I find and start yanking them up my legs, bouncing on one foot. "Then I can pick him up? Where is he? I'll leave right now and—"

"Please, Avery. There's more. He's been involuntarily admitted to a psychiatric hospital for a forty-eight-hour observation period."

"What?" I fall to the bed, jeans tangled around my ankles. "Why?"

"When the police arrived, he was violent and incoherent. It's likely he was on something, but we won't know until they run a urinalysis at the hospital."

*Oh, Ethan. What have you done?*

"Then what happens? I mean, if he—"

"It's likely he'll be released after the forty-eight hours, but that's entirely dependent on the eval and whether he cooperates with the doctors. If he makes this difficult on himself, they could hold him."

My hands tremble. Up my arms and down to my toes. I

can imagine what Ethan's going through right now. Anguished and confused, so much rage and pain exploding inside him. I should have been there. Somehow, I should have gotten to him. The idea of his spending the night in a psych ward, alone, it breaks my heart.

Then a thought occurs to me.

"Carter, was anyone else with him?"

He's quiet a moment, perhaps debating whether to tell me, until he says, "Vivian Mott was arrested and charged with possession of narcotics. She's being booked and held for arraignment."

After I get off the phone with Carter, I lie awake in bed, staring at the ceiling, anxious and breathless, trying to think of what to say. I don't want to screw this up again, drive Ethan farther away when he's at his most vulnerable. The last thing he needs is a lecture or someone else pointing out all the ways he went wrong. There's time for that later, once he's released and he's had a chance to recoup. Once he's home and I can make him understand that I'm not fighting him.

I know what addiction does to people. How it changes us, controls us. We aren't bad people, we're just sick. Our minds aren't our own when we're chasing our next fix—whatever it may be. It's tunnel vision that filters out everything that isn't what we're after. Anything that gets in the way is an obstacle to be destroyed. We sacrifice everything to maintain the high. Most of all, the people closest to us. They're the easiest targets. Because at its core, addiction is hatred. We hate what we become because this *thing* has taken control. Every day we wake up and say, *No more. This time I stop. This time, I'll be stronger.*

It isn't that easy.

So we hate ourselves a little more each time we fail, and we take that hatred out on the ones we love.

What's happened to Ethan isn't his fault, but he does have to take responsibility for getting better. He has to want it. Getting sober, no matter how many people stand beside you, is a solitary effort. All the counseling in the world can't change the fact that 90 percent of the fight happens in our own minds. Every day is a choice. He has to want to make the right one.

If not, I can't stand by and watch him suffer.

No matter how much I love Ethan, and I still do, I can't sacrifice my recovery for his vices. It nearly derailed me once, and I can't take that chance again.

The last several days, I wake in a cold sweat, dreaming of the rush and numb euphoria. I imagine the pure, excellent bliss when it hits my bloodstream and calms every nerve. How perfect and peaceful it is when the rest of the world melts away and there is only light and beautiful warmth. Ethan used to give me that. Without him, the repressed parts of my mind yearn for another source. Every old instinct screams at me to find the thing that fills the void. Sometimes I go to sleep afraid I'll wake up with a needle in my arm and no memory of how it got there.

The only thing harder than getting clean is doing it again. There's nothing on this earth that could make me go through another round of detox. Not for love or money or the promise of curing world hunger. It really is that fucking bad—the parts I can remember. The parts I can't are worse.

# 27

# A Parting Gift

The bed dips beside me. Warm fingers trail across my shoulder and down my arms. I know it's a dream when I feel his body pressed against mine. That I'm hallucinating his lips at my neck, his arm draped across my stomach. He traces patterns beneath the hem of my shirt as I clench my eyes shut and try to hold on, not to wake up. It smells like him, his skin. I feel that indescribable energy that wraps me in light when he's near. A tear falls down my cheek and my chest constricts. I want to roll over, weave my hand through his hair, and feel the strands between my fingers. Want to touch his lips, soft and tender. Taste him on my tongue. To look into his deep-water eyes and remember what home feels like. But it's a dream, and if I move, if I breathe, disturb the fragile, formless moment, it'll disappear like smoke.

"Avery," he says, tucking my hair behind my ear and brushing his fingers down my neck. "Baby, I'm home."

His arm around my waist tugs me, turning me toward him.

I open my eyes, morning light bleeding in, and he's still there.

"Ethan?"

A spike of adrenaline rushes through my body.

"I'm here."

I throw my arms around him, fingers digging into his back. Face buried under his chin, I inhale. He takes my leg and hitches it over his hip, arm firm against my back. We can't get close enough. Can't feel enough of each other. We cling tighter, straining to kill the space between us.

"I thought you weren't getting out until this afternoon," I say, my tears dripping on his shirt.

"It is afternoon."

I've slept all day, exhausted from insomnia and worry, still so delirious I almost can't believe it's real.

"I'm so mad at you," I cry against his chest, voice strained. "I'm so fucking mad at you. What the hell were you—"

"Baby, I know. I'm sorry." His hand tangles in my hair, massaging the back of my neck. "I'm so, so sorry, Avery."

Fisting his shirt, I want to scream. Scream into his chest and let out all of this anxiety and anger and all the ways he's tortured me over the last three weeks. Now that he's back, he's safe, I'm overwhelmed with the need to…I don't know. Break something just to hear it shatter. Destroy something. Blow it up and burn the remains.

"I hate you so much. I hate you for leaving and for never calling me back when—"

"It's okay. You can hate me if you have to."

So I do. Minutes or hours, I don't know. But lying in bed, tangled in each other, I hate him. While he's kissing me and stroking my back. While he tells me he's sorry and I cry, aching, pressing my hand against his chest to feel his heartbeat. Until I don't have the energy left in me.

"Where did you go?" I ask, fingers combing through his hair.

"Nowhere."

I would demand an answer, an explanation of where he was and who was with him and how the hell it got so bad, but I think I already know. And now that I've calmed down, I don't want to chase him away again.

"Why didn't you call? Just to let me know you were okay."

"I wasn't okay." Ethan closes his eyes and exhales. He's ragged. Color absent from his face, dark circles under his eyes. There are new lines and creases that weren't there the last time I saw him. He's been through the wringer and come out worse on the other side.

"I was angry," he says. "At you, at first. My father and my mom and everyone else. But then I was just angry at myself, and I didn't know how to talk to you. I was pissed off and ashamed, and I didn't want to be that in front of you."

Gazing into my eyes, full of sincerity, he cups my face to run this thumb under my bottom lip.

"Avery, I never wanted you to see me like that, and I am so embarrassed that I let it get so ugly. I hate that I hurt you. The longer I was gone, the more I convinced myself that you'd left and there was nothing worth coming back to. I'd torpedoed our life and the only thing left to do was drink myself to death."

"None of that matters to me. All I cared about was that you were in pain and you wouldn't let me help. I've been here, alone, worried that you weren't coming back or you were lying dead somewhere. I've never been this scared in my life."

He rolls onto his back and tucks me under his arm, the blankets draped over us. His heartbeat slows, deep breaths making his chest rise and fall.

"Avery, am I too late? I need to know if I've ruined us. You don't have to stay with me out of some sense of obligation or pity. You can be honest with me. Can you still love me despite everything I've done?"

It's an easy answer. And also not.

I still love everything he's been to me since we met. I still love how he brings me to life when he holds me in his arms. The feel of his body next to mine and his voice when he whispers in my ear. How he's always there to stand up for me, always has my back. All the love he has trapped inside him and the adoration in his smile. Ethan is a good man, and I know, completely, he never meant to hurt me. He'd rather throw himself off a cliff than cause me pain. But sometimes we can't help ourselves. We all have demons, that innate human nature to destroy. Ethan's worst target is himself.

"I love you," I tell him. "I never stopped loving you, and I don't think I'd know how to stop if I wanted to."

"But?"

"But I can't stay with you if you're drinking."

"You're breaking up with me." There's no argument behind his eyes. Steely and calm, he doesn't flinch.

"Because I think it's the best thing for both of us. I failed you because I didn't recognize what was happening right in front of me. Now I do, and I can't ignore it. Ethan, I want so badly for us to be together, but I have to respect myself first. And so do you."

He swallows, muscle flexing in his jaw. I know how an addict's mind works. I see the gears turning, searching for an excuse or rationalization or some bargain he can strike with himself that adheres to the spirit of the deal if not the letter. He opens his mouth to speak, but I press my fingers to his lips.

"I love you, and I will always be your friend, but this is something you're going to have to do alone. I can't make the decision for you, and I won't hold a gun to your head. When you need me, you'll always be able to find me. However long it takes, no matter how bad it gets, I will be your friend. But you have to make an effort for yourself. And you have to stay away from Vivian. She's poisonous."

There's nothing about their parasitic relationship that I enjoy, but I do understand it. Addiction loves company. Ethan fills the black, empty space in Vivian's hollow life. She provides all the reinforcement he needs to feed his destructive cravings. And I never did anything to stop it.

"Whatever else you decide," I tell him, "please, let her go. Trust me when I tell you I know how that story ends. You deserve so much better."

I don't let him respond right away. I'm not after a quick surrender that turns to regret and resentment when the sun comes up. So, for tonight, we just enjoy being together again. We order pizza and watch Netflix. I cheat at gin rummy and laugh when he catches me. I take his hand and lead him back to bed when he goes to the fridge, standing in front of the open door, and realizes what he wants is a beer and it isn't there—he can't have it. These are profound moments for addicts. Confronted with limitation. When they reach for their drug and see, for the first time, how unconscious and ingrained the need truly is.

That night we lie in bed, wrapped in blankets and darkness. With his arms around me, my head on his chest, I sense we're both holding our breath, in fear of the same impending cliff: What if this is the last time? What if he chooses his addiction and I choose myself, will we ever have this again? Comfort and security of being in the arms of the one we love. The trust and compassion of the person who sees through our faults. I can't bear to look down, peer over the edge at the black uncertainty.

"Ethan?" I say, sliding my hand up his bare chest, to his cheek, tracing the lines of his face and curve of his jaw. "I love you. Whatever you decide, I'll always love you. Even when we're apart. Even when you hate me. That's a promise."

"Avery." He captures my hand and kisses my palm, holding it firm. "I wouldn't know how to hate you."

Pulling myself on top of him, straddling his hips, I kiss my way to his lips. I peel off my shirt, we toss our clothes to the floor, and I bring his hands up to touch me, hold me. Remember the feel of my skin when he enlivens every nerve. How my breath escapes me when his mouth explores my body. The rhythm of my pulse when he's inside me and there's nothing we don't understand about each other.

We only have a few hours to daylight, and with it a decision that will irrevocably change our lives. So, if this is all there is, all we have left, I don't want anything left unsaid. If this is our last memory, I want it burned on my heart.

"I'll get better," he says, whispering against my lips. "Just don't give up on me."

I hope that's true. For both of us. But as we fall asleep, I begin to prepare myself for life post-Ethan. The farthest distance between two points is desiring sobriety and achieving it.

* * *

Sitting in his truck outside the rehab facility upstate, a cozy, wooded estate on a lake, Ethan grips my hand. Or maybe I'm holding his. The program is six weeks, during which time we won't call, we won't write—this is his time to concentrate only on his recovery without the crutch or distraction of me. It's a painful requirement, but a necessary one. He has to step out on this ledge alone if he's going to find his balance.

"I am so proud of you," I tell him as he stares out the window. I know the war churning within him, and what a profound step it is to make it this far. "Remember that."

"The only thing I'm afraid of is letting you down," he says. "When I was gone, every second of it I wanted to call you. So many times I almost picked up the phone. But I was ashamed—those things I said to you. Fuck, Avery." He drags his hands through his hair and presses his palms to his forehead. "The look on your face when I took off. It's still in here. Every time that image pops in my head, it guts me. It was like I was someone else, watching it happen, and I couldn't stop myself. I'd make the decision to come home, and then that look would flash in front of my eyes, and I couldn't do it."

"It's over now. We're past that." I don't want to think about it any more than he does. "The important part is that you're trying."

"I fucked up, Avery." He drops his hands to look at me, eyes red and stricken.

"I forgive you." I take his face in both hands, insistent that he hear this. "All I care about is that you get healthy. And you're going to have to forgive yourself. The guilt will cripple you. Trust me. The only way this gets any better is if you accept the mistakes and learn to let go. I promise it gets easier."

"How can you love me this much?" Leaning his face into my hand, he closes his eyes, a deep crease through his brow. "Why are you still here?"

"Because you made me love you. Every word. Every moment we were together. One mistake doesn't erase all that." Reaching into my pocket, I pull out the shell casing and tuck it into his fist. "I'm giving this to you. It's every battle I've fought and every lesson I've learned. It's my strength and commitment. Keep it with you, and when you think it's too hard, when you start to doubt, when you're in so much pain and anguish you don't think you'll survive it, remember this. Remember me. Because I want it back. I need it back, Ethan. But only when you don't anymore."

Ethan wraps his hand around the back of my neck, tugging me closer. He kisses me, deep and desperate. All his fear and uncertainty in one vulnerable, precious gesture.

"One day at a time," I tell him. "I'll be right here when you're ready."

"I won't fail you," he says, forehead pressed to mine. "I fucking swear, Avery. I'll never fail you again."

# 28

# IN LOVING MEMORY

The last words Ethan said to me still ring in my ears, echoing in my dreams. It's been almost four months since he entered rehab and I moved back in with Kumi. Her father became more reasonable once I offered to pay my fair share of the rent and utilities, and Kumi threatened to drop out of law school if he didn't agree.

Still not a word from Ethan. Every day I think about calling him, checking in to make sure he's okay, but I stop myself. We aren't together anymore. That was my decision, and I have to stick to it. It's important for him to have this time alone. And for me, too.

"You're getting an award?" my mom says, the sound of running water and clinking dishes in the background. "Echo, that's fantastic!"

Saturday morning, I stand in front of the mirror putting on my makeup in the bathroom with my phone on speaker.

"I've been nominated by the magazine. Along with about

a hundred other writers across the country. It's for journalists under thirty-five, and I'm up against C.J., so I'm not holding out a lot of hope. But it's an honor to be nominated."

Actually, getting to say those words does feel like its own small prize.

"Still a big accomplishment, honey. I'm so proud of you."

That's not a bad prize, either.

"Thanks, Mom."

She's come a long way recently. My mom's learned to accept that I've made my choice, for better or worse, to stay in Manhattan and pursue my career. And though she'd still prefer I become a beekeeper or make organic soap for a living, ideally somewhere quiet and secluded, she understands how important it is that I find my own path.

"So work's great then. What else is going on?"

That's her way of asking if I'm seeing anyone.

"Nothing's changed."

I go back to my bedroom and pull the plastic dry cleaning cover off my modest black dress.

"Honey, I know you don't want to hear this." And yet she's going to say it anyway. "But maybe it's time to get back out there, try meeting people."

"I work fifteen hours a day. When I come home, all I want to do is crash. I wouldn't have time to date if I wanted to."

"Echo..."

"I'm not ready."

She's not alone on this. Everyone tells me I should move on, get laid. I'm not there yet. Meeting new people seems like entirely too much effort.

"I know you loved him, Echo, but at a certain point you have to think about self-preservation."

That's exactly what I'm doing.

"I'm not saying we're getting back together. I'm not sure I want to, honestly. But that doesn't mean I'm ready to think about being with someone else. It just feels…wrong."

"Oh, honey. You can't be certain if you don't try. Give it a chance."

"Please. Stop. Let me do this in my own time, okay?"

The water running in the background shuts off. I hear a chair scrape the floor and her exhale through the phone.

"Echo, I want you to really think about this." Her voice changes. A tone I haven't heard in years. "Sometimes the people we fall in love with aren't who we thought they were. We want so much to see the good that we create a blind spot for the bad. I don't want to see that happen to you, honey. You are a bright and beautiful soul; you deserve every happiness. Don't waste this time in your life on a wish that might not come true."

Her message isn't lost on me. My father ruined her when the great love of her life turned out to be a monster. He killed her ability to trust—in herself or others. Whatever great dreams and ambitions she had for her life were stolen by pure evil. So I don't blame her for pushing, for trying to spare me the same heartache and betrayal. But Ethan isn't Patrick. The two couldn't be more different. And as hard as it is to argue that she's wrong when all evidence points to the contrary, I know Ethan and I had something real. Until the resonance wears off, I'm not ready to let someone else into that space.

"Mom, I know you worry, but I'm okay. Whatever happens, I'll be all right."

My phone chimes to alert me I have a text from Carter telling me he's downstairs. It's just as well. Once the topic of Ethan comes up with my mother, it's all downhill from here. So we say goodbye until the next time we'll have this same conversation then I finish getting dressed.

*  *  *

A caravan of black limousines lines the road through the cemetery. Carter drives until we see the crowd of people gathered. It's a blustery, frigid day, the wind whipping my hair around my face and lifting my black trench coat as we step out of his car and he takes my arm to escort me to the open grave. Carter was the one to tell me Linda had died. At first I was apprehensive about attending the funeral, certain that if Ethan wanted me here he would have called himself, but Carter convinced me. At the very least, I want to pay my respects and offer her family my condolences. Though I spent very little time with her, Linda was always kind to me. Welcoming and sweet. And I know her death is a difficult setback for Ethan, inevitable as it was. I want him to know I'm still here, if he needs me.

As we approach, I spot him seated beside Paul. Dressed in a tailored black suit, wavy chestnut hair tugged by the wind, he looks good—healthy. Though he hides his eyes behind dark sunglasses, I can see in his face he's gained some weight back from the thin, gaunt man he'd become. Carter and I stand at the back during the service. At least forty people are gathered on three sides, huddling together and braced against the cold. Huge sprays of flowers teeter on their stands around the casket while the pastor gives his sermon.

Then as Ethan stands to speak, a flash of color catches my eye. Walking up from the road, where a yellow cab is pulling away, Vivian wears black jeans and a leather jacket. And a fresh coat of that neon pink dye job. The sight of her induces a sharp, stinging rage. Heat flames my face as I'm suddenly burning in my coat. Everything about her is offensive to me. That she isn't in prison is repulsive. Quietly, I break away from Carter and stalk toward her. She isn't going to ruin this for Ethan. I won't let her.

"Turn around," I say when I reach her several yards from the graveside. "You can't be here."

She stops, appraising me behind reflective aviator sunglasses. "That's really not up to you."

"I mean it, Vivian. Slither back into whatever sewer you washed out of and don't let me see your face again."

"He hasn't spoken to me in months. I don't know what you said to him, how you twisted him against me, but I was his friend long before you showed up. He needs me."

"Listen to me." I grab her wrist and push her back a few steps, concerned that our voices might carry and disturb the service. She tries ineffectually to shake my grip. "If I have to break your arm to keep you away from him, I'll do it. There is no version of this where you take one more step past me."

"Avery." Carter comes up beside me, tall and intimidating. His hand brushes open his jacket as he puts his hand in his pocket, revealing the sidearm concealed in its shoulder holster. "There a problem?"

"Vivian was just leaving."

Standing there, she appears to debate whether to test my resolve. And perhaps it's the threat of a law enforcement officer that finally convinces Vivian this isn't a fight she can win. I release her, and she turns to skulk away, back down the road out of the cemetery.

"If you ever consider a career change…" he says as we walk back to rejoin the service.

"Me with a badge and gun would be a terrible idea."

After the funeral concludes, we linger out of the way. I'm having second thoughts about approaching Ethan, and the idea of talking to Paul has my fingers going a bit fuzzy. This might have been a horrible idea. The death of a loved one is a solemn, private affair. Showing up without an invitation is awfully uncouth. But just as I'm about to insist Carter get me out of here, Ethan spots us. He stands there, frozen for a moment. Hands in his pockets, shoulders high and tense, I'm afraid I've upset him. Then he moves, coming toward us in long, confident strides. My heart races as I search for the right thing to say.

"I'll give you two a minute," Carter says, and he walks off before I can tell him not to leave me here alone.

Once Ethan's looming over me, I can't speak at all. He smells the same: mint and eucalyptus. His presence, like the day we met, sucks all the air from the space around us and I'm trapped in his overwhelming gravity. My skin buzzes with awareness—the memory of him and how he touched me.

How good we were when it was good. How red and desperate his eyes were the last time I saw him. The pain when he left me and the heartbreaking relief when he came back. Now he's here, and I have nothing and everything to say.

"Avery," he says, soft and almost reverent. "I'm glad you came."

"Carter." I clear my throat, blinking away the sting in my eyes. "He thought I—"

"Thank you." He tucks my hair behind my ear and the gesture is nearly enough to collapse me. "It means a lot to me that you're here."

Wrapping my arms around my stomach, I don't feel the wind or the cold, only the need to be closer and the ache of how unnatural this feels, being apart.

"I'm so very sorry, Ethan. Your mother was a lovely woman. I'm grateful I got the chance to meet her."

His lips attempt a smile, but it's barely a twitch. "She was quite fond of you. We talked about you at the end. Good things. I promise."

I wipe my eyes, glancing away to seek out Carter, who's standing beside his car. "Well, I wanted to pay my respects, and, uh, I should probably let you go so—"

"Are you coming back to the house?"

"Oh, um…"

"Please." He cups my cheek, running his thumb under the ridge of my bottom lip. Every part of me wants to lean into him. To be held in his arms again. Safe and warm. "I need you with me."

I promised I would. And I will.

\* \* \*

Hundreds turn up for the reception at the Ash townhouse following Linda's funeral. When I arrive with Ethan, the street is clogged with limos dropping off passengers. Inside, the entire first floor is overcrowded with people dressed elegantly in black, sipping drinks, and nibbling on finger foods. Half the wealthiest men and women in America are here, including several celebrities. But Ethan wants nothing to do with any of them. He takes us up to the second floor and his childhood bedroom, now converted to a simple guest room. He stands at the window, jacket open and hands shoved in the pockets of his tailored black pants, framed in dim gray light as clouds blanket the city. I'm content to watch him, to absorb the sight of him, refilling the empty space where the memories had begun to fade.

"This morning was the hardest day yet," he says, his back to me as I sit on the edge of the bed. "I was clawing out of my skin. If there'd been any liquor at my place, I'd have drowned in it."

"But you didn't."

"No, I didn't. Because I hoped I'd see you, and I wanted you to be proud of me."

A knife twists in my chest. "I am proud of you, Ethan."

He turns, ocean-blue eyes shining behind withheld tears. He manages half a smile, wistful and sad.

"I'm still sober. Not a drop since my arrest."

"That's fantastic. You should be proud of yourself, too."

Coming toward me, there's a restrained fierceness about

him. He's a powerful animal held behind thin glass. Ethan stops at the edge of the bed, inches away. Intense, palpable energy tugs at me. It's suffocating being this close to him. He's regained that ineffable potency that shrinks the room around him, demanding attention.

"You're all I think about," he says, running his fingertips down my arm. "I can't close my eyes without seeing your face. Sitting in a quiet room, I hear your voice. I barely sleep, and when I do, I dream about you lying next to me. Then I wake up, touch the cold space in bed, and I remember why you left me."

"Ethan…" I should walk away now. Stop this before I can't. But…

"It's killing me, Avery. I've tried, but I can't stay away from you any longer."

He bends and takes my face between both strong, warm hands. His lips meet mine, soft and tender. Like they've always been there. A heavy, crushing wave of relief and want pull me under. I'm not capable of resisting him. Not when I've thought about this moment and almost nothing else for months since we last touched. When he grabs my hips and pushes me up the bed, draping his body over mine, I weave my fingers into his hair and hold him to me. If only I could make this moment last. Stay here, suspended, unconcerned about a tomorrow that will never arrive. Here, everything is as it should be. For this brief and eternal moment, the pieces fit together, and I'm whole again.

"Fuck, Avery." Ethan breathes against my lips, harsh and strained. He grasps the back of my leg, hitching it up around his hips as my dress gives way to his hand sliding upward. "I've fucking missed you."

I hate myself as I push the jacket off his shoulders then dig my fingers into the crisp fabric of his shirt. We can't do this. It's horrible timing and a worse venue. More than that, he isn't ready. Nor am I. Neither of us has proven we can adequately function without the other. If he's still clinging to me as his reason for sobriety, he hasn't come to terms with taking responsibility for his own recovery. And until I can go to sleep at night and wake up in the morning without thinking of him first, I'm not strong enough to support him, or walk away again if I must, if he falls off the wagon.

"Ethan," I say, pushing at his chest. "Stop."

He pulls back, staring down at me through thick lashes. Hair falls over his forehead and his chest heaves against mine.

"Come home," he says. "Please."

"I don't live there anymore."

"It's still your home. Wherever I am, you'll always have a home there."

I turn my head, staring out the window as tears prick my eyes. "Don't say things like that."

"Why? Why do you want me to pretend I don't love you? What point is there in entertaining a reality where you aren't the last woman I'll ever love?"

The tears fall down my cheeks, and I can't bear the weight of him anymore. I push him off, scrambling to my feet.

"Because I can't leave you twice. I can't suffer this agony a second time. You broke my fucking heart, Ethan. You made me sit there and watch you kill yourself a little bit every day and it tore a piece of me away that I can't get back. I love you so much, and I hate what you did to us."

"Hey." He lunges at me, capturing me in his arms and holding tight when I try to break free. "I know I fucked up. I know I hurt you. But I'm better now. That's over. I'm never going to be that guy again. I swear, Avery. I'd rather throw myself off a building than ever put you through that again. You have to believe me. I need you."

"That's the problem," I mutter against his chest. "You have to stop needing me and start a life that doesn't include me."

"I don't want to. I don't want that life."

"I'm sorry." Pushing away, I step out of his arms. "Please understand, this isn't about forgiveness. I forgave you a long time ago. But I have to put myself first, and you have to make decisions for you, not anyone else. The only thing that's going to allow that to happen is time."

The impassive mask falls into place as Ethan stares at me, hands sliding into his pockets. "So that's it. You're walking away."

"I'm not going anywhere. I've always been right here. I said I'd be your friend, and I always will. But right now, we can't be together. You have to learn to live without us."

No matter how much I love him, his sobriety is more important than my pain. I'd take a lifetime of anguish and separation if it meant keeping him from ever going down that dark path again. It's what you do when you love someone.

"I should go." I straighten my dress and wipe my eyes, taking in one last look to save for the uncertain time ahead of us. "If you need anything, please call me. This isn't goodbye."

Just as I'm about to walk out the door, Ethan stops me. He holds my hand, running his thumb over my knuckles.

"You got me this far," he says. "Don't give up on me."

I close the distance between us and rise on my toes to kiss his cheek.

"Never."

Because I'm still holding my breath, waiting for that day when I don't feel like I'm Ethan's relapse waiting to happen.

# 29

# THE CHEATERS

Come on," Kumi whines from the bathroom as she curls her hair. "You can't spend our first New Year's Eve in the city at home alone."

"Can, too." With a box of vegetable lo mein, I sit on the couch watching the *Twilight Zone* marathon on TV.

"Come with us. You can be my midnight kiss."

"Tempting, but I think Navid might get jealous."

There's no part of getting dressed and party-hopping all over Manhattan that sounds appealing to me. Freezing my ass off and rubbing my toes raw in a pair of ankle-killing heels. I've never been much of a social creature, and New Year's Eve gets old fast when you're the only sober person in the room.

"Have you heard from him?" Kumi walks into the living room wearing a tight sequined dress that's sure to bring Navid to his knees.

A knot twists in my chest. The ever-present ache that is the empty place where Ethan isn't.

"Not since the funeral."

Almost two months ago. I thought we'd hang out, act like friends, but Ethan's kept his distance. It's what I told him to do, I know. All the same, I miss him.

"You're sure I can't convince you?" Kumi considers me with sad, sympathetic eyes. "Even just for a few hours?"

"I'm sure." I've been looking forward to having the place to myself for a night. Sit around in my pajamas, eat junk food, and fall asleep by eleven. "Have a good time. Be careful. Call if you need bail money."

The doorbell rings. Kumi grabs her purse from the kitchen table then blows me a kiss as she and Navid head out. A few minutes later, I get a text from Addison. Rather than another plea to join the festivities, it's just a link and an order to read it. Tapping on the link sends me to an essay in the *New York Times* Modern Love section.

## Find Yourself a Girl Who Cheats at Scrabble

By Ethan Ash

*I've known two truly extraordinary women in my life. One recently departed this world after a long and painful battle with cancer. The other I chased away in my determination to drink myself into an early grave—beat my dying mother to the void. Both women were exceedingly kind, brilliant, loving souls who, among their many achievements, made me a better man for having known them. And both shared a common trait, a quirk I've come to identify as a singular, valuable hallmark: both cheated at Scrabble. Find yourself a girl who cheats at Scrabble, because a person who cares enough to fight for the little things will be the last one standing when it matters...*

*...Find yourself a woman who cheats at Scrabble, and try to be worthy of her.*

\* \* \*

I try calling him, but the number I have for Ethan has been disconnected. There's no answer at his loft, where Vivian's mural has been painted over with stark white primer. Then as I'm about to dial Carter, the answer occurs to me. There's only one place Ethan would be.

It's nearly midnight when the cab pulls up the driveway of the house in Montauk. I find him standing at the edge of the cliff, staring out at the starry sky. Chilling wind lashes at my face as I approach him. He's illuminated by moonlight and the glow bleeding from the house. At a distance, I watch him for a moment. Statue of a man, frozen against the horizon. It's how we first met, me staring at his back, catching him in a candid moment. Despite his scars, and also because of them, I still find him no less daunting. He can still shrink a room, the entire coastline, with only his presence. He still has a gravity that bends everything else around him. I look at Ethan, and I see a man who remakes the world just by waking up.

"You could have just called," I shout.

Slowly, like he's not sure it wasn't the wind talking, he turns to see me walking through the tall grass that thins into bare dirt. A cautious smile plays across his lips. But it's his eyes—still vivid and alive.

"I wasn't sure you'd come," he says.

I stand beside him, watching the waves rush up to meet the shore and retreat again.

"Where've you been?"

"Here, mostly."

"Why?"

He runs his hand through his hair as I stare up at his shadowed profile. It seems like ages since we last stood here. Almost impossible to believe it wasn't yesterday.

"Working on a new book, actually. Decided it was best to take a step away from the news business for a while." He turns to face me, something anxious behind his eyes and in the set of his jaw. "I've thought a lot about what you said, and what I've decided is that I can't meet your expectations."

"I don't—"

"Please," he says. "Let me say this. Loving you has changed me, Avery, and I can't go back to a place where I'm living only for myself. Every decision I make includes you. Six, seven times a day I still want a drink, but I don't do it because the only thing more painful than the craving is the idea of disappointing you. You said you want me to stop needing you, and that's just not possible. I've fucking tried, Avery. I really have. It's exhausting. I'm tired. Aren't you? No matter how long we're apart or how far away I get, you don't wear off."

I wanted Ethan to do this on his own, find that part of himself that would motivate him to stay sober. But I haven't done any better at letting go. So many times, I've tried to split myself in half and create a new person from the leftovers, pretending it was enough. This time, there aren't enough threads without him. Loving him is an exchange—he took part of me with him, and gave me a piece in return. The truth is, that part of himself I wanted him to find…he's decided it's me.

"This whole time," I tell him, hugging my chest against the cold, "I've been waiting for that day I wake up and I've almost forgotten to miss you, but it doesn't come. No matter how hard I pretend it will."

I chose him because he's everything I've wanted and something I didn't know I needed. He makes me whole again. Has given me back the parts of my identity that I'd hidden for so long because he saw something beautiful in them.

"Avery…" He takes my hands in his, stroking his thumbs over the backs. His brow creases, and an odd shift plays across his face. "You've given me my life back. I wouldn't be standing if it weren't for you. And no matter what you decide, I'll always be grateful."

"Ethan…" Shivers skitter down my spine. "You're, uh, doing it again…"

"Every day I find a new reason to love you. You're the thought that gets me up in the morning. You're the dream that helps me sleep at night."

Staring into his deep, earnest eyes, his face fading into shadow, my fingers fill with static and my knees go a little sideways.

"Ethan, I love you, too. Okay, babe? You don't need to—"

He drops to one knee. My breath catches in my throat.

"You've made me a better man. You've had faith in me when

I couldn't find it in myself. For as long as you'll have me, I promise to never take that faith for granted. Avery…" Ethan reaches into his pocket. Then prying open my clenched fist, he places the shell casing in my palm. "Will you be my girlfriend again?"

The tension in my chest snaps, and I suck in a breath.

"Fuck, Ethan. You scared the shit out of me."

"Well, that's an encouraging response."

"No, fuck you," I say as he gets to his feet. Smirking, he wraps me in his arms. "You're unhinged, you know that?"

The strange thing is, I hadn't even realized that I'd forgotten to miss the shell casing. Somewhere along the way, I stopped needing it. Perhaps because Ethan gave me a reason to look forward rather than back. I've found a different kind of strength that isn't based in fear and regret. He's replaced the broken pieces of me, fit them back together while I wasn't even looking. And with his belief in me, I've come to know myself not for who I was, but for what I'm becoming. The biggest changes were in the smallest details.

"But you haven't even seen the fireworks yet."

Seconds later, huge bursts of color explode over the sky. Whistling, screaming up from the darkness, they scatter and shine.

"I hate you so much right now."

"I love you, too."

# About the Author

Tyler King was born and raised in Orlando, Florida, and graduated from the University of Central Florida with a degree in creative writing. As a journalist, her work has appeared in *Orlando* magazine and *Orlando Business Journal*, among other publications. She is a proud army spouse currently living in Virginia with her husband.

Learn more at:
   TylerAKing.com
   Twitter, @TylerAKing
   Facebook.com/TylerAKing

PLEASE TURN THE PAGE FOR AN EXCERPT
FROM TYLER KING'S

*The Debt*

AVAILABLE NOW!

# Prologue

## Session 3

Our conversations always began the same way. This woman was only interested in the worst parts of me. The ugly. Shame and contrition and all the ways I'd found to abuse myself since...

"Why are you here?"

These rooms made me anxious. The claustrophobia of one woman's undivided attention. She still smelled like the walk across campus: damp denim and wet grass in the tread of her shoes. She watched my knee bounce. Watched me drive the serrated edge of a plastic knife into the cast wrapped around my right hand. Her fingers tapped across the screen of her iPad to the rhythm of my tongue piercing flicking between my teeth. And she waited patiently for an answer. A still, quiet patience that only irritated me further. She was a fucking wax statue of perfect fucking patience.

"Why are you here?"

"Because I fractured a man's jaw." And broke my hand for the trouble.

"Why are you here?"

"It wasn't my choice."

"But why are you here, Josh?"

Because eighteen years ago a woman I only remember by the back of her head left me on a public bus. No matter the answer I gave, it wasn't good enough. Not humiliating enough. She wasn't interested in my remorse. I had none. This woman wanted to cut me open and watch me writhe on the floor.

"Why are you here?"

"Are you going to start every conversation with the same question?" The end of the knife snapped off inside my cast. Goddammit.

"Josh…"

"Asked and answered."

She wanted to sigh. I could see it in her eyes. The boredom in this room was contagious.

"A violent outburst put you in that chair, but I want to know how you got here." She set her iPad aside and crossed her legs, entwining her fingers in her lap. "What is it like?"

"What?"

"The panic attacks. How do they feel?"

I closed my eyes, flexing my wrist against the severed shard of the knife. "Like waking up with your hands tied behind your back and a plastic bag cinched over your head. It feels like dying in terror."

"Let's start there…"

# Chapter 1

I stood in the shower with the lights off and my forehead pressed to the tiles. My palm lay flat, fingertips gripping the thin grout trench for support. Scalding spray beat against my back, but it could not chase away the frigid, crackling sting of ice pumping through my veins. I held my semi-flaccid dick in my hand, trembling as my lungs ached to push past the boulder lodged in my throat. My body caved in on itself, shrinking. Gravity squeezed me. It pressed and it pushed until the weight was so much, the pain so great, I collapsed to the bottom of the tub, naked and shivering. The room spun forward and back, end over end. I grit my teeth, clenched my fists. Static filled my head and numbed my face. The sick, black poison of nausea seeped its way into my gut. Bubbling. Boiling. I heaved and clenched, vomiting acid and whiskey, leaving me a huddled clump of shaking agony in a soup of sweat and putrid bile swirling around the drain at my feet.

The water ran cold before I could move again. A silent sob

cracked through my chest. Coughing, I choked on the air filling my lungs. Exhaustion was a relief.

When the panic attack subsided, I reached for the soap and rubbed it between both hands, then lathered and rinsed my body from face to feet. I hated it. Hated touching my skin with wrinkled fingers while my nerves were still raw.

Withered, I planted my hands on the tiles and climbed up the wall to stand on trembling legs. My muscles were mud. Wobbling out of the shower, I reached for a towel.

In my room, a naked woman lay asleep in my bed. I dropped the towel on the floor and slipped under the covers.

But sleep wouldn't come.

Hours later, just after 8:00 a.m., I was still awake when the woman next to me stretched and reached for her phone on my nightstand. Propped up against my headboard, I watched the silhouette of a leggy blonde dressing at the foot of my bed. She shoved her tits into a push-up bra and wiggled her way into a tight black dress.

"It was fun," she said. "See you around, MacKay."

"Later."

She tiptoed away with her shoes in her hand and closed the door behind her. I knew I shouldn't have brought Kate home, but at the time I didn't have the clarity of mind to do otherwise. Women had always been transient in my life. This one was no different.

I pried myself from the covers, then crossed the room and stood at the floor-length mirror beside my dresser to inspect the new ink peeking around the right side of my rib cage. The skin there was still tender and swollen, a result of six hours under the needles to continue the design that decorated my back. Bear was an artist with an implement of pain.

My eyes fell to the framed photo lying facedown on my dresser: a younger me in a tux, standing onstage with my adoptive parents beside a piano before my first sold-out concert. It was one of the happiest days of my life, and I couldn't bear to look at it.

I was skinnier then, and lanky. Hadn't yet grown into my body. Next to my pale, freckled parents, I stood out like one of those exotic adopted children of yuppie celebrity parents. Dark skin. Black hair. Green eyes. People told me I was "interesting" to look at, to gawk at. So little by little I covered all the pretty bare flesh in tattoos.

The first piece I ever had done was of a raven with its wings spread wide across my chest. The tips of each broken wing nailed down. I was seventeen then. After my first sitting, I came to understand why people said tattoos were addictive. I suppose I became a glutton for pain, because when Bear's wife offered to put a hole in my lip, I let her stick a needle through my face. For shits and giggles. At twenty-one, I had two full sleeves. My dad only asked that I keep the modifications within reason. I was a bit fuzzy on that definition.

From the top dresser drawer, I grabbed a tube of antibacterial ointment and applied two fingers' worth to the new tattoo. My stomach growled. It was empty and angry from last night. So I sifted through the field of laundry-pile bunkers scattered around my bedroom until I found a black shirt and dark jeans on the passable side of clean.

When I hit the landing at the bottom of the stairs, I felt

a pair of knowing brown eyes watching me from the living room. Nothing good ever came from the morning-after ritual. Even so, I couldn't help but glance at my roommate curled up on the leather couch with her laptop open and earbuds hidden under her long dark hair. She held seven fingers over her head. Hadley averted her gaze back to the computer screen rather than look for my reaction. Like she didn't give a fuck.

"Don't you have anything better to do than wait for the walk of shame?"

"Don't you have an appointment to get your dick swabbed for STDs?"

"Fuck off."

"Get bent."

And so everything was par for the course on a Sunday morning. I held out my middle finger as I turned toward the kitchen. *That was fun. Let's do it again next week, shall we?* I had yet to decipher her scoring system. Asking for clarification would only validate her participation in my sex life.

Neither of us enjoyed living together. My parents' house in the middle of nowhere was too big for two people and not big enough for the both of us. Since my dad left to take a job in New York during our freshman year of college, every day was a special kind of torture. But Hadley needed me. And as much as I couldn't stand being near her, I wouldn't abandon her again.

Besides, that girl could cook. I walked into the kitchen and pulled the tinfoil off the food Hadley had left for me on the stove. After I poured myself a glass of orange juice and prepared my plate, I took a seat at the granite breakfast bar that framed the gourmet kitchen. Her scrambled eggs, bacon, and cinnamon toast were reason enough to get up in the morning.

Hadley wasn't so bad. I knew I could be a surly, inconsiderate bastard. Our spats weren't entirely her fault. For the most part, we were resigned to grin and bear it for the next two years until graduation. Hadley was set on moving to Boston for her master's degree. I was going to New York the second I fulfilled my promise to my dad and had my bachelor's in hand. No one was under the misconception that this arrangement would last forever.

"You're an asshole." Hadley walked in to lean back against the counter beside the stove. She wore my black Tool sweatshirt with the sleeves rolled up and the hem brushing her legs just at the apex of her thighs. And those tiny black shorts that made my dick twitch every time she bent over. Those fucking shorts.

Reaching toward me, she swiped a piece of toast off my plate, never mind the three pieces still sitting on the platter. She did that all the time, and it drove me up the wall. Since she was the one doing all the cooking, I'd given up trying to break her of the habit and teach her to keep her thieving fingers to herself.

Rather than answer, I shrugged one shoulder and shoveled another forkful into my mouth.

"Stephanie Slater has sent me three text messages asking me to ask you to call her." Her dark eyes looked past me or at the floor, anywhere but my face. "Do your own dirty work. I clean up after you enough as it is."

"You know how much I dislike confrontation."

"This is a new low, even for you. If you screw your friend's sister, you could at least take her calls."

"I'll keep that in mind."

"And stop fucking the crazy ones. She's giving off a stalker vibe."

"Anything else?"

"If Scott shows up with a hatchet, I'm not covering for you." One corner of her lips turned up in a wicked smirk.

I gave her a wink. Hadley laughed, rolled her eyes, and sauntered off with my last piece of bacon.

I never went out of my way to piss Hadley off, but I rarely exerted too much effort to stay on her good side, either. That ship had sailed, hit an iceberg, taken on water, snapped in half, and dragged all souls aboard down with it a long time ago.

Half the time I wanted to throttle that girl. The other half I wanted to wrap her in blankets and swear undying allegiance if she'd smile again. I cherished the rare moments when Hadley was relaxed, laughing, and more like her old self. I had a debt to Hadley that I'd spend the rest of my life repaying. I owed her my head on a platter. And if ever given the chance, I'd take a bullet for her.

\* \* \*

After breakfast, Hadley sat on her bed with a sketchbook on her lap. The shard of charcoal between her fingers rubbed across the page, making a soft scratching sound in the otherwise silent space. I enjoyed watching her work. The expression of intense concentration she wore. Bobbing her head to the music playing through her earbuds.

I sat on the edge of the bed. Hadley flipped her sketchpad when I tried to steal a peek. Reaching over, I tugged one of her earbuds out. The sound of Fiona Apple's voice sprang from the tiny speaker.

"I've got to take the Les Paul to the shop. You want to come along?"

"How bad is it?"

"The neck is loose. It sounds like shit. Vaughn will have to strip it down and reset it."

"What an asshole."

Not Vaughn. The asshole was the drunken bastard at my show last week who jumped onstage to give us his best Slash impression. He grabbed my Gibson Les Paul, so I decked him and tossed the guy to the floor, but he managed to take my guitar to the ground with him.

"We can run by campus to pick up our textbooks and hit the grocery store on the way back."

"You're going to class this semester?" She arched a sassy eyebrow.

"I go when it's necessary."

"Right. What could an institution of higher learning possibly teach the prolific Josh MacKay?"

"I'm still waiting to find out."

Hadley rolled her eyes and swatted me with the back of her sketchpad. "Swing us by the art supply store and you've got a deal."

Really, Hadley never asked much of me.

"Sure. You need me to wait outside first?" I got off the bed and shoved my hands in my back pockets.

"Nope." She stood to put her sketchpad away in her nightstand. Hadley tied her hair up in a ponytail and wrapped the wires of her earbuds around her neck. "I'm good."

She proceeded mechanically toward her bedroom windows that looked out on the woods behind the house. In the same order, always the exact routine, Hadley unlatched and latched the locks five times, clicking back and forth. Her hand lingered for a few seconds. Fingers squeezed and twitched to repeat the action. Then she took a breath and spun around to continue throughout the house.

To every window and door, I followed behind as Hadley performed her ritual. I never rushed her, was never impatient about her process. I'd done this to her. It was my job to assure her later, when she teetered on the edge of an anxiety attack, that she hadn't missed a single point of entry.

She had done well today, and I smiled at her when we made it to the alarm keypad in the foyer in less than four minutes. I felt like an arrogant shit for trying to offer her my approval, but Hadley seemed to take some level of pride on the days when we didn't make two or three trips mid-ritual back to the second floor to start all over again.

She keyed in the code three times, disarmed the alarm three times, and didn't hesitate to take a step back when she was ready for me to finish up. Definitely a good day.

At the front door, Hadley locked up and only jiggled the handle for seventeen seconds before she sighed and plastered on a calm expression. I held open the passenger door to my black '65 Mustang, watching as Hadley got in and brought up the security app on her phone to check again that the system was armed.

In the car, she sat with fists clenched and knuckles white as the engine groaned and came to life. One finger pried its way free to tap the stereo to cue Black Keys at an earsplitting decibel. Her attention was aimed straight ahead at the tree-lined dirt driveway that spanned a hundred yards out to the two-lane road.

When the stone-faced house was no longer visible behind us through the thick surrounding forest and my front tires crunched over the last of the uneven dirt and gravel to the flat pavement, I hit the clutch and slammed the stick shift. Hadley rolled down her window as we exceeded the posted speed limit toward the highway. She liked it when I drove fast, so I was more than happy to oblige.